SPECIAL MESSAGE TO READERS

THE SOLDIER'S WIFE

Dan Riley, a major in the British Army, is back from a six-month tour of duty in Afghanistan. He's coming home to his wife Alexa and his daughters, who he adores. The world views those reunions as a taste of heaven after months of hell. But are they? Life for a returning soldier is rarely straightforward and Dan finds it hard to adjust to home life in the Wiltshire camp. Can a man trained to fight, readjust to family and domestic life? And if he can't, how will the family cope? Can Alexa, Dan's wife, sacrifice her own needs and fulfilment to support his commitment to a way of life that demands everything — not just of him, but of her and the children as well?

Books by Joanna Trollope
Published by The House of Ulverscroft:

A SPANISH LOVER
THE BEST OF FRIENDS
MARRYING THE MISTRESS

JOANNA TROLLOPE

THE SOLDIER'S WIFE

Complete and Unabridged

CHARNWOOD
Leicester

First published in Great Britain in 2012 by
Doubleday
an imprint of Transworld Publishers
London

First Charnwood Edition
published 2013
by arrangement with
Transworld Publishers
a Random House Group Company
London

British Library CIP Data

Trollope, Joanna.
  The soldier's wife.
  1. Large type books.
  I. Title
  823.9′14–dc23

ISBN 978–1–4448–1485–9

Published by
F. A. Thorpe (Publishing)
Anstey, Leicestershire

Set by Words & Graphics Ltd.
Anstey, Leicestershire
Printed and bound in Great Britain by
T. J. International Ltd., Padstow, Cornwall

This book is for all those who gave me their invaluable time and help in my research: Alice, Sarah B, Jason K, Eliza and Rupert, Sophie, William and Charlie, Sarah and Andrew, Sam, Ally, Tiggy, Joan, Denise, Nick S, Patrick H, Joanna W, John S, Fiona S, Richard M, Alex H, Tom N, Gemma, Julie, Chrissie, Toni and Corporal Wallace. Thank you all, and so much.

1

Even before her eyes were open, Isabel could tell that the house was awake. The water was thumping away in the pipes behind the wall in her bedroom, as it had done ever since Maintenance — now contracted out to some civilian firm in Liverpool that Isabel had heard her mother say was useless — had come to stop the shower leaking, and she could also hear the twins twittering away somewhere, in the sort of bird-speak they had developed for private communication.

It was annoying, really. It was annoying to be the last awake, and not the first. Isabel had discovered that if she could steal a march on the day — even by fifteen minutes — she could manage it better, get a grip on herself. At school — best, really, not to think about school if she could help it — she had devised this method of taking charge of herself deliberately and methodically, as a way of dealing with homesickness. Wake before everyone else, go through the wretched mental photo gallery of home and Mum and the twins and the dog, and the smells museum of the kitchen and Mum's sweater drawer and the awkward cupboard where the bed linen lived, whose door would never shut, then gulp, sniff, wipe eyes, sit up and breathe. Breathe and breathe. Eyes shut, then eyes open. Swallow. Find hairbrush and begin to brush, reminding herself how amazingly lucky she was to have long, thick, straight hair and not the curly or frizzy kind that got you despised for something that you couldn't possibly be blamed for in the first place. Put hairbrush back. One more deep breath. Up.

Isabel put her fingers lightly across her eyelids, and opened her eyes slowly behind them. She was not, of course, at school. She was at home, in her own bedroom, at number seven, the Quadrant, Larkford Camp, Wiltshire, which had been home now for nearly two years. Before that home had been a bit in Germany, and a bit in Yorkshire and a bit in London, and before that, when it was just Mum and Isabel on their own, a bit in another part of London in a high-up flat with the top of a tree right outside the windows, which Isabel believed she remembered with a passionate nostalgia. There'd also been schools to go with all these places, school after school.

'Five schools by year six,' Mum had said to Isabel, trying to make the case for boarding school. 'It's too much. It's too much for you. It isn't fair. You make friends and then you move and lose them. Don't you think you'd rather have continuity, even if it means sleeping away from home?'

Isabel didn't know. Even now, technically settled into boarding school, she didn't know. She wanted to feel steadier, she wanted to please, she understood that if Dan got promotion they might move again — but then, if he didn't, if they didn't, why was it necessary for her to be away from home when home wasn't, after all, changing? And then there were the twins. The twins went to a local nursery school, and when they were five would go to the local primary.

'But the twins — ' Isabel began.

Mum looked at her. Isabel could see she understood and hadn't got a real answer. She just said, 'We — can't plan, you see. Not if we want to stay together. As a family. But if you go to boarding school, at least you know — I know — that one thing, at least, will go on as before. That's all.'

In Isabel's experience, it was only the small things that went on as before, like the smell of the linen cupboard and the twins' refusal to eat anything orange and the way one fingernail on her left hand grew at a very slight angle. The big stuff, like what was going to happen next, to all of them, was always a giant question mark hanging in the air, affecting everything, every mood. And even when the question mark was answered, it was always replaced by another one. Like today. Today was a big day, a day they had been looking forward to for six months, a day that was circled on the kitchen calendar, and for which the twins had made a huge messy paper banner randomly stuck with patches of shiny coloured paper and scraps of pink feather from a dressing-up boa.

Today, Dan was coming home from Afghanistan, with his whole battery. That, Isabel knew, meant about a hundred soldiers. Plus Dan. Plus all the other soldiers, from the other batteries, from the regiment. Planes and planes of them, all coming home together, in transports like flying sardine cans, Dan said, only huge. So Dan's coming home took away the question mark of would he be killed or wounded while he was away, which was a huge relief because Dan had always been kind to Isabel, and she appreciated that. But now there was another question mark in place of the would-Dan-be-killed one, and that, although not as awful, was still a deep anxiety.

Isabel took her hands away from her face and stared hard at the ceiling above her. People at school talked about what might happen to their soldier fathers a lot. Nobody was supposed to look at or listen to the news at school, but people did, all the same, and then whispered about it. There'd been a helicopter crash in Afghanistan last term, and the radio announcer had said, 'All killed. The relatives have been informed,' and Libby Guthrie, whose father was in the Army Flying Corps and who had gone quite white, said, 'Oh, phew. Relatives have been told. So we're OK then.' They'd all screamed then, and got hysterical with relief, jumping about with their arms round each other, and Isabel had felt an intense, brief, heady sensation of belonging.

But she didn't feel that now. She felt very separate and very apprehensive. Dan was coming home and Mum would be thrilled and the twins would be thrilled, and she would be pleased. But what, the new question mark asked, would he be *like*?

★ ★ ★

4

In the kitchen, Alexa had the fridge door open. The interior was immaculate, the contents arranged with precision and by category. The kitchen floor — Army-issue vinyl printed to resemble outdated Italian floor tiles — shone. So did the windows. The walls, which she had painted pale blue herself, although she knew she would have to return them to magnolia when they left the quarter, were smear-free except for the twins' exuberant Welcome Home Daddy poster. There were flowers on the table, the tea towels were ironed and her hair, still damp from the shower, had possibly never been cleaner. Her friend Mo had been round the evening before on her way to an Army Benevolent Fund early Christmas fair — 'Twenty quid for tepid curry with the Old and Bold — you're so lucky you can't get a babysitter and come with me' — and had shouted with laughter at the flawless state of the house.

'God, we're pathetic. What do we think we're doing? Last time Baz got back from exercise he was completely, utterly filthy, and as rank as a polecat, and there I was, spotless in every crevice, not a hair on my body. I *ask* you!'

Alexa said, surveying her manicured hands — no varnish, but no torn cuticles, either — 'I suppose it's relief. And excitement. And — ' She stopped.

'And what?'

'Army habit. Keeping up appearances. Smart at all times.'

Mo gave herself a quick glance in Alexa's hall mirror. She pulled down the hem of her

5

embroidered sweater. 'I should be wearing a dress. To satisfy the Old and Bold. They'll be in Jaeger and regimental brooches, *comme toujours*.'

'You look great,' Alexa said.

'Better on a horse, though. It disguises my low centre of gravity.' She leaned forward and gave Alexa a quick kiss. 'I'll be thinking of you tomorrow. It'll be weird but wonderful. Have a row to clear the air as soon as you can — it'll get him out of his cave. We usually schedule it for day four.'

Alexa picked a booklet out of a tidy pile on the hall table, and held it out. 'That's what Welfare recommend, only more circumspectly.'

'What on earth's that?'

'Homecoming,' Alexa said. 'Welfare briefing on how to manage men going away and then men coming back again.'

Mo didn't try to take it. 'What a hoot.'

'None of it's a hoot.'

There was a small pause, and then Mo opened the front door. She blew Alexa a second kiss. 'But we have to get on with it, don't we? The house looks a peach and so do you. Lucky Major Riley.'

The door had slammed behind her, and Alexa heard the second slam of her car door, and then the car reversing and roaring away as if she were late to catch a train. Dan said Mo was at her happiest in an emergency, and Alexa had opened her mouth to say that maybe the visible and urgent expenditure of energy was more like a coping mechanism, and had then, for no reason she was very proud of, shut it again. Dan admired people who coped in emergencies. Emergencies were, after all, what he was trained for. And that was just one of the many things she had had to learn.

Something else she had learned now lay before her in the fridge. The food for a man sated with nourishment in foil pouches. Simple proteins — steak, chicken — beers, fruit and vegetables, powerfully mature Cheddar. He would probably eat nothing for a day or two — although the beers would vanish and no doubt much of the bottle of supermarket whisky she had bought — and then he would eat ravenously, whatever straightforward, un-messed-about food she put in front of him, liberally doused in Tabasco sauce. The British Army, she sometimes thought, could absorb as much Tabasco sauce as Avery Island, Louisiana could produce. The twins played shops with the rinsed-out miniature Tabasco bottles provided in every 24-hour Army ration pack — dozens of them, perfect replicas of the originals down to the McIlhenny label. Alexa pictured soldierly insides glowing and fire-hardened from years of pepper sauce which reduced everything, in her view, to a blazing similarity. Which was, perhaps, what soldiers wanted — a hot, peppery mush you could shovel in straight from the microwave or a pan of hot water. Certainly, if you shopped in the little supermarket which served the blocks behind the wire where over three thousand single soldiers lived, the freshest item you'd find there would be a foot-long sausage roll — no preparation, no

7

unfamiliarity, no need for cutlery.

The fridge let out a bleat of alarm at being left open so long. Alexa gave a little start and banged it shut. What was she doing, standing gazing at marshalled rows of yoghurt pots with wet hair and none of the children either dressed or breakfasted? She was doing, she supposed, what her mother had done before every diplomatic party, checking and re-checking, feeling faintly sick and distinctly choked with anxious expectation, and possessed by a simultaneous conviction that she could not cope with what lay ahead and nor could she cope with it not happening.

She crossed to the window and held on to the edge of the sink below it. Rough autumn grass — she had mown it, she hoped for the last time that year, three weeks ago — stretched from the front of the house to the ragged hedge which separated them, and the house they were attached to, from the narrow asphalted road that ran round the Quadrant. There was a big circle of grass in the middle of the Quadrant, and a clump of beech trees through which the unmistakeable figure of the Brigadier's wife — small, upright and purposeful — was making her way with two liver-and-white spaniels at her heels. She was the only officer's wife in the regiment, Alexa thought, not to have Labradors — black Labradors — but she had grown up with spaniels, she said, she understood them. She also had cats.

'Pansy animals, possibly,' she once said to Alexa. 'But bright. I like a clever creature.'

Alexa turned her head. Behind her, keeping a

8

watchful eye but not moving until instructed, was Dan's black Labrador, Beetle. He was not a clever creature, but he was biddable, kind and reliable. He was also the first dog Alexa had ever lived with, having had a wandering diplomatic upbringing that never seemed to allow for more pets than a tank, once, of tiny turtles, which had proved, after the initial wonder at their size and perfection, to be no more interesting to own than a box of slightly animated stones. Beetle was the first living thing Dan had introduced to Alexa — before any friend, before his father — and he had also proved to be the route that Isabel could take to accepting that Dan was here to stay in their lives, in a role she only really associated with a photograph.

'Good dog,' Alexa said.

Beetle's tail moved very slightly in polite acknowledgement. He was perhaps the only one in the house whose reaction to Dan's return would be entirely uncomplicated. Even the twins, Alexa could not be entirely sure of. Dan had been away once for only a month's training, in Canada, when they were not yet two, and when he returned and swooped down to hug them they had been terrified of this unfamiliar giant and fled shrieking behind Alexa. Dan had been devastated. Alexa had found him in their then German garden, on a broken bench, his head in his hands, not able or inclined to be reasonable. It was a week before Tassy, the bolder of the twins, had instructed him to bath her. And another week before Flora had silently offered him her shoes to put on. And all that time, Dan hardly spoke. He wasn't sulking, he was just somewhere else — 'in the zone', he called it — and there was nothing for Alexa to do but wait.

This time, of course, she had waited for six months. She had looked after the children, walked Beetle, cooked and cleaned, serviced the car and the lawn mower and the disobliging central-heating boiler; she had mopped up the girlfriends of the junior officers, who had frequently not even met their boyfriends' parents, cut the grass, watched countless DVDs in the evenings, joined in endless small female social diversions in the days — 'He's in the Army,' her father had said with forced joviality when she told him she had decided to marry Dan, 'so you'll end up an Army wife, measuring out your days in coffee spoons!'; she had tried not to write daily emails to Dan, and certainly not ones that even hinted at the bizarre mixture of feeling both trapped and insecure that haunted her, and was never separated from her telephone.

Once a week, there'd been a satellite phone call to Dan, in Afghanistan. If there was any crisis or sudden action, all the communications would shut down, and if you missed your turn, you missed it and were rewarded with a particular intensity of anxiety that persisted until the men were permitted to communicate again. Worries about Isabel's misery at school, about Flora's lazy eye (she wore miniature spectacles with a patch over one lens which gave her a sweetly scholarly air), about the lump on Beetle's

10

side, had to be choked down even if the phone connection worked, because Dan was mentally in another place, on quite another planet. This tour, he hadn't even taken photographs of them all, nor the drawings the twins had done for him.

'I can't bear to,' he said. He was standing among the precise piles of his kit, in their bedroom. 'I couldn't look at them last time, and I felt a shit because I couldn't. So, better not to take them.' He gave a half-laugh. 'I feel shit about enough, as it is.'

As well as those calls — as vital as they were unsatisfactory — Alexa rang her girlfriends on the camp daily. She rang Mo, and Franny and Sara and Prue. She also rang Dan's father once a week, out of affection, and her own parents, out of duty. And she rang Jack. She rang Jack almost as often as Jack rang her, which was every day or two.

Jack Dearlove had been in Alexa's life since she was seven. His father had been a minor diplomat, like hers, and their peripatetic careers had brought their children together, quite by chance, in several postings, the last of which was Bonn, just before both Jack and Alexa went off to university. And at his university — Newcastle — Jack had made a friend, a close, slightly older friend, whom he had introduced to Alexa in a jazz café on the Fulham Road which specialized in live music. The friend was called Richard Maybrick, and it was his photograph, taken on a walking holiday in France with his hair ruffled and his teeth gleaming in a wide, untroubled smile, that his daughter Isabel kept on her chest

11

of drawers at number seven, the Quadrant, Larkford Camp.

Richard Maybrick had died of a brain tumour in the neurological hospital in Queen Square, in London, when Isabel was only a baby. The tumour was diagnosed when he was twenty-six and his wife Alexa was pregnant with their first child, and it killed him eighteen months later. Throughout those months, the stocky, comfortable figure of Jack Dearlove was never far away. He was there after the consultations, he was there after every intense and terrifying bout of treatment, he was there when Alexa came out of Richard's last hospital room and said, bleakly, 'It's over.'

Alexa's parents supposed that their daughter would then, after a decent interval, become Mrs Dearlove. Alexa's mother, who had always minded very much about appearances, had even commented upon what an attractive surname it was. Preferable, actually, she said carelessly, to Maybrick. But Alexa, although she saw so much that was loveable in Jack's warmth and dependability and sturdy set of principles, saw nothing either romantic or exciting in him. In any case, Jack himself, devoted as he was to his mate Richard's widow and baby, was in love with an Ethiopian model of startling, etiolated beauty, whom he captured, and married, and then lost again, but never ceased to yearn for. He became, as Alexa's friend Franny put it, the perfect brother-friend. He had seen Alexa through Richard's illness and death. She had seen him through Eka's surrender, and then flight

12

— insofar as he would let her. He was designed, Alexa knew, to pick up the scattered and shattered pieces of humans other than himself.

He'd picked *her* up often enough, after all, quietly materializing just when she needed him, with the extraordinary faithful reliability of the best kind of sister in a Jane Austen novel. In fact, she often thought, he represented a continuity of presence and support in her life that, quite literally, no one else had been able to. Not girlfriends. Not even Dan. Jack had always been there, even when he was physically in London, a sort of cheerful, dependable, affectionate human hand-rail.

He had rung early that morning, before he set off on one of his runs. He was always running, or spinning, or lifting weights, at the gym in Chiswick, near his flat. It was, as he cheerfully admitted, all part of the endless battle he waged with his weight, having inherited his father's lack of height and his mother's lack of a usefully swift metabolism.

'I just *look* at a doughnut,' he'd say, 'and it immediately adds itself to my outline.'

That morning, he'd greeted Alexa with 'Sick as a parrot, are you?'

Alexa, on her way to the shower, shampoo bottle in hand, had smiled into the telephone. 'Sicker.'

'Exciting, though.'

'Yes.'

'Are you in a corset and fishnets?'

'I'm a mother of three,' Alexa said. 'In a fleece dressing-gown that my grandfather-in-law chose

13

for me himself, last Christmas, in Elys department store on Wimbledon High Street.'

'Elys, eh?'

'He likes it there,' Alexa said. 'He doesn't like anything too up-to-date, like coffee shops. On the third floor in Elys, they give you strong tea in a metal pot, and a toasted tea-cake. Just the one, to be eaten slowly.'

'I hope you'll eat. Breakfast, I mean.'

'Thank you, Nanny, but I couldn't possibly. It'll be coffee with a longing look at the brandy bottle.'

Jack said, in mock amazement, 'You have brandy?'

'*And* weedkiller.'

'Wow,' Jack said. 'You live life to the full, down in Wiltshire.'

'We do,' Alexa said, 'the fleece dressing-gown and me. And now I'm going to wash my hair.'

Jack's tone changed. 'I'll be thinking of you.'

'Please do.'

'Ring me tomorrow.'

'Of course.'

'And a high five to the old hero.'

Alexa dropped her phone into her pocket, and then dropped the dressing-gown off her shoulders. She stepped into the shower — tiles on the wall were missing and the plastic tray at the bottom had a fine, wavering crack across it — and found herself humming. Talking to Jack was like finding a forgotten fiver in the fruit bowl. He never failed to make her feel better.

★ ★ ★

14

'Mummy?'

Alexa turned from the sink. Isabel, in the outgrown nightie patterned with cherries that she insisted on still wearing, was standing in the doorway.

'Hi, darling.'

'I feel a bit weird.'

'We all do.'

Isabel drifted towards the table and leaned on it. Beetle sat up in his basket, wagging, and waited for her to notice him.

'D'you think Dan does?'

'He probably feels weirder than anyone. Camp Bastion, then up to the air head, and then twenty-four hours in Cyprus, and then home.'

Isabel wound herself along the table edge until she was opposite Beetle's basket. His tail was a blur of wagging. She knelt beside him and put her arms round his neck. Alexa said, 'Try not to let him lick you.'

'I like it. What happens in Cyprus?'

'It's called decompression. They get a shave and a shower and a comedy show and something like a barbecue — '

Isabel closed her eyes so that Beetle could make a thorough job of washing her face. 'Do they get drunk?'

'I don't know, darling. I think they're only allowed five cans each.'

'And then be sick?'

'Izzy, might I persuade you to have some breakfast?'

Isabel unlocked her arms and got to her feet. 'Have the twins had breakfast?'

15

'Just yoghurt so far.'

'At school,' Isabel said, 'Libby Guthrie's little sister, who's only five, said to me, 'Is your daddy dead yet?' and I said yes. I said he'd been dead for ages and then Libby whispered to her sister why and Bella didn't get it and said, 'Did someone shoot him or blow him up?''

Alexa came across the kitchen and put her hands on Isabel's shoulders. Then she pushed her gently before her until they were standing in front of the fridge. 'Now. Yoghurt, banana, cereal. Or cereal and an apple. Dan is coming home today and he is all in one piece and there's not a scratch on him. We are *not* going to talk about dying.'

Isabel said nothing. Alexa reached into the fridge and put a pot of strawberry-flavoured yoghurt in her hand. 'Eat,' she said. 'I'm going to get the twins.'

★ ★ ★

Dan had said, please don't come to Brize Norton. Just wait at home. It'll be heaving at Brize and I don't want to see you all again for the first time in public.

Alexa had thought of saying, I think I've done enough waiting, and then she thought, if I've waited six months, why can't I wait a few more hours, if he's asked me to? And he was right, anyway; it was so much better to see him come home, privately, than to be part of the massed, emotional, tearful chaos of men and kit and babies and children and women and the

16

wonderful, awful exhilaration of reunion. Wasn't it? She had, of course, planned to go to the airbase. She had washed the car, and hoovered crisp crumbs out of the child seats, and cleaned the dashboard with some patent spray cleaner that had left the interior smelling like a cheap beauty parlour. But two nights ago, ringing from Cyprus — safe in Cyprus! Safely out of Afghanistan! — Dan had said, please don't come to Brize. Be there for me at home, where I can picture you. I'll whistle for Beetle. Let Beetle out when you hear me whistle. Four-ish, I should think. Maybe earlier.

She wasn't sure how she would have got through the day, if it hadn't been for Franny. Franny just appeared, after breakfast, and looked at the girls and said, 'Round to mine, babies,' to the twins, and 'I need you,' to Isabel, and then she said to Alexa, 'I'll bring them back about three thirty.'

'How do I ever repay you?'

'You have my horrible boys when Andy flies into a mountain.'

'He won't — '

'He might. He's another being in that chopper.'

Alexa looked at Isabel. She had put on small denim shorts over purple tights and the dumpy sheepskin boots that were an off-duty uniform for her school.

'OK, Iz?'

Isabel nodded. She bent her head so that her inappropriately shining eyes were not evident. Franny's older boy, Rupert, gave Isabel the

17

distinct feeling that he had somehow noticed her. And he was almost fifteen.

'She'll be fine,' Franny said. 'It'll give me a day of girl power, having your three.' She looked down at the twins, who were whispering away together in their particular language. 'These two fascinate my boys. Even if they'd rather die than say so.'

When they had gone, Alexa toured the house for the twentieth time, straightening and adjusting, wrenching the dripping shower head to its furthest Off position, polishing the draining board with kitchen paper. In the hall, she paused, and took the homecoming leaflet from the Welfare office off the table, and opened it.

'Why learn about homecoming and reunion?' it began brightly. 'Everyone is affected, that's why — service members, spouses and children all feel the stress, as well as friends and relatives. After all, everyone changes. It's only natural that those who have been away, as well as the spouses and children, family and friends, will have changed with time. They won't, any of them, be exactly as you remembered.'

She put the leaflet down, and looked at herself in the mirror Mo had glanced in the night before. Was she different? Did she *look* different? A bit thinner, maybe, but the same height, obviously, and hair more or less the same length, and even if her jeans were newish, they were a familiar kind of jeans, and her hoop earrings had been given to her by Dan, soon after they met — he'd said that he thought big earrings went with long hair. She moved her head slightly. Her clean hair swished across her shoulders. Still long, if not quite as long as it had been when she went — so reluctantly! — to a party given by a work colleague at the school where they both taught, and there was this tall young man gazing at her from the other side of the room until she'd had enough to drink to go up to him and say, in a slightly pantomime voice that she was ashamed, in retrospect, of using, 'Can I help you in any way, sir?'

'Yes,' he'd said. 'You can leave this party with me, right now, before anyone else nabs you.'

And she had. They'd gone to a pub, and then to a Chinese place to eat, and then for a walk in a park she didn't know because it wasn't in her part of London, and he'd kissed her, suddenly, in the middle of a public path, right under a street lamp, and here she was, eight years and two babies and five house moves later, waiting for him to come back with all the sick excitement she had felt in that second, in the night-time park, before he kissed her, and when she had known with complete avidity that he would.

Beetle shot suddenly past her out of the kitchen, and stood, quivering and taut, by the front door, his tail a blur of wagging.

'Nonsense,' Alexa said. 'Nonsense. He won't be back for hours yet.'

Beetle took no notice. He focussed on the door as if he could see through it, every particle of him poised and straining.

'I'll show you,' Alexa said. 'I'll open the door and show you. And when it turns out to be someone else, you'll feel pretty silly.'

19

She leaned across Beetle and unlatched the door. Beetle, unable to bear waiting for even another fraction of a second, shoved the door wider with his shoulder and bolted out towards the road. Alexa looked up, across her badly mown lawn, over the ragged hedge, towards the beech clump. Coming across the central grass of the Quadrant, in desert combats and burdened with his grip and his Bergen rucksack, was — Dan.

2

George Riley had planned to go down, quietly, to Brize Norton when the planes came in from Cyprus. He'd had no intention of joining Alexa and the children or in any way compromising their exclusive and primary right to welcome Dan home, but he thought he'd just like to be there, in the crowd, to see the lad safe back with his own eyes, and then melt away, satisfied and relieved, to begin the laborious public-transport journey back to Wimbledon, where he could then go round to the old man's flat and report Dan's return and they could celebrate together with a beer.

But when Alexa rang to tell him that Dan wanted their reunion to take place at home and that she wasn't driving anywhere, it had seemed a bit sneaky, to George, to travel down to Brize, even if he didn't make himself known, so he went round to see his father instead, to tell him of the change of plan, and the old man said, don't ring him. Don't ring him for a couple of days.

George said, 'What if he doesn't ring me?'

Eric Riley had never lost the manner of the regimental sergeant major he had once been. 'Then he doesn't.'

'But — '

'You wait,' Eric said to his son. 'You just bloody *wait*. When I got back from Aden the

21

families had to wait till the boys wrote them a bloody *letter*.' He put a not entirely steady hand out for his teacup. George thought his father drank more tea than anybody else in the universe. First thing in the morning, he'd make a brew. Last thing at night, he'd make a brew. In between, George suspected that the kettle never had time to cool down, and the teapot Eric used — squat and metal, encased in the crocheted wool cover George's mother had made decades ago, striped in regimental colours — was as black as a coalmine inside, from all the tannin. 'When you got back from the Falklands,' Eric added, after a gulp of tea, 'I don't recall you ringing. I don't recall you being in any bloody hurry to let your mum and me know you were home.'

George looked at his father's teacup. Once out of the Army, Eric swore he'd never drink a brew out of a mug again; he'd drink it in a civilized manner, out of a teacup. And he always had. Just as he took the antimacassar from the back of his armchair, embroidered in cross-stitch, to the launderette with his washing, and went to the barber every three weeks, and shined his shoes with spit and polish and a bone worn as dark as the teapot. Standards, he said.

'I was in a twitch about Lisette, I should think,' George said. 'What she'd been up to while I was away.' He leaned forward and put his arms on his knees. 'Well, we know now, don't we?'

Eric gave a snort. 'Well shot of that baggage, you are.'

'She's Dan's mum, Dad.'

'There's mothers and mothers,' Eric said. 'Those who think they've done it all just by giving birth, and those who think that's where it starts. What kind of mother runs off to Australia with her fancy man and leaves a little lad behind?'

'I'm glad she did, Dad.'

Eric gave his cup a little shove. 'Fill me up, lad.'

George stood up. It was too hot in Eric's flat, as usual, and the smell of dusty, fusty old fabrics and carpet gave the air a peculiar, slightly sickening density. If he opened the window, though, he knew that not only would Eric complain of a draught, but it would let in the equally thick, cheesy smell of the neighbouring dairy, whose milk floats were lined up docilely in the afternoons, as neatly as toy trucks in a children's cartoon. His mother Eileen, Eric's late wife, had regarded the flat as convenient, but only temporary. Her dream had been, one day, to cross the Queens Road and live in a part of Wimbledon she had always aspired to.

'Trouble with your father,' she'd said to George, only days before she died, 'is that if it isn't to do with the Army, he's got no more ambition than a potato.'

George picked up Eric's teacup. His mother hadn't been a Wimbledon girl, any more than Eric had been a Wimbledon boy. They'd ended up there because of Eric's brother — his one, much older brother, whose memory Eric revered, and who'd been killed at the very end of

23

the First World War — October 1918 — and whose memorial headstone was in Wimbledon, in the Gap Road Cemetery.

Eric hadn't even known Ray. Ray had died four years before Eric was born, but there was something about the bad luck of being killed less than a month before the Armistice that impelled Eric to choose to live near by, and to keep his memory company with regular visits. And it was only his memory. Ray's body, like that of every soldier killed after 1915, was not repatriated after his death. There were too many of them, the authorities had decided, and most of them were too mutilated even to identify. So they were hastily buried where they had fallen, and this wretched fate, this horrible anonymity, had added to Eric's resolve, which he felt in the core of his being and would never have dreamed of analysing.

Anyway, Eric liked the Gap Road Cemetery. It wasn't always quite as tidy as he would have liked — 'There's over twenty-four acres of it to keep up, you know,' a Council gardener had protested one day when Eric complained about grass clippings not being picked up — but he couldn't fault the care the War Graves Commission took of the services headstones. The word he used to himself — a word he'd heard his granddaughter-in-law, Alexa, use — was meticulous. It was meticulous to spray the headstones regularly with fungicide so that they stood out, bright white, the lettering on each one sharply visible. 'R. C. Riley,' Ray's headstone read, '17660. Private Army Pay

Corps. 14th October 1918. Aged 20,' and then underneath, a big, simple, deeply incised cross. Eric didn't ever take flowers when he went to see Ray, except on Remembrance Day, when he took a few red paper poppies from the British Legion and stuck them in the earth at the bottom of the headstone in a neat, stiff little row.

Eric and Ray's mother had been eighteen when she'd had Ray and forty-two — and deeply ashamed to be pregnant, since it told the world that she and Eric's father still had relations — when she had Eric. She died when Eric was the age Ray had been when he was killed, but by then Eric was overseas, with the Army, in the Second World War and was offered no more concession for grieving or adjustment than half an hour with the padre and his mates holding back on the customary abuse for a couple of days. When he came back to England, he married the daughter of the couple who'd lived next door to his parents, whom he'd always got on well with.

'Might as well,' she said, when he suggested they marry. 'At least we know what we're getting into, what with the war changing everything, like it's done.'

That had been in 1945. The following year, George was born and Eric was promoted. He went on being promoted, up and up the non-commissioned ranks, until September 1965, when he went out to Aden as a regimental sergeant major, where he stayed till June 1967.

'Best years of my life,' he'd say silently to Ray's headstone. 'Bloody knew what I was there for. We lost a good battery commander in a helicopter crash, but apart from that, we showed them what's what. Bloody useful.'

George put the refilled teacup down in front of his father. 'Bit stewed, Dad.'

'You know I like it stewed. Stewed's how I've drunk it all my life. You spoken to Alexa?'

George sat down again opposite his father in the chair scratchily upholstered in cut moquette. 'That's how I know Dan didn't want the family at Brize.'

Eric eyed him. 'Was she cut up?'

'I think she's so relieved he's out of Afghanistan she didn't care one way or the other.'

'Bloody curse, these mobile and email whatsits,' Eric said. 'You know too much. You have to tell too much.'

George thought back to the blueys of his soldiering days, those fragile airmail letters that invariably had too much depending upon them. And what you didn't read, you imagined, like him imagining all the things Lisette was doing — getting up to, more like — which she never mentioned but which somehow haunted her carefree, careless handwriting like shadows and whisperings. When he'd been down in the South Atlantic in 1982, he hadn't known whether to long for a bluey or to hope the next one never came. At least nowadays you knew the day-to-day stuff, it wasn't all such a big deal. And you got the football results almost as soon as the match ended. He said, 'It's never easy, coming back. Not for them, or us.'

His father drank some tea with relish. 'It was easier on those bloody ships. Took for ever. Plenty of time to readjust, get bored. Now it's decompression like a bloody diver, wham, bang, out of ops and back in your own bloody bedroom with the wife wanting the moon and stars.'

George said reprovingly, 'You don't think that of Alexa.'

Eric grunted. 'I think the bloody world of Alexa.'

'The tops,' George said softly.

When Dan had brought Alexa to Wimbledon, they'd both been bowled over. She wasn't a beauty, necessarily, but she had class. She was tall and smiling, with all that hair down her back, and she was a widow. Twenty-six, and a widow. They couldn't get over that. Bloody shame. Where was the justice in a lovely girl like that being a widow at twenty-six in this day and age when the doctors can do almost anything? But then, if her husband had still been alive, Dan mightn't have stood a chance. He might be the apple of his father's and grandfather's eye — Ministry of Defence-sponsored place at Welbeck College, Military College at Sandhurst, first commissioned officer in the family — but a girl like Alexa, married with a baby, might still never have given him a second glance. Just another typical bloody soldier, she might have thought. Why would I need one of them when I've got my nice civvy husband already?

But then the poor bugger had died, hadn't he? And horribly, from this tumour on the brain.

And there was Alexa, trying to look after her little girl, trying to hold down her teaching job, trying not to ask her parents for help, and she goes to this party, not in a good mood, and there's our Dan, standing by the wall, drink in his hand, eyeing up the talent, and he spots her as soon as she comes in, and he thinks, that one's got my name on, and he waits and watches and waits and watches, and blow me if she doesn't bloody well come right up to him and ask him if there's something he wants. Wants? *Wants?* When what he wants is standing there right in front of him? Bloody marvellous.

There'd been much debate as to where Dan should bring Alexa to meet his father and grandfather. George's austere little flat had been dismissed as having all the domestic charm of a hospital waiting room, and the café in Elys, which Eric so favoured, would indicate that they didn't have a home to take her to. So it was a teatime occasion, in the end, in Eric's flat, with Eric's teacups, and a plate of cakes from the French patisserie at the top of the High Street, all a bit uncomfortable, a bit awkward, until Alexa produced a bottle of whisky from her bag and set it down without comment next to Eric's teapot.

George thought he'd probably fallen in love with her at that moment. He knew his father had. And Dan was so deep in already he was almost drowning. George had looked at the four of them, sitting round the whisky and grinning, and felt suddenly, recklessly, that all the pains of the past, all the loneliness and anxiety and disappointment, had been swept away by the presence of this young woman and her — her sheer *style*. When he looked at Dan, the lad seemed to have a glow round him. A captain already, and soon — no doubt about it — to be beiged for a major. And now this girl, pouring whisky into Eric's late wife's sherry glasses and licking cake crumbs off her fingers. Her father was something in the Foreign Office, her mother — well, she was one of those ladies who knew how to arrange flowers and talk comfortably to strangers about nothing, from the sound of her. Meeting them might not be something any of the Rileys exactly looked forward to, but, hell, what did that matter? And if they could produce a girl like this, he could forgive them anything. He'd raised his whisky glass and looked at Alexa over it. 'Here's to you, ma'am,' he'd said, and meant it.

★　★　★

As it turned out, the meeting between the Rileys and Alexa's parents was quite successful. Dan refused to get worked up about it, saying that his future parents-in-law were just like the Army great and good who came to the regimental drinks parties the garrison held at Christmas — 'You know the type, Dad.' Eric wanted to wear his suit, so George wore his, too, in case his father looked out of place; but when they got there, to this very classy flat in a vast building on the Marylebone Road — small but formal, with little sofas and a lot of lilies — Alexa's father was in a jacket and tie and her mother was in pearls, so the suits looked appropriate. Alexa, bless her heart, was in jeans and a velvet jacket, and her little Isabel was in gumboots which she refused to take off. Her grandmother said things like 'Not on the sofa, darling' quite often, but neither Alexa nor Isabel seemed to take any notice, and when Morgan Longworth offered George a drink, Alexa said, 'Don't do your global cocktail act on George, Pa. He drinks beer or whisky,' and Morgan, smoothly, not batting an eyelash, said, 'Sensible man.'

Eric had asked for tea.

Dan said easily, 'Granddad doesn't drink in other people's houses.'

'On principle?' Elaine Longworth said archly.

Eric, ramrod straight in his suit, looked at her and smiled. 'If I'm going to make a bloody fool of myself, ma'am, I'd rather do it in my own home.'

After they'd gone — Alexa declining to reveal where Dan was taking her and Isabel — Morgan Longworth gave his wife enough time to plump up all her handsome cushions and then he said, 'Well?'

Elaine straightened. She put her hands on her hips. She said, not looking at Morgan, 'Not sure what I was expecting . . . '

'But?'

'I don't think I've ever had three such good-looking men all together in my drawing room before.'

Morgan waited. He picked up Eric's teacup and George's whisky tumbler.

30

'Of course — ' Elaine began and stopped.

'I know.'

'Richard was . . . well, better educated. More . . . more sophisticated.'

'Certainly,' Morgan said.

He took the cup and the glass out to the sleek little galley kitchen. When he came back, Elaine had picked up one of the cushions and was holding it against her, as if for comfort. She said, 'I couldn't help liking them.'

'Especially the old man. Didn't he remind you of Bombardier Prout?'

'In Hong Kong? Yes, exactly. Do — do you think she'll be safe with him?'

'With Dan? As houses.'

'But this Army thing. We saw so much of it, didn't we? Yearning for a settled home, not knowing whether to be with the husband or the children — '

Morgan adjusted the glass coffee table one inch. 'Just like us, then.'

'We weren't — '

'We were. I remember you were in a frightful state when Lex had to board.'

Elaine put the cushion back at a precise angle to its pair. 'You didn't like it either.'

'I hated it,' Morgan said. 'Poor little girl. First an only child and then sent off to boarding school in a wretched climate.'

'She was an only child,' Elaine said on a dangerously rising note, 'because I was forty when we married and forty-two when she arrived. She was something of a *miracle*.'

Morgan threaded his way between the sofa

31

and the coffee table so that he could put an arm round his wife's shoulders. 'My observation was not meant as an accusation. You know that. She was a miracle indeed. And,' he said, increasing the pressure of his arm, 'you were loyally following me all over the place.'

There was a small silence, in which both of them did a little diverse remembering. Morgan recalled — as he often did, pleasedly, privately — the one time he had achieved deputy head of mission, in Jakarta, and the very brief period, in Paris — Paris! — when he had stood in as a minister at the Embassy, during someone else's illness. Elaine, in the circle of her husband's arm, remembered the unspoken reason, all those long travelling diplomatic years, for persistently accepting posts overseas. If Morgan was overseas, he was graded as an A2 — he loved that — which would not have been the case had he remained at a desk job in the Foreign Office in London. She also remembered, after a brief battle with self-control that always accompanied the recollection, that except for two briefly glorious temporary appointments in Jakarta and Paris, Morgan had, more often than not, been a counsellor. Three years here, three years there — Athens, Hong Kong, Reykjavik, Buenos Aires, all over the place. She swallowed. Morgan was seventy-eight, now, and she was seventy-six, and there was absolutely no point in wishing that their lives had been either different or more candid.

She moved, very slightly, to elude Morgan's

arm, and said, 'Dan's done very well. In the Army.'

'And weren't they proud of him!'

'He's sweet to her,' Elaine said. 'And to Isabel. Perhaps he'll be a good influence. Perhaps he'll persuade Lex that letting a child grow up without many rules only makes for unhappiness all round.'

'You mean the gumboots.'

Elaine cast a quick look at her cream sofa. 'So — *odd*. And Lex in jeans.'

'She's always in jeans.'

Elaine looked across the room. On a reproduction eighteenth-century French console table against the far wall was a photograph of Richard Maybrick, the same photograph that his daughter Isabel would have, eight years later, in her bedroom at Larkford Camp.

'She's been through so much,' Elaine said. 'I just don't want there to be any more. No more worries and separations and choices. I wish Dan wasn't a soldier. I wish he was a lawyer or a doctor, someone who came home at night, someone with a career and not — not a *calling*.'

She turned her head away. Morgan put his arm back round her shoulders and offered her a clean white handkerchief.

'I know,' he said.

★ ★ ★

'I think you should ring Mrs L,' Eric Riley said to his son.

They had moved on from tea to beer. George

was drinking his from the can; Eric, from a glass. They were each on their second beer. They never drank more than two, and if George went to the pub on his way home for a top-up, he never mentioned it to his father.

'Why me?'

'They'll be wondering, that's why,' Eric said. 'It's bloody manners.'

'But Alexa'll ring them — '

'Not with Dan back, she won't. She won't ring anyone. Get on that phone and tell Mrs L the plane's landed and we can all breathe easy.'

'I'll do it from home.'

Eric pointed across the room to where his telephone sat on the small cloth-covered table where George's mother had first put it, eighteen years before.

'You'll bloody well do it now.'

George put his beer can down and stood up. 'I've got nothing to tell her — '

'You have. Dan's back in England. That's all she needs to know. Get on with it.'

George moved reluctantly towards the telephone. He hated telephones, always had. He preferred to walk miles to deliver a message, rather than say it down a phone line.

'Can't remember the number.'

'It's on the wall. On my list. Third one down.'

'Dad — '

'You're useless,' Eric said, heaving himself out of his chair. 'Bloody useless. Just as well you didn't apply to Signals or Logistics, they'd have laughed in your bloody face.' He came slowly across the room, shuffling slightly in his leather slippers, the backs trodden down as they had been in all the identical pairs of slippers George could remember him wearing, all his life. He held his hand out. 'Give it here, you moron.'

George handed him the telephone. He was grinning. 'Thanks, Dad.'

'Sing out the number.'

George watched his father's big fingers jabbing at the numbers on the handset. If your hands looked at home ramming a shell up the breech of a gun, they never looked quite right when required to do anything domestic. It still amazed George to see his father making a sandwich. It was as surprising as finding an elephant able to do it.

'That you, Mrs L?' Eric shouted into the receiver. 'Good. Good . . . Yes, not too bad, thank you, nothing death won't take care of . . . Yes. Yes. That's why I'm ringing. His plane's landed, and he should be on his way home, or home by now . . . No. He didn't want that. He wanted them at home, waiting for him . . . No idea, Mrs L. Who's to say what's in a man's mind after six months in the bloody desert? . . . No. No, I shouldn't. Leave them to ring you. I've just said as much to the boy's idiot father. Your first family comes first, and the rest of us just have to wait. But he's home. He's safe . . . You, too, Mrs L. Regards to His Excellency.' He took the phone away from his ear, squinted at it, punched a button and handed it to George. 'Useless woman,' he said. 'She'll never get it. She talks as if he was home from some bloody business trip, no more to worry about than writing a report and getting his shirts washed.'

'You like her,' George said reprovingly.

'Of course I bloody like her. She's Alexa's mother, isn't she? But a lifetime's poncing round Embassy cocktail parties is never going to help you understand soldiering, is it?'

★ ★ ★

In her drawing room above the Marylebone Road, Elaine Longworth sát holding her telephone. Morgan was out at some reception at the Argentine Embassy — he loved those parties still, but she only went with him these days if there was a very particular reason to — and she was alone in the quiet flat, with the comforting rumble of traffic from below and the silk-shaded lamps lit, throwing her carefully arranged pieces of South-East Asian sculpture into dramatic relief. There was a precisely mixed gin and tonic beside her, on a rosewood table acquired in The Hague, but she hadn't touched it. Nor had she opened the evening paper, or put on her reading glasses. She was simply sitting, on one of her cream sofas, in a pool of lamplight, thinking.

It had been during a car journey, in the dense heat and traffic of Jakarta, that she had mooted to Alexa that she might — would — have to go back to England, for schooling. To boarding school. She would come out to Indonesia for the holidays, of course, travelling on the aeroplane with a label round her neck advertising her as an unaccompanied minor, but in the term time she would be at a school where lots of diplomatic

36

children went, so there would be lots of girls, *lots*, who were in the same position as Alexa.

Elaine put the telephone down beside her on the sofa and closed her eyes. When she thought about Jakarta, she remembered their house (lovely) and their staff (even lovelier), but the things that brought it back most vividly were the details, like the sound of sandals slapping against bare heels and the intense fruit taste of mangosteens. And like that moment in the car, when she faltered in painting a rosy picture of English boarding-school life to Alexa, and at the same instant the car stopped at some traffic lights and was at once surrounded by distressing hordes of barefoot children, begging and beseeching, and the driver wound down his window far enough to throw out a handful of rupiah coins, as light and inconsequential as sequins. And Alexa had turned to her and said, 'If I have to go to England, why don't you come with me?'

She remembered that she had looked out of the window away from Alexa. The car was moving forward again, and what with her tears, the faces of the children outside the window were elongated into brown blurs. She wanted to blurt out, 'I can't, I can't,' but instead she said in a slightly choked voice, her face still averted from Alexa, 'I have to stay with Daddy, darling. You know that.'

Alexa hadn't replied. She sat staring at the back of Pak Hari's sleek black head. Elaine had reached out for her hand, and although she hadn't refused to let her mother take it, she didn't respond, and her hand lay in Elaine's, warm but inert. Then, after a polite interval, she took it back again.

Elaine had wanted desperately to say sorry, but she had felt, obscurely, that apologizing for this decision would somehow be betraying Morgan, and she had promised herself on her wedding day in Chelsea Registry office to show no kind of disloyalty that wasn't private to herself alone. Morgan had been forty-two then, and it was plain that he would never, for all his talk and mild self-delusion, be anything more than a useful minor diplomat. She could see that, but she would never countenance anyone else making it plain that they had seen it too. Especially not Alexa. Daddy's job was paramount. Daddy was paramount. Without Daddy, we wouldn't get to travel and live in interesting places and eat mangoes in the bath and learn to say thank you in Bahasa. Daddy's life made our lives possible, and that had to be remembered and accommodated at all times. Otherwise she, Elaine Jackson, might still be the spinster personal assistant to a senior partner in a firm of solicitors in St Mary Axe, specializing in disputes between air-freight companies and their carriers.

Alexa had not mentioned going to boarding school again. When they got home, she had climbed out of the car — Pak Hari holding the door for her, respectfully — and run down to the compound gate to talk to the guard and his friend in the dusty street outside, who sold chicken soup from a barrow with smeary glass walls and a violently bright kerosene lamp. And when she came back to the house, she joined her parents for dinner — nasi goreng, with prawns and chilli — with the air of someone who had won some kind of inner tussle and would definitely not welcome further discussion on the matter.

Elaine opened her eyes. That was over a quarter of a century ago. Alexa was now thirty-four with children of her own. But feeling for her, on her behalf, didn't seem to get less acute just because they were both older. She still couldn't bear to think of Alexa leaving for school and England, any more than she could bear to think of her now, at once heady with relief at Dan's safe return and simultaneously faced with getting to know him again, and then bracing herself for the next departure.

She picked up the evening paper. Don't ring them, Eric had said. Don't. She opened the paper and stared at it, unseeing, without her spectacles on. She wouldn't. It was the least she could do. And the least was so much better than, as in the past, the wrong thing.

3

Dan was so thin. When Alexa, unable to conceal her shock, pointed it out as he emerged from the shower, he gave a little bark of laughter and shook water out of his hair. He said deprecatingly, 'We all look pretty shabby.'

'You didn't,' Alexa said, misunderstanding him. 'You got home shaved, laundered — '

Dan ran a thumb down his visible ribs. 'I meant this. The fitness — '

'Oh,' Alexa said, and then, as if correcting a mistake, 'Of course.'

'The body armour weighs a ton. And then all the kit. The heat — '

'Sorry, Dan. I know.'

He smiled at her. He said, quoting, 'Selfless commitment'.'

'Don't remind me.'

'What comes next?'

''Respect for others',' Alexa said, quoting the military mantra and trying to keep the smallest hint of disrespect out of her voice. ''Integrity, loyalty, discipline and courage'.'

'Word perfect, Mrs Riley. You'd make a fine soldier.' He leaned forward and kissed her mouth.

When he took his mouth away, she said, 'Lunch?'

He shook his head. 'Seeing someone.'

She intended not to say 'Who?' and failed.

He moved past her, wrapping a towel around

his waist, and made for their bedroom. 'Gus.'

'But you saw Gus — ' Alexa said, and stopped.

Dan didn't reply. He dropped the towel on the bedroom floor and began to dress, rapidly and neatly, but not in battledress, she noticed. He was putting on barrack dress — khaki drill trousers, shiny shoes, the blue ribbed sweater that looked like a garment belonging to a dated Action Man.

She said, 'Why formal? Why barrack dress?'

He didn't turn round. He was buttoning his epauletted shirt in front of the mirror which — Army issue again — had never been long enough for people of their height to see themselves in, except in sections.

'Two CO's orders. He doesn't want us going berserk just because we're home.'

'Oh,' Alexa said faintly.

She looked at Dan's back, then she looked at their bed. She had been married to Dan for seven years and she still could not always look at their bed, or him, with much equanimity. Four days ago, when he got home, he had carried her up there — *carried* her, all five foot ten of her — and he'd hardly said a word. He wasn't saying many words now, either.

'But — but can't someone else do whatever you have to do? Won't the sergeants supervise all the unpacking and sorting of stuff?'

'Of course.'

'But — '

Dan turned round. He had his red-and-blue side hat in his hands. He said, 'I need to see Gus.'

'OK.'

'And the young officers. Set them up a bit not to wreck their leave. Sort out their money. Remind them about drink driving. You know.'

'And Gus?'

'You know about that, too.'

Alexa looked at the ceiling. A water stain like a great, blurred grey cobweb covered one corner, where a pipe from the water tank in the attic above had leaked six months ago. Gus was Gus Melville, another battery commander, another major, a friend of fifteen years' standing.

'My bezzie mate,' Gus often said of Dan, standing beside him, almost leaning on him. 'The man with whom I can, and do, speak in tongues.'

Dan put his side hat on with precision, without glancing in the mirror. He came round the bed and put his hands on Alexa's shoulders. He said, looking straight at her, 'My ears are still ringing.'

'I know. I didn't mean — '

He bent, very slightly, to kiss her again. 'All those boys of mine,' he said. 'That big slug of Scots folk dying to get home. But they're useless. Their risk threshold is completely out of whack. I've got to talk to them before they go, or they'll get arrested. Or die on the roads. And I've got to talk to Gus.'

She stood aside. 'You go.'

He paused for a second. Then he said, 'I'm not with it yet. Bear with me,' and ran down the stairs at the speed of an adolescent setting himself a record.

The front door slammed shudderingly. Alexa went slowly along the landing and into the twins' bedroom, and picked up a slipper and a doll and a length of mauve Christmas tinsel from the floor. The twins were at nursery school until lunchtime. Isabel was back at boarding school after half-term. She had gone back with another child, driven by another mother, and she had not looked out of the car window as they pulled away, but had seemed to engage in animated conversation with the other girl as if to indicate that home, where all the rest of her family was now reunited and together, was of no real consequence to her. Alexa had turned to Dan. He'd held her.

'She'll be OK,' he'd said.

'I don't think so. She hates it. Hates it.'

'Everybody hates saying goodbye. Look at us.'

She'd glanced up at him. 'Dan?'

But he was already looking somewhere else. He was thinking about something else. The arms that were round her were still holding her, but remotely, as if her body was anyone's. She gently detached herself. Dan had said that deployment on active service made you long for extremes, either the supreme domesticity of home when you were away from it or the violence of action and danger when you were back. You couldn't just halt the pendulum, he said, you couldn't stop it crashing from side to side, often out of control. Even if it sometimes hit her — or the children — as it swung.

It was over an hour until she needed to collect the twins. They would run out of school towards her, on a high, and then squabble in the car, because they were hungry. She had planned to say, 'Daddy'll be there at lunchtime,' but she couldn't, because he wouldn't be. He'd be with Gus and the other officers, in the officers' mess, with the silver Chinese dragon on the table and the sentimental narrative paintings of regimental defeats and moments of noble and fruitless heroism on the walls, drinking soup and speaking in tongues, that Army patois of acronyms and specific slang which was as bonding and exclusive as the twins' private cheeping. He would not be thinking about the twins. Or her. He would be — as they all described it — in the zone.

She looked round the room. She had painted it corn yellow and put up cork boards for the twins' energetic and random artistic efforts. Their beds, German and ingeniously converted from their original cot form, had been a present from her parents. Two little beds, two fleece dressing-gowns, two sets of slippers with animal faces on the toes, two hairbrushes, one plastic pot of hair slides and clips, umpteen soft toys. It was, as she stood there holding the slipper, the doll and the mauve tinsel, eerily quiet. She hadn't left a radio on downstairs and Beetle, disappointed at not being taken with Dan, would be burying his suffering in sleep, in his basket. The silence, now that she was really listening to it, was enormous.

Of course, the telephone hadn't rung for four days. Neither the landline nor her own mobile. All her friends, respectful of her and Dan's reunion, were carefully leaving them alone. So were his family, and her parents. They would all be imagining the household alive and vibrating with relieved energy — even, as Mo had pointed out, the energy of rows. They would be visualizing meals together, and walks together, and hilarious subterfuges to get to bed together with a pair of lynx-eyed three-year-olds in constant attendance. They would not be picturing this solitude, this silence. The only person Alexa could think of in a similar position, except that both her children were away at school, was Gus's wife, Kate Melville — although Kate worked in London three days a week and had never — loudly — let the inflexibility of the Army stand in her way. Today was one of her London days. She would not have altered that, even for Gus's homecoming.

Alexa bent and put the doll on a bed and the slipper beside its pair. Then she balled up the tinsel and put it in her pocket. Kate Melville was energetic and impressive and focussed, but she did not seem to need Sara and Prue and Franny and Mo as Alexa did; she did not appear to suffer from doubts about validity, or visibility. She ran a cancer-research charity in London, and in her crisply expressed opinion, her work had all the importance and consequence of her husband's.

'Gus may wear the uniform,' Mo said of the Melvilles, 'but Kate wears the trousers!'

Alexa went slowly downstairs and into the kitchen. Beetle remained in his tight curl, in his

45

basket, but a faint tremor of his tail acknowledged Alexa's entrance. Dan would probably come back after lunch and collect him, to take him up to the battery offices, and she would see Beetle being completely fulfilled by this small attention. There was a lot to be said for emulating the attitude of a Labrador — take what's on offer with a glad heart, and if nothing's on offer, go to sleep. Franny's boys were like that, robust and cheerful, easy to handle and prone to sleeping when bored.

'Too sad,' Franny'd say, looking at them. 'Pure cannon fodder. Cookie-cutter Andys, both of them. My genes didn't get a look in.'

Alexa took her telephone out of her jeans pocket. Maybe she'd ring Franny. But then, if she rang Franny there'd have to be some good reason, however small, for doing so, otherwise Franny would immediately guess what was the matter.

'Give him time,' she'd say. 'They are on Planet Afghan when they get back. Give him time.'

And she'd be right. Only the afternoon before, out in the garden with the twins so that Flora could show her father that she had learned to propel herself on the swing by herself, a woodpecker — unexpected, out of season — had suddenly started drilling into a tree fifty yards away, and Dan had let go of Tassy, whose hand he was holding, sprinted across the grass and dived under the garden table. The twins, shrieking with delight, had thought it was a game. Alexa had known that it wasn't. When Dan crawled out and stood up, shaking and shamefaced with the little girls jigging and squeaking round him, Alexa had wanted nothing so much as to hold him and comfort him. But that would have been the last thing he wanted. He simply stood there for half a minute, mastering himself, and then he said to Flora, 'OK, now, show me,' and walked past Alexa back to the swing as if she hardly existed.

She looked down at her phone, pressed the buttons to reach her Favourites list, and dialled, on impulse.

'I should be in a meeting,' Jack Dearlove said, without preamble.

'Are you?'

'No. Instead I'm not eating a prawn-mayonnaise sandwich that is sitting on my desk.'

'Oh, Jack — '

'It never ends, this battle with the body. I put my bathroom scales in a suitcase behind a whole lot of stuff in my bedroom cupboard and then I got them out again. Pitiful. How's the hero?'

Alexa looked out of the kitchen window. 'Thin. And spaced. Not with me in spirit.'

'But in body?'

'None of your business.'

'So that's OK then. Give him time.'

'I am.'

'Give him,' Jack said, '*loads* of time.'

Alexa felt a sudden urgent desire to argue. She swallowed hard. 'I need to talk to him.'

'Nothing that can't wait?'

'Well,' Alexa said, 'there's all the old stuff. Isabel's homesickness, Flora's eye, the state of the car, more lumps on Beetle. I suppose that can all wait till he can switch his sights round to us again. But — '

'But what?'

'There's something else,' Alexa said.

'You're not pregnant!'

'Work it out, Jack. If I was, I'd be huge by now.'

'I meant — '

'By someone else?'

'Well,' Jack said, 'it happens — '

'Not to me.'

'OK. Sorry.'

'Frustration is one thing. Fidelity is quite another.'

'I said sorry,' Jack said. 'What other thing, then?'

Alexa looked across the kitchen. On the dresser which she had bought for ten pounds at a car-boot sale in Wincanton, propped against her cherished row of polka-dotted pottery mugs, was a long white envelope. She cleared her throat. Then she said, precisely, 'I have been offered a job.'

'Good for you.'

'No, Jack,' Alexa said. 'A proper job. Full-time assistant head of languages at a private school near by, with a real salary and real responsibilities.'

'Oh.'

'It's nearly as good as the job I had when I met Dan. It means health insurance and perhaps a place for Isabel — '

'You can't do it,' Jack said.

'What?'

'You can't. You have the twins, and Dan'll get posted somewhere or start a course in Shrivenham or something. You know you can't.'

There was a short silence. Then Alexa said, 'Are you *listening* to yourself? Or are you just thinking about that sandwich?'

'I am thinking about you.'

'And telling me that I can't even consider — '

'You can't.'

Alexa closed her eyes. 'I'm having a pretty awful day. And you are making it much worse. I think I'm going to ring off.'

'Do that,' Jack said. His voice had none of its usual warmth. 'Just do that. And see if it makes you feel any better.'

'I really thought that you, of all people — '

'You *chose* Dan,' Jack said, interrupting. 'You *chose* this life, you traded freedom for security, you *know* you did. When the twins are bigger or Dan gets a regiment or something, *then* you can think of working. But not now.'

'What's come *over* you?'

'Reality,' Jack said. 'Hunger. Anxiety about you. Facing living with the consequences of my own decisions. All of it. None of it. Fed-upness. Thursday. I don't know. I only know that you can't indulge yourself right now, so don't burden poor bloody Dan with it, fresh from being bombed out of his skull.'

She heard the line go dead. She looked at the screen on her phone. 'Call ended,' it said with the kind of complacent obviousness that seemed to be the chief hallmark of modern technology. She put the phone back in her pocket. She was shaking slightly and found she was swallowing hard and repeatedly, as if to keep something uncontrolled — rage? tears? — at bay. She crossed the room to the dresser and picked up the envelope. It was addressed to her, Mrs Alexa Riley, and it had the school's name and elaborate crest printed in the top left-hand corner in dark blue. She knew the contents by heart, and there was absolutely nothing to be gained by re-reading them. In the space of five minutes Jack had managed to take her enterprise in even applying for the job, and her achievement in being offered it, and reduce both to a handful of dust. You can't, he'd said, and by implication, it wouldn't be fair. It wouldn't be fair to the man who has, quite simply, rescued you.

Alexa unhooked the car keys from their place among the mugs on the dresser, and motioned Beetle to follow her. He sat up, but hesitated, indicating that if he stayed where he was, Dan might return to collect him, which was, if it was all the same to her, his preferred option.

'Only if Gus is coming back this way,' Alexa said to him, reading him. 'He went with Gus, you see. I have the car and I thought you might like to collect the twins with me.'

Beetle stayed where he was, his tail quivering apologetically. Dan's dog, attuned to Dan, for all his manners and kind-heartedness.

'I wish I was like you,' Alexa said to him. 'I wish what I had was always enough.'

Beetle lay down again in his basket and propped his chin on the edge. He was going faintly grey around his muzzle and sometimes his eyes had a blueish milky film to them. He was ten; quite an age for a Labrador.

Alexa knelt down by his basket, filled with sudden fear and remorse. 'You know how important you are, don't you?'

Beetle looked embarrassed. He gave her outstretched hand a brief lick.

Alexa stood up again. 'Won't be long.'

He didn't look up as she left the room.

★   ★   ★

Dan had left the driving seat of the car pushed right back, as was his wont, and the mirrors re-angled to suit the seat's new position. There was also a chocolate wrapper on the floor, as well as a Lottery scratch card and an empty can of Red Bull. The radio was tuned to Heart FM, or something she never listened to, and there was a pair of men's aviator sunglasses with a broken earpiece in the shallow well above the dashboard. The only thing that was heartwarming in her present frame of mind was a Simply Red CD in the disc player, the *Stars* album, produced in 1992 when neither she nor Dan had had any idea that the other one even existed. He'd given her the album on their third date, because he said that the words of one of the songs was what he felt about her already.

'Listen,' he'd said. 'Listen to this. The line about not believing in much but utterly believing in one other person. That's me. That's how I feel. I believe in you.'

Alexa adjusted the seat and the mirrors and

51

started the engine. It was ten minutes to the children's school, through the garrison village — beauty and tanning salon, off-licence, video store, small supermarket, barber, Gurkha Variety Store — and out into the shallow hills that ran down towards the main road that led eventually, through Dorset and Devon, to Cornwall. On good days, the idea of a road running all the way down to Cornwall was exhilarating, like being in an airport and seeing Shanghai and São Paulo listed on the Departures board, but on bad days, such a road seemed merely to taunt her with the confirmation that escape was not for her, that her present choices were entirely circumscribed by her earlier choice, which she had made without really having any idea of the consequences.

It had been a history teacher at that long-ago boarding school who had pointed out to her class that patterns in life and events are only visible in retrospect. Life lived day by day, he explained, appeared a shockingly random business, and it was only looking back that gave a clear view of the steady rise and fall of cause and effect. He had been a white-haired man in an old-fashioned tweed suit and a green corduroy waistcoat, the retired headmaster of a local prep school, and he talked to the girls he was teaching as if he was merely musing, thinking aloud as he wandered up and down in front of the blackboard. Most of his pupils thought he was just a caricature old granddad, but a few of them, including Alexa, had a sense that they were in the presence of a mind that knew too much to be shocked or surprised by any revelation. Alexa had even been able to talk to him about the violent homesickness caused by being at school on the other side of the world from her parents, and he had simply said, looking at her kindly but dispassionately, that she should try to enjoy these years before she had to shoulder the burden of making her own decisions.

'It's a liberty,' Mr Stonelake had said, 'not to have to live with the results of your own mistakes. You won't see it now, of course, but when you look back, you'll see it as one of the great freedoms of childhood.'

But she had, instead, ached for childhood to be over. At some level during those years at school, she had decided that the only way of getting through this period of her life was to accelerate herself somehow to the next stage, to hurry childhood and its dependency up by starting to take her own decisions, make her own choices. As an only child, there were, after all, only adults in her intimate world, and they seemed to make rules that suited themselves, rules that others then had to fall in with. And the falling in had, it was plain to Alexa, everything to do with money; the sooner she could pay for herself, the sooner she could decide for herself. Looking around at the worlds of work that she knew — diplomacy because of her father, teaching because of school — it seemed obvious to opt for learning to teach some of the languages she had acquired during the travels of her childhood. Even the Mandarin she had picked up in Hong Kong was an up-and-coming language, and then there was her Spanish from Buenos Aires, and the French she had excelled in at school. She allowed her parents to congratulate her on her admirable A-level results and then she announced that she was going to teacher-training college.

Her parents were horrified. Morgan had visualized the next phase of his daughter's life taking place in medieval libraries in Cambridge; Elaine had had a hazier vision of a punt on a dawn river, with Alexa wearing a ballgown and accompanied by a young man straight out of *Bridesbead Revisited*. Neither castle in the air featured anywhere remotely as prosaic as a teacher-training college.

'But you can't. Without a degree — '

'I'll get a degree,' Alexa said. 'I'll do a degree alongside gaining qualified teacher status. It will take three years. I can do it in London.'

Elaine said wildly, 'But who will fund it?'

Alexa looked at her coolly. She knew her mother had worked before her marriage, but her own rigorous view of work led her to consider Elaine's wifely supporting role during the last twenty years as not even beginning to count as work. She transferred her gaze deliberately to her father.

'You will,' she said.

There had been a few seconds of suspenseful silence, and then Morgan had said courteously, meeting his daughter's eyes, 'Of course.'

She knew they were disappointed. Whatever grandiose ambitions they had harboured for her were plainly difficult to relinquish, ambitions that manifested themselves in the — to her eyes — ridiculous formality of their domestic lives and the unbending stateliness of her father's bearing, even when encountered in a dressing-gown and slippers. There was nothing for it, Alexa decided, but to show them what muscular application she was capable of and what Real Life, as she termed it to herself, was all about. She deliberately chose a modest college in South London and was allotted a room in a hall of residence which had not seen one iota of modernization since it was built in the mid-seventies. She focussed on work, radical culture and mild political activism, on a sartorial diet of street markets and second-hand shops, and a physical one of anything in her local supermarket with a reduced label on it. She emerged, after three years, with a first-class degree and the offer of a job in the language department of a significant London girls' school. Her parents, by then newly retired and installed in their careful flat on the Marylebone Road — within walking distance, Alexa noted, of Harley Street and its attendant range of private medical services — took her out to dinner in Mayfair to celebrate. Her mother was in grey silk and pearls. Alexa wore embroidered jeans and a second-hand fur jacket. Her father, his champagne glass slightly raised towards his daughter, made an elegant speech about parental pride and the satisfaction of being proved wrong by one's only and much beloved child. The child in question heard him in silence.

The following year, the day after being offered promotion, despite her youth, to assistant head of department, Alexa had joined her childhood friend Jack Dearlove at a jazz café on the Fulham Road and been introduced to Richard Maybrick. He was OK, Alexa thought — nice enough, nice enough looking, cleverish, but he couldn't hold a candle to her exhilaration at being promoted. He was just part of the audience that night, another smiling, congratulatory face in a pleasurable sea of them, and if he didn't take his eyes off her, well, hey, that was just how it was that evening. She could have got high on tap water that night, she could have swung from the moon. She had rung her parents to tell them the news and her father had said, for the first time in her life, 'I am so proud of you.' Not 'I want this for you' or 'I wish you would do it this way,' but simply and at last, 'I am so proud of you.'

The next day, Richard Maybrick was at the school gates. He took her out for supper, explained that he had read geography at Newcastle University, where he met Jack, and was now interested in becoming a marine biologist. He came to the school gates five times in the next ten days, and then he asked Alexa to come up to the Lake District with him at the end of term, for a week's fell walking.

She had gazed at him. '*Fell* walking?'

'Yes.'

'In what?'

'Boots,' said Richard Maybrick, and reached under the café table. He put a stout paper carrier on the table. 'These. Your size.'

'Wow,' she said. She looked at the bag. 'How do you know my size?'

'I looked,' he said. 'I bet I know your dress size too.'

'And my bra size?'

'I can guess.'

'Are you — moving in on me?'

He smiled. He had a wide smile and strong, even teeth. 'If you'll let me.'

She'd looked back at the carrier bag containing the boots. There was suddenly, after all the years of endeavour, of solitary enterprise, of ostentatious frugality, an unspeakable appeal about surrender. She could put her feet into those boots, chosen by Richard, and be taken up to the Lake District, where she had never been, by Richard, and then follow Richard up and over those mountains and hills, as if — as if she was, for a heady moment, just handing the responsibility of being herself to someone else. From where she sat, right then, the prospect seemed to promise a new and unexpected kind of liberty. She put her hand on the carrier bag and pulled it towards her. 'OK,' she said.

Learning to love Richard Maybrick had been a profound but unalarming experience. His parents worked in medical research, his sister was a doctor and he himself was in no hurry about anything. He laid his emotional cards on the table, made it plain that they would not change, and then waited to watch — not see — if she picked them up. It was all so easy, in retrospect: his strange, distant, industrious family, his personal ease, his support for her ambition. He had been brought up with working women, and expected, he said, nothing else. When he gained a place at London University's Marine Station on the Isle of Cumbrae in Scotland, it did not cross his mind to suggest that Alexa make any changes to her life and work. He would, he said, commute to the best of his ability, and he'd bend his mind to that just as soon as he'd got these headaches sorted. His sister had said they were probably eyestrain but that he wasn't to leave it. So he wasn't, he said. He also felt slightly sick a lot of the time. He was smiling as he spoke. There was, after all, plenty to smile about. He had been accepted at the Marine Station and Alexa was twelve weeks pregnant. Even commuting while he did his second degree wouldn't be a problem, he assured her. Problems and Richard Maybrick were unknown to one another. Promise? Promise.

Even now, Alexa couldn't look back on those two years with any equilibrium. Richard's visit to the doctor about his headaches had segued immediately into a taxi ride to University College Hospital and then, almost before he had time to communicate what was happening to Alexa, to an operating theatre for the removal of an astrocytic tumour, grade four. And after that, the skies fell in. Richard came home, went for X-rays and scans, was ordered back to hospital, came home, was scanned again and sent back to surgery, over and over in a grisly rollercoaster ride of anxiety and waiting and fear. Alongside him, Alexa worked and tried to remember that she was pregnant, constantly shuttling from school to hospital or home, to an empty bed, or one in which Richard lay waiting for a reason to resume his habit of steady optimism. Isabel was born in one London hospital, attended by her distressed maternal grandparents, while her father lay on the operating table in another, attended by his sister, who was burdened with her own unkind superfluity of medical knowledge. By the time Isabel had started to pull herself up against armchairs and sofas, her father was dead and her odd, hardworking, undemonstrative paternal grandparents and aunt had retreated from her life, and her mother's, in a complete paralysis of unarticulated grief and shock. At twenty-five, Alexa found herself not so much free to choose as floundering in a marsh of utterly unwanted autonomy. She remembered looking down at Isabel in her cot, humped up on her knees in her preferred sleeping position, and thinking that if it wasn't for the need to provide for her, there really would be absolutely no point in troubling to draw another breath.

They moved to a cheaper, smaller flat at the top of a North London building whose redeeming feature was a pair of immense old plane trees outside, which grew to the height of the roof. Alexa found a day nursery for Isabel and spent her evenings either marking or sifting through the chaos of invoices and legal letters and trying to work out how she was to settle the debts Richard Maybrick had accumulated in his short life, and of which she had known absolutely nothing. He had left no will — it had not crossed either of their young minds to consider needing anything so elderly or depressing — but he had left three credit cards, maxed to their limit, and not a single useful asset beyond his personal possessions in the shared flat. He had also, Alexa discovered, been in the process of negotiating an unsecured and outrageously expensive loan to finance his time on the Isle of Cumbrae.

The only person who knew of her situation was Jack Dearlove. She was insistent that no parents should be told, nor the school where she worked. It was agreed between them that if Jack lent her the money to settle, and cancel, the credit cards, she would repay him within a year. No hurry, he said, *please*, two years, three years, don't cane yourself. 'A year,' said Alexa. 'A *year*. I have to be free of it.'

'Don't — don't think badly of him,' Jack said. 'I'm sure — ' He stopped.

She'd looked down at Isabel, sitting placidly on her knee picking studs of chocolate out of a brioche, and said furiously, 'Oh, don't worry. I don't think badly of *him*. It's myself I'm angry with. For believing him, in the first place.' She paused and then she said, half smiling, 'And I'm proud of myself for digging us out of the pit he left us in. I've — I've *worked* myself free.'

And sixteen months later, the debt triumphantly repaid and a party invitation reluctantly, recklessly accepted, there was Dan. A *coup de foudre*, of course, but then there were so many subsequent reasons for not just dismissing it as no more than that. Dan's life, his personality, his

60

father, his grandfather, his dog — all a seduction. There was everything to like about Dan, there was everything to yield to in the certainty of his work and his situation, never mind the unbelievable luck that such a personable man had got to the age of almost thirty without acquiring a wife and children.

Alexa swung the car into the narrow road in front of the twins' nursery school, with its bright fence of stylized wooden flowers and the banner in the window which read 'Happy Days!'. She pulled over to the kerb and switched off the engine. She remembered, briefly and with a pang at her own naivety, being deeply stirred, during her early encounters with some of Dan's friends, with a beguiling senior officer, by a sense of the *rightness* of Army life. She took the key out of the ignition. She'd heard Claire, the Brigadier's wife, say in an interview once, 'As the wife of a soldier, you just adapt your skills and career ambitions to the Army,' as if doing so was no harder than making supper out of whatever you could find in the fridge. It was wonderful, while it lasted, to believe that, heady and inspiring. And agony to feel the conviction slipping away as the other real urgencies of life raised their voices, ever louder, especially one voice which seemed to ask her, over and over, 'Why, after Richard, did you think acquiescing to another man's life would be, in the end, any different?'

She opened the car door. The children would be lined up inside the classroom, pent up like puppies, waiting for the hysterical moment of collection. Those twins, her and Dan's children, whose needs were as valid as their father's. Or hers. She got out of the car and locked it.

'Hiya!' someone called.

She turned. A girl in a pink faux sheepskin jacket was waving from the entrance to the school front garden. She was familiar, the wife of someone in Dan's battery — Ros? Rosie? — someone presumably going through exactly what Alexa was going through right now. She smiled back, filled with a sudden rush of fellow feeling. Ros or Rosie shouted with forced cheeriness, 'Nothing stops for the school run, does it?'

Alexa put her car keys in her pocket and straightened her shoulders.

'Nor should it,' she said, and laughed.

4

Dan was stopped halfway up the battery offices stairs — deep-blue vinyl treads, paler blue walls — by the regimental adjutant, a spare and eager young man who gave the impression of being permanently poised to sprint somewhere.

'Part one orders are through, sir,' he said breathlessly. 'You'll find them on your email. Leave starts in ten days, after regimental PT. A Friday, that is. Sir.'

'Thank you, Nick.'

'And the CO says we can sleep some of the boys and girls of 40th regiment tonight. He says why not? More bar profits.'

'Thank you, Nick.'

'And your BK is waiting to speak to you in your office, sir.'

'I know that, Nick, thank you. That's why I'm on my way up there.'

'Of course. Sir.'

Dan nodded to show that the exchange was over, and proceeded up the stairs to the battery command floor. It was soothing up there, an area of rigid protocols and hierarchies, where every man knew his duty and his place, and the walls were comfortably lined with photographs of every battery commander the regiment had had since 1845, as well as those of more recent glories. Outside Dan's own office hung a colour photograph of the latest regimental recipient of the Military Cross, complete with its blue-and-white ribbon: a modest young gunner of extraordinary bravery who was unable to articulate anything very much except that he wished to be left to get on with life as one of the lads and in no way to be made a fuss of. He could not, Dan reckoned, have stood more than five foot four in his stockinged feet, and was two months short of his twenty-second birthday. He had a mother in Parkhead in Glasgow and a brother in a young offenders' institution, and no idea where his father was. The lieutenant in charge of the troop reported that the father hadn't been seen in twenty years and that the mother regularly saw too much of the bottle.

In Dan's office, Paul Swain, his battery captain, was on the telephone. He was a thickset man in his forties, once a regimental sergeant major and now a late-entry captain whose own photograph, displayed modestly behind the door, bore the little silver oak leaf awarded for being Mentioned in Dispatches. He stiffened slightly in acknowledgement as Dan came in, said to his phone, 'Yes. Yes, fully agreed. Sorted,' and put the phone down. He said, 'Gunner McCormack's going to lose that foot.'

'Shit,' Dan said.

'He'll get less than nine grand a year for that as compensation.'

'Double shit. Poor bugger.'

'Sounds chirpy enough, though. Says he's always got another foot.'

Dan bent to move the cursor on his screen to access his emails. He said, 'Let's hope his attitude carries him through the next stage, poor blighter. I've just been in the gun park. They live, breathe and eat that hardware, don't they? Every bolt gleaming. You'd never think those guns had spent the last six months in the dusty arse end of nowhere.'

There was a brief pause, and then Paul Swain said lightly, 'Missing it?'

Dan looked steadily at his screen. He said, 'Here they are. Part one orders. And it's not going to be eight weeks' leave in one slug. Look. A month, then back here, then another month.'

Paul Swain came to look over Dan's shoulder. He grunted.

Dan said, 'Probably wise. The lads'll only blow all their money and then get into trouble.'

Paul grunted again. He said, 'I've got a farm to see to. I want to take the kids shooting rabbits.'

Dan turned to grin at him. 'More jam to make?'

'Chutney this time of year, Major. I make a first-class chutney, I'll have you know.'

Dan looked back at the screen. 'It's a rum old cycle to handle, this, isn't it? Three or four years of being on ops, then relax, then start training, then hard training, then ops again — '

'That's what you joined for.'

'I did. But — '

Paul Swain waited a moment and then said, 'Change of gear. Never easy, but never dull.'

Dan stood up. He said, too forcefully, 'I just don't want the unit to lose cohesion. They fight so much better in small groups. I don't want them all getting scattered on leave.'

'I see, Major.'

'I do miss the smell of cordite, though. I love it. I'd wear it as aftershave if I could.' He moved to the window and looked out. The boys in the gun park had been silently at work with their oil and wadding, and on closer inspection had been clammily pasty with hangovers.

'Had a good time, Denny?' Dan had said to one of them.

The boy paused for a moment. He stood straight. 'Honking, thank you, suh.'

Dan smiled at him. He felt an enormous affection welling up and out of him like the warmth from a brazier. 'Celebrating, were you?'

The boy risked a smirk. He caught the eye of his mate working on the other side of the gun trails. 'Completely spangled, suh.'

Dan smiled again now, just thinking of them. They loved being in a band of brothers; they loved doing what they had been trained to do. It was so important, at all times, not to fail in front of them, not to give them cause to doubt, even for a second, that their very best endeavours would be both noticed and rewarded.

He had given Gunner Denny a brief nod. 'Take note of what the sarnt says to you about celebrating. He won't be wrong. Letting off steam and getting into trouble is the good and bad of getting home.'

Denny didn't flinch. 'Suh.'

'Dan?'

Dan turned round. Paul Swain was still standing by Dan's computer.

'You wanted to discuss the homecoming parade?'

'I did, Paul. I do. The CO says medals to be awarded on the polo field. We must get McCormack back for that. And a family day. We must think about that. Family. All that fanfare. OK?'

Paul Swain smiled. 'OK.'

'A few pink jobs in with the blue ones — '

'I hear you.'

'Happy?'

Paul Swain gave a sketchy, slightly mocking salute. 'Home-coming parade, Major. Medals. Particular attention to the wounded. Family day. Action.'

★　★　★

'Can you stop the car a moment?' Dan said.

Gus pulled the car into a muddy space beside the road, under a scrawny belt of larch trees. 'You OK?'

'Yes,' Dan said. 'Just — not quite ready to go home.'

There was a short pause. Gus switched off the engine. 'Me neither.'

Dan glanced at him. 'Anyone there? At home?'

'Nope.'

Dan waited.

'Kids are at school,' Gus said. 'Kate is in London. Tuesdays, Wednesdays, Thursdays, Kate's in London.'

Dan said quickly, 'Come and have supper at ours. Alexa'd love it.'

'Thanks,' Gus said, 'but I'll grab a bite in the mess. I'll go back there when I've dropped you.' He grinned briefly. 'I might catch a sight of the new girl subbie they've appointed to target information. She has a habit, apparently, of coming down into the mess at night in her pyjamas and coolly picking up a plated meal to take back to her bedroom.'

'A looker?'

'Blonde,' Gus said shortly.

Dan said, 'I'm not going to have a drink tonight.'

'Oh?'

'I — I can't concentrate. I'm still too amped to concentrate. Drinking makes it worse.'

'Or bearable.'

'Maybe.'

'What Kate doesn't get,' Gus said, staring straight through the windscreen, 'is that I don't drink to blot out the bad stuff I've seen and been a part of. I drink because — because I miss the good stuff.'

'We haven't been back a week yet.'

'I know.'

'The trouble is,' Dan said, 'that on ops, everything is important. *Everything*. Nothing is taken for granted. You can trust the next man with your *life*, for God's sake.'

'I expect,' Gus said, a little sadly, 'that you could trust Alexa with yours.'

'When I was out there,' Dan said, 'when I wasn't thinking about the battery, I was thinking about her. And the girls.'

Gus grunted.

68

Dan said, 'It was a bit crackpot, I suppose, but I sort of told myself I was protecting them.'

Gus turned to look at him. 'You bloody *what?*'

Dan stared straight ahead too now. 'Didn't you feel that? Didn't you think that even if you couldn't justify killing for its own sake, you could always make a case for killing to protect people you love?'

Gus shook his head. 'Mental . . . '

'It's not,' Dan said. 'It's just understanding that if you are protecting something precious, you can get your head to a place where anything seems justified.'

Gus sighed, as if arguing with Dan would be a complete waste of breath and effort. He said, 'Would you say that to Alexa?'

'Nope,' Dan said.

'Why not?'

'More protectiveness. I don't want her to know what we saw and did. Especially the close shaves. I most *definitely* do not intend for her to know that. If I tell her something, even something with a happy ending, like the medic who told me to grind my knee into Flasher's thigh, between his wound and his heart, to stop the blood flow, and it worked, I'd still leave her with the image, wouldn't I, and then she'd be wondering what I hadn't told her, what happened that *didn't* have a happy ending. She'd be picturing the blood and the piss and the — '

'Stop it, Dan,' Gus said. 'You're fucking sweating.'

'I don't want to sweat in front of Alexa.'

'At least,' Gus said, 'she's *there.*'

'Fuck *me*,' Dan said. '*Fuck* me. So *sorry* — '

'Maybe it's for the best, Kate sticking to her routine. I don't want to be a nuisance round her. I'll have adjusted a bit more by Friday.'

Dan bent forward and put one forearm across his eyes. Gus put a hand on his shoulder. 'You OK?' he said again.

Muffled, Dan said, 'I should be asking you that.'

'I'm no more OK than you, mate. Brave face, fighting talk. That's what we do.'

Dan raised his head. He said, 'You long for home, don't you? You fight for it. But what you forget when you're away is that ordinary life won't kill you, except by accident, so of course everything looks pretty small here by comparison. And pretty dull.'

'There are some advantages, though.'

'Name them.'

'Booze,' Gus said.

'OK,' Dan said. 'Sex.'

'Beds. Pillows.'

'Food on a plate.'

'Girls out of uniform.'

'No fleas,' Dan said.

'Showers.'

'Not,' Dan said, 'lying for hours in some fucking desert waiting for action and having to roll on your side to pee.'

Gus nudged him. 'Families?'

Dan looked at him. They grinned at each other. 'OK, altar boy,' Dan said. 'Families.'

'Look at the guys who haven't got them. Look at someone like Denny in your battery. The regiment's the first family he's ever had.'

'Your kids,' Dan said.

'I'll see mine on Sunday. You've still got your little bombshells at home.'

'Isabel isn't.'

'Isabel — '

'She's a great kid,' Dan said. 'I'm relieved she's away at school. She needed the stability.'

Gus leaned forward to turn on the ignition. 'What if you're pinked? If you're promoted?'

Dan looked at him sharply. 'Why d'you say that?'

Gus shrugged. 'I know you're thinking of it. We both are. We're the age to start thinking about promotion, aren't we?'

Dan said, 'I don't want it to come between us — '

'It won't.'

'It might. They'll be writing up the command reports already and we can't all be on target.'

Gus put the car in gear and peered into his side mirror. 'We're young yet. We've got eight years or so.'

Dan said, 'I've done about seven already. As a major.'

The car swung into the road.

Gus said, 'I never thought about it while we were away. All those tensions just vanish. Now we're back and eyeing each other up already.'

Dan said firmly, 'Nothing'll happen before February.'

Gus swore briefly at an unsteady cyclist. When he was past her, he said, 'Just as well. There's plenty to cope with right now, don't you think?'

Dan walked across the grass in front of his house in the dusk, treading softly out of the sightline of the kitchen windows. He moved until he was against the wall of the house and could see in, hoping that Beetle's acute and unerring instinct for his presence would not betray him. But Beetle was by the kitchen table, his back to the window. He was sitting on his haunches but his every nerve was strained to focus on what was going on just above him, where the twins, unimpeded by over-large plastic aprons tied over their clothes, were earnestly pressing cookie cutters into an irregular rectangle of brownish dough. Their hair was gathered up with plastic bobbins on top of their heads in absurd little tufts, and Flora had smudges of chocolate on her spectacles as well as on her face. Tassy simply had a broad smear of it across her mouth, like badly applied lipstick. Opposite them, and visibly restraining herself from assisting them, stood Alexa, in jeans and a tight cardigan, with a blue muffler looped round her neck like a cowl. She looked about eighteen.

There was a sudden flurry and Beetle leaped briefly into the air, snapping at a fragment of dough that had skidded over the edge of the table. The twins shrieked. Beetle, appalled at himself, dropped flat on the floor and quivered.

'Smack him!' Tassy demanded.

'Certainly not,' Alexa said.

'He took my cookie!'

'You pushed it.'

'It slipped!' Tassy screamed. 'It did *that*, and he *took* it!'

'He's a dog. He's a Labrador — '

'He's *naughty*!' Tassy roared.

Flora looked at her sister. Then she picked up another piece of dough and offered it to her. Tassy glared at it, seized it and hurled it across the room.

'NO!' Alexa said to Beetle, before he moved, and then to Tassy, 'What an ungrateful and horrible thing to do.'

Outside the window, Dan waited. The scene within made his heart turn over, even Tassy's face, now scarlet with fury, her mouth a square of howling. He would give Alexa a minute more to cope alone and then he would go in, unannounced, and be the great and marvellous distraction. He watched her pick up Tassy and carry her, sticky and screaming, from the room, while Flora, having clocked the whole upset calmly from behind the one open lens of her spectacles, was proceeding with her cutting with ostentatious tranquillity. Slowly, with the air of one uncertain of his reception, Beetle rose from the floor and resumed his steady, avid watching.

Alexa came back into the room and retrieved the thrown piece of cookie dough. Flora didn't look up. She laid two perfectly executed rounds beside one another. '*I'm* not screaming,' she said.

'Nor you are.'

'I'm just doing *good* cutting.'

Dan could not bear to be a watcher any more.

He stepped sideways and tapped on the window. Flora took no notice, but Alexa and Beetle were galvanized into action. Beetle rushed barking to the front door and Alexa came to open the window.

She leaned out to kiss him. She said, in a voice that seemed to absolve him from all events earlier in the day, 'Would you like to come in and deal with your own home-grown Taliban?'

He held her shoulders. She smelled of baking and shampoo. 'Sorry I was so long.'

'It was six months last time,' she said, 'so what's half a day?'

He felt limp with something close to adoration. He said, 'Sorry all the same.'

'I must go and open the door for Beetle. He's going mad.'

She straightened up and ran across the kitchen towards the hallway.

'Hello,' Dan said to Flora, through the open window.

She turned to regard him briefly. 'When these are cooked,' she said, 'you can have one. *If* I say so.'

★ ★ ★

'Sorry I haven't rung earlier,' Dan said, into his telephone.

He was lying on the sofa in the sitting room, across the room from the television, which was turned on, with the volume down to mute. Alexa had done something to the room while he was away, but he couldn't quite put his finger on what it was that made it look so much warmer and more coherent. His Union Jack cushion was still there, and the brass shell case on the hearth, which now housed a collection of mad wooden tropical birds on sticks rather than a poker and tongs, but there seemed to be more colour somehow, and it looked softer. Were those different curtains? And was the striped rug new or just from another place?

'I didn't expect you to ring,' George said mildly, from Wimbledon. 'I knew you were safe. Your granddad would've shot me if I'd bothered you.'

'I would too!' Eric shouted from the background.

'Are you at Granddad's now?'

'Yes, lad,' George said. 'It's Tuesday. I'm here Tuesdays and Fridays. Wednesday he goes to bingo.'

'Not a soul under seventy there!' Eric shouted.

'I'm fine, you know,' Dan said. 'I'm lying on the sof — the settee, with my boots off.'

'And a beer, I hope.'

'Actually,' Dan said, 'having a dry night. I tend to cane it a bit when I get back.'

'I remember,' George said. 'I remember getting wellied for nights and nights.'

'It was that bloody woman!' Eric bellowed.

Dan raised his voice slightly. 'You're speaking of my mother, Granddad.'

George laughed. 'He never misses the chance, does he? You sleeping?'

'On and off.'

'Sometimes,' George said, 'I didn't want to

75

close my eyes. That's when all the pictures came back.'

'It's certainly an adjustment.'

'How's Alexa?'

'Angelic,' Dan said. 'And the kids are so funny.'

'So you're all right, then?'

'Dad,' Dan said, 'I'm all over the shop, as you can imagine, but I'm fine.'

Eric shouted from the background, 'How many did you lose?'

'Shut up, Dad,' George said, taking his mouth away from the phone. 'What kind of bloody question is that?'

'Tell him too many,' Dan said. 'Tell him that counting them makes me want to commit murder.'

'Poor buggers.'

'It's the limbs blown off, Dad. At one point we were losing a limb a day.'

George said, 'They do wonderful work now, prosthetics and all that.'

'It isn't the same as having the arms and legs you were born with. I'll keep going to Headley Court to see them.'

'That's right. That's got to be right.' George paused, and then he said, 'Any . . . any chance of seeing you?'

'Of course, Dad. I just can't quite make plans — '

'Or maybe we could come down to Larkford. If that's easier. I'd love to see the kids.'

Dan closed his eyes. 'I'll ask Alexa.'

'Wouldn't want to be a trouble — '

'You wouldn't be. She'd love it. It's just we've got all this homecoming stuff right now. Parades and things. I remember seeing you get the South Atlantic medal. I went with Granddad.'

George turned to his father. 'Remember taking Dan to see me get the South Atlantic medal?'

'Course I do,' Eric said. He held out a hand. 'Let me speak to the boy.'

'Granddad,' Dan said, automatically sitting up straighter. 'How are you?'

'Grand,' Eric said. 'Now you're back. Grand.'

'Me too.'

'You can't be,' Eric said. 'Not when they take you off one planet and dump you on another in twenty-four hours. Bloody madness. We took weeks to get back from Aden, bloody boring but you got adjusted. Don't take it out on that lovely girl of yours.'

'Hang on a sec, Granddad — '

'I'm not saying you are,' Eric said, interrupting. 'I'm just saying bloody watch it. Whatever you're dealing with, ain't her fault.'

'I hear you.'

'Good,' Eric said. 'Good. I heard something the other day, down at the Legion. The boys called Iraq the Gifa — the Great Iraqi Fuck All. And you've been in the Gafa — the Great Afghan Fuck All.'

'Yes, Granddad.'

'Take it slow, lad. Day at a time. Give my love to your girls, great and small.'

'I will.'

Eric's voice broke a little. 'Take care of

77

yourself, boy,' he said hoarsely and then the line went dead.

Dan sat and stared at his phone. They'd be together in Eric's stuffy sitting room, his granddad mildly bullying his dad, as ever, and then they'd crack open another beer and get a bit sentimental, and then George would go home to that bleak room he'd lived in since God knows when, past the pub where he'd probably stop for a whisky and never let on to his father that he had. They were timeless, the two of them, in their habits and routines. He'd try to go and see them, he really would. Maybe for Remembrance Sunday. They'd love that — suits and medals and a serving son and grandson with sand from a real desert still practically in his turn-ups. And they'd stand round the war memorial at the top of Wimbledon High Street, and the inscription on it would move them all to inward tears even if none of them could be shed in public.

'*All these were honoured in their generation and were the glory of their time.*'

Dan swallowed. He could cry now, thinking of it, and of his father and grandfather, and their own histories and their pride in him. Oh God, the number of people who could not ever, ever be let down . . . It was wonderful, of course it was, it was a reason for going on, always going on, better and better, higher and higher; but sometimes it was just . . . just —

The door opened. Alexa was standing there, holding her mobile phone. She looked odd, as if she'd seen something unexpected and upsetting.

Dan got up off the sofa, and stood up. 'Are you all right?'

She hardly looked at him. She just held out the phone wordlessly. He took it from her. At the top of the screen it said 'Isabel', and below it was a text message, just a single word: 'Help'.

5

To her relief, Isabel wasn't made to sit on a chair in the corridor outside the headmistress's office. The old headmistress had had a row of chairs in the corridor, and when you were sent to see her you had to sit out there in public, so that anyone going past could see that you were in trouble. But Mrs Cairns, the new headmistress, had made a lot of changes. She was younger than Mrs Arbuthnot had been, and she drove a cool car, an old Morgan sports car, and she wore high heels and make-up and red-framed spectacles. There wasn't a detail of her appearance or manner that wasn't subjected to a forensic-style scrutiny in assembly every morning, and minutely analysed afterwards. But so far, she'd met with general approval, if only because she was a refreshing change from Mrs Arbuthnot, who had seldom smiled and wore gross mohair cardigans and even grosser Celtic jewellery. She was determined, it seemed, to signal that relations between staff and girls should move on to a more informal, more humane footing, and to that end, when you were summoned to see her you didn't have to sit humiliatingly in the corridor, but were allowed an upholstered seat in the outer room to her office, where Mrs Cairns' secretary sat at an L-shaped desk in front of her computer.

Isabel wasn't sure if she should speak to the

secretary. She had said 'Thank you' when told where to sit — in a corner, under a watercolour of a cottage garden — but as the secretary said nothing further to her, she decided that it would look as if she didn't know she'd done anything wrong if she were to initiate any further discussion. In any case, the secretary, a solid middle-aged woman with an iron-grey bob and a penchant for what the girls called art-teacher shoes, with instep straps, had been inherited from Mrs Arbuthnot, and was palpably not in favour of many of her successor's changes.

So Isabel sat on her chair, with consciously good posture, and tried to deflect her frightened thoughts by wondering what would happen if the watercolour of a cottage garden suddenly fell down on her, or a mouse emerged from behind one of the William Morris print curtains and ran over the secretary's foot. She leaned out from the back of the chair, very slightly, so that when the picture fell it wouldn't hit her on the head, and stared at the carpet so hard that she could almost picture a mouse darting across it from the cover of the curtain to the shelter of the desk. Then she remembered how excited Beetle got if ever there was a mouse in the kitchen, and her throat tightened at the thought. She would not cry, she must not cry. No more thoughts of Beetle, or how Flora looked if you offered her carrots, or —

Mrs Cairns' door opened. She stood in the doorway, holding it. She wasn't smiling, but she wasn't scowling, either.

'Isabel,' she said.

Isabel scrambled awkwardly to her feet.

The secretary said, 'Mrs Arbuthnot always used the intercom.' She didn't add Mrs Cairns' name.

Mrs Cairns looked at her with a wide smile. 'And sometimes I will too, Jean. It depends upon whom I am seeing.' Then she looked back at Isabel. 'Come in, please.'

Isabel had only been in the headmistress's office once before, when she and Alexa and Dan came to see the school together. Mrs Arbuthnot had spoken mainly to Dan, who had said quite plainly that he was only Isabel's stepfather, but Mrs Arbuthnot had taken no notice and afterwards, in the car, Alexa had said, 'My God, she's just like the Queen, isn't she, much prefers action men.'

Dan had glanced round at Isabel, in the back seat of the car, and said, 'What did you think, Izzy?'

And Isabel, feeling powerfully that a decision had already been made and that asking her opinion was merely a courtesy, said bravely, 'Well, it wasn't exactly Hogwarts, was it?' and Dan had laughed.

The room looked a bit kinder than she remembered it. There were flowers, and photographs of Mrs Cairns' nearly grown-up children, and the furniture seemed to be smaller and paler and less alarming than last time.

'Why don't you sit there?' Mrs Cairns said.

She indicated an armchair beside a low table by the window, with another armchair opposite it. Isabel looked at it doubtfully. She had been expecting to sit on a hard chair across a desk from Mrs Cairns.

'There?'

'Of course,' Mrs Cairns said. 'Even if the talk is uncomfortable, there's no need for our bodies to be as well.'

Isabel lowered herself carefully into the armchair and sat upright, careful not to lean back. She stared at the table top. It was completely empty, except for a plastic bottle of water and two tumblers.

'Water, Isabel?'

Isabel shook her head. 'No, thank you.'

Mrs Cairns sat down opposite her. 'Could you look at this, please, Isabel?'

Isabel raised her head, very slowly. Mrs Cairns was holding out a pink plastic Nintendo DS.

'Do you recognize this?'

Isabel nodded.

'Could you speak, please?'

Isabel swallowed. 'Yes.'

'Who does it belong to?'

Isabel swallowed again. 'Libby Guthrie.'

'Did Libby lend it to you?'

'No.'

'Isabel, did you ask Libby if you could borrow it?'

'No.'

Mrs Cairns put the DS down on the table beside the water bottle. 'But it was found, after Libby had reported it missing, in your locker.'

There was a brief pause. Then Isabel said, with difficulty, 'Yes.'

'Can you explain how it got there?'

In a whisper, Isabel said, 'I took it.'

'Can you tell me why?'

Isabel shook her head.

'Please try, Isabel.'

'I don't know.'

'Did you want to attract Libby's attention?'

'No.'

'Do you want a DS of your own?'

'No.'

'Are you jealous of Libby Guthrie?'

There was another pause and then Isabel said, 'I don't think so.'

Mrs Cairns leaned forward. She had taken off her spectacles and they swung round her neck on a fragile jewelled chain that caught the light. She said, with slightly more severity, 'And you haven't apologized to Libby, have you?'

Isabel said nothing.

'Have you? Please answer me, Isabel.'

Isabel said miserably, 'I didn't want to upset her. I didn't mean to. But it . . . it just happened.' She looked up for a second and said in a rush, 'I couldn't stop it.'

'Of course you could.'

Isabel shook her head dumbly.

Mrs Cairns leaned back a little. Isabel felt herself being surveyed and her face growing hot under the scrutiny. It was impossible to explain the sensation of knowing she had done wrong while knowing just as strongly that she almost meant to.

'Isabel,' Mrs Cairns said, 'you say you don't want a DS. You say you aren't trying to get your own back in some way on Libby. You didn't try

84

to hide the DS when you knew your locker would be searched. Can you please tell me something, anything, about what was going on in your head when you stole it?'

Isabel gave a huge sigh. She shot Mrs Cairns a quick glance and then she looked past her, at an engraving on the wall of what the house where the school now was had looked like in the nineteenth century, with a carriage and horses standing on the drive and ladies in crinolines being handed down the steps.

'I . . . just did it,' Isabel said, and waited.

* * *

'No,' Alexa said into the twins' darkened bedroom. 'No more water, no more songs, no more *talking*. You are going to *sleep*.'

Tassy said something incomprehensible to Flora, and Flora sniggered faintly.

'Daddy?' Tassy then said clearly, to Alexa.

'When he's home, he'll come up and kiss you. But if I hear one more sound out of either of you, he won't.'

There was a powerful silence, and then Flora said, 'Beeldy-buss.'

'Flora,' Alexa said warningly.

Tassy said, giggling, 'She wasn't talking to you.'

Alexa pulled the door shut until there was only a crack for the light from the landing to shine through. She stood for a moment, eyes closed, collecting herself, and then she walked slowly down the narrow landing and even more slowly down the stairs. Dan had said that he hoped — *hoped* — to be home by seven. It was now seven forty-five. She had promised herself that she would greet him without a hint of reproach, however late he was, not least because she wanted to talk to him — the kind of talking that required both participants in the conversation to focus — about Isabel.

Mrs Cairns had telephoned to ask if Alexa had any views on the DS episode. Alexa, who had tried unsuccessfully to speak to Isabel without the latter either crying or saying, over and over, that she didn't know, she didn't know, she didn't know, had said that she would like to come and see Mrs Cairns, and Isabel herself, as soon as possible.

'We would *both* like to come,' Alexa said, not having asked Dan. 'Isabel's stepfather as well. He's known her since she was tiny. None of this is remotely in character.'

Mrs Cairns had made an appointment for three days' time. She had sounded to Alexa as if she wasn't in the kind of hurry Alexa would have liked her to be in.

'What will happen to Isabel in those three days?'

'Completely normal routine,' Mrs Cairns said.

'But if Libby Guthrie — '

'We are perfectly observant,' Mrs Cairns said. 'And I have no intention of allowing the situation to escalate.'

Alexa had felt rebuked. Add that to a powerful desire to leap into the car and drive madly to Isabel's school and somehow snatch her from it, and it was hard to concentrate on anything much. She had snapped at her mother, on the telephone.

'But I've waited six days,' Elaine said plaintively. 'It's almost a week since Dan got home, and while I do try not to pester you, I think you might consider how it feels to wait for news as long as that.'

'You knew he was home,' Alexa said irritably, her phone tucked into the angle of her neck and shoulder while she folded the twins' interminable little duplicate clothes. 'Eric rang you. George told us Eric rang you.'

'It isn't the same,' Elaine said, pacing her words for emphasis, 'as hearing, from you, that Dan is safe home and that you are all reunited. Nor is it the same as actually *speaking* to Dan. I haven't heard his voice in six months.'

Alexa picked up a tangle of khaki socks. Was it wonderful to have socks to pair up again, or were they just another reminder that the man might be back in person, but hardly seemed to be in spirit?

She said, less crossly, 'I'm not apologizing for him, Mum.'

'I don't expect you to.'

'I think you do. But I won't. I can't. It's very hard for them, coming back. Why don't you ring him in his office?'

'Oh!' Elaine said, as if appalled at the notion. 'I couldn't interrupt him there!'

Alexa laid two cocoons of sock beside the twins' laundry. She said silently, to the air, 'But it's fine to have a go at me about him, isn't it?'

'Are you still there?' Elaine asked.

'Yes,' Alexa said. 'Sorting socks, with soup in the blender, a clean kitchen floor and an agenda as long as your arm for when he — ' she stopped.

'When what?'

Alexa added more socks to the pile. 'Nothing. Nothing. I shouldn't have — Mum, I'm just a bit overdone with the domestic round. I'll get Dan to call you.'

'It would be nice,' Elaine said, 'if he felt calling us was a pleasure, rather than a duty.'

'I can't promise you perfection,' Alexa said, flaring up again. 'Why can't you take what's on offer without always wanting *more*?'

There had been an injured silence and then Elaine had said, in a voice that made Alexa feel she had stupidly revealed far too much, 'I will ring again in a few days, when you have both had time to sort yourselves out,' and then added, infuriatingly, 'Daddy sends his love. Of course.'

Alexa had ended the call without saying goodbye properly. Rude, childish conduct. Rude, childish conduct that gave her no satisfaction beyond the brief, delicious spurt of temper as she clicked her phone off. Her mother's call was just one more thing, albeit a relatively small one, to add to the ever-growing list of things to talk to Dan about. She glanced across the kitchen, to the white envelope still balanced among the pottery mugs. Hah! In her current mood, hah! was the only response to the ironic notion that anyone might stop the pursuit of their own ends long enough to consider whether she, Alexa

88

Riley, perfectly intelligent and professionally qualified, might not merit a chance to fulfil herself as much as everyone else around her assumed they had a perfect right to do.

From an apparently profound slumber in his basket, Beetle suddenly sat up, ears pricked, and whimpered.

'Go,' Alexa said tiredly. 'Go and be nice to him.'

Beetle dashed past her to the hall at the moment when car headlights swung into the drive. Alexa stood with her hands resting on the piles of laundry. Do not snap, she told herself, do not sigh, do not be sarcastic or chilly or unhelpful. The man now opening the front door is, as all the other wives would say, *your* man, and you knew what you were taking on. Even if you didn't, because nobody could know what being in the Army is really like until they've lived it.

'Hi, there,' Dan said, from the doorway. Beetle was right behind him, nose pressed to the back of his knee, eyes shining.

Alexa didn't move. She tried to smile. 'Hello.'

'I'm late.'

'I know.'

He came across the kitchen and turned her away from the laundry so that he could hold her. 'Sorry, doll.'

'It's OK,' she said into his shoulder. 'I kind of knew — '

'When they've all gone on leave,' Dan said, 'it'll be better. It's just this getting-back-and-going-off thing — '

'I know.'

'Twins asleep?'

'I hope so.'

Dan let her go. He said, 'I'll just go up and check.'

She watched him go out of the room in his combats and boots, his stable belt tight round what still seemed to her too small a waist for a man of his height. When he'd held her, she could feel the padded rectangle of the rank slide on the front of his shirt press into her. In her present mood, that seemed like yet another reminder that the Army was there between them in a way that was peculiarly unbearable, since, if asked, she would have said, almost truthfully, that she believed in what Dan was doing nearly as much as he did.

She crossed the kitchen to the fridge and took out a bottle of white wine. Mo had brought it round, saying she'd won a case in a raffle at the Army Benevolent Fund Christmas Fair the other night and felt like sharing.

Alexa had demurred. 'No, honestly, Mo. It'll keep, you know.'

'Not in our house,' Mo said. 'Safer to give most of it away. Anyway, you've drunk nothing while Dan's been away, have you?'

Alexa looked at the bottle now. She hadn't. She hadn't drunk any alcohol and she hadn't, she realized, touched another adult. For six months. In one way, it had just happened; in another, she had made it happen, as if tiny sacrifices might add up to enough to bargain with Fate for Dan's safe return. And now he was back, really back, kissing his sleeping children in their darkened bedroom. While hers, her firstborn, waited to be rescued.

She reached up on top of the fridge to where the corkscrew lived, in a shallow basket, along with bottle openers and spare corks. From the doorway, Dan said, 'Out for the count, both of them.'

'So they should be.'

He came to take the bottle and the corkscrew out of her hands. 'I'll do that.'

'Thanks.'

'What news?'

Alexa said, too suddenly, 'Mrs Cairns can see us on Thursday.'

Dan pulled the cork slowly out of the bottle. He set the bottle down on the table. Then he said, awkwardly, 'Sorry, sweetheart.'

Alexa said nothing.

Twisting the cork out of the corkscrew, Dan said, 'We can't do Thursday. It's the family day. Parade and all that. We all have to be there.'

Alexa folded her arms. 'I don't.'

Dan put down the cork and corkscrew with elaborate care. 'Lex, I need you there. My family on family day. The battery needs you there. The regiment does. All their families do. It's something we do *together*.'

Alexa let a beat fall and then she said, 'Not, I'm afraid, while there's a crisis with Isabel. She's my priority, even if she isn't yours.'

'That's not fair.'

'And this situation isn't fair to Isabel! Or me.'

'Please don't say that.'

'I *feel* it,' Alexa said. 'Suppose it was one of the twins?'

'That's not fair either — '

'And this situation isn't fair to *Isabel*! Or me.'

Dan opened a cupboard and took out a couple of glasses. He said, 'In just over a week's time, I'll be all yours. We can do whatever you want, go wherever you want — '

'It's never like that in practice,' Alexa said, 'is it? There's always demands, always something needing doing, always other priorities.'

Dan sat down opposite her. He closed his eyes briefly. Then he opened them and said, 'Please.'

Alexa reached out towards the wine bottle. Dan took her wrist in one hand and picked up the bottle with the other. He said, pouring, 'I'd really like to come with you. You know I would. I think the world of Isabel and I'm very upset she's unhappy. I'm not making light of this episode, but I don't think it's such a big deal because she's such a great kid and as honest as they come. I think it's just a blip. And when all the boys have gone off to see their mums and book their holidays in Ibiza, I'll talk to whoever you want and be glad to do it. But I can't do it *now*. I can't do it on *Thursday*. Could you — could you postpone the meeting?'

She looked down at his hand holding her wrist, at his big, impregnable military watch, at his wedding ring. She said, 'Isabel's waiting for me — '

Dan let go of her wrist and pushed a glass towards her. 'Then go and see her on Thursday.

Just go.' He smiled at her a little warily. 'I'll be here when you get back. Promise.'

* * *

Jack Dearlove's flat in Chiswick had a view of the river if you went on to the narrow balcony and hung out over the rail as far as you dared. Jack had bought it as somewhere to sleep and keep his stuff, the same year that he had started his business — contract cleaning of both offices and residential properties — intending to trade up as soon as he could, either to a house or to a better flat actually on the river. His business had prospered, with contracts now stretching down the M4 corridor, but he had somehow never quite found the time or enthusiasm to look for a better flat. There had been a lot of opportunities, since the business was a useful grapevine for property movement, but Jack had never quite got round to exchanging what would do for the time being for something he might actually take pride in.

If he was frank with himself, he knew that he was hoping Eka might return to him. She had never asked for a divorce and was in the habit — between racy and unprincipled lovers who purportedly owned topaz mines in Brazil or motor-racing circuits in Italy — of ringing Jack in tears and saying she was, yet again, out of cash and out of hope, and could he help her. He had learned, painfully, to prevaricate long enough for Eka to be invited on someone else's plane to someone else's island, whereupon the whole merry-go-round would start again. But he was unable, somehow, to be strong-minded enough to give up the fantasy that one day he would be begged by Eka to buy a place in which they could both pursue a life of contentment fuelled by her heart having changed and his having never wavered. It was an idiotic dream, he knew, and he probably wouldn't care for it if it ceased to be a dream and became an improbable reality, but all the same, it gave his life a deeply romantic, unrequited edge, and was the reason for little leaps of excited hope when the telephone rang at odd hours of the night.

He wasn't in bed when it rang on this occasion. He was half asleep on the American reclining chair that occupied the centre of his unremarkable sitting room, eight feet from an enormous television balanced on a couple of removals boxes. He glanced drowsily at the screen on his phone before he answered. It did not say, as expected, 'Eka'.

'Lex?' he said. 'What are you doing ringing at this hour? Are you OK?'

'I wondered if you'd even speak to me.'

'Of course I'll speak to you. I was just off the whole world that day. It's after two in the morning. Where are you?'

Alexa said, 'In the kitchen.'

'Why aren't you in bed with the hero?'

'I was.'

Jack struggled to tilt the chair into a more upright position. 'Have you had a row?'

'Only very politely. I wanted him to do

94

something with me. For Isabel. And he — won't. Can't.'

Jack rubbed his hands through his hair. 'What thing?'

'She's — stolen something. At school. She says she doesn't know why she did it, and she doesn't want the thing. But she won't say sorry. It's all part of the homesickness, I'm sure, and Dan coming back, and the twins being here while she has to be away. But the Head has said she can see us on Thursday, and Dan has other things to do on Thursday. Please don't tell me that his priorities are entirely valid and that I should have thought of all that seven years ago.'

Jack stood up slowly, displacing cushions and crumpled newspapers. He said, ignoring her tone, 'You think Dan is putting his men in a PT session before you and Isabel?'

'It's a homecoming thing, a family day. They always have them and usually I like them, but this time I'm too miserable about Isabel to do my Army-wife stuff. And — it's not just that. It's more that whatever happens to us, it can't ever be the priority. There's always an Army thing that has to come first. I just know that it's always *something*.'

Jack looked down at his recliner. Lying alone on it half-dreaming of Eka was not really so very different from sitting at a Wiltshire kitchen table in your dressing-gown, longing for Dan's attention. Both of us, he thought, craving an intimacy that eludes us. Both of us wanting to be the priority to people whose essential charm for us probably lies in the fact that their focus is

95

often — usually — elsewhere.

He said, disgustedly surveying the debris round the recliner, 'I can see four beer cans and a pizza box on the floor.'

'I'm drinking fennel tea,' Alexa said. 'Which is far more depressing.'

'Not for fat boys,' Jack said. 'It sounds like the unattainable heights of virtue and eleven stone. What can I do for you?'

'I wondered — '

'Yes?'

'Jack, I don't want to go to the school alone. I don't want to get things wrong, say the wrong thing, overreact because I'm wound up about Isabel and make it worse for her. I just don't feel quite steady about it all. It's so maddening, because there I was, coping so well all the time Dan was away, but now he's back I suddenly don't seem able to think straight. I don't seem able to — '

'Of course I'll come,' Jack said. 'I'm her godfather, after all. Or something. I've known her since before her first breath. Are you crying?'

'Not really,' Alexa said. 'But *thank* you. Thank you.'

Jack bent and picked up the pizza box. It was huge. And quite empty. Pepperoni with extra pepperoni. The box was smeared with blotches of orange-coloured oil. Disgusting. He spun it into a corner, like a boomerang. 'My pleasure, Mrs Riley. Now back to bed with you and no sulks with the Major.'

Alexa was laughing. 'You've lightened my heart — '

'I don't want anything to do with your heart,' Jack said. 'Take it upstairs where it belongs. Nighty-night.'

★   ★   ★

While she was brushing her teeth the next morning, Dan came up behind her, already dressed in his combats, and put his arms round her.

'Wait,' she said, mumbling, spitting toothpaste.

He pulled her upright against him so that they could both see their reflections in the mirror above the basin, Alexa with toothpaste on her chin and her hair unbrushed, Dan ready for work and impeccable, even down to his side hat.

He leaned forward to put his cheek against hers. 'Can I ask you something?'

Alexa remembered her resolve of the night before. 'Of course.'

'I'm nervous of that tone of voice.'

'And I,' said Alexa, putting her toothbrush down and rubbing at the smear of white below her bottom lip, 'am nervous of what you're going to ask me.'

He looked straight at her reflected eyes. 'I want to ask Julian and Claire to supper.'

Alexa's eyes widened. 'The Brigadier!'

'He's OK. You know he is. But he'll miss playing with his train sets more than anyone, now we're back. And you like Claire.'

Alexa stiffened a little in Dan's embrace. 'I do like Claire. But does that mean dining room and silver candlesticks, because the dining room is

97

the twins' playroom and we don't own any silver except my earrings.'

'You know it doesn't. Kitchen's fine. Kitchen supper's what they'd like. And the CO. Can we add him and Mary, too?'

Alexa stepped sideways, so that Dan had to drop his arms. 'Mary has a cleaner and a gardener — '

'Well you do, if you're in command. But you're a great cook. We'll do it our way.'

Alexa picked a damp towel off a nearby stool and rubbed her face. 'Do you have an agenda,' she said, 'wanting Julian and Mack for supper?'

Dan grinned at her. 'A bit,' he said. Then, 'Please.'

Alexa dropped the towel. 'Of course,' she said.

He took her back into his arms. He said, against her hair, 'Thank you. Really, thank you. And I am truly sorry about last night, and Isabel and everything.'

There was a brief pause, then Alexa said into his shoulder, 'I'm fine. And I'm sorry, too. Sorry about the family day. Really I am.'

'You're fantastic. You really are. I'll be on message in a week or so, honest.'

'Jack's coming with me,' Alexa said.

Dan's embrace stiffened. Then he took his arms away. 'Jack?'

'Yes.'

'What's he got to do with Isabel?'

Alexa didn't look at him. 'He's known her longer than you have,' she said. 'And he's prepared to make time to come with me,' and then she walked out of the bathroom.

6

'Ah,' Mrs Cairns said, holding her hand out to Jack, 'Isabel's stepfather.'

Jack was wearing a tweed jacket checked as loudly as a horse blanket, and a scarlet muffler. He looked, Alexa thought, like a round and cheerful bird. He smiled at Mrs Cairns and took her hand. 'Actually not,' he said. 'Godfather. Stepfather is still defending the nation.'

Mrs Cairns glanced at Alexa. Then she said, 'I am so glad somebody's doing it,' and motioned them towards the armchairs where Isabel had sat four days previously.

Alexa said, 'I had hoped to see Isabel first . . . '

'She's in class, Mrs Riley. French for year seven will finish at twelve forty-five.'

'She does nothing but cry on the phone.'

'I have the impression,' Mrs Cairns said, pulling up a third chair and seating herself in it, her red spectacles as dominating as a gash of scarlet lipstick would have been, 'that she is absolutely aware that she has done wrong. She has even said she stole and she knows how wrong stealing is. But nothing will make her apologize. She seems very distressed at having upset Libby Guthrie, but she won't say sorry to her. She isn't particularly stubborn or angry. She's just determined.'

Jack leaned back in his chair. He appeared to be taking in every detail of Mrs Cairns' appearance, and considering his reactions. He said slowly, 'Her father has been home for ten days. Just ten days.'

'But she saw him.'

'She was there the day he came home,' Alexa said.

'And she was pleased to see him?'

'Thrilled,' Alexa said, and then, glancing at Jack, 'apparently — '

'Why do you say that?'

'Because this isn't like her. Because this whole episode is so completely out of character. She's never drawn attention to herself, she's never done anything underhand.'

'She has two younger sisters?'

'Yes.'

'Who are at home?'

'Of course,' Alexa said, more crossly than she intended. 'They are three.'

Jack leaned forward. He had unwound his muffler and it lay, loosely coiled, on his lap, part vanishing under the pressure of his bulk as he bent over it.

'Can't you just forget it?' he said to Mrs Cairns. 'Forget the whole thing?'

She turned her red spectacles towards him. 'Of course not.'

'Come on,' Jack said. 'A good child like Isabel, a good, hard-working, conscientious child, flips a bit under temporary family pressure. That's all it is, isn't it? I mean, she didn't try and pass the thing off as hers, she didn't try to sell it, she just took it so that you'd all notice she's a bit wound up right now and maybe you'd do something to make her feel better. Why don't you just drop it, and let us take Isabel home for a while?'

There was a pause. Mrs Cairns turned her spectacles on Alexa. 'Is this a view you share?'

'More or less, yes.'

'But you must see that it's impossible.'

Alexa sat up a little straighter. 'Why?'

'There is no value to the moral code of a school like this without consistency. The whole school knows what Isabel did and, I imagine, that she won't apologize. There are consequent factions. Girls like factions, so this is a golden opportunity for them. At its most basic, simply setting this whole episode aside encourages more bending and breaking of rules. I can't do it.'

Jack spread his hands. 'This whole school is full of Army kids. You must have crises all the time.'

'We do,' Mrs Cairns said. '*Serious* crises. Wounded fathers. Fathers who will not come home ever again.'

Alexa cried out suddenly, 'Don't try and put me in my place, Mrs Cairns!'

'I am doing the *reverse*, Mrs Riley. I am trying to make you see the seriousness of Isabel's case. I can't dismiss it and I don't want to be disproportionately heavy-handed. But she must have privileges withdrawn and she can't go home with you.'

'Can't — '

Mrs Cairns stood up. 'No. She isn't ill, she does not need home rest. It won't help her or anyone else if she is not required to face what she has done.'

Alexa got unsteadily to her feet. 'But she's so homesick.'

'I'm afraid quite a lot of them are. And I'm also afraid that it can't be an excuse, even if it's often a reason.'

Jack rose too, dropping his scarf. Bending to pick it up, he said, 'So where exactly has this interview got us?'

Mrs Cairns looked at him. Her glance was not particularly friendly. 'Closer, I hope,' she said, 'to understanding what is best for Isabel.'

'And for your school?'

Mrs Cairns didn't flinch. 'And the school,' she said, and walked towards the door.

★ ★ ★

'I just felt — *rebuked*,' Alexa said.

She was sitting at a table in a little café attached to a garage where they had stopped for petrol. Jack had brought her tea in a paper cup and was sitting opposite her, nursing a can of Coke Zero. He said, 'I wasn't much help.'

Alexa reached out to pat his hand briefly. 'She out-gunned us. She knew what she wanted before we even got there. Pathetic smother mother put in her over-emotional place. These are Army children and they have to learn to *bear* things, don't they?'

'I'm OK,' Isabel had said, over and over, during the brief time she was allowed to see them before lunch. 'I'm OK.' She was pale and weary looking, but she didn't cling to Alexa and she didn't cry.

'Has Mrs Cairns been talking to you?'

'No.'

'And is Libby avoiding you?'

Isabel looked sideways. 'Not really.'

'Are people whispering and being horrible?'

Isabel shrugged. 'A bit.'

'Darling — '

'I'm OK,' Isabel said. 'I'm *OK*.'

'Why won't you say sorry?'

Isabel sighed. 'Because I'm not.'

'You're not sorry? But you took something that didn't belong to you.'

Isabel let a beat fall and then she said, 'I didn't want it.'

'What did you want?'

Isabel said nothing.

Alexa moved to try and put her arms round her and Isabel, without drama, stepped sideways. 'Izzy. Please. What did you want? What *do* you want?'

Isabel cleared her throat. 'I can't have it. I tried, but I can't. So I'll get used to not having it. I'm OK.'

'Darling, please tell me — '

Isabel hopped backwards. 'I've got to go to lunch now.'

'I can't bear you to be unhappy.'

'I'm OK,' Isabel said. 'I'm OK.'

'I can't believe she didn't cry,' Alexa said now. 'I've cried enough for both of us, God knows. What a ghastly morning.'

'I'm good in meetings,' Jack said. 'I don't know what happened to me. It was those specs. And being in a headmistress's study. I went to pieces.'

'No, you didn't.'

'I was a chocolate teapot, Lex. And I can't comfort myself by saying bloody woman, because she wasn't.'

'And I,' Alexa said, 'can't comfort myself by saying I know what's right for my own daughter, because she made me feel I don't.'

Jack nudged his Coke can. 'We should be drinking something much stronger than this.'

'That would be fatal.'

'What'll you tell Dan?'

Alexa looked straight at him. 'That I was outclassed by a true professional.'

'We were.'

'Not your responsibility.'

'I came to support you.'

'Jack,' Alexa said, 'think of the state I'd be in if I'd been through that alone.'

'Does he think you were alone?'

'No.'

'Did he know I was coming?'

'Yes.'

'And?'

'Not — not pleased.'

Jack gave a groan. 'Lex, don't *do* this.'

'Don't do what?'

'Don't play him off like this. Don't challenge him all the time.'

'Challenge him?' Alexa said, her voice rising.

'I agreed to come to support you. I didn't agree to come to annoy him.'

'His annoyance is his affair.'

'Oh my God,' Jack said. 'Oh, *Alexa*.'

He stood up. She was staring down at the

cooling tea in the paper cup.

'I'll drive you home.'

'Look,' Alexa said, her eyes still on the tea. 'Look. I have to fight Isabel's corner. I have to fight my own corner. I want to be loyal, I have no trouble being loving, but I can't always put myself aside for some more demanding requirement, I can't abase myself, *obliterate* myself because of what Dan has to do. And *wants* to do. Don't forget that. He *loves* the Army. Loves it. He is fulfilled by it. I love to see him fulfilled, I promise I do. But I can't live purely on *his* fulfilment. I'm a person too, with a brain as well as a heart, and all the ambitions and hungers and curiosities that brains have. I also can't live on the emotional crumbs that fall from Dan's table after his men have finished eating the main meal. I know he loves me. He probably loves me more than he's ever loved anyone. But he's got me now, so he's free to love all this other stuff, this soldier stuff, and that has all the urgency and thrill of the chase that I can't possibly have now that I'm his wife and the mother of his children. He's back, but he's not back, not in any sense that's any use to me or his family. And if one more person tells me just to give him time, or that I knew what I was taking on, or that I'm so lucky to have the security, I will just . . . just *kill* them.'

Jack leaned down. He said quietly, 'People are listening.'

'No, they're not.'

'Three tables round us are neither drinking their coffee nor eating their pecan Danish, they

105

are *listening*. Open-mouthed.'

'Let them.'

'Lex, I'm not unsympathetic — '

'You just wish you were a soldier. Most men do, I should think. 'Every man thinks meanly of himself for not having been a soldier.''

'Who said that?'

'Dr Johnson.'

'I don't believe him.'

'He's right. You're all fascinated by soldiering. All the he-man, boy stuff. Boots and guns and blood and sweat and bonding.'

'Get up, Lex,' Jack said. 'I'm taking you home.'

Alexa rose slowly from her plastic chair. She said sadly, 'Little Izzy — '

'She's OK. She told you so.'

'I felt . . . ' Alexa said, 'I felt as if I was — losing her.'

'They grow up.'

Alexa looked at him. 'I don't like you much today, Jack Dearlove.'

He took her arm. He gave her a rueful smile. 'Join the club,' he said.

★ ★ ★

'Two weeks ago,' Gus said, 'we were in Helmand. Can you believe it?'

Dan grunted. They were both in his office. Gus was sitting in Paul Swain's chair with his feet on the desk in front of him, and Dan was leaning against the wall opposite, with his eyes closed.

106

'All that endless, endless desert — '

'But you could always see the mountains. Wherever you were, you could see the mountains.'

'Great colours. Remember Ranger Beattie and his little tin of watercolours?'

'Bloody good, some of them.'

'And the irrigation ditches,' Dan said. 'Everywhere. And the tree lines. Good cover.'

'And just as good cover for laying IEDs. How's that poor lad of yours?'

'Lost a foot,' Dan said shortly. He opened his eyes. 'I spoke to his mother today. She said, 'You sort of accept they might die, but you never imagine this happening.' I didn't like to tell her about Tommy Stanway losing both his fucking legs.'

Gus took his feet off the desk and stood up. He walked slowly to the window and stood looking out. Then he said, without turning round, 'Makes you . . . ashamed, really.'

'Ashamed?'

'There's these kids,' Gus said, 'or even the older ones, like Sergeant Matthews — shattered pelvis, colostomy bag, wife still with him but only just, saying he isn't the man she married — ' He stopped.

Dan let a short pause fall, and then he said, 'Is this somehow about Kate?'

'Kind of.'

'What then?'

'Well,' Gus said, turning round from the window and folding his arms, 'she's got an award ceremony tonight and some meeting or other tomorrow, so she won't be back till Saturday now.'

'Oh.'

'She's done brilliantly. She's won this award for her recent fundraising campaign. Signed up more subscribers than anyone has ever achieved in a single year. I'm really proud of her.'

Dan hitched himself on to a corner of the nearest desk. 'Of course,' he said politely.

Gus raised his hands and put the heels of them into his eye sockets. He said, 'Please don't read between the lines.'

'It's where the important stuff is, though.'

'I just want to see her,' Gus said. 'I just want her to be there. She doesn't have to do any lovey-dovey stuff, she just has to be *there*.' He took his hands away and blinked. 'I'm pathetic.'

'No, you're not.'

'A whinging wanker — '

'Gus,' Dan said, 'she's your wife. You love her. You missed her.'

'D'you think she missed me?'

'Course she did.'

Gus gave a half-hearted smile. 'That didn't sound quite convincing. Or convinced.'

'I meant it to,' Dan said. 'I mean it. Kate's very pragmatic, and pragmatic people don't do sensitive, as a rule.'

'Am — am I sensitive?' Gus said.

'You are.'

'Sod it. Are you?'

Dan got off the desk. 'Chronically. In some ways.'

'Does Alexa know that?'

'She does.'

'How — ' Gus said, and stopped, then started again, 'How's it going?'

Dan flicked a glance at him. 'In what way, precisely?'

'You know perfectly well in what way, you tosser. With you and Lex.'

Dan went over to his computer and began to fiddle with the mouse. He said, his eyes on the screen, 'We are, shall we say, feeling our way towards one another again.'

'I could do with a bit of feeling.'

Dan straightened up. 'Come down to the mess and have a drink.'

'It's only five forty-five.'

'We'll have a drink at six and maybe one while we're waiting.'

Gus came and stood beside Dan, looking at his computer screen. 'Why don't you talk to me about Alexa?'

'Nothing to tell you, Augustus.'

'But — '

Dan put an arm across Gus's shoulders. 'We have some domestic wrinkles that won't be ironed out until I've counted all my boys out with clean faces and dire warnings.'

'Really?'

'Really.'

'Let's get that drink. My dad used to look at his watch at dead on six every night and say, 'Thank God. Dear old gin.' Never drank wine, though. Odd, that.'

They emerged on to the floor of the battery offices. The central desks were empty, the noticeboards cleared of everything except battery minutes and an irritating recent directive from Health and Safety pinned with absolute precision against the green baize.

'Eerie. End of term.'

'I still love this place.'

'Me too.'

'"The culture of the battery — "'

'"So important — "'

'"To young soldiers."'

'Yes, *suh*!'

'What would you be,' Gus said, putting his side hat on, 'if you weren't a soldier?'

Dan paused in front of the colour photograph of the young MC. 'Probably a very frustrated policeman. Or a mercenary. You?'

Gus linked his arm in Dan's. He said cheerfully, 'A right mess.'

'Well, then. How lucky that we do what we do.'

'Lucky indeed,' Gus said with fervour.

★　★　★

Kneeling beside the bath while she soaped the twins, Alexa felt her phone vibrate in the pocket of her jeans. She sat back on her heels and dried her hands along the bathmat. The text on her phone screen read, 'Gus bit down so cheering him up. Back 7.30 latest. xx'.

'Daddy?' Flora said with unerring instinct, rising out of the bath with clots of foam clinging to her like shreds of cotton wool.

'He'll be back to kiss you.'

110

'No!' Tassy shouted.

'Don't you want him to kiss you?'

'I want him to *read* to me! I want him to read me my *story.*'

'Tomorrow — '

'Now!'

'Now, now, now!'

The twins exchanged glances and began on a bellowed chant, 'Now, now, *NOW,* now, now, *NOW!*'

Alexa put her hands over her ears. 'Stop it!'

'Get him,' Tassy demanded.

'I can't, he has the car — '

'Ring him!'

Alexa felt rage rising in her throat like incipient tears. Suddenly she couldn't trust herself to speak naturally to the twins, but only artificially, as if making a formal public speech to an audience of adults.

'Do you know,' Alexa said, 'I am reluctant to do that. I quite see the force of your reasoning, but there's some sort of pride in me which prevents me from ringing to say you promised and yet again your promise wasn't worth the breath it was uttered with, if you see what I mean?'

Tassy stared at her for a moment. And then, without warning, she reached up, whipped off her sister's spectacles and threw them into the water.

'Tassy!'

'To clean them — ' Tassy said.

'I don't want them clean!' Flora wailed.

Alexa rolled her sweater sleeve up to her

armpit and felt about in the water for the spectacles.

'You're tickling!' Flora shrieked, and then, 'I can't see, I can't see, I can't — '

'I'll look for you,' Tassy said.

Alexa retrieved Flora's glasses and began to dry them on a towel. They were alarmingly frail and also bent out of shape by the violence of their lives. She knelt up to hook the side-pieces back round Flora's ears. 'There.'

'I can't see,' Flora said, more calmly. 'They're all drippy.'

'They'll dry.'

'I want Daddy!'

'I want Daddy!'

'Please,' Alexa said. 'Please — '

From downstairs, Beetle began to bark. The twins stopped chanting. 'Daddy coming!'

Tassy stood up too, now, and began to scramble over the edge of the bath. 'Daddy, Daddy!'

'I don't think so — '

'Wait!' Flora screamed. 'Wait! I want to see Daddy!'

'Sorry,' Mo said from the doorway.

Alexa turned awkwardly from where she knelt on the bathmat. 'Mo!'

'And Franny,' Franny said, appearing behind her. 'Hello, Riley girls in your bubble bath.'

'Hello, hello, hello!' the twins shouted, slippery and excited. 'Hello, hello!' They slithered past Alexa and ran across the room.

'I can't pick you up without a towel, you wet nonsense — '

112

'Here — '

'Hello, little Miss Four Eyes. Are you clean or just wet?'

Alexa got to her feet. 'What are you both doing here?'

'Aren't you pleased to see us?'

'Thrilled. Absolutely thrilled. But — '

Mo was bundling Tassy up in a towel. She carried her across the bathroom and sat on the closed lid of the lavatory with Tassy on her knee. 'Instinct, babe.'

Alexa looked at her. 'Instinct?'

Mo didn't look back. She was rubbing Tassy briskly with the towel. 'Rub-a-dub, rub-a-dub, small wet person. Not a cheep out of you for ten days, Mrs Riley. And Fran and I thought, heigh ho, many mattress moments going on at number seven, good-oh, and then the time went on and we saw Dan here and there in the car alone, and we looked at each other and we said, not sure we like the non-communication, not altogether reassuring. Let me do those piggy toes, Miss Tassy. So we thought we'd just boldly come and see.'

She set Tassy, pink and naked, on the floor by her feet. She gave her bottom a little pat. 'Didn't think you'd mind.'

Franny, holding Flora against her in another towel with one hand, adjusted Flora's spectacles with the other. 'We knew you'd be here. We knew it was bath time. So here we are.' She glanced at Alexa, and winked. 'OK? Pleased?'

Alexa subsided back on to her knees in the middle of the floor. She pushed her hair off her face. 'Thankful,' she said.

113

'We brought a bottle,' Mo said. 'Army wives, full of forethought and advance planning. You'll find it in the fridge.'

Alexa opened the fridge door. She said, 'The twins have never, ever been so biddable about going to bed.'

'Three adults to two children is about the right ratio.'

'Makes me long for girls,' Franny said. 'Almost as much as I long never, ever to be pregnant again. And I have such huge babies. At five foot four, it isn't funny.'

Alexa put the bottle of Muscadet on the table, and the corkscrew beside it. 'Sit you down.'

'We are.'

'Sorry, it's a reflex. I'll be saying drink up and you may not get up till you've finished any minute.'

'You look tired, Mrs R.'

Alexa turned away to find glasses. 'Not really.'

'Tense, then.'

'Thank you.'

'It isn't a criticism,' Franny said reasonably. 'It's merely an observation.'

Mo took the wine glasses out of Alexa's hands and put them in a neat row on the table. 'These homecomings can be just fiendish.'

Alexa sat down at the table and leaned her elbows on it. 'I can't get anywhere near him.'

'Not even sex?'

'Well,' Alexa said, half-laughing, 'there's quite a lot of that, but I wouldn't say it was exactly conversational.'

Franny took the wine bottle and the corkscrew and poised it to take out the cork.

'It's a screw cap,' Mo said.

'You are so helpful.'

'I brought a screw cap in *order* to be helpful. It's such a pity you two don't ride. Riding is such a release when you are seething with frustration.'

'Except,' Franny said, 'that the stables are such a hotbed of bad behaviour.' She took the cap off the bottle and began pouring. 'Can't you just run Dan up against a wall and make him focus? I do it to Andy, but then he isn't as tall as Dan, and living with just boys makes you a bit physical in all your solutions.'

Alexa sighed. 'I just want him to tune in to me. I've got some big stuff to tell him.'

They both looked at her.

'Like what?'

'Like the acuteness of Izzy's homesickness. Like I've been offered a job — '

'You *what*?'

'A job,' Alexa said. 'A proper teaching job in a fairly proper private school fifteen miles away.' She glanced towards the dresser, where the envelope still sat among the spotted mugs. 'The letter came the day before Dan got back. I rang them and said I couldn't decide till I'd talked to him and explained the circumstances, and they were very nice and said they could wait two weeks. Two weeks is up in three days' time.'

Franny pushed wine glasses towards Mo and Alexa. 'Wow.'

'Clever girl.'

Alexa said to her wine glass, 'I'm beginning to think that the clever bit was brazening out the interview and getting the offer. Because I don't see how I can accept. I mean, there's not just poor Izzy, there's the twins, and all these demands on Dan's time, and then, because of him, on mine. Like this dinner party — '

'What dinner party?'

Alexa picked up her glass and put it down again. 'Dan wants me to have the Brigadier *and* the CO to dinner. Plus wives.'

'You'll walk that.'

'They're all OK.'

'It's not that,' Alexa said. 'It's just that his request comes on top of him not connecting with me or the children, really, for one single minute since he's been home.'

Mo sat up suddenly and looked towards the window. At the same second Beetle lurched out of slumber and his basket in a single purposeful movement.

'There's his car — '

'Don't go — '

'I have no intention of going,' Franny said. 'We're married to the breed, remember?'

'He knows nothing about the job.'

'OK.'

'And very little about Izzy — '

'Fine. Fine. No inquisition coming up, promise.'

The front door opened and slammed shut, and there were the sounds of Beetle's rapturous welcome and Dan's response, and then he appeared in the kitchen doorway.

Mo said, beaming, 'Welcome home!'

Franny raised her glass. 'Hear, hear!'

Dan was smiling broadly. He said cheerfully, 'Got a fourth glass?'

'I'm sure we can find you one.'

'You won't want this — girl drink.'

'I'll drink anything, Fran. How's my mate, Andy?'

'Aren't you going to kiss your wife?' said Mo.

'Andy's good, thank you. Will be better for a sight of you, when you have a moment.'

'D'you have a kiss for me, wife?'

'Goodness, Dan, Helmand sure peels the pounds off you,' said Mo.

Alexa held up her face. Dan smelled of chewing gum and whisky.

'Sorry I'm late. Did I miss — '

'You did.'

'Are they still awake?'

'I so hope not.'

'I'll just go and check.'

'In a minute,' Mo said. 'When we've gone. Which we'll have done shortly. Can we ask how you are?'

'You can ask,' Dan said, smiling at her, his hand on Alexa's shoulder, 'but I'm afraid it doesn't mean you'll get an answer.'

'So if I said was it worth it?'

'I'd say I bloody well hope so!'

'You're no use,' Mo said, getting to her feet. 'We all hope that. It's just that we'd also like to know that our own effort is worth making.'

'I do know that,' Dan said, suddenly sober.

There was a short, powerful silence. Dan's

117

hand moved briefly from Alexa's shoulder to her hair and then he said, 'I really am going to check on those girls.'

'We'll say goodbye,' Mo said.

Franny stood too. She moved to stand in front of Dan and reached up to kiss him. 'We were allowed to bath your peaches.'

'Minxes, more like. My best to Andy.'

'Will do.'

Dan looked at Mo. 'And a high five to Baz.'

'We're not speaking,' she said. 'He's booked on a three-week course without telling me.'

Dan glanced down at Alexa. 'Try six months.'

'Oh, we have.'

He crossed the kitchen to the hall doorway. 'Come again soon,' he said, and vanished.

★ ★ ★

'Have they gone?' Dan said.

Alexa was laying the table for the two of them, opposite one another as usual, with candles in the glass candlesticks George had brought back from a British Legion trip to Copenhagen.

'As you see.'

Dan came to stand quite close to her. 'Were they here to make a point?'

Alexa put down her handful of cutlery and stood up straight. 'No,' she said. 'They were here because they're often here. They got me through the last six months, them, and Sara and Prue, and sometimes Kate when she wasn't too busy. If you remember, Franny had all the girls the day you came back.'

118

Dan put his arm round Alexa's waist. 'I do remember.'

'If wives didn't stick together — '

'Well?'

'You know what I was going to say. There's no point saying it yet again.'

'Look, sweetheart, I am truly sorry I was late again. Truly. It was just that poor old Gus is in a funk about Kate. She's got all these work commitments and she won't be back now till Saturday. And it's really got him down. Right down.'

Alexa took one step to the right so that Dan's arm slipped from her waist. 'Dan, there's me too. There's us — '

'I know that.'

She looked at him. 'I don't think you do. Or if you do, you don't act on it.'

'Sweetheart, you know how it is, you know I can't — '

'Please stop.'

'I mean, I hated Jack going with you the other day.'

'But you didn't ask!' Alexa cried. 'You didn't even *ask* me about it afterwards!'

Dan stared at her. 'Didn't I?'

'No! You haven't asked about anything, you haven't really looked at me or listened to me or wondered what it's been like for me or what I've been doing or feeling or thinking, you haven't got your head back from wherever it's been all these, months, and I'm afraid it looks to me as if you haven't even been *trying*!'

Dan looked stricken. He held his arms out. 'Please — '

She shook her head. 'I can't. I can't talk to you till you can hear me.'

'I'm listening.'

'You're scared,' Alexa said. 'You're afraid of what you might have done. I'll talk to you when you're over that, I'll talk to you when you're back in the world that the rest of us have to inhabit. But until you can get your priorities sorted, I don't want to open my heart to someone who is, to all intents and purposes, still miles away doing something so alien to ordinary life that it might as well be on the moon. Do you realize, I don't even really know what *that*'s like? I don't know, in any detail, what you did, or, more importantly, what you felt about what you did. You come back here, full to the brim with something, and even if I can guess at some of it, it's only a guess. Dan, we're *married*. Marriage means, among a lot of things, *sharing*. How can I know you if you tell me almost nothing, and ask me even less?'

Dan looked on the verge of tears. 'Sorry,' he whispered. 'So sorry.'

'I know you are. Or at least, I know you want to be.'

'Can't we — '

She shook her head again.

'I thought — '

'What did you think?'

'I thought,' Dan said, unwisely, uncertainly, 'that you understood.'

Alexa picked up the cutlery again. She was shaking. She said with a visible effort to keep her voice steady, 'There's a difference between trying very hard to understand something that doesn't come naturally to you for the sake of someone you love, and having that understanding pushed so far that it begins to look very much like exploitation.'

There was a silence. Then Dan said, 'Is that how you feel?'

She turned to face him. 'Right now, yes.'

He rubbed a hand over his face and through his hair. 'I don't . . . really know how to respond to that.'

'I know,' Alexa said. 'I can see. That's my point. And when you can see the whole picture from my point of view as well as from your own, so that you *do* have an idea of how to respond to all the things that are crowding into my mind right now, then we'll talk.'

She resumed laying the table. Dan stood and watched her, his expression one of complete dismay. Then he reached out and picked up the Muscadet bottle.

'Drink?' he said uncertainly.

7

George Riley bought himself a National Express coach ticket to Salisbury. Using his senior travel card it was gratifyingly cheap, so much so that he suggested to Eric that he might like to come too.

They were sitting in the third-floor café in Elys on Wimbledon High Street, with a pot of tea and a toasted teacake each, which Eric was eating at a pace slow enough to irritate the mildest of men.

'Eat up, Dad, do. It'll be like leather. Why don't you come with me?'

Eric, chewing with exasperating thoroughness, shook his head. 'Can't. Can't sleep in any bloody bed but my own.'

'Don't you want to see them?'

'Course I do,' Eric said, swallowing with deliberation. 'Don't be bloody ridiculous. But I can't sleep away from home. Which you know bloody well. Anyway' — he paused and took another measured bite — 'they'll be up here as soon as Dan's leave starts. I'll see 'em then. Take the little girls to South Bank Gardens, though why they needed to bloody modernize it — '

'Don't start, Dad.'

'That stupid caravan thing, selling *gelati*. What's wrong with bloody ice cream, I'd like to know?'

'So you won't come to Larkford?'

'And that Mums Meet Up nonsense, grans

122

and granddads welcome. I bloody ask you.'

'Dad,' George said, leaning forward, 'have you taken it in that I'm going to see them, even if you won't come?'

Eric stopped chewing. He looked at his son. 'What you doing that for?'

'I told you,' George said. He picked up the teapot on the table between them and poured tea into both their cups. 'I told you. It's all gone a bit quiet and I — '

'Leave them be.'

'I know what you think, Dad.'

'Leave them bloody be!'

George added milk. Before he met Alexa he used to put the milk in tea first, but she had pointed out that if you did that, you couldn't judge how dark you wanted your tea.

'I'm going, Dad,' he said, 'whether you like it or not. I've got an uneasy feeling and I want to be proved wrong.'

Eric's look changed to a glare. 'You're a bloody nosey-parker, George Riley.'

'Well, come with me and prove me wrong yourself.'

Eric muttered something.

'What?'

'Nothing.'

'Suit yourself,' George said. 'I spoke to Alexa and she is going to pick me up in Salisbury. She said I could have Izzy's room. I'll only be away the one night.'

Eric looked down at his plate as if the half-eaten teacake had appeared there without his consent. 'Bloody thing's cold,' he said.

123

★ ★ ★

George took a small rucksack on the coach, with a change of shirt and socks, his shaving things, a tube of handcream for Alexa and two small packets of candy-covered chocolate buttons for the twins. Dan had always been difficult to buy presents for, and George planned to take him out for a beer instead, if that proved possible. He would have liked to take something for Isabel, having a distinct sympathy for both her situation and her personality, but she wasn't at home, was she? She was shut up in that school and learning to grit her teeth, as Army kids had always had to do. At least boarding school for kids like Isabel was probably reasonably kind, these days. When he looked back at those great blocks where the other ranks lived in the garrisons, in Germany, when he was stationed out there, the soldiers' wives were not only up for anything once their men had been deployed, but were, in George's view, hardly exemplary mothers. Tough kids, those were, those kids in the blocks, tough and self-sufficient. Maybe it was good training. Maybe it taught you to stand on your own two feet and never to expect too much. That way, you didn't get disappointed. George felt he knew a lot about disappointment and, if nothing else, it had taught him to value the good things. Like how well Dan had done, and what a great wife and family he had. George really esteemed them — another of Alexa's words. Which was why he was now on a coach travelling down the M3 towards the A303, because he had a small, uneasy sense that things at number seven, the Quadrant were not as uncomplicated as his father wished to think or Dan wished to imply.

He took a paperback out of his rucksack. *Eight Lives Down* by Major Chris Hunter. It was set in Iraq, not Afghanistan, and was about bomb disposal, not artillery. But George had picked it up because he liked war memoirs as a genre, and the man who'd written this was a major, like Dan. There was a glossary at the back of all the military acronyms. It was comforting just to read some of them, like 9 milly for a 9 mm pistol. He could feel the pistol in his hand, just thinking about it. What a sad old soldier he was, smiling to himself at the mere memory of having a gun in his hand.

He glanced up. Across the aisle, a vividly made-up middle-aged woman in an electric-blue jacket with brass buttons was plainly waiting to catch his eye. She smiled at him. 'Mind if I slip in beside you?'

George indicated his book. 'Sit where you like,' he said, 'but I'll be reading.'

* * *

The twins had chosen several of their soft toys to put in Isabel's bed for George. This process involved unmaking the bed that Alexa had made up for him in order to be able to tuck a white nylon fur owl, a green plush giraffe and assorted bears and rabbits in against the pillows and under the duvet. This became such an absorbing game that Alexa felt safe to go out on to the

125

landing, to the corner at the top of the stairs where the mobile signal was strongest, and make the telephone call that had been preying on her mind for several days.

She had been pleased when George rang to ask in his straightforward and diffident way if he might come down to Larkford for a night. He had simply said that he'd like to reassure himself that the lad was really in one piece and Alexa, grateful for anything that helped bring Dan's leave closer by even half an hour, said warmly that they'd love to see him. It was true, in any case, always. Her relationship with her father-in-law was one of the least complicated of her entire life — he seemed to ask for so little and to be pleased and satisfied with so little, making him as peaceful and undemanding a presence in the house as Beetle.

Dan, when told, had simply said, 'Oh. Fine,' and Alexa, practising her newly self-imposed rule of leaving molehills as molehills instead of instantly, dramatically elevating them to mountains, had merely smiled and continued to slice the mushrooms she was about to add to a chicken casserole. She had held her breath while she smiled, which she knew was hardly evidence of a complete surrender to true nonchalance, but at least she hadn't used her breath for another tirade. She found, having dialled the number now, that she was holding her breath again.

'Thornhill School?' a female voice said on a rising note.

Alexa let her breath go, too suddenly. 'May — may I speak to Mr Johnson?'

'Who shall I say is calling?'

'Mrs Riley. He's expecting me.'

'One moment.'

There was a silence. Then, faintly, almost as if it was there by mistake, Vivaldi's Four Seasons could be heard. Alexa strained to catch it properly. It was so faint, it was hard to tell even which season it was. Clearly nobody at the school had listened to it for ages as, played that indistinctly, it could only serve to increase the anxiety or ire of any parent ringing the school. Was it Spring? No, no, it was Summer, surely —

'Mrs Riley?'

'Oh, Mr Johnson — '

'I was hoping you'd ring. To tell the truth, I was going to ring you if I hadn't heard from you by the end of the day. How are you?'

'I'm fine — '

'And you've had time to think the matter over?'

'I should have written — '

'No, no,' Mr Johnson said, 'an email would have done. But I'm glad you rang, I'd rather speak to you, I'd rather explain myself.'

Alexa pressed her phone to her ear and stared along the narrow landing. 'Explain?'

'I always believe,' Mr Johnson said warmly, 'in explaining things in person. Especially tricky things. I'm sure you know how impressed we were at your interview.'

'Yes.'

'You ticked so many boxes, Mrs Riley. The thing is — '

'Yes?'

'I could see,' Mr Johnson said, his tone almost cosy, 'that the commitment was going to be hard for you. I could just see it. Mind you, I've every sympathy. I've a niece married to a sailor, and it's hard enough for her to carve out a life for herself. The Army's even more demanding, I know that.'

'So,' Alexa said, interrupting too hastily, 'you've had second thoughts?'

She could almost see Mr Johnson's concern seeping down the phone line, like syrup.

'I have to tell you, Mrs Riley, that — '

'You've found someone else.'

'Not with your qualifications — '

'But someone else.'

'Yes, Mrs Riley. I'm so sorry. It was just that we really needed full-time commitment. I'd so hoped we could work on the hours you could give us, but on consideration, it wasn't a workable hope.' He paused. She pictured his kind, mobile face crumpled up with reluctance to say what he was saying. 'I really am so sorry.'

Alexa looked at the ceiling, stared at it hard for a second or two. 'Mr Johnson, thank you. Actually — '

'Yes?'

'Actually, I was ringing to tell you that I was afraid I wasn't going to be able to accept the job, anyway. My twins are so young, and the nature of my husband's work. All the moving . . . '

'Of course.'

'And possible promotion. You never quite know . . . '

'Indeed.'

'It didn't,' Alexa said, choking down mortification and gathering bravado, 'it didn't seem fair to the school to offer a commitment I simply might not be able to fulfil, however much I wanted to.'

'I'm relieved, Mrs Riley. I really did not want to be the bearer of bad news.'

'I'm relieved too,' Alexa said untruthfully.

'Of course, I may well be very grateful for some part-time help, covering maternity leave and so forth?'

'Oh, thank you.'

'No, thank *you*, Mrs Riley. I am really sorry. And regretful. Really.'

'Thank you, Mr Johnson.'

'I'll be in touch, if I may? You would fit in so well with our community here. All the best, Mrs Riley.'

'Thank you.'

'Goodbye for now.'

'Goodbye.'

She clicked her phone off and leaned against the wall. Then she slid down it until she was crouched on the floor with her arms round her knees and her head bent.

Tassy came out of Isabel's room holding a large felt rabbit with embroidered goofy teeth. She came and stood by her mother. 'Are you crying?' she demanded.

Alexa looked up, sniffing. 'No.'

'Why are you on the floor?'

'Just felt like it.'

'I should get up,' Tassy said. She put out the arm not holding the rabbit and hooked it in Alexa's. 'Upsy daisy,' she said firmly.

Alexa rose unsteadily to her feet.

'Blow your nose.'

'Yes, I will.'

'Hard,' Tassy said.

Alexa looked down at her. She had Dan's colouring and her maternal grandmother's face, in miniature.

'When I've done that,' Alexa said, brushing her hand across her eyes, 'we'll go and collect Grampa, shall we?'

'In the car?'

'Of course.'

'With Rabbit?'

'Sure.'

Tassy thought a moment. 'OK,' she said.

★   ★   ★

Dan carried two pints of bitter across the loudly patterned carpet of the pub's saloon bar. George had found them seats at a small table under a crude painting of two shire horses pulling a plough up a field as neatly ribbed as brown corduroy. He set the glasses down on the table.

'There's a treat,' George said, looking at them. 'Your granddad and I only ever have halves.'

Dan settled on a padded stool opposite his father. He said, 'I'm not having halves of anything right now.'

'Don't blame you.'

Dan raised his glass towards his father and took a deep swallow. 'How's Wimbledon?'

'Much the same.'

'And Granddad?'

130

'He doesn't change,' George said affection-ately. 'He was in a temper yesterday because the Y had fallen off the front of the library building, and of course he has to go in and tell them about it, doesn't he, and they said they knew and he was about the fiftieth person who'd told them. Then he came out and had a right sound-off. You know him. It's all change and nothing for the better and all you can do is live the way you know to be right, live by the rules, nothing's like it used to be, what about Plough Lane Stadium — '

'I remember Plough Lane,' Dan said, smiling. 'When we had that flat off Durnsford Road, remember? Plough Lane and Wimbledon FC. I was sixteen.'

'You were, lad.'

'And now there's no stadium and just a memorial.'

'Your granddad hates that memorial,' George said. 'You should hear him. Snorting about 'artwork'. He's better off with swords and crosses. Like the sword in the war memorial in the Gap Road Cemetery.'

Dan looked at his father. 'Does he still go there?'

'Every week. Shirt and tie, polished shoes.'

'I understand that,' Dan said.

'Do you? He never even knew his brother.'

'It's not about that, though, is it?'

George let a beat fall and then he said, 'Not about what?'

Dan sighed. 'It's not about respect for the dead. I mean it is, of course it is, but it's about

131

fellow feeling, isn't it? Anyone with a sense of decency can respect someone who's died while serving their country, but only another soldier can really understand what that entails.'

George said, staring at his beer, 'In the South Atlantic I just remember not wanting to let my gun crew down.'

'Exactly.'

'What about you?'

'What about me?'

George glanced up. 'You want to talk about Afghanistan?'

Dan smiled again, easily. 'Not really, Dad.'

'Nothing to say to me?'

'Nothing,' Dan said carefully, 'that I need to say to you.'

'Fair enough.'

'Sorry.'

'You can only do what comes naturally,' George said.

Dan picked his beer glass up. He said to it rather than to his father, 'Not sure Alexa'd agree with you.'

'No,' George said.

'Has . . . has she been talking to you?'

'A bit.'

'And?'

George gave his son a steady look. 'I'm no go-between, lad. But something's not right.'

'Is that why you wanted to buy me a pint?'

'It's always easier to talk,' George said, 'if you have something to do.'

Dan gave a little shrug. 'I don't need to talk.'

'Ah.'

'I just need to get all my folk off on leave, then I can focus.'

'Fair enough,' George said again.

'What did she say to you?'

George suddenly looked very like his own father. 'I've told you, I'm not a go-between. You need to talk to her yourself.'

'Drink up, Dad.'

'I'm a slow drinker. Trained by your granddad.'

Dan leaned forward. 'And don't — don't bloody meddle.'

George stared back at him. Then he lifted his glass, drank and set it down again. He said, as mildly as if he was commenting on the weather, 'You never did like being in the wrong, did you?'

★ ★ ★

The digital clock on the front of the radio by her side of the bed read one forty-seven in angular green numbers. Beside her, on his back, one arm flung above his head and one down by his side, where it had slipped an hour ago from resting on her hip, Dan lay in apparently profound and tranquil sleep. Shortly after midnight, he had begun twitching and muttering in his sleep and had let out a yelp or two, and then laughed, and Alexa had put her arms round him and held him, and said the soothing and anodyne things she said to the twins, until he relaxed against her and then turned to lie on his back, like a knight on a tomb, one hand on her hip. She had lain, still and wakeful, beside him for over an hour until the urge to turn over became irresistible and she had rolled gently away, feeling his hand slip limply from her and lie against her back as impersonally as if it had nothing to do with either of them.

Almost an hour further on into this long night and she was still awake. When Dan had been away and she couldn't sleep, Alexa had devised rules to prevent herself picturing a situation she could only imagine in a landscape she could only imagine and Dan, in some terrible state of mind, or body, or both, in the thick of it. But tonight, with his physical presence heavily beside her, no anxiety-prevention rules seemed to hold any sway over her scurrying mind. She should not have confided in George about the lost job. Or if she had, she should not have emphasized that she had decided not to take it because of the exigencies of Army life. Neither should she have described the visit to try and rescue Isabel, or blamed Dan's skewed priorities for the failure of that mission. George had stood beside her at the sink, drying the pans and utensils she had dumped, dripping, on to the draining board, and listened. She might have consoled herself by reminding herself that Dan had gone back to the garrison yet again, because of some trouble in the blocks, and that George could always have indicated that he didn't want to hear any more, but two in the morning was no time for consolation of any kind. She had abused George's affection for her, and she had been disloyal to Dan, and she felt terrible about both. Almost as terrible, in fact, as she did about not getting a job because she was in no position to accept it.

Tomorrow, driving George back to Salisbury, she would apologize, and ask him to forget what she had said as far as he was able. Put it down to the reunion, she'd say, we're all a bit wired, in fact we were warned about it, how we'd all be a bit mad for a while. So sorry, George. I should never have opened my stupid mouth. I don't mean it. Of course I don't. Why should I? Look at all I've got. Except —

What was the definition of frustration? Being thwarted, certainly, being discouraged and dissatisfied, having a strong sense that one's capacities and capabilities were being wildly, exaggeratedly, hugely unfulfilled. Alexa took her eyes off the green numbers and shut them firmly. At this moment, lying there tense and agitated beside the slumbering Dan, she was the very epitome of frustration. I could, she thought, have *invented* the word.

★　★　★

George found Dan polishing his shoes by the kitchen sink.

'What was the trouble last night?'

Dan was burnishing a toecap with brisk, practised strokes. 'Oh, just some pre-leave happy high jinks.'

'You can tell me,' George said. 'I've been a soldier and I've been in charge of them. What took you behind the wire at nine o'clock at night?'

'Drugs,' Dan said shortly.

'Drugs?'

'Well, we're not sure yet. But some nonsense with drugs, maybe. There's a lot of smoke and mirrors, of course. Infuriating.'

George picked up a yellow duster and offered it to Dan. 'Your granddad still bones his.'

'You need to, to get the best shine.'

'Dan?'

'Dad,' Dan said, brushing on.

'I want you to take me back to the bus. Not Alexa.'

Dan gave a little grimace to his shoe. 'Sorry, Dad, no can — '

'Yes, you can, lad.'

Dan stopped brushing. 'Excuse me?'

'You can take an hour off to drive me to the bus. That girl of yours has done it all so far. I'm your father, not hers.'

'But I'm afraid — '

George put the duster down. 'We need to leave at two forty.'

Dan stared at his shoe.

'Don't tell me,' George said, 'that the sky'll fall in on the battery in just one hour.'

★ ★ ★

'So,' Dan said, swinging the car out into the main road, 'do you want to get whatever it is off your chest?'

George, zipped into the blue windproof jacket he had been wearing as long as Dan could remember, said nothing. He sat composedly in

136

the passenger seat, gazing out at the late-autumn hills through the windscreen, his hands relaxed on his thighs.

Dan tried again. 'Well?'

'I wanted to ask you something.'

Dan changed gear, accelerated past a van with energy and changed back down again. 'Fire away.'

George took his time.

'It's hard, coming back — '

'Oh please, Dad, don't start that again. And don't say 'When I was in the Falklands'.'

'I wasn't going to. I wasn't thinking about the Falklands, even.'

'Well,' Dan said sharply, 'what then? What were you thinking about?'

George said dreamily, 'Alexa.'

'Alexa! What about Alexa? What *has* she been saying to you?'

George glanced out of the side window. 'Oh, it's not that. It's not about what she's said and done. It's about you. It's about what you think of her.'

Dan gave an angry little bark of laughter. 'You know bloody well what I think of her.'

George turned his head so that he could look at his son. He said calmly, 'Your granddad would say that as usual I've made myself as clear as mud. What I meant was, how did you think about her when you were away?'

There was a brief silence and then Dan said, 'I missed her.'

'Course you did. But how did you think about her? What part was she playing in what you were doing?'

'What on earth do you mean?'

'You know what I mean,' George said steadily.

'D'you — d'you mean did I think what I was doing out there had some — some relevance to her?'

'Sort of.'

Dan looked sideways at his father and grinned. 'You are one weird old bastard.'

'Maybe. But I'd like an answer, all the same.'

Dan said, 'We discuss this sometimes, Gus and me. We talk about — well, about this protection thing.'

'Protection?'

'Of Alexa. All our girls. Keeping them safe.'

'Of course. And?'

'What do you mean, and?'

'You don't want them messy,' George said, 'do you? When you're in the middle of a big mess on ops, you want everything at home to be pure, don't you? Pure as driven snow. That way you can cope, can't you? Imagining all that purity back home that you're defending. Them being pure and innocent makes it all worthwhile.'

Dan glanced sideways again. 'Heavens, Dad, I never thought — '

'You never asked. I never thought to mention it. Didn't need to. But it rings a bell?'

'A whole peal of them.'

'Trouble is,' George said, 'the families only stay innocent if they don't know anything. And if they don't know anything they can't talk to you. And then lines of communication go down.'

They slowed for a roundabout. Peering right and left, Dan said tensely, 'So this is, in fact, a bollocking for not treating Alexa the way you think I should treat her.'

'Trouble is,' George said again, ignoring him, 'that if you treat families as innocents, you end up treating them like children. And that's no good for communication. It may be all very well for *you* to want to protect them because it suits some high falutin' ideas you have, but it's not so good for them.'

'Enough, Dad.'

'Talk to her, boy. *Talk* to her. Tell her what you've been through. Ask her what she's been through. That's all.'

Dan changed gears badly and the car briefly rocked and jerked. 'I am *certainly* not telling Alexa some of the stuff that goes on. I never have. I never will.'

'You're patronizing her — '

'I am *not!*' Dan shouted. 'I am not! I am protecting her from stuff that will only give her nightmares — images of dead kids, betrayals, accidents. I'm protecting her from all the ugly stuff, just as I protected her from all the wild stuff when I was a junior officer and — '

'She's a grown woman, Dan.'

'That's just it! That's it exactly! What grown woman wants to know about a bunch of guys getting blind drunk together, getting naked together, having jerking-off competitions in the mess together — '

'Don't talk disgusting, Daniel.'

Dan beat the steering wheel with the heel of his left hand in exasperation. 'I give up.'

'What?'

'Talking to you. Trying to get you to understand. Sometimes it amazes me you've ever been a soldier.'

'Insults'll get you nowhere.'

'But Dad,' Dan said, 'are you so besotted with Alexa that you can't even remember what you felt about trying to shield someone like her from knowing something that will only distress them because they can't do anything about it?'

They were entering the outskirts of Salisbury. Dan slowed the car until the speedometer needle was trembling on thirty.

'That wasn't my point,' George said.

'Oh my God. And your point was?'

'It's not about protection. It's about getting through to her. If you can't tell her anything, then ask her how she is.'

'I *know* how she is. Finding it bloody difficult to have me back, and no wonder.'

'Just ask her,' George said.

'What?'

'Ask her how she is. Ask her what she's thinking. What's been going on.' He looked ahead. 'Just drop me here. I'll walk the last stretch.'

'No, Dad, let me — '

George put his hand on the car door handle. 'I'll get out here. Stop the car.'

Dan slowed the car to a halt outside a small newsagent's shop.

'I'll pick up a paper. Crossword for the journey.'

'Dad?'

'Yes?'

'I'm sorry I shouted. You know what she means to me and I know I'm hopeless right now, but I'll make it up to her, promise.'

George opened the passenger door. He turned back to look at his son. 'Mind you do.'

'I will.'

'You're a good lad, but you need to do a bit of thinking.'

'OK.'

George reached out and patted Dan's shoulder briefly. '*Talk* to her,' he said.

8

'Hello, stranger!' Alexa said, delighted.

Kate Melville stood on the doorstep. She was wearing a tailored suit and sunglasses, and was carrying a huge bunch of mop-headed chrysan-themums. She took off her sunglasses and smiled.

'You look wonderful!' Alexa said.

Kate held out the flowers. 'Bronze, please note, not white, so you didn't think of Chinese funerals. How are you, babe?'

Alexa laughed. 'Up, down, round and round. You know. Where've you been? These are gorgeous.'

'Working,' Kate said. She stepped into the house and kissed Alexa.

'To some effect, I hear,' Alexa said.

'Well, it's nice to see one's efforts repaid a bit.'

'Gus is so proud.'

Kate looked her up and down. 'You're thinner.'

'Never a bad thing.'

'Much thinner.'

'Even better. Coffee?'

'A quick one,' Kate said. 'I've a train to catch.'

'Back to London?'

'It's Tuesday. Back-to-London day. How are the children?'

'Two good,' Alexa said, leading the way into the kitchen, 'one not.'

'Isabel?'

'Isabel.'

'This wretched boarding thing — '

Alexa put down the flowers and picked up the kettle. She said, without turning, 'I thought you liked the boarding thing. I thought you said the children loved it.'

'I think they do. Or at least they make the best of it because they know they've got to. But I'd love them to be at day schools. I really would. Good London day schools.'

Alexa indicated a chair and put two mugs on the table. She said, 'Dreamland. Like the house I fantasize about.'

'Don't you get sick of that?'

'What?'

'Fantasizing about what you can't have because the Army is just so inflexible?'

Alexa switched on the kettle and came to peer into Kate's face. 'Are you OK?'

Kate avoided her gaze. 'So so. This wasn't good, was it?'

'What wasn't?'

'This homecoming. They only want to see each other.'

'That'll wear off.'

Kate looked directly at her, suddenly. 'Don't kid yourself.'

'Kate!'

'I'm just fed up.'

'You've hardly given Gus a chance,' Alexa said, sitting down in the chair next to Kate's. 'You've hardly been home.'

'What do you know?'

143

'Enough. Dan's never here because he's always consoling Gus. Because you're not there.'

'Whose side are you on?' Kate demanded.

Alexa said unhappily, 'I really don't know.'

'Then don't go for me.'

'I wasn't.'

Kate stood up. She straightened her suit jacket and said, almost melodramatically, 'I'll go.'

'But you've only just come.'

'I don't want,' Kate said, 'to be confronted by any more toe-the-Army-line stuff.'

'I was only trying to put across another point of view.'

'Dan's.'

'Kate,' Alexa said, getting up too, 'what is the *matter* with you?'

Kate picked up her sunglasses. 'I thought you might give me a bit of a steer.'

'On what? On Gus? I haven't seen Gus, apart from so briefly — '

'Sorry,' Kate said. 'I shouldn't have come.'

'You came for a reason.'

'Not really.'

'But one you've decided not to tell me about. One you've had second thoughts about.'

'Alexa,' Kate said, 'you're lovely but you're kind of brain-washed.' She put her sunglasses on and turned her blank dark gaze on Alexa. 'Gus says you are having the head honchos to dinner, even.'

'Dan asked.'

'Course he did. And you said yes.'

Alexa said, suddenly furious, 'And you'd have refused? If Gus had asked you?'

Kate looked away, a half-smile on her face. 'Probably.'

'Jesus, Kate — '

'It must be nice,' Kate said in a tone of mockery, 'to congratulate yourself on being such an excellent Army wife.'

'Stop it!'

'Even helping Dan to get promotion.'

'Stop it!' Alexa shouted. 'What on earth's got into you?'

Kate picked her bag up slowly and slung it deliberately over her shoulder. She said, in a more normal voice, 'I just can't believe in it any more.'

'In what? In the Army? In Gus?'

Kate said, her head bent, 'Any of it.'

Alexa took a deep breath. 'Is that what you came to say today? Armed with flowers, you came to tell me you'd had enough? Not two weeks after Gus gets home?'

There was a pause. Kate fiddled with the clasp on her bag. 'No.'

'Well, then. Well?'

Kate said, more sadly, 'It's — it's all so difficult.'

Alexa snorted. 'Tell me about it!'

'I'm sorry,' Kate said, 'I shouldn't have come. I shouldn't take it out on you. Sorry. I didn't mean — ' She stopped.

Alexa turned and picked up the flowers and held them out. 'You have them.'

'No, please.'

Alexa shook the flowers with emphasis. '*Take* them. And come back when you're not so crazy.'

Kate stepped forward, not looking at Alexa, and retrieved the flowers. She laid them along her forearm as if she was cradling a baby. 'Thanks,' she said, and then, with a short half-laugh, '*If.*'

★ ★ ★

When the telephone had rung mid-morning, Elaine had supposed that it would be her friend Verity, calling to confirm matinée tickets for the National Theatre. Verity had said she would ring before midday, and she was the kind of person who telephoned when she said she would, as well as being the kind of person who made arrangements, down to the smallest detail, months in advance of any activity, and became personally offended at the mere suggestion of any subsequent change. Plans made with Verity could be relied upon with utter confidence to work, but also carried an undertone of menace.

'You wouldn't,' Verity was inclined to say if her proposals were met with any hint of a desire for modification, 'want to let me down, would you?'

But the call had not been from Verity, but from Alexa. An Alexa apparently standing in her kitchen surrounded by cookery books and lists, in a state of uncharacteristic turmoil.

'But, darling,' Elaine said, not having done more than assemble a meal for a bridge four in a decade, 'what's to faze you about supper for six?'

Alexa had said, too vehemently for the situation, that Elaine didn't understand.

'What don't I understand? The etiquette of

having a colonel and a brigadier for dinner?'

No, Alexa said, yes, well both, really, and on top of everything — she had stopped mid-sentence, as if she had suddenly flung her hand up over her mouth.

'Everything, darling?'

In a more measured voice, Alexa said she'd just rung for some menu suggestions. Things that looked as if you'd spent ages on them when you hadn't really, because you hadn't got ages to spend, and anyway were feeling so distracted and preoccupied with things —

'What things?'

'Oh,' Alexa said, sounding on the verge of tears, 'just the domestic round. You know . . . '

'I don't,' Elaine said, truthfully. 'Not like you do. I never have. Where's Dan?'

Alexa said neutrally that he was up at the offices.

'Again?'

'There's some bother with drugs. They did some random testing on some of the soldiers and two of Dan's lot tested positive. They swear they took nothing, they insist they just got the fumes from other people at a party. It's really — hard for Dan.'

'Is it?'

'He's told them he'll stand by them if they tell him what happened. But they won't.'

'Oh dear,' Elaine said. She was about to say, sympathetically, 'It's always something, darling, isn't it?' and checked herself. Instead she said, 'What news of Isabel?'

'Oh, Mum.'

'What, darling?'

Alexa said, through sudden tears, 'She's just — just enduring it. Sends pitiful little messages about being fine. I feel so *awful*.'

'It isn't your fault.'

'It is! It is! If I hadn't married into this life, Isabel wouldn't be suffering as she is!'

'She might be suffering because you weren't as happy as you are with Dan.'

There was a prolonged silence, not broken even by sniffs from Alexa's end of the line.

Elaine said, 'Darling? Are you there?'

'Do you think,' Alexa said, more resolutely, 'that avocado something is too much of a cliché?'

Elaine grasped the phone tightly. 'Would you like me to come down?'

'What?'

'Shall I come down to Larkford and help you? I easily could.'

Alexa said carefully, 'I — don't think so.'

'Why not?'

'We'll come to London when Dan's on leave.'

'But this supper party.'

'I'll manage.'

'Alexa,' Elaine said, putting on her reading glasses for emphasis, 'you rang me because you *weren't* managing.'

'I am now.'

'Despite Isabel? And Dan?'

Alexa muttered something.

'What?'

'I said,' Alexa said, 'I shouldn't have rung.'

Elaine replied reproachfully, 'I'd like to have helped, you know.'

'I don't mean to be ungrateful.'

'No.'

'I just rang,' Alexa said firmly, as if she had never wavered, 'for a few recipes, you know?'

When she had put the phone down, Elaine went into her bedroom and sat at the dressing-table Morgan had given her when they were first married, because, he said, it was an exact replica of the one his mother had always used. That knowledge had, Elaine recalled, been violently irritating to her forty years ago, but now, as with most irritating things, her reaction to it had mellowed. It was as if, she sometimes thought, she no longer had the energy to resent things and disapprove of things and battle against contempt. Even the soft sepia photograph of his carefully feminine mother that Morgan still kept on his chest of drawers was no longer an annoyance. If she found Verity's behaviour over theatre dates a real hindrance, she surely wouldn't go on putting up with it, would she? Wasn't it, really, just a measure of the calmer waters of being older, of liking routines and familiarity, and even — dare one acknowledge it — the serene self-indulgence of monotony?

She sat down at her dressing-table, on its matching stool, and surveyed her reflection in the triple mirror between two lamps made of silvered cupids that Morgan had found on a holiday in Venice. Alexa had not inherited her face, but Alexa's little Tassy had, as had Flora, in a more blurred version. Elaine did not feel she knew the twins very well, any more than she

149

knew Dan, or the child Isabel had grown into since she was sent away to school. When she thought about them, or even more emphatically about Alexa, all the calm and surrendering thoughts about her civilized and well-managed daily round in the Marylebone Road were exploded by immediate agitation. She laid both hands flat across her stomach, pressing hard against her neat, discreet merino cardigan. Alexa had sounded all over the place on the phone, distressed and uneven and as defensive as ever. Elaine stared at herself in the mirror. Her face seemed to be melting, dissolving, blurring between the cool, gleaming orbs of her pearl earrings.

Oh my goodness, Elaine thought, letting go of her stomach and snatching a tissue from their lace-covered box, oh my goodness, I'm going to cry.

★　★　★

Julian Bailey turned to smile his handsome, direct, soldierly smile at Alexa. 'Delicious,' he said. 'And I never eat pudding as a rule. Ask Claire!'

He looked startlingly different, Alexa thought, out of uniform. They all did, of course, to a certain degree, but Julian Bailey, as spare and slight as a jockey, was an altogether changed physical proposition in corduroy trousers (rust-coloured) and a cashmere V-neck (navy blue) than he was in battledress and side hat with his hardly enormous feet, now shod in immaculate

150

suede loafers, magnified and masculinized by Army boots.

He was clever, everyone said, extremely clever. He wore rimless glasses, behind which his blue eyes shone with great intensity, and he had a reputation for reading and an encyclopaedic knowledge of opera. His wife, Claire, to whom he deferred with elaborate public gallantry, was built on the same scale and balanced his intellectual powers with formidable practicality and capability. Alexa suspected that despite making all the conventional noises of delighted approval, Claire would have guessed that the sauce on the chicken contained a can of condensed soup because Alexa had only discovered at the last moment that she had forgotten to buy cream. Claire was wearing tailored trousers, not jeans, and a white shirt under a velvet waistcoat embroidered in gold thread, which Julian had brought home from Afghanistan. She had gold stud earrings, no other jewellery but her wedding band, clear skin and freshly washed hair. The effect on Alexa and, plainly, on Mary Mackenzie, the Colonel's wife and something of a professional pretty woman, was to make them feel they had put on the wrong clothes and too much make-up.

Alexa smiled back. 'Good. So glad you liked it. A terrific apple year, of course.'

'Of course,' Julian Bailey said, still smiling. 'When we left Helmand, it was apricot time. You'd be amazed how beautiful the countryside out there can be. Mountains with these lovely valleys between, filled with little white farms and apricot orchards. Under a blue sky, quite fabulous. I expect Dan has told you.'

Alexa glanced down the table. Dan was leaning towards Mary Mackenzie to refill her glass. She was saying 'No, no,' but not really stopping him, and he was smiling and pouring, and Claire Bailey was holding out her own glass in mock indignation at Dan's not noticing that it was empty.

'Oh, yes.'

'I was so sorry,' Julian said, 'that you couldn't make the family day.'

'Yes, me too.'

'They're so crucial these days. Aren't they, Mack?'

The Colonel on Alexa's left put his pudding spoon down with regret. He said, 'No nonsense about not eating pudding in my department, Mrs R. That was fantastic. But then I'm the one who eats the biscuits out of my rat pack before anything else.'

'The family day, Mack. So important to be able to be inclusive. To demonstrate to the families how vital they are to our morale — '

'Awful piece in the paper today. Did you see? *Guardian*, I think — '

'I only ever read the arts pages in the Saturday *Guardian*, Mack, as you well know.'

'It was headed 'No Medals For Those Left At Home', or something.'

Alexa took a gulp of wine. She said as mildly as she could, 'Well, there aren't.'

Julian Bailey turned his shining blue gaze on

her. He said pleasantly, 'Did that have anything to do with your not attending the family day?'

Alexa looked back at him. 'No. It was Isabel.'

'Isabel?'

'My oldest.'

'Oh, of course. Stupid of me.'

'My children,' Alexa said, raising her voice very slightly, 'come first.'

'Naturally.'

'Well, not naturally, actually, as far as the Army's concerned.'

Julian glanced down at the table. 'I suppose Claire has always shielded me from most of that. She's always said that her role is to ease the children through life with as little disruption and as much happiness as possible. Luckily they like school.'

'Unluckily,' Alexa said, 'Isabel doesn't.'

'I am truly sorry to hear that.'

'Yes.'

'Perhaps,' Mack said, his eyes on his senior officer, 'you should speak to Welfare?'

'Good idea. I'm glad you mentioned it. Let me set it up.'

'Lovely man!' Claire called from Mack's other side. 'Walt the Welfare. You should have shouted earlier.'

'I hoped — ' said Alexa.

'You should have come straight to me,' Julian said, 'or Mack. Why didn't you?'

Alexa glanced at Dan. 'You were all so busy.'

'Never too busy for our own families. Where would we be without you?'

'I thought I could sort it.'

'Well, let us help you do that. How are yours, Mack?'

'My one, Julian.'

'I know that. How is he?'

'Ask Mary.'

'You're no help. And no advertisement.' He picked up his pudding plate, as if to signal both that he would like to help and that he would also like to move the conversation on.

Alexa stood up. Dan was telling Mary Mackenzie a story, and she was laughing and shaking her head, and her long dark curls were becoming entangled with her earrings. Dan paused and looked up at his wife. 'Darling?'

'I was just going to ask,' Alexa said, 'if anyone wanted tea or coffee? And if so, which kind?'

⋆ ⋆ ⋆

'That was a stunning success,' Dan said. 'Stunning. You were amazing. Wonderful dinner. They all loved it.'

'Good.'

'I mean, look at the time! Twenty-five past midnight! It was a triumph. It really was.'

Alexa, pulling her hair up into a ponytail, turned to the sink. 'I'm glad.'

Dan was marshalling wine bottles — a considerable number — on the table before putting them in the recycling box by the back door. He paused, a bottle in each hand. 'What's the matter?'

Alexa turned the hot tap on full blast. 'Nothing.'

154

Dan put down the bottles and came across the kitchen. He reached past her and turned the tap off. 'It's not nothing. What's the matter?'

Alexa held on to the edge of the sink, her shoulders hunched. 'You know what's the matter, Dan. You *know*.'

'I don't.'

'Don't you?'

'No,' he said, 'I really don't. You put on an amazing meal for the two senior people in my life and their wives, and everyone has a wonderful evening and eats and drinks like there's no tomorrow, and stays till after midnight, and you can't be as pleased as I am?'

Alexa turned to him. 'Of course I'm pleased it went well. Of *course* I am. They're nice people.'

'But?'

'But it doesn't help anything.'

Dan spread his hands and gave a shout of derisive laughter. 'Darling, it does! It helps me a hell of a lot. You know how well the battery did the last six months, you know what the future means to me — '

Alexa shouted, interrupting, 'I didn't mean that!'

There was sudden silence. Then Dan said, 'What do you mean?'

'I mean you. You and me.'

'Sweetheart, we're getting there — '

'No, we're not!'

'Lex, give me time — '

'I have! I have! I've given you eight years, of which the last six months and two weeks have been particularly hard to bear!'

155

'I know you're upset about Izzy.'

'Yes!' Alexa screamed. 'Yes! And why aren't *you*?'

'I am, *I am*. I hate her to be unhappy.'

'But not enough to stop doing whatever you do all day up at the offices and pay the problem any real attention. Not enough to give up one of those endless hours you spend with Gus to come to the school with me.'

Dan stepped back. He said tiredly, 'I wish I'd come. I really wish I had now. But I couldn't. You know I couldn't. It was the family day and it was re — a bit awkward you weren't there, as it was. But I would rather have come with you. I wish I'd been able to, I really do.'

'What's the point of that?'

'I just want you to know I was wrong. I should have come. We should have made Mrs Whatsit see us another day. Or *I* should have. I hated Jack going — '

'Just stupid male sexual jealousy,' Alexa spat. 'Nothing to do with Isabel.'

Dan glared at her. 'You are so wrong!'

'I am so not! It's been you, you, you ever since you got back. You haven't asked about Flora's eye, you haven't asked about Beetle's lumps, you haven't asked anything about me, what I've been feeling, what I want to do with my life, have you? Nothing. *Nothing*. It's all the battery. Or Gus. It's just Army, Army, Army. Because that's all that really matters to you, isn't it? You are good at your job, in fact, very good at your job, and that has obliterated everything else, hasn't it? All the people who make it possible for you, all the people who facilitate this career of yours so that you can go on climbing up and up the ladder until you are where Julian is now, with three stars on your shoulder, and you can tell yourself that you have earned every single one of them. Well, I'm telling you, Daniel, you might earn them as a *soldier*, but you certainly won't have earned them as a *man*.'

She stopped. She was shaking. Dan had retreated behind the kitchen table and was standing there, behind the palisade of empty wine bottles. He said, quietly, 'That's not fair.'

Alexa shrugged. She took a tea towel off the back of the nearest chair and blew her nose on it.

Dan said, 'You and the children mean everything to me. Everything.'

Alexa wiped her eyes.

He said, 'I love Isabel dearly.'

'I know.'

'I do what I do, as you bloody well know, because I *believe* in it. I believe I'm making the world a better place, in however minuscule a way, for you and the children to live in. I thought you understood that.'

Alexa sniffed, folded her arms and regarded the ceiling. 'Understanding it is one thing, Dan. Living with it is quite another.'

'I can't go on if you don't get what I do.'

Alexa's head tipped down again. 'Don't dump the responsibility on me!'

'But — '

'I've got more than enough to do without carrying your beliefs as well as my own!'

157

'I didn't mean — '

'You've got your job, Dan! You've got what you do and your men and Gus and Mack and everyone! You've got a support system! What have I got?'

Dan came round the table and put his hands on her shoulders. 'You've got friends and the children and all our parents. And me.'

'You.'

'Yes. Me. I love you.'

Alexa looked at him. 'But no job.'

'Well, not at this moment. But you did have. You had a good job and you were great at it. And you'll have another.'

'When?'

'Some day. Soon. Some day, soon, I'm sure you will — '

'Dan.'

'Yes?'

'I had one,' Alexa said.

'What?'

'I had a job. I was offered a job while you were away, I applied for a teaching job, a head-of-languages job, and I was offered it. But I couldn't take it, could I? It was a fantasy even to apply for it. But I couldn't take it because of the twins, and because you're coming to the end of your time with the battery and will probably get promotion, and then we'll move. So I couldn't. And in the end, they couldn't have me, could they? Because I couldn't be reliable.'

Dan stared at her. He said in a whisper, 'I had no idea — '

'No.'

'Why didn't you tell me?'

Alexa stepped back, so that Dan's hands slipped from her shoulders. She put her chin up. 'Why didn't you *ask?*'

9

'You're in here, in front of me,' Dan said, 'because I want to give you one last chance before you see the CO.'

Gunner Rigby, shorn red hair barely visible beneath his side hat, stood stiffly to attention in front of Dan's desk. Behind him, equally stiffly, stood Paul Swain and the regimental sergeant major. All six eyes were fixed on a point on the wall behind, just above Dan's head.

Dan himself, also in battledress, was seated. He had nothing on the desk in front of him apart from the rug, in Hunting Robertson tartan, that Paul Swain spread on it for interviews, to remind the interviewees of the supreme importance of regimental loyalty.

'Are you listening to me, Rigby?'

'Suh.'

'I don't want you to have to go to the CO. Leave starts after PT tomorrow, as you know, and if you have to go and see the CO he is likely — in fact, bound — to tell you that your leave will be permanent. If you can't be open with me, Rigby, you will be facing discharge from the Army before the end of the day. Is that clear?'

'Clear, suh.'

Dan leaned forward, his forearms on the desk, his hands linked. 'Shall we go over it, one more time?'

Rigby said nothing. His gaze at the wall did not waver.

'You and Gunner Wharton were asked to a party. The invitation was sent by text message, and the word 'party' had a capital T. Is that correct?'

'Suh.'

'I am unfamiliar with the jargon, Rigby, but I gather partying in this context means drugs will be available, and a capital T indicates the presence of crystal meth. The use of this substance also indicates that there will be no women present at such a party, only men.'

Gunner Rigby gave a small shudder but remained mute. Dan sighed. He said, looking at his linked hands, 'I am aware, Rigby, that Gunner Wharton has no appetite for a girlfriend. I have no idea, and do not wish to know, if you share his tastes. I am aware you have been a good friend to him and shielded him from abuse and stuck up for him, all of which I commend. But it is taking that loyalty too far to refuse to admit your participation in whatever went on at that party that night.'

Silence.

'You should not have gone,' Dan said. 'And you should not have taken any drug of any kind. If you do not admit to your wrongdoing, you will find yourself out on your stupid, stubborn, bloody *ear*.'

Still silence.

'One last chance, Rigby. You can't, I think, save Gunner Wharton, whatever you do. But you can save yourself.'

Suddenly Gunner Rigby blurted out, 'I'm a good soldier, sir!'

'You are. So, I might add, is Gunner Wharton. But it doesn't stop you being complete and utter arseholes, does it?' He raised his eyes and leaned back in his chair. 'Tell me what happened, and I can help you. Stick to your bone-headed denial and misplaced loyalty, and I can't.'

'I'm a good soldier,' Rigby said again, almost in a whisper.

'Then be one. *Tell* me.'

Rigby sighed. His body seemed to sag briefly, and then he straightened again so hard that his thin, pale neck, rising above the open collar of his battledress, was almost corded with the effort. 'Suh.'

'Nothing?'

Rigby stared mutely ahead.

Dan stood up slowly. 'Very well, then. Off you go, Rigby.'

'Suh.'

The RSM barked something unintelligible. Rigby jolted himself into a salute and then swung round and followed the RSM out on to the main floor of the offices as briskly as if he had received a reprieve rather than a sentence.

'Bloody hell,' Dan said disgustedly to Paul Swain.

'A complete shambles.'

'Can you imagine, throwing away an entire career for the sake of an evident lie told by someone else? They were at this party, they took this stuff, they — '

'Please! Don't go there, Dan,' Paul Swain said.

'The whole episode's just a heap of shit, frankly.'

Paul Swain moved down the room towards his own desk. He said as he went, 'And he wasn't wrong. He's a good soldier. So's poor sodding Wharton. Part of our best gun crew.'

Dan said sadly, 'The cause doesn't really have to be right, or winnable, does it? We saw that time and time again in Helmand. Men will choose to die in battle with their mates rather than flee to survival. They only need to feel loved and valued by each other to fight for a cause they don't know about or care about. I'd bet my bottom dollar Rigby isn't gay. But he's lonely. Usual hopeless chaotic family situation. Wharton befriended him. Wharton's funny and quick and most of the boys love him. He's their camp mascot. Rigby cannot bring himself to fail him.'

Paul Swain stooped to reactivate his computer. He said, 'You did all you could.'

'So did his subbie.'

'Poor guy.'

'Why poor?'

Paul Swain grimaced. 'Girl trouble.'

'What, Freddie? I thought he'd got a gorgeous girl.'

'He has. She is. But she's one of those independent ones. Wants civvy life and an Army boyfriend.'

Dan was silent. Paul looked down the room at him. 'Dan?'

'Yup.'

'Dan, I repeat, you did all you could for Rigby. *All*.'

'Wasn't enough.'

'It was more than most would have done.'

Dan put his hands briefly over his face. When he took them away, he said, 'It still wasn't enough. Seems — ' He stopped.

'Seems what?'

Dan shrugged. 'Seems the story of my life right now.'

★ ★ ★

'Hello, there!' Jack's text read. 'Anyone at home? Lights seem to be on but no reply. Call me.'

Alexa flipped her phone shut and dropped it into her pocket. She was halfway round the supermarket, the huge one right in the garrison village, so close, in fact, to her friend Prue's married quarter that Prue said she could see what was on Buy One Get One Free without stirring from her kitchen window.

'It's a lovely quarter,' Prue said, 'but it's a truly horrible location. Welfare should try living on the flightpath of every drunken soldier.'

Alexa had hoped to find Prue at home for a therapeutic cup of coffee before she tackled the weekly supermarket shop, but Prue's house was locked and silent, almost reproachful, it seemed to Alexa in her current mood, to a person without a job and in dire need of another perspective. If she'd thought it through, of course, she'd have remembered that Prue would be out. Mondays through Thursdays, Prue worked as a physiotherapist at the local military hospital, where she provided, it appeared to

Alexa, as much a counselling service as a physically therapeutic one for her soldier patients.

'They'll tell me all sorts of stuff, big stuff, but they won't report it. They think any plea for help will go on their reports. And they are really suffering. Lots of it is relationship stuff. If that's going badly, they can't cope with anything. I've had them break down on me while I'm trying to sort them. A loyal girl is more important to them than she'll ever know.'

A loyal girl, Alexa thought, dumping packets of pasta into the trolley. A loyal girl, faithful and firm in allegiance. Faithful, yes, as far as she was concerned, tick. Firm in allegiance, half a tick. Maybe, actually, no tick at all. Did firm in allegiance mean not screaming at your husband among the dirty dishes that he, not three weeks out of the juggernaut of boredom and terror of active service, was utterly failing you in every aspect of a loving partnership? Did it mean controlling yourself, subduing yourself, repressing yourself, until you felt yourself to be not only at breaking point but a mere distorted shadow of the woman he'd married?

She looked at the serried rows of tea packets. Every kind and colour of tea, packaged to make you feel that nothing stood between you and self-enhancement but the purchase of a neat, bright box. Calm, some of the boxes promised, easy sleep, relaxation, serenity, tranquillity. Just add boiling water. Lie back in your recliner chair with a steaming mug and hey presto, what was unmanageable becomes manageable. In her pocket, her phone bleeped again.

'Hello,' Jack texted. 'I know you're there. Call me or I'm coming to get you.'

Alexa dialled. 'What does valerian taste of?'

'I have no idea. It's a rhizome.'

'In my hand,' Alexa said, 'it's a box of tea bags.'

'From the Latin, *valere*, to be strong.'

'It's trying to be strong,' Alexa said, putting the box back, 'that's all but finishing me off at the moment.'

'Why haven't you rung me?' Jack demanded.

'I have.'

'No. Categorically not. For over a week.'

'I'm shopping.'

'You can talk to me with your other hand. How's Izzy?'

'Bad,' Alexa said.

'And you and Dan?'

Alexa said nothing.

'Ah.'

She pushed her trolley up against a shelf of shiny sacks of dog food.

'Is that why you haven't rung?' Jack asked.

'I don't think so.'

'A row? Or, should I say, *the* row?'

'I don't think,' Alexa said again, 'that I can talk about it. Even to you.'

'My God. That bad?'

'I feel so bad. Furious with him. Furious with myself. Why aren't I coping? I live in this camp with hundreds of women who are coping. Even those poor Fijian wives in the blocks cope better than I do. I don't know how they endure it. They

166

can't even drive, to get off the base, for God's sake. They have a good old catfight every so often and clear the air, and instead I simmer and mutter and then explode and yell at him like a madwoman.'

'Did you?'

'Yes.'

'D'you want to tell me about it?'

'Only,' Alexa said, leaning against a vast sack of complete diet for the older dog, 'if you can reconcile me to what I feel and what I've done and turn Dan back into someone who can entertain one single idea other than the Army.'

Jack put on a fluting female voice. 'There were three of us in this marriage. Him, me and the Army.'

'I don't feel like being teased today.'

'Lex,' Jack said, 'please stop being so melodramatic. I think I'll come down to darkest Wilts and take you out on the lash.'

'No, thank you.'

'You worry me.'

Alexa took her shoulder away from the sack of dog food. She said, 'I tried to see my friend Prue before I began on this. She's a physio. Her brother's an Army surgeon, still out there. He told her in an email that he's cut off more arms and legs in the last three months than he'd expect in a lifetime on civvy street. And the awful thing is that these shattered limbs aren't accidental, like they used to be. They're *intentional*. They mean to maim. They mean to maim our boys.'

'Our boys?'

'Yes. Boys from the British Army.'

'What,' Jack said, 'are you trying to say to me?'

Alexa sighed. 'That with all that in Dan's head, how's he ever going to hear me?'

'Did you tell him about the job?'

'Yes,' Alexa said.

'And?'

'He looked appalled. He didn't really say anything. I'd been screaming and I cried. He got me a brandy. I thought maybe we'd cleared the air a bit, anyway, and tried to talk to him this morning, you know, trying to build a bit, but he was back in the cave, as they say, with these boys of his on their drugs charge. I am stuck, Jack, really stuck. I can't think what to do next, I can't — '

'Why don't you come to London?' Jack said.

'The twins — '

'Just for a day?'

'Dan's leave starts tomorrow.'

'Oh,' Jack said heartily, 'great. Super great. The famous POTL. Post-Operative Tour Leave. Weeks of it. Things'll look up. You'll see. No uniform, different mindset.'

'Maybe.'

'Course they will. Wonderful. Call me in a day or two.'

'And you?' Alexa said. 'And . . . and Eka?'

Jack gave a brave imitation of a laugh. 'Eka? She is in a palazzo in Bologna with a man who owns a shoe factory. An old palazzo and an old factory and an old man. Very old.'

'How — '

'Sixty-one.'

'Not very — '

'Shut up,' Jack said. 'Go back to your teabags. Think outside the box. Start again. New day, new Dan. Leave and life start here.'

'OK.'

'Darkest hour before dawn. You've done the worst bit. It'll get better now and you and Dan can go together to rescue Izzy. Clouds roll away. Dawn breaks. Sun rises — '

'*You* shut up now,' Alexa said.

'You'll see, Mrs Riley,' he said, 'you'll see. You'll look back on these three weeks and wonder what on earth all the fuss was about.'

★   ★   ★

Showering after games, Isabel abruptly felt, if not exactly happy, at least much less unhappy. It had been an unexpected afternoon of quiet triumph, all because Chloe Miller, always picked as goal shooter for netball, had had to go to the surgery to have an ingrown toenail dealt with, and Miss Hoxton, who usually looked right through Isabel as if Isabel only existed in her own solitary imagination, had suddenly focussed on her and said, in her commanding, cheerful PT way, 'You take Chloe's place this afternoon, Isabel. Let's see what you're made of.'

At first, Isabel had been horrified. She wasn't one of the naturally sporty ones in her form in the first place, and had only earned a place in the team — sometimes — by marking her opponent so doggedly that she was deemed grudgingly to be useful. But she had never aspired to be goal shooter. She wasn't collected enough, or steady enough, and invariably stood at just the wrong place or at the wrong angle.

'No objections,' Miss Hoxton said briskly. 'How will we ever know what you can do unless you try? On that court. At the double, please. And no discussion from any of you, thank you.'

And then something almost miraculous had happened. Isabel's instinctive panic had resolved itself into an unheard-of focus and energy. She had found herself in the circle with an equally anxious girl who represented no threat, and she had caught the ball, smoothly and without fluffing, every time it came her way, and had put it neatly and cleanly into the net on four separate occasions. She had scored four times. Four. Her side had won, four nil. At the end of the game she had bungled nothing and achieved everything. On the way back from the netball courts to the school buildings, several people had banged her on the shoulder and said nice, congratulatory things, and Libby Guthrie, running past, had even turned to smile and give her a thumbs up. It was the first smile Libby had thrown her way since, since — well, since *then*.

Isabel stood in the shower, eyes closed, drenched in thankfulness. When she was alone, after, she would text Mum and say with appropriate nonchalance that she had done quite well at netball that day and people seemed to like her a bit, in consequence. She turned so that the water — never hot or fierce enough — could run down her back. Apart from texting Mum, it was going to be quite important not to show anyone that she felt her triumph that afternoon had brought her any kind of salvation. She mustn't mention it, or even look at all pleased. She must compose herself with all the quiet apology she had been trying to convey recently, and if anyone said anything, or was friendly, she mustn't leap on them like Beetle if offered a titbit, all wagging enthusiasm. She must, she resolved, just let any rehabilitation the afternoon had brought happen of its own accord.

She turned off the shower. In the next cubicle two people had obviously been showering together, which was strictly forbidden. She recognized their voices — Libby Guthrie and a new girl who everyone was very keen on, on account of her acceptable kinds of prettiness and cleverness and her remarkable prowess as a gymnast. The two were talking in a familiar, breathless way about the boys they were or were not going to allow as friends on Facebook when the new girl said, in her light, attractive voice just faintly spiced with an Australian accent, 'She was OK, today, wasn't she?'

'Who was?' Libby said. Her voice was slightly muffled, as if she was towelling her hair.

'Isabel.'

'Isabel!'

'Yeah. Well, she was OK, right? Cool score, yeah?'

Libby grunted a reply that Isabel could not catch.

'Come on,' the new girl said. 'Come on. She's

171

OK, isn't she? You can't carry a grudge for ever, can you? She's a bit pathetic, but she's OK, right?'

'What?'

'I,' the new girl said in her laconic, offhand way, 'don't mind her. Do you?'

There was a pause. In it, Isabel stood, naked and dripping and frozen to the spot.

'I think,' Libby Guthrie said at last, 'that if I were you, and I thought anything as mental as what you've just said, I'd keep pretty quiet about it.'

There was the sound of someone being given a shove, and a brief small cry.

'OK?' Libby said. 'Get it?'

★   ★   ★

The twins were drawing after lunch, at the kitchen table. Flora was drawing her usual tiny, contorted pictures in the corners of sheets of paper, and Tassy her preferred huge abstract scrawls that often swept over the paper's edge and across on to the table. Alexa, on her way upstairs to distribute ironed laundry among the bedrooms, had left them comfortably bickering about the text from Isabel that she had read out to them. It had been a very factual text about her netball triumph, and at the end she had written, 'Don't ring. I'm fine. A bit busy.'

'She was the winner,' Tassy said to her sister, kneeling up on her chair in order to be able to use her whole arm for a great swirl of red wax crayon.

172

Flora, her nose almost on her minute, crabbed scribbling, said nothing but just breathed noisily, as she was wont to do, through her mouth.

'At football,' Tassy added.

'No,' Flora said.

'Yes!'

'No.'

'Yes, yes, yes! She was the winner at *football*.'

Alexa paused on the stairs to listen. After a second or two, Flora's audible breathing stopped long enough for her to say, 'Neckball.'

'Football!'

'Neck — '

There was the sound of a car pulling up outside. Alexa called down, 'Twins! Daddy! Daddy's back!'

There was a stampede from the kitchen, led by Beetle. From almost the top of the stairs, Alexa watched for a moment as dog and children scrambled together to get the door open. Then she put the basket of ironing down on the stair above her and began to run down.

'Ow!'

'Stop him, Mummy! Stop, Beetle — '

'Let me, let me — '

The door burst open and Beetle charged through, followed by Tassy. Flora lay on the doormat, her spectacles half off, her mouth open and wailing.

Alexa crouched beside her. 'You're OK, darling. Let me put your specs on.'

Flora fought to resist help. 'No.'

'Yes. Just so's you can see where you're going.'

'Daddy!' Flora screamed. 'Daddy!' She battled

her way out of Alexa's arms and began to run after her sister.

Alexa stood, smiling, full of the cheerful resolve she had been cultivating since her phone call with Jack. In the driveway, Dan was getting out of the driver's seat, laughing at the exuberant tangle of dog and children that greeted him. And out of the passenger side, at the same moment, slowly climbed — Gus.

A stab of sheer fury streaked through Alexa, almost briefly blinding her. How could he? After all they'd been through, all he'd said to her, all he'd promised about things being different once leave started? How he would be able to forget everything to do with the Army and focus on all the human and domestic matters that she had been dealing with alone? How could he be so clumsy, so insensitive, so utterly *obtuse* as to start this precious period of rebuilding by bringing Gus, of all people, home with him? Gus, who represented to Alexa, right now, all the reasons for Dan's remoteness and absences and deafness to family concerns. It was as if, she thought wildly, bitterly, Dan had no intention of his leave being in any way different from his working life. She stood in the front doorway, her arms folded, unable even to raise the smile of courtesy required, by unspoken but insistent Army custom, for one's husband's colleagues.

She waited for Dan to pick the twins up, as he usually did. But he didn't. He stooped to kiss them and to fondle Beetle's ears briefly, but then he went round the car to the passenger side, put an arm round Gus's shoulders and closed the car

174

door with his other hand. Then he began to make his way back, almost pulling Gus with him, looking down with the greatest concern. Alexa unfolded her arms. Was Gus ill? Was he hurt? He looked as if he was almost stumbling, within the circle of Dan's arm. Had he done the typical male show-off thing at final PT and strained himself?

The twins, jabbering and jumping, attached themselves to Dan's free side as he came round the car. Alexa waited. Now that she could see him, Gus looked awful. Greyish, haunted. He wasn't as tall as Dan and he was stockier in build, but he looked as if he'd suddenly shrunk, as if the air had gone out of him. Dan raised his head and, for the first time since he got back, looked straight at Alexa. And then he lifted his free hand and put a warning forefinger against his lips.

Alexa hurried across the grass. She put a hand on Gus's arm. 'Gus. Are you OK?'

He nodded. 'I'm fine.'

'Are you ill? Has something happened?'

Gus glanced at her. His brown eyes were as lugubrious as Beetle's were when commanded to stay in his basket. 'Not ill,' Gus said, with a fleeting attempt at a grin.

'Daddy, Daddy, Daddy!' the twins sang, seizing Dan's trousers in order to tow him into the house.

'What's happened?'

Dan said, 'He'll tell you. I'll take these two upstairs for a moment. Gus'll tell you.'

Alexa put her hand out. 'Gus?'

He looked at her. She saw, to her horror, that his eyes weren't just sad but full of tears. He clutched at her hand and said, in a hoarse whisper, 'She's left me.'

★ ★ ★

'Of course, there's someone else,' Gus said.

He was hunched at the kitchen table, his hands round a mug of tea. His hands, those big, capable, military hands set off by a big, capable, military watch cased in black rubber, made a weird contrast to his face and to his normally disciplined hair, which now stuck up in awkward little tufts as if it had been chopped at randomly while he slept, for a prank. He stared at the table top. 'There's been someone else for a year. Or more. For quite a time before we deployed, anyway.' He flicked a glance at Alexa. 'I half want to know nothing and I half want to know everything. I thought she'd have talked to you. I thought that if she talked to anyone, it'd be you.'

Alexa said sadly, 'I've hardly seen her. All the time you were away, she was working. Or seeing the children — '

'Both those things. And more. Much more. He runs a company that's one of her major donors. Some money thing. Hedge-fund manager or something. I don't know what. I don't understand money. Never have. She said to me, 'Do you realize you've never paid a bill in your life?''

'Dan doesn't either.'

Gus took his hands away from his mug and

propped his elbows on the table. He said, not looking at Alexa, 'What did she say to you?'

'Nothing much, Gus.'

He shot a look at her. 'I can't believe that. You girls — '

'I've said, I've hardly seen her. All the time you were away, she was the one I didn't see. She came for the first time in ages, the other day.'

His head jerked up. 'Did she?'

'Gus, she was in a funny mood, very spiky and edgy, but she didn't say anything that made me think that this was in her mind. She just said it was all so very hard.' She paused. 'Which it is.'

Gus gave a little groan and put his forearms down on the table, and then his head on them.

'I'm as surprised as you are,' Alexa said. She gave the ceiling a quick glance, as if she could somehow will Dan downstairs to assist her.

Gus mumbled something. She bent towards him. 'What?'

Gus said, slightly more distinctly, 'It's not a surprise.'

'Gus!'

He raised his head and said wearily, 'She's been telling me forever. Not about someone else, but about how she can't hack patch life, how she can't sacrifice her career to mine, how she can't believe any of it's worth it.' He blinked. 'I could put it out of my mind, out there. Or, at least, I could put it out of my mind most of the time. And when I did think about it, I'd tell myself that I'd make it up to her when we were back, I'd tell her one more promotion and then I'm out, and we'd live wherever she wanted and she

177

could have the prime career and I'd do everything to support her, everything.' He gave a grimace. 'I've never looked at anyone else. Not since I met her. I thought that she felt the same, in spite of our differences. But she said last night that it wasn't lack of love, it was lack of respect. She said Dan and I are the last of the dinosaurs and the new uni-educated officer boys are respectful of their partners' lives and don't live and breathe the regiment the way we do. She said how can she respect someone so unworldly, so unquestioning' — he turned his mournful brown gaze on Alexa again — 'and I expect she's right.'

'Did she tell you this face to face?'

'No,' Gus said, 'on the telephone. I rang her to say I was coming up to London this afternoon and she said, don't, and I said, why? and she said, there's nothing to come up for any more, we're through.' His face crumpled and he buried it in his arms again. 'Not sure I can stand it.'

Alexa said, 'Would you like a whisky?'

Gus shook his bowed head. 'That was another thing. She said she couldn't stand the way booze was part of Army life. I thought she got it. I thought she knew good hard partying was only second to good hard sport as a coping strategy. I mean, she seemed fine when I was president of the Mess Committee. No complaints then, or at least none I heard. She seemed to like the parties, she really did. I thought she was OK with that. With me. With — well, everything. But then,' he lifted his head again and gazed gloomily at Alexa, 'I read all the runes wrong, didn't I?

178

Bouncing around on my own little cloud and never seeing the storm gathering. Lex — '

'Yes?'

'What am I going to do without her?'

Alexa put a hand out and laid it on Gus's nearest one. He turned his hand over at once and gripped hers so hard she thought he'd crush it. There were steps on the stairs, running down.

'Dan's coming,' Alex said, aware her tone indicated that he could somehow solve everything. She glanced across the room.

From the doorway, Dan said, 'I've made a very impressive Lego castle. Come and see.'

Gus let go of Alexa's hand and got slowly to his feet. Dan held out his own hand to him, as if he was a child. He said to Alexa, 'Won't be long, sweetheart.' He smiled at her. 'I've said Gus can have a billet here for a bit. Can't have him rattling round in an empty quarter, can we? Put him in Izzy's room for now. OK?'

10

Alexa parked the car outside the Larches Social Centre. It was situated beside its namesake, a stand of lanky larch trees, just beyond several lines of the grim, dank terraces of outdated married quarters for other ranks, interspersed with strips of broken hardstanding and shabby grass, that in their dismalness could only contribute to family breakdown, Alexa thought. There were no curtains at some of the windows, and sagging sheets were pinned carelessly across others. MacDonald Gardens, they were called. Gardens! They were as garden-like as the bleak car park in which she was standing. What a way to live. What a way to try and keep a family together, let alone bring it up. OK, so the terraces were condemned as unfit for purpose and would be demolished in time and replaced, but in the meantime, there they were, sodden with rain and gloom, a few hundred yards' buggy push from the usual Army shopping parade of cut-price supermarket, off-licence, barber, kebab joint and tanning salon. Tanning salon! Did any profession in the universe spend quite so much time looking at itself in the mirror as this one?

She got slowly out of the car and locked the door. Dan was home with the twins, while she, at the urging and arranging of Dan's two senior officers, had an appointment with the regiment's welfare officer, Walter Cummings. It was, she felt, shameful to be doing this, but if she had refused — as Kate Melville would surely have refused — then it would look defiant to the point of destructiveness. She had said to Dan, attempting to be reasonable, attempting to show she was not supinely giving in to yet another Army insistence, 'We should be going to this together, you know,' and Dan, spooning yoghurt into Flora, who was intent upon being a thorough baby and was sitting, sweetly helpless, on his knee, said without looking up, 'Who'd look after the twins? I'll come next time. If there is a next time.' He scraped the spoon expertly along Flora's lower lip. 'In any case, Gus'll be back from playing squash soon. Let's hope hammering the hell out of a squash ball and Freddie Stanford will make the poor bugger feel a bit better.'

Alexa looked round her now. There were few people about — just an overweight girl pushing a double buggy with her phone clamped to her ear, a woman leaning against a nearby bus stop, smoking, and a youngish man in battledress, gazing at the display in the window of the video store. In front of her was the social centre — Pilates classes advertised, coffee mornings — and beside it the dental practice, and beyond that, the welfare service building. Reddish-brown bricks, rain-streaked concrete, with avenues of lime or chestnut planted everywhere, with absolute precision, in an attempt to ameliorate and soften the necessarily functional appearance of a community which had been created for a purely, crucially, inflexibly pragmatic reason.

181

How many of the inhabitants of MacDonald Gardens — and even of the slightly classier NCO quarters, and flimsy middle-ranking-officer houses with their tacked-on garages and patios — were relishing the prospect of this long leave? How many of them would, like Alexa, actually make an appointment to see someone on Walter Cummings's staff? Almost none of them. Why would they? How could they justify it to themselves, in any case, with all the soldiers needing help, all those men peeling away from a war zone with their heads full of noise and horror. TRIM, it was called, the ongoing service they were offered. Trauma Risk Management. 'A consultative process,' it was referred to in welfare speak. How many men would ever admit they needed it? And would she, if left to herself? Would she, Alexa Riley, be standing here on a late November morning, with the sky like a grey duvet laid across the low and depressing rooftops round her, unless Dan's commanding officer had, with the greatest skill and courtesy, not given her any option? What, in fact, was one admitting to, by having an appointment to see Walt the Welfare?

He was an affable man, she knew that. The Chaplain General, a surprisingly young and sinewy man who always looked as if he was longing to be allowed to break the Army's rule of padres not being permitted to carry a weapon, approved of him, and said so in public loudly and frequently. But, for all his huge significance as families welfare officer, Walter Cummings would only be in that role for a couple of years.

After all, no soldier wanted to be a welfare officer. It was, in the eyes of the military, definitely a pink job, and even the trust displayed in being chosen for it didn't compensate. When Walter Cummings was appointed, he had said jovially to anyone who would listen, 'Suddenly I'm supposed not to shout but listen! I ask you!'

He was waiting for Alexa in his ferociously orderly office, his desk surface empty apart from a pad of paper placed parallel to the nearest edge, and a rollerball pen aligned exactly beside it. He held out a hand. 'Good to see you.'

Alexa regarded him. He was of the same build as her grandfather-in-law, with the same open countenance. 'Sorry — '

'What do you mean, sorry?'

'I mean,' Alexa said, 'that I'm sorry to be here. I'm sorry it's thought that I should see you.'

'Ah-hah,' Walter Cummings said.

A girl in battledress and Army boots appeared in the doorway, her hair pulled back so tightly that it almost hurt to look at her.

'Tea?' Walter said to Alexa. 'Coffee?'

'Neither, thank you.'

'Oh, come on,' Walter said. 'It'll make it easier. Miriam's got sod all to do this morning, have you?'

'I wish,' Miriam said, with emphasis.

'Tea, then. Thank you.'

'Milk, ma'am?' Miriam said. 'Sugar?'

'Neither, thank you.'

'He,' Miriam said, tossing her head in Walter's direction, 'takes *everything*.'

When she had gone, Walter motioned Alexa to

the wooden-armed chair in front of him. 'Make yourself comfortable. I have to say — '

'What?'

'I have to say, Mrs Riley,' Walter said, 'that I'm pretty surprised myself, to see you here.'

★ ★ ★

Dan and Gus were watching the late news on television. Gus had spent a long time, that evening, talking to his sons on the telephone, who had been, he said, completely brilliant for kids of ten and twelve, even the younger one, who said, even though he couldn't help having a bit of a weep about the situation, that he hoped it all meant that Mum would be a bit happier now and that he, Dad, could get on with soldiering without having to worry about her so much any more.

The conversation had made Gus a bit tearful again. He had sat at the supper table and said that the younger boy was longing to join up, had always wanted to, was a born soldier just like Franny and Andy's two, that he wasn't the kind of pad brat who had a teenage rebellion and kicked off just to spite his parents, but had always been a good kid, one of the best, and here he was now, putting his old Dad's feelings before his own. He drank his soup and said, between swallows, that he didn't know what he'd done to deserve kids like that, and Kate was a bloody good mother, he had to give her that, and maybe he hadn't appreciated how good she'd been, and hadn't told her often enough that he thought the job she'd done on the boys was bloody marvellous.

They'd cleared up after supper together, the three of them — Gus had learned, with astonishing speed and efficiency, the layout of everything in the kitchen — and then Alexa said she was going to sort out the twins' clothes for the morning, and Dan said he'd just catch the news with Gus and he'd be up straight after, promise.

'No beers,' Alexa said to him, in an undertone.

'Why d'you say that?'

'Because you and Gus have been up after midnight every night since he moved in. And I want to talk to you.'

Dan looked at her warily.

'I want,' Alexa almost whispered, 'to talk to you about this *morning*.'

He put a hand out and squeezed her arm briefly. 'Of course.'

So she was now sitting on their bed, fully clothed, listening to the murmur of the television and Dan's and Gus's occasional voices from the sitting room below. She looked at the clock. She would give Dan another ten minutes. Then — then, however typical it was, however Wronged Wife she appeared, she would go downstairs and say, quite loudly if necessary, that she needed to speak to Dan, and she wanted to do it *now*.

She lowered herself back on the bed until she was lying flat, staring at the ceiling, her feet still on the floor. Walter had been kind to her, very kind. He had sympathized with her predicament, he had understood her frustration, he had said

185

he knew from personal experience what it was like to feel one had no choices. And, of course, it was going to be worse now leave had started because everyone would want a piece of Dan, the families and so forth, so it was no wonder Alexa was feeling she never got a look in. Ask my wife!

Alexa said awkwardly, 'It isn't really that. I mean, it's only partly that. It's more . . . more . . . ' She glanced at him and looked away again. 'I mean, what am *I* supposed to do?'

Walter Cummings looked politely puzzled. 'Come again?'

'I shouldn't be asking you this. It's not up to you to sort out the wives like me, the ones with resources. But . . . '

'But what?'

Alexa looked down at her lap. 'We're married to men who know what they're doing all the time because they're told so. And we have to fit round that. Part-time wives. Part-time earners. Even part-time mothers — '

Walter Cummings picked up his rollerball pen and looked at it intently.

'Sorry,' Alexa said. 'It's just that as far as self-fulfilment goes, it's close to impossible. And our children. It's so unfairly hard on all our children. This boarding-school thing — '

He cleared his throat. He looked like someone who was being asked to solve an intractable problem that they had never signed up for in the first place.

Alexa took sudden pity on him. 'Sorry,' she said again. 'Sorry, sorry. I'm not helping. I'm all over the place, none of that was connected — '

186

Walter sighed.

Alexa read his sigh. She said, 'And you've heard it all before?'

He nodded. 'Doesn't mean I don't feel for you.'

'But?'

Walter sighed again. He picked up his pen and put it down again. Then he said, 'There are changes coming.'

'Changes?'

'You know about the Army Families Federation?'

'Of course.'

'Well,' Walter said, 'they are fighting what they see as a government attack on conditions of service. They say the forces are a special case because of the willingness of forces personnel to lay down their lives, and therefore their conditions of service should be special, too.'

He glanced up at her. She was sitting very still.

'The last government presided, shall we say, over the dismantling of regiments and all the subsequent humanitarian fallout that that entailed. Charities can't possibly pick it all up, and they aren't. There are fashionable, discretionary fights right now, and charities like Help the Heroes do a great job for them. But what about the wars of the past? Trouble is, the military covenant has never been written down, and now there aren't enough funds.'

Alexa leaned forward slightly. 'I don't quite see — '

'I'm coming to it,' Walter said. 'I'm coming to something that might affect you and, in its way, help by limiting your choices. There's been a recent doubling of operational allowance, as you know, and a huge improvement in services for mental health. But we're all having to look right across the demands. At present, you get the continuity-of-education allowance, don't you? Something above five grand a term.' He raised a hand as if to pre-empt being interrupted. 'You may hate boarding school for your daughter, but a lot of money goes towards keeping her there. In all, the Army spends £1.8 billion keeping its kids educated. So something like the Harriers, which cost £1.2 billion, have to be deleted. D'you see what I'm driving at?'

Alexa nodded. A grey wave was rising in her with terrible familiarity, a sense of having made an inappropriate fuss at an inappropriate time.

'I'm very sorry,' Walter Cummings said, 'if anyone feels betrayed. I really regret we can't satisfy everyone. The continuity-of-education allowance is under review right now. You may have your answer to one problem in your life made for you. And I'm sorry, as I say, that I can't do anything for you. I haven't got any solution, especially at the moment. There isn't one.' He grimaced. 'To be frank with you, Mrs Riley, if you weren't an officer's wife, I'd probably be saying to you, in as nice a way as I could think of putting it, that your husband will do as he's told and you'll have to accommodate yourself to that. Finish. I could offer you a 15 per cent discount on Relate sessions, I suppose, but I don't somehow think you'd take me up on that, would you?'

She had let a little silence fall when he finished speaking and then she had stood up, just as there was a knock at the door and Miriam came in with two white cups on a tray. Then she said, with as little vehemence as she could manage, 'I never thought there was anything you could do. Not your fault. Not mine. Just — just the system.'

They had drunk their tea and coffee still standing, talking gently and unthreateningly about how the Army was going to reconcile its needs for better equipment and housing with the cuts being imposed on and by the Ministry of Defence. Walter had taken her cup from her and put it back on the tray, and had held the door open for her, indicating that he was going to accompany her out of the building. His whole physical bearing was solicitous, as if she were very frail or very old, his hand hovering at her elbow at every step or unevenness in the surface on the way back to the car park.

She'd held out her hand to him. 'Thank you.'

He'd grimaced. 'Rocks and hard places come to mind.'

'I know,' she'd said, as if it was for her to comfort him, and then she'd driven home and found Dan in front of the computer with a twin on each knee, watching a website that showed you the daily round of life in the penguin enclosure at Edinburgh Zoo. All three were laughing.

And now it was the evening and there had not been a moment alone with Dan. She looked sideways across the bed at the clock. It had been

189

almost half an hour since she made her resolution. She sat up and ran her fingers through her hair. Was it unfair, was it unproductive? . . . Oh, come on, she thought in almost the same breath, come on, go downstairs and just *do* it.

She got off the bed and straightened her sweater. Then she went out on to the landing, strode purposefully down the stairs and across the hall, and pushed open the sitting room door. On the sofa sat Gus, still watching the television, and by his side Dan was sprawled, head back, among the cushions, mouth slightly open and deeply asleep.

Gus switched his gaze from the television to Alexa in an instant. Then he grimaced, pointed at Dan and spread his hands out in a gesture of hopelessness.

'Sorry,' he mouthed at her.

★ ★ ★

When the alarm clock rang the next morning, it took some seconds for Alexa to disentangle her mind from a disconcerting dream involving her father, Mrs Cairns from Isabel's school and her own long-ago bedroom overlooking an immense, fan-shaped palm tree in Jakarta. She opened her eyes slowly to the expanse of remarkably unblemished tawny skin across Dan's naked shoulders. He had not been in bed with her when she finally fell asleep. And she had not woken when he slid in beside her. She pulled his hand from its sleeping position across his chest and held it in hers. 'Dan?'

He grunted.

'How — how did it go?'

There was a pause, and then Dan said, 'How did what go?'

'Talking to Jim Rigby.'

Dan rolled slowly on to his back. 'That was days ago.'

'I know. I forgot to ask.'

Dan yawned. He freed his hand to rub his eyes. He said from behind both hands, 'I got nowhere. Nor will he, now.'

'He wouldn't admit to anything?'

'Nothing. Stuck to his denial. They both got hauled out of parade and dismissed. End of.'

'So what will happen to them?'

Dan sat up slowly. He said, dully, not looking at her, 'God knows. The usual. They'll be on a high for a week, then they'll sink, then they'll fall to pieces. You know the story.'

Alexa said, 'Can't the Army help them?'

Dan began to get out of bed. He said, 'We can help anyone who wants to be helped. But not those who refuse it point blank. You can't sacrifice those poor bloody guys at Headley Court for a few losers who can't see a priority when it stands up and hits them on the nose. All the time and money and effort that went into training Rigby and Wharton! Think of that. Back from Afghanistan without a scratch on them. Think of that, too. Think of that, and then think of Gary McCormack, who thought he'd only lose a foot, but he's got an infection and it now looks like his leg will have to go, to the knee.

Makes me livid. *Livid.*'

Alexa slid out of bed and stood up. Reaching to put on the dressing-gown Eric had given her, she said, 'I can understand that. Of course I can,' and then, after a beat, 'Dan?'

He was standing naked by the window, absently scratching. She thought briefly, irrelevantly, of his telling her about the dogs' flea collars they'd worn in Helmand round their ankles.

'What?'

'My turn,' she said, 'for you to ask me a question.'

He blinked at her. Then he smiled. He came round the bed and ruffled her hair and kissed her, sleep mouthed and stubbly. 'About what?' he said.

★ ★ ★

Blimey, George Riley thought, looking about him. This is the kind of place, if you were very rich, you'd come to die. All this carpet, and those dinky little pictures hung on painted panelling and that squeaky clean chandelier up there, glittering enough to take your eye out. He'd pressed a bell outside, a bell in a long, highly polished brass panel of bells, next to a little printed card behind glass that read 'Longworth', and Mrs L, who sounded as surprised to hear him as if he'd been a rhino from the zoo from over the road, had said come in, come in, take the lift to the seventh floor, and a buzzer had sounded, and here he was, standing in this

192

bloody great hallway as if he'd landed in another world.

He'd been here once before, of course, years ago. When Dan had first met Alexa. But he'd been in a bit of a moither then, frankly, worried that Dad would say something out of turn and that they would both look right eejits in their suits, and he hadn't really taken in what the place was like. But he was now. Beige this, beige that, heat pumping out of radiators behind fancy grilles, quiet as a church or a library. Bloody suffocating. He moved cautiously down the thickly carpeted hallway and pressed the button for the lift. The lift doors were also polished. He could see himself reflected as clearly as in a looking glass. Well, he thought, you mightn't be able to breathe in here, but you can't fault them for looking after this place.

There was a discreet series of muffled clanks as the lift arrived and the doors slid politely open. The interior was panelled, with a single small mirror let into the far wall — so that, George supposed, stepping in and instinctively running the palm of his hand over his hair, you'd got time to pick the spinach out of your teeth before you confronted the lady wife. Rum do, the whole thing. Reeking of money, of course, but why would you use that money to buy yourself a padded cell?

Elaine Longworth was waiting on the seventh-floor landing, the front door of the flat open behind her. She held her hand out. 'George!'

He grasped it, smiling. She said, 'We weren't

193

expecting you. Why didn't you ring?'

He said, still smiling, 'I never ring. Can't abide the phone.'

'We might have been out.'

'I'd have waited,' George said. 'I wouldn't have minded. Time's the one thing I've got plenty of.'

She led the way into the flat and closed the door. The sitting room was as George remembered it, full of furniture and flowers, which gave it, weirdly, the air of a bedroom, not a living room. It was, to George's mind, a lady's room, but there, in an armchair by the window, reading the *Daily Telegraph*, was Morgan Longworth, who looked, in his collar and tie and immaculate V-necked sweater, perfectly at home. He rose as George came in and held out his hand. 'My dear fellow — '

George said, 'Sorry not to give you warning. I'm not much of a one for telephones.'

Morgan motioned to the nearest sofa. 'No inconvenience. On Thursdays we have neither bridge classes nor hair appointments. What can we get you?'

'Just ten minutes.'

'Tea?' Elaine said. 'Coffee?'

She looked, George thought, as if she could do with a brew herself, and a good heart-to-heart to go with it. Pity, in a way, that Morgan was at home. He smiled down at her. Nice woman. Nice-looking woman, well kept. He said warmly, 'Well, if you're making a brew . . . '

'Of course,' she said. 'Of course.'

George sat down where indicated on the sofa and hitched up his trouser knees. Then he leaned

194

back and crossed his legs. He saw Morgan glancing at his toe caps. They were as shiny as if they'd been varnished. He grinned at Morgan. 'Dad's work,' he said. 'Didn't trust me to come and see you without shining my shoes.'

Morgan leaned forward and took off his reading glasses. 'I imagine,' he said, half smiling, 'that we can guess why you've come.'

George nodded.

Morgan said, his voice slightly lowered, 'Have you plans to see them?'

'No,' George said.

'Have you spoken to them?'

'Hardly,' George said. 'Dad insists I don't. I'd even face the telephone for that. In fact, I did. I rang and I went down. Just for a night. But Dad always says, leave them, you've said your piece, now leave them be.'

'Your piece?'

'I just wanted our lad to talk to her. *Talk* to her. I went down one day and came back the next.'

'We,' Morgan said with emphasis, 'have not seen anything of them since Dan came home. We haven't actually even spoken to Dan.' He glanced towards the kitchen. 'It puts a great strain on Elaine.'

'That's why I've come,' George said. He cleared his throat. He wasn't used to the constriction of wearing a tie. He looked at Morgan. 'We think it's gone on long enough. Dan's been home weeks now. We may be sick with pride in the boy, but it's not all about him now. He's got to wake up and think about other

195

people. If they won't come to you, you should just go down to them. Just go. Put her in the car and go.'

Morgan hesitated. He said, 'I've been telling her not to ring.'

'Dad's the same. Or, at least, he was. But he's changed his mind. Wouldn't have shined my shoes otherwise.'

'I'm a bit of a protocol man,' Morgan said doubtfully.

'Tell me about it! But it's time for action.'

Elaine was coming out of the kitchen, bearing a tray of tea. 'Action?' she said.

George sprang up to take the tray from her, fractionally ahead of Morgan. 'Yes,' he said, setting the tray down on a glass coffee table next to an orchid and a pristine hardback book. 'Time to rescue that girl.' He saw alarm spring at once to Elaine's eyes. If Morgan hadn't been there, he'd have put a hand on her arm, or even maybe an arm round her shoulders. He said confidingly, 'Nothing blinkers a man like soldiering. Nothing.' He paused and then he said, 'I should know.'

★　★　★

'I'm emailing you,' Kate Melville wrote to Alexa, 'because I can't quite face ringing you. I think you might put the phone down on me, and I can't risk that happening. Of course, you might delete this without reading it, but I won't know that, will I? It won't be as painful just to get no reply as to hear the phone go down.'

196

The house was very quiet. The twins were at nursery school and Dan and Gus had driven off in Gus's car to Gus's boys' school, where, both men had indicated to Alexa with apparently staggering insensitivity, the headmaster was displaying exemplary concern and accommodation. She was alone in the kitchen with Beetle, her laptop on the table, a mug of coffee cooling beside her. It had amazed her, momentarily taken her breath away to see Kate Melville's name in her inbox, but it had not crossed her mind, even for a nanosecond, to delete the message unread.

It was a long message. It filled the screen almost to the bottom, without paragraphs. Alexa had discussed with Franny and Mo what their reaction would, should, could be, when — if — Kate got in touch, and when Mo had said, without particular heat but firmly, that she was sorry but that was *it*, if only because Kate's timing was completely unforgivable, just as Gus got back, Alexa had glanced at Franny and seen the irresolution on her face that she felt was written plainly on her own.

'You can't just write her off . . . '

'I'm afraid I can.'

'But she won't have no reason — '

'We all have a reason, for God's sake!'

'But Mo — '

'He's a bloody *soldier*! What did she think she was marrying? If she wanted a nine-to-five bank manager, she should have married one.'

'You don't really know what it's like,' Alexa said, 'till you're in it. You don't really know what they're like, how they'll be — '

197

Mo had set her jaw. 'In three months' time,' she said, 'I'll have the lot, won't I? I'll have horses, dogs, children and a husband in Afghanistan. When he comes back, in nine months' time, I'll have a frigging lunatic for a bit, too, like Alexa's got now. But I won't be pushing off to London, saying it's all too much. I promise you that. It's not what I signed up for, especially after Baz warned me. He *warned* me when he proposed. He *told* me. Just as Andy told you and Dan told you and I bet, I *bet*, Gus told Kate.'

When she had gone, Franny and Alexa had sat in silence for a while, and then Franny said softly, 'She's frightened.'

'Frightened? Mo?'

'Of course she is. We all are. Something like this rattles our cages.'

Alexa said, 'Will you speak to her?'

'Who?'

'Will you speak to Kate? If she rings?'

Franny thought a moment, twisting her wedding ring round and round. 'I — don't think so. Not for a bit, anyway. It's not about her, really. It's about Gus. And all of us still here.' She looked up at Alexa. 'Will you?'

Alexa had picked up her mug and taken a gulp of coffee. 'Yes,' she said, and put the mug down again. 'Yes, I will.'

And now here was the email. 'Dear Alexa,' it started like a letter, 'I'm emailing you because I can't quite face ringing you.'

Oh, Alexa thought, I can guess how you're feeling. I can imagine having transgressed, or wanting to transgress, having such an irresistibly powerful urge to break the rules, defy the conventions, upset the traditional, time-honoured apple cart, that transgression becomes the only option. And then, when you've struck out and done it, having to turn and face not so much the music as the baying of outrage, the ferocity of people who believe that your defiance has cost them the security of their own unthinking acquiescence. She looked back at the screen. She remembered Kate standing in that kitchen, cradling her flowers — a picture, she now realized, of conflicted guilt and determination.

'I don't want to justify myself,' Kate wrote, 'but one day, if you'll let me, I'd like to explain. Or try to. I know my timing was atrocious but, believe me, I didn't intend that, I didn't mean to go the moment Gus got back. But I just couldn't stand it. I suddenly couldn't bear it another second, his being so remote and so needy all at once, and I snapped. I shouldn't have, and I did. I know I risked far more than just leaving Gus when I went, I know none of you will ever forgive me. And I'm not asking that. Already, away from it all, I feel better and stronger. I don't say I wouldn't like understanding or forgiveness, because that would be both untrue and arrogant, but I don't need it. I don't need approval from an institution I can't respect any more. But — and it's a big but — I'm really, really sorry about what I said to you the other day. I wish I hadn't sounded like such a bitch. I didn't mean what I said. I may not respect the Army any more, but I do respect you. I do. And I respect you for sticking with it. Please don't throw me over. Please come and see me in London. I'm staying with Mel, Freddie Stanford's lovely girlfriend. You should meet her. Please think about it. And whatever you think of me, remember what I think of you. Love from Kate.'

Alexa sat and stared at the screen. Then she scrolled the email back to the beginning and read it again.

'Army marriages,' Mo had said, 'must be some of the strongest. They have to be.' She had shrugged. 'I was earning more than Baz when we met. I told him I wasn't moving. But you have to compromise. You *have* to.'

And then, Alexa thought, you get to a point where you can't. Or you're the kind of person, like Kate, who never could and who had struggled to try, and had been unable to struggle any longer. No mention of the new man in her email. Hardly a mention of Gus, either. Silence on the children. Did she even know Gus was staying with them? Did she know — or care — what an acute case of walking wounded she had left for them all to cope with in the aftermath of her departure? It was enough, Alexa thought angrily, to make her press the Delete button and banish Kate Melville and her bitter resentment of the Army to the great obliterating spaces of the limitless ether. What was Kate after, anyway, flattering her and beseeching her? Why should she, a relic of the old life for which Kate apparently had nothing but contempt, be of any consequence whatsoever to a reinvented shiny new Kate, occupying the spare bedroom of a

200

junior officer's unknown girlfriend?

She moved the cursor and then held it there above the Delete icon. Who was this girlfriend? Freddie Stanford was an amiable young man, nice looking, nicely mannered, good with his troop, whom Alexa had hardly distinguished in her mind from all the other nicely mannered, capable captains. But Kate, instead of going to stay with a colleague when she fled, or an old school friend, or even a sister, had elected to stay with Freddie Stanford's girlfriend. Who in turn had presumably invited her. What was going on? Why should Kate suppose that she, Alexa, would ever want to meet this girlfriend? Why?

Alexa swallowed. She glanced at the clock. Ten minutes before she needed to collect the twins. She looked down at the keyboard and then put her finger on the mouse mat and moved the cursor from Delete to Reply. And pressed.

Beside her, vibrating against the table top, her phone began to ring. She picked it up and looked at the screen. 'Franny,' it said.

'Fran?' Alexa said. 'I'm just off to get — '

'One second,' Franny said. Her voice was unnaturally level. 'Don't go anywhere.'

'But — '

'Listen, Alexa,' Franny said. 'Listen. Go and get the twins, and then come straight to me. Don't panic, nothing to panic about, but you need to come straight to me after you collect the twins. The thing is — well, the thing is — she's fine and she is at this moment eating a cheese sandwich — but I have Isabel here. She just — turned up.'

201

11

The twins were overjoyed. They sat leaning over the edges of their car seats so that they could touch Isabel, sitting in the space between them, and when they reached home, they wanted her to come straight to the playroom and build a castle, dress up, read to them and play hospitals, all at once. Isabel, extremely composed, seemed calmly happy to acquiesce.

'Don't grill her,' Franny had said to Alexa. 'Don't fire questions at her. She's in a funny state, but it's not an upset one, as far as I can see. She'd worked out a route online to get home by bus, and she'd saved up until she could buy a ticket. She'd planned it. It was all organized.'

Alexa had rung the school, before she went to collect the twins. The school secretary had sounded suspiciously as if she had no idea that Isabel was missing, and then Alexa had spoken to Mrs Cairns, who said Isabel had pleaded a severe headache and had been sent to lie down shortly after breakfast. Her absence had been noticed half an hour earlier, and a thorough search was still ongoing.

'We need to talk,' Alexa said, gripping the phone.

'Mrs Riley — '

'No more of that,' Alexa said furiously. 'No more patronizing of parents and sweeping real problems under the carpet. We need to talk. Or rather, *I* need to talk and you need to listen.'

Then she had dropped her phone into her bag, seized her car keys and raced for the car, leaving Beetle in a confusion of anxious obedience, rooted miserably in his basket.

Isabel hadn't flung herself at her mother. She was wearing school uniform with her own hooded blue fleece over the top, and she had brought nothing but her school backpack with its jingling collection of key rings and charms. Her hair was pulled back with both a plastic Alice band and an elasticated loop, and although she was pale, she wasn't red-eyed or visibly exhausted. When Alexa had come in, almost stumbling over the excited twins, Isabel had stood up and allowed herself to be hugged, and then she had freed herself and bent down so that the twins could thrust their morning's artwork at her and jabber at her in competition, their voices rising almost to screams.

'She's eaten a round of cheese sandwiches,' Franny said, 'and a banana and a KitKat. I offered her bacon and eggs, but she said she'd wait till she got home.'

'Why didn't she *come* home?' Alexa said, whispering. 'Why didn't she come straight home?'

Franny looked across her kitchen at Isabel and the twins, now on the floor together admiring angel pictures decorated with tissue-paper wings. 'I don't know.'

'Didn't she say? She must have said *something*.'

'Only,' Franny said, 'that she didn't want a

fuss. She thought it would be easier if I told you than if she just appeared.'

'Suppose you'd been out?'

'She'd thought of that. She was going to go to Mo, and if Mo was out, to Mary or Claire, and if *they* were out, she was going back to Mo because she'd have come home some time, to feed the dogs.'

Getting them all into the car, Alexa had tried to hug Isabel again. 'Darling, I am so thankful to see you.'

Isabel merely stood in her embrace. 'Yes.'

'Will you tell me? Will you tell me later why you did it? Will you tell me why you didn't telephone?'

Isabel began to get into the car. 'I can't keep saying.'

'But you haven't said anything to me yet!'

'I said something to Fran,' Isabel said. She climbed past Tassy's car seat and settled herself in the middle. 'I don't want to talk about it. *Please.*'

And now they were home, and the three girls were in the playroom, and Dan and Gus were not back, and she was roaming agitatedly round the kitchen, picking up the packet of mince she had got out of the freezer to thaw and putting it down again, and replaying in her mind the second conversation with Mrs Cairns in which she had reiterated that Isabel would not be returning to school before they were sure what had impelled her to run away, and even more sure of her reception if — *if* — she returned. It was impossible to settle to anything sensible. She got items out of the fridge to give the twins lunch, and found she had weirdly put a jug of stock, a leftover stuffed pepper and a jar of olives on the table. She would ring Jack, she thought. She would ring Jack and tell him what had happened and he would say how awful, poor kid, don't let her anywhere near that place again, d'you want me to come down? And she'd say no, not really, and he'd say, where's Dan? and she'd have to say out, out with Gus and I don't know when they'll be back, what's new? and Jack would get that anxious, defensive tone in his voice and she'd realize that she shouldn't have rung, that there was nobody to ring, that the only other person who would have felt as she did about Isabel — her father — was dead, and that Isabel was *her* problem, *hers*, and she had failed her, and made her stay in a place that she had hated and feared so much that she —

'Mummy?' Isabel said.

Alexa looked up, startled. She indicated the table, vaguely. 'I was just . . . '

'I'm starving,' Isabel said.

★ ★ ★

Dan and Gus were in high spirits when they returned. They had had a reassuring visit to the school — the boys, Gus reported, were being absolute bricks — and had paused on the way home for a late pub lunch of beer and pies and were in a mood to treat Isabel's appearance as a marvellous and unexpected treat. They both hugged her and picked the twins up and turned

205

them upside down until Flora's glasses fell off, and generally created enough noise and exuberance for it to be a full five minutes before Alexa could say, almost despairingly, thrusting herself into the mêlée until she was almost nose to nose with Dan, 'Dan. Dan, *listen*. She's not here on an exeat. She's not here with anyone's permission. She *ran away*.'

Dan lowered Flora slowly to the floor. 'What?'

'You heard me. She ran away.'

'I didn't,' Isabel said. 'I *walked* down the drive. Then I got three buses. Then I walked to Fran's house. I had a timetable. And I've got three pounds forty left. I didn't *run*!'

There was a silence. Gus put Tassy down too. Dan looked at Isabel. Then he looked at Alexa. 'What's going on?'

'I don't know.'

'What d'you mean?'

'She hasn't told me. She won't — '

Dan turned to look at Isabel again. He said, quite gently, 'Won't you?'

Isabel flipped her Alice band down on to the bridge of her nose, and then pushed it back again. 'No.'

'Why not?'

'Because,' Isabel said steadily, 'I want to tell *you*.'

★ ★ ★

'Right,' Dan said, 'here I am. Fire away.'

Isabel looked round her bedroom. It was — though very neatly — definitely overlaid by

206

Gus. His boots and shoes were lined up by her bookcase, his clothes hung from her cupboard, there was a tidy stack of his shirts and sweaters on the chair where she usually piled her soft toys, and her bed had a tight, flat, alien look, with a folded T-shirt and boxer shorts on the pillow and a battered clock radio on the table beside it.

She sniffed. 'It smells funny.'

'We'll move him,' Dan said. 'He can sleep on the sofa. We'd have moved him already if we'd known you were coming.'

Isabel sighed. She sat gingerly down on the edge of her bed. She said, 'If you'd known, you'd have stopped me.'

'We might not, you know. We'd have wanted to know why.'

Isabel said simply, 'I hate it.'

Dan lowered himself to the floor and put his arms around his bent knees. 'Yes,' he said. 'That's what Mum says. Home-sickness.'

Isabel laced her fingers together. 'You don't know what it's like.'

'Maybe I do.'

'If you do,' Isabel said clearly, 'you chose to be away. I didn't choose. I was sent.'

'We thought it was better. We thought you'd had enough of chopping and changing.'

'Not my family,' Isabel said. 'That doesn't chop and change. All the other stuff doesn't matter. I can do that, if I can be at home.'

Dan looked up at her. 'What other stuff?'

Isabel shrugged. 'Doesn't matter.'

'It does, Izzy. It *does*. What other stuff?'

Isabel took off her Alice band and bent the two ends together. 'People not talking to me,' she said. 'Whispering about me. Not sitting next to me. Not wanting me in their team.'

'Since . . . '

Isabel put the end of the Alice band in her mouth and clenched her teeth on it. Through her teeth, she said, 'Worse since then.'

'Have you told anyone?'

'No.'

'No one at school?'

'No.'

'Have you told Mum?'

Isabel removed the Alice band from her mouth. She said softly, 'Not really.'

Dan leaned forward. 'Why not?'

'No point.'

'No point?'

'No,' Isabel said, 'there's no point. It makes her feel awful and there's nothing she can do. There's nothing anyone can do, except — except you.'

There was silence. Then Dan got off the floor and came to sit beside Isabel on her bed. He didn't touch her. He looked at her for a long time and then he said, 'Is that why you wanted to talk to me?'

Isabel nodded.

'Could — could you make yourself completely clear? Can you tell me what you think I've done?'

Isabel spun her Alice band away from her across the room. It landed with a light clatter against Gus's Army boots.

'OK,' she said. She sounded quite composed. 'OK. We live here because of you. We lived in all the other places because of you. We stay here, waiting, because of you. We'll probably have to move again, quite soon, Mum says, because of you. I'm at boarding school because of all this moving, because of you. So, if you're the one making all these changes happen, you can make them stop, too.' She flicked a glance at him and then she looked down at her feet. 'Can't you?'

*   *   *

Morgan Longworth had long considered, privately, that the secret of a successful married retirement was for one of you to be an owl and the other a lark. Many years of diplomatic entertaining had reinforced his own owl tendencies, so that the late night hours, after Elaine had gone to begin the lengthy ritual of the end of her day, had come to represent something almost luxurious, something certainly to be looked forward to. The television, carefully considered — for the elegance of the jokes and the moderation of the political opinions — emails to ex-colleagues around the world, books and a leisurely whisky and soda combined to give each day a particular beckoning charm, because the conclusion, however tiresome the preceding hours, was so very pleasurable. He thought he also detected a certain relief in Elaine, when she stood up from her chair on evenings when they were at home together and announced that she would turn in. She was, he suspected, as thankful to be leaving him for a few hours as he was to see her go.

So when he got up from his own chair at the same moment as she did from hers and announced that he'd like to say something to her, she had looked quite annoyed for a few moments, before she recovered her habit of perpetual courtesy.

'What, now?'

'Yes, dear, please.'

He could see her picturing the bath in which she liked to lie for the length of the Radio 4 bedtime serial. If he delayed her, she'd miss it. He said, modulating his voice in the way he used to when using the official telephone, 'It won't take a moment.'

Elaine flounced back down into her seat. 'You've had all evening — '

'We were listening to the Bach.'

She gave a little exclamation of annoyance. 'Morgan, you can be so affected.' She turned to look briefly at him. 'What is it?'

He removed his patient smile and said, in far more straight-forward a tone, 'Alexa.'

Elaine flung her hands up in the air and let them fall heavily into her lap. 'As if I've thought about anything else for days!'

'Have you spoken to her?'

'You know I haven't.'

'I have a plan.'

Elaine didn't turn to look at him. She was staring across the room at the photograph of Richard Maybrick. She said, almost sarcastically, 'Do you now?'

'Yes, actually, I do. I think George was right.'

Elaine said nothing. Morgan knew she had a soft spot for George and Eric Riley, a soft spot he had no intention of indulging as a general rule. But in this case, George had given Morgan both an idea and an opportunity.

'I think he's right,' Morgan repeated.

Elaine smoothed her skirt over her knees. 'In what way?'

'His suggestion that we should go down there.'

'Oh,' Elaine said in exasperation. 'Oh, well done.'

Morgan allowed a small reproving silence to fall. Then he said, 'Except that I think that *I* should go.'

'What!'

'I think,' Morgan said, 'that I should drive down to Larkford and see Dan. Talk to Dan. By myself.'

Elaine at last turned to look at him. 'Really?'

'Yes,' he said. 'And that I should encourage Alexa to bring the twins here to London, to stay with us. Even for a night.'

Elaine began to play agitatedly with her pearls. 'But they should be *together*, Alexa and Dan. They've been apart so much. They should be together now.'

Morgan cleared his throat. He looked at the ceiling. 'Or maybe not.'

'What d'you mean?'

'I mean to surprise them,' Morgan said. 'I mean to surprise Dan, especially. I mean to be . . . ' he paused and then he said, 'a thoroughly unexpected element in an apparently intractable situation.'

'I should leave,' Gus said.

'No, mate, no. It's fine. As long as you don't mind the sofa for a night or two.'

'Course not. Great sofa. But I think I'm in the way.'

Dan handed him a beer bottle. 'The reverse is true. Anyway, you'd upset Alexa.'

'She's pretty upset already.'

'It would be worse,' Dan said, 'if you left now. She'd feel terrible.'

'She's got enough to cope with.'

'Actually,' Dan said, flipping the top off his own beer, 'I'm dealing with that.'

'With what?'

'With Izzy,' Dan said.

'Jeez.'

'All under control,' Dan said. 'She's a sensible kid.'

Gus leaned against the kitchen table. Upstairs Alexa was settling the twins, aided by Isabel, who had promised to read three — no, four, Tassy had shouted, four, five! — Charlie and Lola books.

Gus said, 'It's not just that.'

'Not just what?'

'It's not just being in the way . . . '

'Which you're not.'

'It's watching all this.'

Dan grunted. Gus took a swallow of his beer. He said, 'All this family stuff.'

'So you'd be better brooding on your own?'

'Got to face it sometime.'

212

'Right now? Right after she goes?'

'I should have seen it coming,' Gus said. 'I should have. I knew how she felt. I knew how hard she found it. I remember, when I was a subbie, my old CO describing the wives as 'excess baggage' in front of her. He was sort of joking, trying to be jolly. But she hated it. You could see from her face, even if she didn't say anything then. It was later, when she'd had a bit to drink, that she dared him to tell her to know her place. He said to me afterwards that she'd never make an Army wife.'

'Stop it, Gussie.'

'She's got all the qualities Mack has, or Julian has. She could run a brigade, no trouble. You can't tell a woman like that what to do.'

'But you didn't — '

'No,' Gus said. He took another swallow. 'But the Army did.' He gave a sort of snicker. 'You're bloody lucky.'

'Yup.'

'She's a great wife for a soldier, your Alexa.'

Dan let a brief pause fall and then he said, 'She isn't happy.'

'Go on!'

'Izzy isn't happy at school and Alexa isn't happy at home. Or with me.'

Gus put his beer bottle down on the table. He said loudly, 'Bloody nonsense.'

'It's not.'

'Don't do this to me,' Gus said. 'Don't do it. I can't lean against the only fucking tree left in the forest and have it fall over.'

'I'm not falling over.'

'But you said — '

'I said,' Dan almost whispered, glancing at the ceiling, 'that I have problems. I might not look as if I do, but I do. But I'm going to solve them.'

'Are you?'

'I am. I'm taking Isabel back to school, and then I'm taking Alexa and the twins away somewhere. Disneyland Paris, maybe. Legoland. Haven't thought it through. But that's what I'm planning.'

'Well, that's a relief. Can't have my bezzie mate falling to pieces just when my world goes to buggery.'

'I know,' Dan said. He indicated the beer bottle on the table. 'Drink up.'

Gus looked at the bottle. He said, 'Remember Mark Troy?'

'I do. Poor sod.'

'He's out of jail. On some rehab course. He just lost it on discharge, sleeping rough, bottle of vodka, bottle of sherry, umpteen Special Brew every night, arson, fights, you name it. I don't want to go that way.'

'Bloody hell, Gus,' Dan said. 'What's got into you? Course you won't. Troy had no family, or at least, none who were any use to him.' He picked up the beer bottle and held it out. 'You've got family, a job, friends. You'll be a new man in three months.'

Gus took the bottle. 'Maybe.'

'And in the meantime, you're staying here. You can look after old Beetle while we're away.' He came round the table and clinked his beer against Gus's. 'You, mate, are going nowhere.'

Through the wall, Isabel could hear them arguing. They weren't shouting or anything, and Mum wasn't crying, but she could tell from the way their voices were going on and on, often side by side as if they weren't listening to each other, that they were having a barney. And even if she couldn't hear their actual words, she knew that they were arguing about her going back to school.

In a funny way, Isabel had known she'd have to go back, even while she was walking down the drive with her phone and her bus money in her pocket and the thrilling, energizing panic of waiting to hear footsteps running after her — but she had made herself walk normally, at a brisk but not terrorized pace, and had planned, had she been caught, to return, and then try again, and again, and again, if necessary, until she made it back to Larkford.

'Are you really OK?' Franny had said to her. 'You seem so OK, it's almost unreal.'

'I'm fine,' Isabel said. 'I couldn't stand it and I got sick of saying so. That's all.'

She knew Mum got it. She knew Mum might not have all the details but she had the general picture. But she was stuck. Isabel saw that. Mum was stuck in a way that she hadn't been before she met Dan, a way that Isabel didn't want to dwell on too much because blaming Dan for everything wouldn't work. Dan was nice. It was a pain that he liked being a soldier so much, but that didn't stop him being someone Isabel couldn't picture being without. Any more than she could picture being without the twins. The twins and Dan and Mum and Beetle were, Isabel pictured, in her castle, her private castle. The problem was her being, because of school, shut out of her own castle. And this problem, she had decided, had to be solved by her, because nobody else, it was perfectly evident, either could or would come up with a solution.

So when Dan had announced that he was going to be the one who took her back to school, she had been perfectly fine with that. It had been horrible seeing Mum so upset and wanting to come too, and Dan saying no, and Gus offering to look after the twins, and Tassy completely losing it at the very idea and roaring that she didn't want Gus, ever, ever, *ever*, but it hadn't made Isabel want to cry. She wondered if she had cried so much at school that she'd almost built up an immunity, like having a vaccination against rubella, and the steady, resolved mood she'd been in recently had come to save her from going completely round the bend with the despair of no one doing anything about her situation. It had only dawned on her quite gradually that, in the complete absence of adult help, she was going to have to help herself. She was going, she had decided, to keep leaving school — she refused to think of it as running away — until they all got it into their thick heads that she was not, simply *not*, going to stay. They could take her back as often as they liked. Mrs Cairns could talk to her and devise her pet 'community service' punishments till she was blue in the face. Libby Guthrie and her gang could be complete cows as much as they wanted. It wouldn't matter. She wasn't, *wasn't*, going to stay. And tomorrow, when she was alone in the car with Dan, she would tell him so. It was only fair, she considered, and he was, after all, a man who set great store by fairness.

The voices through the wall were fainter now. There was, in fact, the odd bump and thump instead. Oh my God, thought Isabel, not that, not *that*, I shall be sick, la-la-la, fingers in ears, turn on iPod, volume up, up further, drown it all out — Her phone beeped, in the dark, on the little table where Gus had had his radio. She put a hand out from under the duvet and pulled the phone into the bed with her.

There was a text on the bright small square of the screen.

'Hi,' it read, 'Rupert here. They can't make you. OK?' And then, amazingly, two Xs. Rupert. Franny's Rupert.

She held the phone hard against her cheek, her eyes closed. 'They can't make you.' No, she thought, dizzy with a sudden astonishing happiness. No, they can't. And they won't, either.

* * *

'I should leave,' Gus said, this time to Alexa.

He was tidying up the kitchen with her. The twins were in front of the television, with their thumbs in, and Dan was driving Isabel back to school. Alexa had managed not to cry when

Isabel got into the car, and, astonishingly, Isabel had looked as if not crying was hardly costing her any effort.

'See you soon,' she'd said to Alexa when she kissed her.

'Nearly the end of term, darling, not long, not long.'

Isabel had settled herself beside Dan, buckling her seat belt. She was clutching her phone but she looked fine, almost serene. Dan looked masterful, in charge again, putting the car smoothly into gear and reversing fast and accurately, his arm along the back of the passenger seat.

'You've got to stand back a bit when they come home,' Mo had said to Alexa, the day before Dan got back. 'It's a complete pain, but you have to. They have to be able to resume control again. Or, at least, to think they have.'

When the car had gone, Alexa had taken the twins into the sitting room and promised them half an hour of CBeebies to compensate for the extravagant grief of Isabel's departure, and then she and Gus had cleared up lunch together, and Gus had put the kettle on to make coffee, and said that he thought he ought to go home now.

Unlike Dan, Alexa didn't say, don't even think of it. Instead, she said, 'Are you ready?'

Gus tossed the tea towel he was shining up the glasses with over his shoulder and said jauntily, 'I'll never know till I try, will I?'

Alexa put two mugs on the table. She said, not very forcefully, 'It's OK, you being here. Honest.'

'You've been so great.'

'No.'

'You have,' Gus said. 'You both have. Fantastic. And it's not easy for you especially. I know that.'

Alexa thought of Dan and Isabel in the car together, and what he might have to tell her — candidly, at last — when he got back. She said, 'Maybe not.'

'Not easy at all,' Gus said, hurrying on. 'What with being close to Kate and all that. It's hell having divided loyalties. And, of course, I share your feelings, I really do.'

'Do you?'

'That's the complete shit of it, really. I think Kate is wonderful. I always have. I mean, I couldn't believe that a girl like Kate would agree to marry someone like me. That's what's killing me, if you want to know. I've never thought I was good enough, and now I've had the proof.' He paused and looked at Alexa. 'You two have been an absolute lifesaver.'

Alexa spooned coffee into the cafetière. 'I'm glad.'

'I'm sorry I've monopolized old Dan so much. Really sorry.'

'That's OK.'

'And I'll do anything I can to help while you're away.'

'Away?'

'Yes,' Gus said. He came and stood next to her. 'Probably shouldn't have said. Dan's planning to whisk you off somewhere.'

'But the twins — '

'Them too. All of you. Lovely family jolly. I'll

keep an eye on the house and Beetle. Be glad to, in fact.'

Alexa turned away to pick up the kettle. She said despairingly, 'That's not . . . '

'That's not what?'

'That — going away — won't solve anything.'

'Oh, come on.'

'It won't,' Alexa cried. 'It won't, it's just another diversion, another way of not facing me, not talking, not listening. Oh damn, damn, damn, I'm going to cry.'

She stood by the kettle, shoulders hunched, battling. Gus came over and put a tentative arm round her shoulders.

'Hey,' he said. 'Hey.'

She turned towards him to say something further, and as she did so, his face moved suddenly closer and his mouth skidded clumsily across hers. She leaped away, as if she'd been scalded. Then she turned, her fists clenched, and hissed at him.

'*Don't*,' Alexa said.

12

Driving back to Larkford, Dan rehearsed what he would say to Alexa. He was practised at this sort of rehearsal, having decided years ago — as he suspected most of the men of his regiment had decided — that it was unfair to the point of cruelty to describe some aspects of being on operations to loved ones on return, merely because it provided a brief personal relief to unburden. All that was achieved in the long run by telling too much was to leave the person you loved — wife, girlfriend, family member — with a series of ghastly images of, say, torn body parts scattered across the desert grit after an IED had blown up, and a subsequent inability not to link those images with the fear of you being more than likely to suffer the same fate. Editing reality was now pretty well automatic.

Anyway, however fascinated — and horrified — your family and friends were to hear about it, they could never, any of them, really get it. No one else could, unless they'd done it. A squaddie who'd actually served in Helmand, even if he could barely string two words together, was a more satisfactory audience, when home again, than the most adored or articulate companion who had stayed behind. One of the things Dan had immediately fallen for in Alexa was that she didn't ask him stuff, she wasn't demanding, she wasn't, as so many of his Army friends' girlfriends were, high maintenance. It was, he'd recognized early on, a huge plus.

To have a gorgeous girlfriend — and soldiers were amazingly candid about wanting and feeling entitled to gorgeous girlfriends — who didn't pester or sulk or whine was completely wonderful. Alexa had even said, once, when he got back from exercise, filthy and happy and exhausted, with streaks of egg from the final egg banjo decorating the front of his battledress, 'Before you start telling me what you've been up to, can I say that I only want a severely edited version, thank you very much!'

That, of course, was a long time ago now. That was before the twins, before the twins were even thought of, when he was newly a major, and she was making yet another dismal married quarter charming, and teaching Isabel to read, and entrancing him unexpectedly, sometimes with stockings and high heels under a trench coat or a dressing-gown or, once, his own battledress. Better not to remember that, right now. Better to focus on the driving, and that conversation with Isabel, and exactly how much, and in what way, he was going to report of the last few hours to an Alexa who had recently — or was it longer, if he'd been really paying attention? — begun not just to ask but to indicate quite forcefully that he was failing her in some profound and important way, letting her down, neglecting something so crucial that it amounted to a dereliction of duty.

He had asked Isabel as they approached the school if she was OK. She said undramatically that she felt a bit sick, but that was all right, she probably wouldn't *be* sick, and anyway, it wasn't for long. Dan said, slightly too heartily, no, not long at all, only a month till the end of term, and Isabel, looking away from him out of the passenger window, said that it would be sooner than that.

'Will it? Is there another home weekend?'

Isabel hadn't turned back towards him. She said to the hedges speeding past outside the window, 'I'm not staying, you see.'

'Not staying?'

'No,' Isabel said. 'When I've planned the next time, I'll do it again.'

Dan struggled to take this in. 'You'll — '

'Yes,' Isabel said, 'I'm not staying. I suppose they could lock me in a room or something, but they couldn't really do that because of child protection and everything, could they? So I'll just make another plan.'

There was a farm gateway coming up beside the road. Dan indicated left and swerved into it. He stopped the car and put the handbrake on.

'You — you are already planning to run away again?'

'I didn't run,' Isabel said patiently. 'I walked. You know why. And I'll keep doing it till you all realize that I mean it.'

'Ye gods,' Dan said. He sat for a while, staring ahead of him. Then he said, 'I'll have to tell Mrs Cairns.'

Isabel turned her head at last and looked at him. Then she said levelly, 'You don't *have* to.'

And he hadn't. He could not believe, now, driving back to Larkford, that throughout his fifteen minutes in Mrs Cairns' study — she had been very charming, in the manner of someone hugely relieved to see a sane intervention, at last, in a tiresomely hysterical situation — he had said nothing of Isabel's intention. He had mentioned the homesickness, he had emphasized his distaste for the bullying and an atmosphere that permitted it, and he had — standing now, looming over Mrs Cairns — made it very plain that he wouldn't care to see any retribution meted out to his stepdaughter as a result of her impulsive attempt to improve her increasingly painful situation.

'You should be grateful,' he'd said, 'that Isabel's courage has revealed the flaws in your system to you. Punishment would not be in any way appropriate.'

He had sounded as he sounded when he was reprimanding his gunners for something. They usually looked straight past him while he was talking, rigidly to attention, terrified to catch his eye. Mrs Cairns, on the other hand, seemed to want him to look at her, so that she could, without admitting any wrongdoing on the school's part, assure him that every effort would be made to give Isabel a fresh and encouraging new try at settling in. She had smiled when she held out her hand to say goodbye. Dan had taken her hand, but he hadn't smiled back. The complicity of adults, he wanted to say, won't work here. Isabel's the one with guts.

He swung off the main road and turned for Larkford. A faint unease was settling on him, an apprehension compounded of Alexa's current mood — or moods, really — poor old Gus's broken heart, and his own decidedly mixed feelings about those weeks stretching ahead without the comforting dictatorship of duties. He had only ever seen his mother once, since she went to Australia, and it had been a wretched occasion, in a steakhouse near Charing Cross station, culminating in his — he was sixteen then — walking out, leaving his meal half-eaten, after she had said scornfully of Dan's father, 'I couldn't live with a man who couldn't cope with normal life. I couldn't. And he'll never manage it, never, he's too used to doing what he's told.'

Dan turned his car into the Quadrant. There was an unquestioned luxury in obedience, rather than in having to initiate. The weeks of leave were not going to be easy because this time so much emotional repair work seemed to be urgently crying out to be done. Maybe time away would help that, but also, maybe Alexa would refuse to go.

Whatever she chose, whatever happened, Dan found that he was at least sure of one thing. He slid the car to a halt in the driveway — Gus's car wasn't there, what could he have gone off to do? — and pulled on the handbrake. He would not tell Alexa of Isabel's intentions, and he would not tell her that he had revealed nothing of them to Mrs Cairns, either. He opened the car door and waited for Beetle to be released to greet him. Thank the Lord for the simplicity of dogs.

★ ★ ★

Eric Riley stood by his brother's grave in the Gap Road Cemetery in Wimbledon. He'd left a row of poppies there, before Remembrance Day — he'd so hoped Dan would come to London for that, but there you go, shouldn't lay yourself open to disappointment, hoping things like that — and now he was collecting them to take them home and add to the drawerful he had already. He didn't like it when poppies and poppy wreaths were left out in the wind and rain after Remembrance Day; it seemed disrespectful to the dead to leave them to get battered and faded. They should be there, on graves and memorials, for one week only, bright as blood, and then they should be removed before they were diminished by the elements. He'd put six in a row by Ray's grave, pushing their green plastic stems into the earth. Now he pulled them up briskly, one by one, and put them in his pocket.

It was a gloomy day. The Council workers who looked after the cemetery repaired the buildings and machines in winter, so the whole place kind of gave up, come November, and acquired a dreary, faintly neglected air, all natural colour leached out of the grass, the trees rapidly shedding their last leaves, the only bright spots the bunches of plastic flowers that people left here and there and that Eric so despised. He stood, as he always stood, facing Ray's headstone, his shoes polished, his overcoat buttoned. It was heavy, his overcoat, an old British Warm, too heavy for November, but it was appropriate for visiting Ray so had to be endured. It would probably outlast him, Eric

226

thought, and George, too. If George would ever wear it. Bloody boy liked those anorak things. With a hood. I ask you.

He leaned forward and rested his hands on Ray's white headstone. Ray had died in the mud. Cold and wet, and probably lusting for a fag. Sometimes, in the heat of Aden, Eric had thought about Ray in the trenches of Northern France. He'd wondered if he'd got dehydrated, despite all the rain and mud. It was a real problem in Aden, the dehydration; you could smell it in a man's pee if he wasn't drinking enough. They didn't know much about it, even then. Looking back, Eric wondered at how little they did know, how different things were, how they'd changed. Take ammo, for example, him being a gunner. They'd had some good stuff, but nothing like a modern high-velocity round. Now that was amazing. Amazing. It came so fast that you'd need an 800-yard start on it; a quarter-second to realize it was coming, a quarter-second for your brain to tell you what to do, and half a second to fling yourself flat. Wham. Bloody miraculous. Bloody impossible. Human beings weren't meant to deal with anything coming at them at two thousand miles an hour. In his day, the worst offence on a gun team was a bad ram. If the shell wasn't far enough up, the gun wouldn't fire. A bad ram, that was. Eric looked at his hands, resting on Ray's headstone. He could picture them now, shoving the shell case up, far enough for the copper-banded edge to be just below the rifling. He'd prided himself on never failing to get it right. Rammer Riley. Sarnt Riley. Yes, suh.

He gave Ray's headstone a brief pat and straightened. He felt faintly uneasy most of the time at the moment, as he knew George did. When George got back from Larkford he said that you couldn't quite put your finger on what was wrong, there wasn't anything dramatic going on; everyone was well, the daily round was turning on its usual wheels, but there was something the matter.

'What?' Eric had asked. 'What — sulks, raised voices, avoiding each other? Explain yourself, lad!'

And George, fetching their second beers, had said, sadly, 'They're just not getting through to each other. It's like they're both on the telephone, but not on the same line. And I'm afraid — '

'Yes? Yes?'

'I'm afraid it's Dan, Dad. I think she'd talk if she could get him to focus. His head's still in Helmand and — '

'And what, for bugger's sake?'

'And I don't think he's doing much to bring it back.'

Eric dusted his hands off against one another. If anyone had ever asked him, he'd have said that the best years of his life had been spent in Aden, never mind the heat and the dirt and the danger and losing some of the best buddies he'd ever known. They were good years because he knew what he was doing and he knew what he was there for. He'd had a purpose, and not only had he fulfilled it, he'd known it was of use to his fellow men, both those serving with him and those going about their business back in Blighty. That's what George had probably felt down there in the South Atlantic — although you'd think, sometimes, he'd never been there, the amount he ever talked about it — and it was what Dan was missing so violently now. You could recite every cliché going about the public good and the common weal and productiveness until the bloody cows came home, but nothing took away the fact that those cliches were true, that nothing satisfied a man as much as the sense that he was of real value and visible use.

Eric turned away and began to walk towards the nearest gate. Poor Dan. Poor bloody Dan. Thankful to be back and at the same time intensely homesick for Helmand. And that girl, trying to deal with a man in that state, never mind mother her children and keep up all the age-old appearances of the patch. Of course the rules had relaxed a bit since his day — he remembered the strictures about no PDAs (public displays of affection), no girl soldiers to be seen drinking out of pint glasses — but he'd bet a pound to a penny that the snobberies of rank and demeanour were as rife as they'd ever been, whatever lip service was paid to their passing. That poor bloody girl. If she wasn't getting through to Dan because he simply wasn't on message, who could she possibly turn to?

He emerged into Gap Road and turned for Wimbledon Village. No point going home, he thought, and sitting there going round in bloody circles. Better head for Elys and a pot of tea and a teacake, and see if, in more convivial surroundings, he couldn't cudgel his old wits into thinking of something he might do for them, some way he could help.

★ ★ ★

'Gone?' Dan said.

Alexa was ironing. From the playroom came the peaceable twittering of the twins, absorbed in some curious game of their own devising, which he'd seen as he passed the window on his way in, involving several cardboard boxes and a herd of soft toys. Apart from that, there was just the mild thump of the iron — on his shirts, he noticed — and the radio whispering away in the background, voices rising and falling with the faint artificiality of words spoken in drama rather than in real life.

'When did he go?'

'About an hour ago,' Alexa said.

'But why?'

She paused and put the iron down on the metal rack at the end of the ironing board. She said, folding in sleeves, 'I think he felt he'd just got to stop licking his wounds here, and get on with facing how life looks as if it's going to be.'

'What did he say?'

'Nothing much, really. Just that.'

Dan came over and stood behind her, looking down at his shirt, now a neat rectangle, collar buttoned. He said softly, 'What did *you* say?'

She picked up the shirt and turned to add it to the pile on the table behind her. She said, 'No big deal, Dan. Just — well, he was thanking me and I was saying that's fine, which I meant, it was, and then he — ' She paused and looked at Dan. 'He said that he'd be going anyway soon, because you were planning to take the twins and me off somewhere for a while. Are you?'

Dan shuffled a little. 'I was thinking of it, yes.'

'Thinking?'

'Yes. I thought we needed to get out of here, all of us. We need to — have a change of scene. See and do something different. It's so hard for you, having me come back into a life and a routine you've devised in order to cope with me not being here, I can see that. I just thought we could both do with being out of this context for a bit, even a few days, until we get our bearings again. That's all.'

Alexa turned back to the ironing board and spread out a pinafore dress of Flora's. 'Dan.'

'Yes?'

'Dan, I don't want to rain on your parade, but, *think*.'

'I have thought.'

'No.'

'I have, I've told you, I've thought about what we can do to make the next few weeks an improvement, not just more of the same.'

Alexa banged the iron down. 'No!'

Dan glanced towards the playroom. 'Shh.'

'No!' Alexa said again, more vehemently. 'You haven't thought, have you? You haven't thought that you haven't seen your grandfather or my parents since you got back. You haven't seen your father properly, either. And you haven't thought,

231

have you, that I can't go off on any jolly hols, leaving Isabel in this state. And how was Isabel? How *was* she? You walk in here, and the first thing you do is not tell me about her but ask where Gus is. The first thing!'

Dan moved a step away. 'She's fine.'

'I don't believe you. She can't be.'

'Sweetheart, she's fine. She was great in the car. She was very calm when we got there. I said my piece to Mrs Whatsit and she took it in. Isabel had made her point, and she's fine.'

'Making her point is only half the story!'

'It's in hand,' Dan said. 'Honestly it is. It'll be different now. They'll keep an eye on her.'

Alexa folded her arms. 'God, Dan. Keeping an eye on her might help with the bullying but it won't help with the homesickness, will it?'

In his basket, Beetle stirred uneasily and sat up. Tassy appeared in the doorway. 'I need,' she said commandingly, 'lots of spoons.'

'In a minute, darling.'

'Lots,' Tassy said. 'For their supper.'

Dan crossed the kitchen and picked his daughter up. 'Hey there, bombshell.'

Tassy ignored him. 'Spoons!'

'I can't go anywhere,' Alexa said, 'till I've got some peace of mind. And I can't *begin* to have that until I can believe Isabel has some solution ahead and you are even halfway back to Planet Normal.'

'Spoons,' Tassy said, less strenuously.

Alexa turned round so that she was facing Dan and Tassy.

'It's hard here,' she said. 'Very hard. It was

232

hard all the time you were away, and it's been no better since you got back. While you were away, there were all kinds of problems, which I dealt with because there was only me and I had to. But now you're back, the problems haven't gone away. In fact, they're worse. They're worse because I can't take unilateral decisions any more. I can't because you're here and you are a problem in yourself. If it was down to me, I'd have Isabel out of that school and me in a job of some kind somewhere and living in a proper community and not this — this weird bubble. But it isn't down to me because you're back now, and what *you* do dictates what *we* do.'

She folded her arms. 'What exactly did Isabel say to you? Did she say something you're not telling me? Am I going to discover that on top of all else you actually have the nerve to differentiate between our daughters?'

There was a short silence, then Dan said, as if she hadn't spoken, 'What did you say to Gus?'

Alexa started across the kitchen. As she passed Dan and Tassy, she put her hand to her face, as if she was crying or she didn't want to see them.

'He wanted to go, and I didn't stop him,' she said. 'He said he found our happy family life hard to bear. Hah! The spoons are in the drawer. Where they always are.'

And then she crossed the hallway at a run, and they heard her race up the stairs and along the landing, followed by the slam of a door.

Tassy looked at her father. 'Spoons?' she said hopefully.

233

Gus said he was OK. Fine, promise. Not exactly never better, but managing. And he'd got to. Manage, that is. He'd just been talking to one of his gunners — well, ex-gunner really, who'd decided to leave the Army because his wife couldn't hack it any longer, and he'd said it was strange, leaving with almost nothing. 'Just a couple of day sacks and me Bergen,' he'd said to Gus, and a bed in his mother-in-law's second bedroom. No room to swing a cat. 'It made me thankful for what I've got,' Gus said, not quite steadily. 'I'll be OK, promise I will.'

'See you tomorrow?' Dan said.

'Maybe, mate. Maybe. Got to sort my head a bit. You too.'

'My head's getting there.'

There'd been a pause, and then Gus said guardedly, 'I . . . I'm not sure we can actually say that. Can we?'

Then Dan had gone into the playroom and surveyed the cardboard-box train the twins had made, in which the toys were propped up and being given supper with teaspoons. He lowered himself to the floor and the twins immediately stopped their game and clambered on top of him, demanding that he play with them, read to them, listen to them, sing to them.

'Where's Mummy?' Flora said. Her spectacles were askew again. Dan peered at the skin of her face, at the texture of her hair, and marvelled at their complete purity and perfection.

'Sleeping.'

'But it's not the night time!'

Dan lay down, holding a twin in each arm. 'Sometimes people get tired in the daytime.'

'I don't.'

'But you're not a mummy.'

'Nor are you,' Tassy said.

'No,' Dan said. He gazed at them both, turning his head from side to side. 'No, I'm not. What am I?'

Flora smiled at him. She adjusted her glasses. She said reverently, adoringly, 'You are the *daddy*.'

★   ★   ★

Alexa woke from a brief, deep, bothered sleep. She had yanked the curtains across when she had come upstairs and flung herself on the bed in order to rage impotently, face-down in the pillows, and now found herself, quite unintentionally, waking an hour later with a stiff neck and a dry mouth and a sense of dread at coming to, to face an unchanged everything.

She rolled over. Her mouth tasted disgusting and her eyes felt gluey. The house seemed very quiet, unnaturally so. Maybe Dan had taken the twins somewhere. Maybe he had taken them round to see Gus. No. Better not think that. If she thought that she'd be clutched by rage and revulsion again, rage at Gus's ineptitude and revulsion at his — his whimpering, appalled apologies. Don't think about Gus. Don't think about Isabel. Don't think about Dan's crass suggestion of a holiday. Lie here and count for a while, count to a hundred, and then get up and brush your hair, brush your teeth, and go downstairs and make supper for the twins without further recrimination or accusation. *Enough*.

Someone was coming up the stairs. It was a slow, careful tread, as if the person was uncertain, or maybe carrying something. Alexa lifted her head from the pillow and held her breath. The steps reached the top of the stairs and then came slowly along the landing. Then the bedroom door opened carefully and a slice of yellow light fell in from the ugly overhead bulb on the landing outside, revealing Dan, carrying a teacup and saucer.

He whispered, 'You awake?'

She sat up a little. 'Yes. Just.'

He came round the bed and put the teacup down on the pile of books on the small chest beside her. 'I've brought you some tea.'

'Thank you. Where are the twins?'

'Downstairs.'

'Doing what?'

'Eating toast and jam,' Dan said.

'Eating — '

'Yes,' Dan said. 'They're very jolly. Sticky, but jolly. Come down when you've come to.'

'Yes, I'll — '

'Soon as you can,' Dan said, his voice a little louder. 'When you've drunk your tea. Your father's here.'

13

Franny's Rupert had texted to ask Isabel if she was on Facebook. There had been no kisses after the text, Isabel noticed, but she had to balance their absence against the fact that he had texted at all, and that he had virtually asked her to be a friend on Facebook. She had thought about her response for a long time — at least three hours — before ingeniously replying 'Not yet. Not allowed,' which did not precisely give away the fact that she was not yet thirteen. She was pleased with the reply. It strengthened the impression she did not in the least mind him having, that she was pretty well a complete prisoner of unreasonable adult prohibitions. When she sent the text, she was careful to conclude without kisses, also.

Mobile phones were not permitted during school hours. The rule was that they were to be left in the cubbyhole by your bed in the morning, and only switched on in the evening to retrieve messages, after prep and supper and before lights out. Like most people, Isabel kept her phone on vibrate mode illicitly in her uniform skirt pocket, and the risk of getting caught lent the school day a pleasurable frisson of danger, not unlike the sensation Isabel had had while walking down the school drive. In the middle of double maths, Isabel's phone trembled in her pocket. She counted to twenty and put her hand up. Mrs Twining, who found maths so exciting that she talked about it as if she'd just won *The X-Factor*, asked what she wanted, with impatience. Libby Guthrie and her gang turned to glance and grimace.

'Please,' Isabel said, 'may I be excused?'

In the lavatory cubicle, having already flushed the toilet to create a comforting wall of noise, Isabel read her screen.

'Can u talk?' Rupert had texted.

'Not allowed,' she wrote back.

'!!!' he said. 'Later?'

'Yes,' she said, stopping herself before she wrote, 'Please.'

'OK,' he said. 'Got an idea.'

She stared, smiling, at the screen. '4 me?'

'Yes, thicko!' he wrote, but then he added 'x'.

Someone came into the cloakroom and banged a cubicle door shut. Isabel reached behind her to pull the flush again. 'Thank you.'

'X,' he said.

She stood up, the phone glowing in her hand. She wanted to say 'x' back. But she mustn't.

'Maths,' she wrote. 'Gotta go.'

She put her phone back in her pocket and unlatched the cubicle door. There was nobody by the washbasins and it was quiet, except for the sound of someone peeing from a cubicle at the far end. Isabel paused to lean over a washbasin and examine herself in the mirror. Nobody would ever, ever, in a million years, think she was pretty. Would they?

★ ★ ★

Lying in Isabel's bed, under a washed-out duvet cover from Isabel's childhood, appliqued with an anthropomorphized mouse dressed as a ballerina, Morgan Longworth contemplated an extraordinary evening. When he'd arrived, unannounced as planned, he'd found his soldier son-in-law lying on the floor under a mound of plush animals, like Gulliver among the Lilliputians, while his twin granddaughters — what was the real situation with Flora and her spectacles? — conducted some sort of stately ritual with a plastic tea set over and around his body. Dan had sprung up, scattering hippos and pandas, and Morgan had found himself being welcomed with the bemused amazement he would have expected had he just landed from Mars. He had shaken Dan's hand, kissed the twins, patted Beetle's head, explained that this visit was merely an impulse rather than an emergency of any kind, and indicated that a cup of tea would be very welcome after the drive from London.

He had asked where Alexa was. Dan said, as if there was nothing to be inferred from it, that she was sleeping.

'Like this!' said Tassy, casting herself down on the floor to demonstrate.

'Like this!' Flora shouted, copying her.

Dan made tea and offered his father-in-law some toast. Morgan had declined the toast, and had sat at the kitchen table watching while Dan settled the twins in their chairs and embarked upon the complicated business — which Morgan remembered as being, in his experience, infinitely simpler and less messy — of special mugs for milk, and the *right* plastic plates, and toast and butter and the correct jam — no, not that one, not that one, the red one, the *red* — and having the toast cut into the exact and only shapes in which it could possibly be eaten. What, Morgan wondered, could be going on in Dan's head, cutting toast into stamp-sized squares? How, exactly, did one change mental gears so entirely fundamentally? He had taken a swallow of tea and cleared his throat. 'Might — might we wake Alexa, do you think?'

When Dan had gone upstairs with a cup and saucer — Morgan noticed that his hand had hovered over, and rejected, a mug — the twins had plainly felt it was their duty to entertain him.

'Are you,' Tassy had said, her mouth full of toast, 'the granddad?'

'I am indeed,' Morgan said. 'I am one of your two grandfathers. You know me perfectly well.'

Flora said conversationally, ignoring his last remark, 'We have one called Eric and one called George.'

'You do.'

'So you,' Flora said, jam now even on her spectacles, 'can be the spare one.'

'Thank you. Thank you very much.'

'Are you called Eric?'

'No,' Morgan said. 'My name is Morgan. You know that. I am Grandfather Morgan.'

For some reason, the twins had found this wildly funny. They had looked at each other and collapsed laughing, Tassy's mouth still packed with toast. Morgan had felt unaccountably foolish, somehow, sitting at the other end of the

240

table in solitary and ridiculous state with his tea, so he had got up and brought a chair to sit between the twins and suggested that they stopped cackling and finished their toast.

Flora had turned her single visible blue eye on him. 'Gruffalo Morgan!' she said, entranced by her own wit and daring, and it had seemed to Morgan that the only option open to him was to join in, so that when Alexa appeared, escorted by Dan with evident solicitude, they were all three laughing and, Morgan realized later, examining the sleeves of his cashmere cardigan, lightly and universally jammy.

Alexa didn't look well. She seemed surprised to see him, but not that surprised, giving the impression that she was in a place that was almost beyond the capacity for reaction. Morgan explained his impulsive wish to see them all, and when Alexa said where's Mum, replied untruthfully that she had a migraine and had decided to go to bed as the best — indeed, the only — way to defeat it. Alexa seemed to accept what he said in much the same way as she accepted his being there, and then she absentmindedly helped herself to a square of Tassy's toast, and Tassy shrieked in protest, precipitating one of those scenes that Morgan would later describe to Elaine as being absolutely foreign to the parents of only children. For one thing, two protesting children make twice as much noise as one.

What followed had been, to begin with, rather enjoyable. Dan had made a covert phone call or two, and then he had suggested that Morgan might like to meet his CO and had driven him

241

off to the garrison — behind the wire, no less — to a large Edwardian building called Ranpur House, where the CO and his pretty wife had been extremely welcoming and provided whisky and soda in a room — further memo to tell Elaine — that could only have belonged to a soldier, with pictures hung in completely straight lines and miniature cannons on the mantelpiece. His whisky had been handed to him in a cut-glass tumbler of satisfactory weight, an agreeable dog had decorated the hearthrug and the conversation took the comfortable turn of allowing him to pontificate — self-deprecatingly — on foreign affairs without feeling the constraint of Elaine's publicly loyal but privately sceptical eye upon him. When they finally left, Colonel Mackenzie had said to Dan, 'Love to the lovely Alexa,' and Mary Mackenzie had added, almost too eagerly, 'Oh mine, too!' and Dan had smiled in an easy, slightly proudly proprietorial way that indicated — seemed to indicate, anyway — that he knew himself to be a lucky man in untroubled possession of a complete jewel.

When they returned to the Quadrant, however, the jewel was not in evidence. The kitchen table was laid — rather sketchily, to Morgan's eye — for supper, and there was a pan or two on the hob, but Alexa was absent. Dan appeared to be entirely undisconcerted by this, and settled his father-in-law in the sitting room with a newspaper before vanishing upstairs. It was twenty minutes or so before Alexa appeared in the doorway and said that it wasn't much, she was afraid, but that supper was ready.

Morgan got to his feet. 'Darling. You weren't expecting me — '

'It's just ham and salad, really. Sorry.'

'I didn't come for food. Don't be sorry. I came to see *you*.'

Alexa had looked at him for a moment, as if weighing something up. Then she said, 'I know. All the same.'

He took her elbow, as if to escort her to the kitchen. He said encouragingly, 'And it's been so good to catch up with Dan for a bit.'

'Yes.'

'He's told me a lot of what went on. One wishes it didn't look so hopeless, but of course, history is against us.'

Alexa had said nothing further. In the kitchen, Dan was uncorking wine and there were candles on the table, and a bowl of potatoes from which steam was gently rising.

'Potatoes!' Morgan said, in the tone of voice he might use to say 'Caviar!'

'Oh, Dad,' Alexa said despairingly.

'A rare treat,' Morgan said, 'I promise you. Your mother never buys them. No potatoes, no cream, no white bread, no biscuits.'

Dan pulled out a chair for him. He said, too heartily, 'Welcome to Liberty Hall, then, Morgan!'

And then — well, then an atmosphere had descended on the table as chilling as if a miasma of dry ice had mysteriously been pumped into the room. His own voice, endeavouring to cajole or encourage his daughter and son-in-law into conviviality, sounded ever more forced, and the

243

effort to make more noise than the sound of knives and forks on plates grew unbearable. He had been full of theoretical initiatives on the journey down, buoyed up by the conviction that the situation on the ground would prove infinitely more tractable than it appeared from the anxious distance of London, but now that he was here, he felt both out of his depth and painfully without ideas or ammunition. The walls of silence he was battling were, plainly, not excluding him, but they were manifestly there between Alexa and Dan, and he simply had no idea how to penetrate them. He ate his ham, praised the potatoes again, drank his wine and harangued himself, silently, for having had the ludicrously misguided notion that he would be a more effective negotiator without Elaine. Spearing a piece of underripe tomato with his fork, he wished with all his being that she would suddenly materialize, at this terrible meal, to help him out. Goaded by the futility of this wish and by the sight of his daughter pushing food round her plate like a turbulent child, he said suddenly to her, 'Why don't you come up to London?'

Her head jerked up. 'What?'

'Mum and I would love it. Please do. Just for a night or two. Come to London.'

Alexa gazed at him. Then, after a moment or two, she switched her gaze to Dan. She said — too peremptorily, Morgan thought — 'Can you look after the twins for a couple of days?'

Dan shifted very slightly in his chair. He picked up his wine glass and said to his father-in-law rather than to his wife, 'I was planning to go to Headley Court this week.'

'Headley Court?' said Morgan.

'Yes. To see some of our boys who got invalided out, the last six months — '

'*Terrible* injuries,' Alexa said.

Morgan did not like her tone. He said to Dan, 'This week?'

'I'd like to.'

'With Gus Melville,' Alexa said to her father.

Dan muttered, 'I could always go alone.'

'Oh,' Alexa said, 'no need for that, I'm sure.'

Morgan hesitated. He thought of the spare bedroom in the flat at Marylebone Road with its padded coat hangers and monogrammed bed linen. He turned to his daughter. 'I meant, darling, why don't you and the twins come? We don't see anything like enough of you, as it is. You can come back to London with me. I can drive you all.'

Alexa looked at Dan again. She said to him, still hardly pleasantly, 'Could you manage to look after Beetle, do you think?'

He didn't look back. He emptied his wineglass and set it back on the table with a slight bang. He said tersely, 'Of course.'

Alexa turned to look at her father. She gave him a wide smile, possibly the first smile of the evening, even if it lacked conviction. 'We'd love to,' she said.

★   ★   ★

And now here he was, under the mouse ballerina duvet, conscious of a great external stillness

245

— how used he was, he thought, to the perpetual hum of London — and an immense internal turmoil. There was no sound from the other side of the bedroom wall, only a distinct absence of noise that managed somehow to convey tension rather than slumber, and no sound either from that strange, enclosed, military world outside his window. In the room at the other end of the landing, his small granddaughters were sleeping with the abandonment of the very young. Below, in the kitchen, Beetle would be curled up tidily in his basket. In London, Elaine would no doubt also be sleeping, possibly in the centre of their bed rather than on her accustomed half, in one of the cream silk nightshirts he liked to buy her from a shirtmaker in Jermyn Street, and somewhere twenty miles away, his oldest granddaughter, Isabel, was, he hoped, not awake and miserable in a school dormitory that did not, he fervently trusted, resemble in any way the one he'd had to endure over sixty years ago in a scarcely heated preparatory school in Berkshire. He had tried to introduce the topic of Isabel at supper, and Alexa had merely said, in a tone that encouraged nobody to pursue the matter, that he had better ask Dan, as Dan had taken charge of the situation now and would shortly come up with a solution. Dan had looked very much as if nobody should ask him anything further on any topic whatsoever, so Morgan had simply reiterated how pleased Elaine would be at the news that Alexa and the twins were coming to London, and had then got to his feet and begun to stack the plates on the table as an indication of how much he now wished the evening to be over.

Which it was, but without the subsequent balm of sleep. He turned restlessly on to his side. Could one take three-year-olds to Madame Tussaud's? The zoo, certainly. The penguins would enchant them. Come to think of it, the penguins would enchant him, too. As, indeed, did the prospect of the company of the twins and of manageable little expeditions — the tops of buses, the London Eye, cafés serving strawberry milk shakes. He thought even the cream sofas could be accommodated. And, perhaps, alone with Alexa, he could persuade her to talk more. Perhaps, without each other, she and Dan could find a way — forward? Back? *Around*, even, whatever was the matter?

He picked up his wristwatch from the bedside table and peered at the illuminated dial. Two twenty-two. He put the watch down and closed his eyes with resolution. If only — if only the two of them hadn't looked, that evening, in their various ways, so *lonely*.

★ ★ ★

'I really don't want to talk about it any more,' Alexa said.

She was sitting on the edge of their unmade bed with her back to him, struggling into a T-shirt. Half-dressed himself, Dan stood, a sock in one hand, and watched her. Her pale, smooth back, lightly sprinkled with small dark moles, made him ache to look at. It was so familiar

247

— so vulnerable, somehow — and at the moment completely out of bounds as far as he was concerned. If he knelt on the bed, as he would have liked to do, and touched her, or kissed her shoulder just beside the groove where her bra strap cut very slightly into her flesh, she would probably hit him.

He backed against the nearest wall and lifted his bare foot to pull his sock on. 'I haven't gone back on anything,' he said. 'I'm still working on the Isabel thing. And I did want to take you away, you and the twins. I did. I do.'

Alexa pulled the T-shirt over her head. She said, not turning, 'And then you make this plan with Gus.'

'I haven't made it yet.'

'And you spring this whole Headley Court thing on me in front of my father, so I can't possibly say anything without looking completely heartless.'

Dan lowered his foot to the floor. He said sadly, 'That was just a bad mistake.'

Alexa picked up the sweater that lay on the bed beside her and began to turn it impatiently to find the way in.

'Lex.'

'What?'

'Sweetheart,' Dan said, 'maybe this is all for the best.'

'What is?'

'You going to London for a bit. Me sorting my head out on my own.'

'You won't be on your own,' Alexa said. She pushed her arms down the sleeves of her sweater.

'You'll go straight round to Gus and nothing will progress one millimetre.'

Dan came round until he was standing in front of her. 'What's Gus got to do with it?'

Alexa pulled the sweater over her head. She pushed the hair out of her eyes. 'You tell me.'

Dan bent a little so that he could look at her more closely. 'No, you tell me.'

'Nothing,' Alexa said. 'Your mate, your problem.'

She looked away. Dan waited a moment, and then he said, in a voice that was nothing like as conciliatory as before, 'Lex, what did you say to him?'

★　　★　　★

Gus looked dreadful. He hadn't shaved, and he was wearing a crumpled pair of desert combats with a manky zip-up pullover, and he had no shoes on, only heavy ribbed socks with threadbare heels. His house didn't look much better. He hadn't pulled the sitting room curtains back, and all the sofa cushions were as dented as if someone had slept on them, and there was a slew of food cartons and bottles and cans across the kitchen table. There was even, Dan noticed, a beer can floating in the dog's water bowl. The dog itself, a chocolate-coloured Labrador, was penned in the outside kennel, wearing the pained expression of one who is being punished for something it never entered its head to do.

'Oh, mate,' Dan said, looking in through the

249

sitting room door at the desolation, 'I knew you shouldn't have come back alone.'

Gus looked past him at the sofa. 'Didn't quite make it to bed last night. Meant to. Must have passed out.'

Dan took his arm. 'Come on, now. Come on. Let's sort you. Let's clear up a bit.'

Gus took his arm away. 'You're a champ, Dan. But no. No, thank you. I'll do it myself.'

'Better with two. Quicker.'

'No,' Gus said. 'No. No, thank you.'

'Come on.'

'No!' Gus shouted. He rubbed his hand over his chin. 'No. Sorry. Thank you. My mess, my problem. I'll sort it. I'll shower and shave and sort it.'

Dan turned from the sitting room doorway. 'As you wish, mate.'

'Sorry,' Gus said.

Dan raised a deprecating hand. 'No problem, Gus.'

'I owe you,' Gus said, slightly desperately, 'too much already.'

'No, you bloody don't. Listen. I have a plan.'

'OK.'

'I have a plan,' Dan said, 'to go up to Headley Court. You and me. Alexa's taking the twins up to London to see her parents for a day or two, so I thought we could use the time — ' He broke off. Gus was staring at him. 'What's the matter?'

'Why,' Gus said, 'aren't you going to London?'

'I wasn't asked. There isn't room.'

'Why is she going to London without you?'

Dan took hold of Gus's arm again. 'Man, it's

250

no big deal. She wants to take the twins away.'

'I thought *you* were taking them away!'

Dan let go. He put his hands in his pockets. He said shortly, 'She doesn't want that.'

'Oh, mate.'

'So I have a day or two to kick my heels. OK? You and me to Epsom.'

Gus said sadly, not looking at him, 'I can't.'

'What do you mean, you can't? What else have you got to do?'

Gus leaned against the nearest wall. His eyes were bloodshot, Dan noticed, his breath was awful. He said, averting his gaze, 'Look, I can't come with you, and that's that. I can't explain, but I can't. You'll have to accept it. I'll sort myself out here, you'll see. I'll get a grip.'

Dan moved a little closer. 'Gus?'

Gus made a sudden movement, ducked as if he was avoiding Dan in some way, and bolted into the kitchen. Dan followed him. 'Gus?'

He was leaning against the fridge, the door of which was speckled with tiny black magnetic letters. Above his shoulder Dan could read a message, probably left by one of his sons. 'Welcome Home Dad' it read. 'We are so proud!' The 'proud' was in capital letters.

'Gus, come on. Get yourself decent and we'll go for a beer. Nothing we can't sort that way. You know us!'

Gus rolled himself against the fridge door until his back was turned to Dan and his forehead was resting on the smooth enamelled surface. Then he said, his voice slightly strangled by his position, 'You don't know *me*.'

Alexa had left the house randomly tidy. There was no washing up in the sink, and the beds were made, but there was a scattering of toys here and there, and little heaps of dirty laundry, and trails of crumbs on the kitchen table, and a jar of honey, open, with a knife stuck in it.

None of these things, Dan thought, would signify anything in themselves. None of them indicated anything more than the normal hurly burly of family life with three children and a dog — in equally normal times. But these times were not normal. What had been merely disorientating about coming home had suddenly, like some hideous genie billowing from a lamp, expanded into a horrible and frightening scenario that he had no idea, right now, how to manage. The mild disorder Alexa had left behind assumed, in his present frame of mind, an unpleasant sense of foreboding, as if the crumbs and the knife in the honey were messages of defiance, of — of distance. Add all that to Gus's behaviour and his outright rejection of comradeship, companion-ship, an hour ago, and there seemed little that was reliably comforting at this precise moment except that dear old dog, watching patiently in his basket for Dan to suggest that they might do something — anything — together.

'Give me ten minutes,' Dan said to Beetle.

He went purposefully across the kitchen and switched on the kettle. Then he swept the crumbs off the table into his hand, removed the knife from the honey jar and dropped both into the sink. He picked up a hair slide from the floor, and a small plastic rabbit wearing nothing but a flowered apron, looked at both for a moment and put them down on the table with idiotic reverence. Two pieces of modern expendable trash, but trash that belonged to the twins. His twins. Who were now in the back of their grandfather's car, in the seats that usually lived in the back of *his* car, being driven away from him to London. And he was here, in his military married quarter, on his own.

He made a mug of tea and carried it into the sitting room, Beetle following at a respectful distance. He sat down on the sofa, picked up the remote control, aimed it at the television, and dropped it again. It was awful, being here alone, awful, and he'd been in the house for fifteen minutes. He had the night to get through, and the next two nights, never mind the days, never mind the distraction of a run across to Headley Court. He put his tea down on the carpet by his feet and put his head in his hands.

He'd had a conversation one night, in Helmand, with Mack, after a gruelling day which they had got through by some miracle without anyone losing a limb — or a life. They were exhausted, both of them, and exhilarated, propped against ammunition crates while the stars rose and the temperature dropped in the sudden desert night.

'They're so good,' Dan had said of the men. 'So good. Just making what they need out of what they have.'

There'd been a short silence and then Mack

had said ruefully, 'And they worry that they may have been ruined for normal life.'

It had been an even longer time, Dan remembered, before he could say half-jokingly, emboldened by the strange intimacy and relief of the moment, 'Well, have we been?'

Had he been? He raised his head slowly and looked about him. This room had been made as it was by the efforts of someone else, not him. But *because* of him. 'Because of you,' Isabel had said, over and over. 'You made our lives like this! You sort it.' His brain felt like mush. Where was that clarity and purpose of thinking that had carried him through all the months away, the gorgeous adrenaline rush of blood draining out of the organs and flooding the heart and brain and muscles, until you quite saw how Atlas could hold up the heavens as if they weighed no more than a blanket. Nothing like it. Nothing.

He stood up abruptly, knocking his tea over. Beetle tensed from his waiting and hoping position just inside the door. Dan aimed a violent, pointless kick at his mug and watched it shatter messily in the fireplace.

'Leave it,' he said to Beetle. 'We're going for a walk.'

14

Just being able to walk to the Tube station was exhilarating. Exhilarating but uneasy too, complicated by old feelings of guilt and new ones of disorientation, plus an apprehension that she would shortly wake from this bizarre dream and find herself back in the kitchen at Larkford, with the domestic machine waiting to be kick-started and a shopping list yet again in her head.

The twins, to her astonishment, had agreed to her going out. In fact, disconcertingly, they had agreed with alacrity, and she had left them actually in her parents' bed, in their pyjamas, with their hair brushed, being read to by her father. In the kitchen, her mother had been stacking the dishwasher with plates that had been very nearly entirely cleaned of supper. Her parents were, no doubt about it, glowing with undisguised triumph. Twenty-four hours in London with a few grandparental rules and regulations and hey presto, darling but insufficiently insistent daughter, two good little girls who did not have to be told more than twice not to jump on the sofas, now did they?

'Enjoy yourself, darling,' Elaine said. 'Time off at last. You could do with it.'

She had hardly looked up as she spoke. And the twins had waved only sketchily from their nest of enormous adult pillows. They certainly hadn't cried, or begged her to stay, and when

Dan had rung earlier to say goodnight to them, they had been rather languid and offhand with him, as if a single day of rides in taxis and visits to cafés serving chocolate milk had already ruined them for the dowdy merits of the everyday.

'Are you OK?' Alexa said to Dan, almost out of habit.

'Yeah,' he said, 'I'm fine.'

'What are you doing?'

There was a brief pause and then he said, 'Clearing up. Sorting out. Walking Beetle.'

'He'll love that.'

'And you?'

'I'm — I'm fine, too. We went on the London Eye. They adored it. They were dancing, so happy. And now I'm, well, I'm going to meet Freddie Stanford's girlfriend.'

'Oh?'

'Yes.'

'Why?'

'She asked me,' Alexa said.

'You girls,' Dan said. He was clearly trying to sound indulgent. 'You and your network.'

'Well. Yes.'

'And are you seeing Jack?'

'Not,' Alexa said, 'that I know of.'

Now walking towards Great Portland Street Tube station, she endeavoured to allow the exhilaration of her brief and unaccustomed liberty to overcome the guilt of not being quite straight with Dan. She was indeed going to meet Freddie Stanford's girlfriend, in Freddie Stanford's girlfriend's flat, but Kate Melville would

256

be there too, of course, and it was with Kate that she had made the plan. And although she had not yet made a plan to see Jack, she intended to, and had already left a message for him to say so. Three nights in London. Two complete days. And the second day, as far as the twins were concerned, had already been commandeered by her parents. They were planning to take the girls to the zoo, they said, and although it would be lovely, of course, if she came too, she was not to feel she had to. The licence this conferred was both heady and confusing.

'It's so weird,' she planned to say to Jack, 'to be given freedom and not know what to do with it.' And he would reply, reassuringly, she was sure, 'You, Mrs R, are just thoroughly out of practice!'

Mel Cooper, Freddie Stanford's girlfriend, had said take any old train going east to King's Cross, then take the Piccadilly Line south to Holborn, and it's ten minutes' walk to my dad's flat. Mel's father, a barrister and a member of Gray's Inn, had taken a job in Hong Kong for three years — very lucrative, his daughter said — and left his flat, in an undistinguished postwar building off Theobald's Road, for Mel to use in his absence. It was there, in the second bedroom occupied by not much more than a bed and Mel's father's antiquated exercise bike, that Kate Melville was now living, she said that morning on the phone to Alexa, while she looked for a flat for herself and the boys.

'Won't they stay where they are?' Alexa said tentatively, hardly liking even to consider the question, let alone ask it. 'At school, I mean?'

'No,' Kate said. She sounded rather more like her old self, practical and decided. 'No, with knobs on. If I'm the one who leaves and the Army goes on paying the fees, then the children, in their eyes, belong to Gus. I'm not having that. I'm not stopping him seeing them, but he can't be the main carer. He never has been and he can't start now.'

Alexa had pursued the conversation no further then, standing wedged between the bed and the window in her parents' spare bedroom. They'd all three slept in that bed the night before, and however unsettled it had been, however often she had been woken by the twins' apparent need to sleep horizontally across the bed with their feet in her face, it had been, strangely, a relief. When she opened her eyes at intervals and saw the coppery night-time glow of London round the edges of the curtains, rather than the blank black darkness of Wiltshire, she had felt nothing but a sense of a burden being lifted.

She felt the same now, walking up Procter Street and Drake Street towards Theobald's Road. If she could set aside her feelings about Dan and somehow manage to banish, just for a few hours, the toothache of anxiety about Isabel, she could, perhaps, be for this evening the person she really was, under all the onion layers of relativity in her life. She would, she thought, stop somewhere and buy wine and flowers. Eight o'clock at night, and there were places still open all around her, selling wine and flowers. Life, she thought, needn't stop just because darkness had fallen. Any kind of darkness, in fact.

Mel Cooper was as tall as Alexa, with modishly lavish hair falling glossily over her shoulders. She was wearing knee boots and a brief knitted dress, and Kate, already holding a glass of wine when Alexa arrived, was not in her usual uniform of a purposeful dark skirt suit, but instead in leggings and a tunic, with her hair skewered on top of her head with a couple of scarlet slides. It was, Alexa thought, shedding her coat, handing over the roses and the bottle, like stepping into a women's-magazine prototype of girl bonding: soft lights, some kind of gentle folk rock playing, a big sofa, wine glasses, a fat candle burning in a miniature bucket. It wasn't at all like evenings in Larkford, even in Franny's kitchen or Mo's sitting room, however welcoming both might be. In their case, the women were all together because being together was dictated by an absence. In their conversations, however supportive or confiding they were, the men who were not there but whose occupations caused their women and children to be there pervaded the gatherings like shadows, present even if never or scarcely mentioned. Here, in this undistinguished and functional urban flat, any indication that it belonged to an absent man was obliterated by the life of the current occupant. She lived here in her own right, and by that same right had invited her boyfriend's senior officer's estranged wife to stay for a few weeks. The military hierarchy inherent in the whole thing plainly meant nothing to her, Alexa was to discover, any more than Freddie's devotion to his troop did. She came forward, smiling a wide and confident smile, took Alexa's coat from her, said, 'Hi, I'm Mel,' and managed, by the very way she moved, to indicate that there would be no codes of conduct here, merely an undemanding and satisfying female evening together.

'Wow,' Alexa said admiringly, looking at her.

Mel laughed. From the sofa, from which she had not risen to greet Alexa, Kate said, 'I told you Freddie had great taste.'

Alexa looked around her. 'This is so nice.'

'My father,' Mel said, 'has no eye for anything beyond books and music. He wouldn't even notice if I painted the whole place pink. All the same, I've restricted myself to just this room.'

'Some pink.'

'Freddie hates it.'

'It doesn't exactly seem to stop him coming!' Kate said from the sofa.

She had her shoes off, Alexa noticed, and her feet were bare, the toenails painted almost black. Alexa said to her uncertainly, 'You look great.'

Kate patted the sofa cushion beside her. 'Come and sit down. I'm sorry I was so awful the — '

Alexa made a hurried, dismissive gesture, cutting her off. 'You weren't.'

'I was. I was wild with rage and I had no business taking it out on you.'

'Here,' Mel said. She was holding out a glass of wine to Alexa. Alexa took it and sat down, not entirely relaxedly, next to Kate's gothic toenails.

'Where do we start?' she said.

'I was saying sorry,' Kate said.

'I didn't mean that,' Alexa said. 'I suppose I'm still adjusting, rather — '

'To being out of there?'

'You make it sound like a prison.'

'Well,' Mel said easily, folding herself up into an armchair, 'it's not a prison exactly, but it's certainly different.'

Alexa edged back against the sofa cushions. She said, 'I don't think I've ever seen you at Larkford.'

Mel ran a hand through her hair and let it fall across her face again. 'No. You wouldn't have. Freddie adores it, of course, but it's not for me. Not in *any* way.' She paused, and laughed, and then she said, 'So not,' and took a swallow of wine.

Alexa said, 'Then how did you meet Kate?'

'Here,' Kate said. 'In London.'

'London?'

'Work,' Mel said. 'I went to talk to her charity.'

'You — '

'I work in psychiatry,' Mel said. 'At the education and training centre of the Royal College. We go and talk to people about our training courses. I went to talk to Kate.'

Alexa glanced at Kate. Kate was looking at Mel.

Kate said casually, 'She was great.' She stretched herself on the sofa in a way Alexa had never seen her do before, easy and deliberate. 'We had coffee afterwards,' she said, 'and the soldier stuff just came out, didn't it?'

'My friends can't believe it,' Mel said. 'Me,

dating a soldier! I met him at a wedding. A complete classic, meeting a man at someone else's wedding. I said, at first, no way, soldier boy, but then he turns out to be really bright and really well-read, in fact, he'd be pretty perfect if he wasn't obsessed with this Army thing.'

Kate looked at Alexa. She said, smiling, 'Would you like to say, what a surprise?'

Alexa didn't look back. Instead, she said to Mel, in a voice she knew betrayed her eagerness, 'So what will you do about it, this Army thing?'

Mel tossed her hair back again. 'Nothing.'

'Nothing?'

'He can go and play soldiers. I'm staying here. I had a look at that camp and I thought, no *way*, Melanie, no *way* are you going to live like that. We had dinner with some of them,' — she looked at Kate — 'you know, Colonel Macsomebody.'

'Mackenzie.'

'And they were sweet and lovely, but it was, like, out of the Ark, and everyone was talking in this weird language, and all the wives kind of knowing their place, all in order of rank and stuff, I mean *archaic*. I said to Fred afterwards, if we have a future, babes, it'll be in London, or at least somewhere I can work. I didn't get a degree to moulder on Salisbury Plain being a Stepford wife who's thrilled when some high-up notices her. I mean, no *thank* you.'

Kate said comfortably to Alexa, 'D'you want to hit her?'

Alexa said nothing.

Mel smiled at her. 'Kate says you're brilliant at it.'

'Only,' Alexa said, unable to keep a flash of temper out of her voice, 'because she's feeling guilty — '

'I am not!'

'Well, then,' Alexa said, 'show a little decent remorse.'

'About what?'

Alexa looked at her glass. 'About what you left behind.'

Kate sighed, and pushed herself a little more upright. 'OK, then,' she said. 'How's Gus?'

Alexa went on looking at her glass. She said, deliberately unhelpful, 'How do you think?'

There was a pause. Mel quietly sat more upright too. Kate said, less comfortably, 'I can't be his mother, you know.'

'There's a difference,' Alexa said sharply, 'between loyalty and mothering.'

'I *have* been loyal,' Kate said. 'There isn't another man. That was just a couple of dinners.'

'Gus doesn't think so. He thinks it was much more. You haven't bothered to give him the peace of mind of knowing that much at least, have you?'

Kate looked at Mel. She said sardonically, 'I told you, didn't I? The perfect Army wife.'

Mel didn't reply. She leaned forward and said to Alexa, 'You took him in, didn't you?'

Alexa nodded. Mel said to Kate, 'When you dump someone, you leave a lot of work for other people to do, you know.'

Kate bent forward suddenly, her forehead almost touching her knees. Alexa said, bending too, to see her, 'Are you all right?'

263

Kate brought her free hand to her eyes. Her shoulders were shaking slightly.

Mel got out of her chair and came across to the two of them. She said to Kate, 'Was it just the Army?'

Kate said to her knees, 'He's mad about it. It's his whole life.'

'He's mad about *you*,' Alexa said.

'Then why take me for granted?' Kate cried. She sat up abruptly and swung to look at Alexa. 'And before you tell me he didn't, he *did*. Just as Dan takes you. What they do is paramount. The country loves them for it, the media praises them for it, they're in a win-win situation just by being in uniform with a dirty, dangerous job to do. But what about *us*? This isn't the fucking nineteenth century! We're educated women with a contribution to make and the Army just doesn't care how many of us it . . . *wastes*.'

Alexa waited for a moment and then she said to Mel, 'What'll you do about that?'

'About what?'

'About what the Army wants of you if you stick with Freddie.'

Mel crouched down so that her face was on the same level. 'Freddie won't *be* like that.'

'He will. He will, he's a soldier.'

'No,' Mel said, 'they're not like that now. Of course, there are some who find girls prepared to behave like their mothers. But most of them, if they want a girl with her own life, they're going to have to accept that we might marry them, but we're not marrying the Army. And on the whole they do. If I said to Fred that I'd changed my mind and wanted to live on the patch and have a Labrador puppy for Christmas, he'd think I'd gone mental.'

Kate gave Alexa's arm a clumsy pat. 'Sorry.'

'Stop that. Don't.'

'And thank you for looking after Gus.'

'Don't do that either.'

'I have to, you've been wonderful, you've been a life-saver. I expect he'd have been hospitalized or something, if you hadn't taken him in — '

'Stop it!' Alexa shouted. They both looked at her. She put her glass on the floor and then both hands over her face. From behind them she said, 'He's gone home. In an awful state. We had . . . had a kind of *scene*, him and me. He tried to kiss me, and I yelled at him. Dan doesn't know.'

'What?' Kate said.

Alexa took her hands away. Mel was standing again now.

'*What?*' Kate said again.

'He was lucky I didn't slap him.'

'He tried to *kiss* you?'

Alexa sighed. 'Only because he's missing you. It was nothing to do with me being me. I was just a female mouth in his line of vision.'

'Oh my God,' Kate said, flinging herself back against the cushions. 'I don't know what to think — '

Mel said unexpectedly, 'This isn't about you.'

Kate stared at her.

'It's men,' Mel said. 'It's soldiers. It's all this soldier stuff that messes with their heads.' She looked at Alexa. 'You OK?'

Alexa nodded tiredly. She got slowly to her

feet. 'I think I'll go.' She glanced at Kate and said, 'I needn't have told you.'

'Why did you?'

'To show you what a state he's in. I might understand why you've gone, but *you've* got to understand what *you've* done. Not just to Gus, but to us. And don't say sorry again. Just do something. Do something about Gus.'

Mel went across the room and retrieved Alexa's coat. She said, holding it out for her to put on, 'Fred thinks the world of your guy.' She smiled at Alexa. 'Come and see me at work. I'll show you what we do.'

Alexa pulled her coat up round her shoulders. She glanced at Kate, now huddled up on the sofa, knees bent under her chin, holding her bare feet. 'I get it, you know,' she said to her. 'I really do. It's . . . it's just that you have another life to go to, and at the moment I don't seem to have. I've let it slip away, somehow. I've . . . ' She paused and then she said to Mel, 'Lovely meeting you. And — and, good luck. All I'd say about marrying into the Army is that you actually have to live it to know it. But if you and your generation can change the smallest thing, I'll be the first one cheering. I just doubt you can, I really, sadly do.'

Mel smiled at her again. She flicked her hair. 'All the same,' she said, 'come and see me. OK?'

★ ★ ★

When Alexa rang to say that she would like to come down to Wimbledon, Eric Riley sent

266

George out to buy flowers. She would not be bringing the twins, she said, because they already had a date to be taken to the zoo, and she hoped that wasn't very disappointing. Eric, grasping the receiver and raising his voice as if it needed to carry all across London to be heard properly, said she'd be more than welcome and not to worry about the children this time. 'Not much to offer them here, any road,' he'd shouted. 'Two old men and a brew. Better off with the lions and tigers. Dan loved the zoo when he was a nipper.'

George returned with a bunch of pink Peruvian lilies and box of cupcakes. Eric looked at them both dubiously. 'You sure?'

'No,' George said. 'It was the lady in the shop who said.'

'You'd get talked into buying anything. No bloody mind of your own.'

They put the lilies in a jug and the cupcakes on a plate that had belonged to Eileen, edged in gold and patterned with violets. Both looked incongruous in Eric's sitting room.

'Doesn't look right.'

'She won't care.'

'*She* won't care, but I bloody do. First visit in years and we can't get it even half right.'

'Perhaps I should have bought champagne.'

'*Champagne*? At bloody *coffee* time?'

'I dunno.'

'No,' Eric said, 'you never do. You never bloody do.'

Alexa arrived wearing a tidy mackintosh borrowed from her mother and carrying an elaborate umbrella from the same source, which she left to dry on the communal landing outside Eric's front door. Eric, afraid it would be nicked, made a fuss about bringing it in and wedging it across his bath under a homemade washing line he did not wish Alexa to see, on which his socks were drying in lugubrious pairs. It was a full ten minutes before the three of them were settled in the sitting room, Alexa next to the Peruvian lilies, and looking, they both observed, weary and distracted. Peaky, Eric said out loud. Alexa had tried to laugh and pushed her hands through her hair and said that sharing a bed with two three-year-olds who were never still wasn't exactly conducive to a good night's sleep.

George made tea for his father, and coffee for himself and Alexa. He used his mother's best teacups, put the milk in a jug and then everything on to a tin tray with a picture of Windsor Castle on it. He was hoping that Eric would let the conversation develop a little and that all of them could settle to being together again for a while, before he made their announcement, but he should have known better. Over sixty years of intermittent life with his father should have taught him that if Eric had something on his mind, something he needed to say, he was unstoppable in saying it.

'Good heart,' George's mother always said of him. 'Can't fault him for heart. But he's got the tact of a bull in a china shop.'

Eric had hardly waited until Alexa's coffee cup was in her hands. He had taken a fortifying gulp of his own tea and then leaned slightly forward, elbows out and hands on his knees, and said that

268

he and George had come to a decision. George attempted to slow him down, to suggest that a few questions about Dan and the children might be in order first, but Eric had raised a hand to flap him aside as if he was an irritating insect, and had proceeded to talk a little louder and a little faster, almost closing his eyes, the better to focus on saying what he was determined to say.

The thing was, Eric said, they could see that it wasn't too easy at the moment. None of it. For any of them. Problems all round, as far as he could see, and now Dan wanted promotion and that'd mean a whole new fandangle of moves and courses and whatnot. So he'd put his thinking cap on. And so had George, in so far as he was any bloody use for thinking, and it seemed to them that what Alexa and the children needed was a *home*, not another godawful quarter that'd be inspected for kicked paint and cracked windows, but a proper home, a house that belonged to them where no one could tell them what bloody colour to paint the walls.

But there was a difficulty. Eric knew that. It was the difficulty that had beset every bloody soldier since the dawn of time. Money. Soldiers were always in debt. Always had been. And it was worse for officers, of course, what with their champagne lifestyles on beer money, keeping up appearances, all that bloody nonsense. He suspected Dan and Alexa had no savings. He didn't know a soldier *with* savings, but — and it was a big but — he and George were exceptions. In the last ten years, they'd saved a bit, both of them, because — not to put too fine a point on it

— of having nothing much to spend it on. They'd always thought they'd go on saving and when they popped their clogs they'd leave whatever they'd saved to Dan and Alexa and the children.

'But,' Eric said, grasping his knees and turning his bright-blue gaze directly on Alexa, 'we've decided that you'd have more use for the money now, that you need the money right now, to help buy a house with, doesn't matter where, so you and the kids, at least, have some stability whatever happens to Dan. So that's what we're offering, that's what we want to do. We're going to give you the money for a deposit on a house.'

He sat back then, jubilant, the offer out there, fair and square. He looked at George and winked. He looked at Alexa. He was beaming. 'Well?' he said.

She hadn't touched her coffee while he was talking. She didn't touch it now. Instead she reached out unsteadily to put it down next to the lilies, and the cup rattled in the saucer. And then, without warning and horrifying both of them, she burst into tears.

★　★　★

Jack Dearlove had bought himself a beer and Alexa a glass of white wine. He'd found a good, quiet table at the back of the bar, even with armchairs, and not on the route to the toilets. He thought he might drink his beer quite fast and get another in before Alexa got there, not because he needed to brace himself after the way

270

she'd sounded on the phone, but more because he thought they might be in for what he privately termed a Long and Deep, and he wanted to be able to concentrate on her and not on how much he would like to be able to get up and fetch a second beer.

After all, he hadn't seen her since that unsuccessful visit to Isabel's school. They hadn't even telephoned each other much, partly out of tact on his part, with Dan being home, and partly, if he was honest, because he had been working very hard and also because he had met someone. As tall as Eka, as thin as Eka, but not, mercifully, as commercially valuable as Eka and thus more available. Maia's availability was something Jack was trying to work on with all the restraint he could muster.

When Alexa walked in, wearing some depressing middle-aged raincoat thing, Jack was rather shocked. She didn't just look tired, she looked kind of defeated, beaten. And even he could see that her hair needed attention. The whole bar was full of terrific hair, amazing hair (Maia, unlike Eka, had fantastic long straight hair), but Alexa's just looked dingy.

'I am very, very pleased to see you,' Jack said. 'But I have to say that you don't look too hot. Lukewarm to off-cold, I'd say. And can I ask what you're wearing?'

'It's my mother's,' Alexa said, pulling it off. 'I don't have a raincoat. And it was raining.'

'Ah,' Jack said. 'I got you wine.'

'Thank you.'

'Drink it quite fast and I'll get you another.'

Alexa sat down in one of the armchairs. She picked up her wineglass, put it down again, untouched, and said, 'I don't know what to do.'

'Come again?' Jack said.

'You can't imagine.'

'Try me. Actually, let me finish this and get in another and then try me.'

'I'm so pleased to see you.'

'No crying, Lex. Do not cry. I do not *do* women crying, unless it's after sex and they're so grateful.'

'I'm not — '

'Well, sniff and *stop*. Go to the loo or something while I get my beer.'

Alexa said, out of the blue, 'Eric and George offered me the deposit on a house today.'

Jack sat down abruptly in the chair next to hers. 'Bloody hell.'

'I know.'

'What did you say?'

'I howled my eyes out and said they were completely wonderful but I didn't know if I could accept it, and they said why not? and I said things were so bad and we simply weren't communicating and I was at my wits' end, and Eric said was I going to leave him? and I said I didn't know, I didn't know, I didn't know *anything* and then I rushed out and forgot Mum's umbrella and it was all awful.' She paused and then she said, 'And they'd bought cupcakes.'

'Don't cry again. You can't cry over cupcakes.'

Alexa said sadly, 'They are such lovely men.'

Jack took a gulp of beer. Then he said, 'You

must have terrified them.'

'I think I did — '

'Have you rung them since?'

'No, I — '

'Alexa,' Jack said with emphasis. '*Alexa.*' He leaned forward and peered into her face. 'Where's the girl I knew?'

'I've lost her.'

'Don't be so self-pitying. Don't be so fucking sorry for yourself.'

Alexa stared at him. 'Jack!'

'Well, I mean it,' he said. He could feel his face reddening. He could feel something close to rage beginning to boil up inside him. He leaned closer, close enough to speak to her with vehemence without causing drinkers at nearby tables to turn round and stare.

'Well, Mrs Riley,' Jack said, 'you have to decide what love is, really, don't you? I mean, is it about loving Dan and wanting him to have whatever he seems to need to make him feel whole, or is it about being loved yourself? And if it's the latter, and only, honestly, the latter, what makes you need to put that first?'

Alexa had pulled back a little. When he finished speaking, she said in a much more decided voice, 'And why just me? Why doesn't everything you've just said apply to Dan?'

'That's better.'

'But why?'

'It does apply. It just manifests itself differently. I expect the poor bugger'd like to slit his wrists right now.'

'Jack,' Alexa said, 'what is all this about?'

Jack inspected his beer bottle. There was about half an inch left. 'Decisions. Decisions. You want a house? OK, you go for it. You want a job, you find one. You want Isabel out of that school, take her. You want Dan to be happy, stop wanting him to behave like some bloody metrosexual touchy-feely New Man fantasy. You like him being a soldier. You think being a soldier is sexy. You think Dan is sexy for being a soldier. No,' he said, holding up a hand and getting to his feet. 'No. You are not saying another word. I'm sick of them. I'm sick of all this whiny, going-round-and-round-the-bloody-houses, girly thinking-aloud claptrap. I am going to the bar to get another drink. You are going to drink your wine and ring those poor Rileys and say sorry for behaving like a lunatic, and when I come back — no, no, don't speak, don't utter — I want to do the talking. I'm going to talk and you are going to listen. I've got something to tell you. And she's called Maia.'

274

15

Stephanie Marshall, junior physiotherapist at the Defence Medical Rehabilitation Centre at Headley Court, not far from Epsom Racecourse, was crossing the staff car park on her way to her own car when she saw him. He was obviously services, being in khaki trousers and an epauletted ribbed sweater, but he was sitting under a tree on the ground and he didn't seem to have a coat, and it was, after all, late November, and although it was quite a nice day, it wasn't the right kind of day or weather for sitting outside and on the ground.

Stephanie had joined Headley Court when the new rehabilitation wing had opened. Eight million, it had cost, but it had this fantastic twenty-five-metre hydrotherapy pool, with a floor you could raise and lower, and generally amazing facilities. And the guys were amazing, too. And the girls. It was a girl she had been working with that afternoon, Captain Patsy Philp, twenty-five years old and a double amputee with only one leg and one hand. There'd been two physios with her, one on each side, getting her walking for a news team who'd come down from London with television cameras. The reporters had watched her for a while and then they'd asked her how she felt. She feels like shit, Stephanie wanted to say, it's harder than you can possibly imagine, you stupid boys, thinking you're doing your bit by just wearing Help the Heroes T-shirts, but Patsy had managed a smile and had said, with no evident show of emotion, 'It's tricky. It'll take more than a couple of weeks before I'm running upstairs again.'

Stephanie had wanted to hit the TV crew. It made you like that, working here. It made you so proud and defensive of the people you were treating, and if you weren't careful so contemptuous of all the civvy people just waltzing about taking their arms and legs for granted. There'd been no service people in her family, none at all, until her brother got this bee in his bonnet about joining the RAF, and now here he was at Headley Court, working in the prosthetics workshop, and because of him, she was here too, and it had changed her life, it really had. It had completely changed her way of thinking.

Which was why she wasn't just going to ignore that bloke sitting on the ground under a tree. She'd seen enough, now, to know that not all the wounds were visible. They'd got people in now who couldn't remember anything or decide anything, bleeds to the brain, you name it. She'd swung her car keys in her hand so that their jingle would alert him to her approach and went towards him, and when she was only a yard or so from him, he jerked up and on to his feet as if he'd been almost asleep or something and was reacting to a trained instinct.

'It's OK,' Stephanie said. She was glad her coat was open, showing him her white medical

276

tunic underneath. 'I just wanted to make sure you were all right.'

He was a good-looking bloke, tall, fortyish probably. He wasn't wearing a rank slide or anything, but he'd be an officer of some kind, Stephanie reckoned — major, probably. He seemed a bit dazed.

She said again, 'It's OK. It's just that we're used to people needing a bit of help, here. I was making sure you didn't. That's all.'

He smiled at her at last. He seemed to be focussing a bit better. He said, 'Thanks. Thanks a lot. I was just — digesting what I'd seen in there. That's all.'

'In their own words,' Stephanie said, 'they're awesome.'

He said, 'That's what they say about all of you.'

She made a deprecating gesture. She said, 'Well, if you're OK — '

'I am. Thank you. I am.'

'D'you have friends in there?'

'Two of my men. Or, at least, men I know.'

'They're lucky to be in there.'

'Don't I know it.'

She took a step back. She made a little rattling farewell gesture with her car keys. 'I'll let you get on, then.'

'Thank you.'

She smiled up at him. 'Take care,' she said.

★ ★ ★

George had done something he hadn't done in years. He'd bought a bottle of whisky — it had some pantomime Scottish name but Lord knows, at that price, what it was made from, or where. He'd taken it home, and was sitting in his only and hardly comfortable armchair with his shoes off and the television tuned to a channel he would have died rather than admit to watching, drinking steadily.

He wasn't, at least, drinking straight out of the bottle. He had fetched a glass from the cupboard in his bleakly orderly kitchenette, a thick, cheap tumbler that had come free with something or other — the equally cheap microwave probably — and had poured the first slug out of the bottle and added a measure of water. Then it became too much of a bother to get up and walk six paces to the tap for more water, so he just sloshed the whisky into the tumbler undiluted, and stared at the pitiful, evidently cheaply made daytime quiz show in front of him, and tried to fight off the memories that always engulfed him when he let himself go like this, of that occasion in 1982, at Goose Green in the Falklands, when he'd spent a whole night alone with the body of a gunner, waiting — no doubt about it, either then or ever since — to die himself, not least because it seemed to him that it was the last word in disloyalty and cowardice still to be alive when his mate wasn't. The memories were never conscious things. He never deliberately summoned them up. But when emotional upset or alcohol — or, most fatally, a combination of the two — weakened his defence against recollection, he was back on that cold and stony hillside with his heart breaking, and the sight of little

278

white Argentinian flags of surrender popping up in the dawn light as if — as a last straw — to mock the utterly pointless waste and sacrifice of the boy who lay now across the gun trails at his feet, as lifeless as the ground on which he had fallen. They were demons, those memories, lying in wait for him, goading him to let down his guard by getting in a state and then, heedlessly, stupidly, fatally, throwing a tenner away on a bottle of gut rot. He despised himself, utterly and thoroughly, for giving in to them.

He'd have stayed with Eric, if Eric had let him. After Alexa had gone, he thought his father might work himself into one of his rages, purple-faced and almost foaming with incoherent fury, but he had realized quite soon and with horror that Eric was almost in tears. His face was working and he was fumbling in his pocket for one of the huge old khaki handkerchiefs he still favoured. George had tried to put an arm round him, but Eric had flung him off and had then shuffled to the front door of the flat, knocking over the plate of cupcakes as he went, pulled it open, and made jerky, urgent gestures with his arm to indicate that George should leave him.

George said idiotically, 'What about the umbrella?' and Eric had roared something incomprehensible, and had seized his son's arm in a still-strong grip and had almost flung him out on to the communal landing.

Crashing into the banisters of the stairwell, George had said, 'But Dad, will you be OK? Will you — ' but the door had slammed behind him, and when he rang the bell repeatedly for re-admittance, Eric hadn't even shouted at him to leave off, he'd simply said through the letter box, his voice unsteady with distress, 'Just bloody leave me, lad, would you?'

So George had left him and gone to see Uncle Ray, in the Gap Road Cemetery, who had had nothing to offer by way of explanation or consolation, and from there he'd gone to the pub for a whisky, and then to the supermarket for a bottle of their Spirits Offer of the Week, and here he was, shoes off, curtains pulled, sozzled and out of his stupid, nightmare-haunted mind by early afternoon on a perfectly ordinary Thursday. He aimed the remote control at the television and switched it off. The ensuing silence was terrible. He thought he might be about to weep too. He detested weeping. He picked up his glass and the smell of the whisky rose up and hit him with a nauseating force and he felt the lump in his throat rise up as well, through his whole skull, and then spill, hot and molten, out through his eyes and down his cheeks.

It was a moment or two before George realized that the telephone was ringing. He got up unsteadily. It would be the old man, calling to say he had a new idea, he wasn't giving up, he wanted George round there at once because he had cooked up a new scheme George was going to have to implement.

'Dad,' he said wearily into the phone.

'George?' someone else said.

He hesitated. His tongue seemed to have swollen so that it almost filled his mouth. 'Who . . . who . . . ?'

'Are you OK?' the voice said. 'Is that George?'
'Yes.'

'Good,' the voice said. 'Good. Sorry if I woke you, or anything. I'm a friend of your daughter-in-law. I'm a friend of Alexa's. My name's Jack Dearlove.'

★ ★ ★

On the way home, Dan stopped to buy coffee and a sandwich he then didn't feel like eating. He filled the car with petrol while he was at it, and checked the tyres and screenwash, then he drove the car to the side of the garage forecourt, where he sat with the paper cup of coffee in his hand and the untouched sandwich (ham and mustard) on the passenger seat beside him.

'Come on, sir,' Tommy Stanway had said, leaning forward, grinning. 'It's not the end of the world, honest. At least now, when I'm out drinking my legs stay sober!'

Tommy Stanway was twenty-six. He was a double amputee, both legs having been blown off by a booby-trap bomb in Helmand. When Dan had reached him, three hours before, he had turned one of his artificial legs upside down, with its boot in the air, and was using the sole of the boot to balance a mug of tea on. He was grinning.

'I've got a good mentality, sir. Gunner mentality. There's some Paras and Marines in here, and I'll show them, I will. Me and Micky Munt, we'll show them.' He made a half gesture, as if he had been about to give Dan a consoling pat and thought better of it. 'I've got football field ambitions,' he said. 'Remember? I was playing the night before — well, before life took a different path. I'll get back out there, you watch me. I may be four inches shorter than I used to be, but I'll be a hell of a goalie.'

Micky Munt, missing a foot and a right arm and an eye, had told Dan that he thought he'd recently met the right girl. She was a soldier, too.

'Women don't seem to care about the way folk look, like blokes do. And she's never known me with two of everything, has she? I'm good, sir. I'm fine. The only thing that gets me is that I feel I've let the boys down, coming home early like this. And the dreams, of course.'

'The dreams?'

The young men had exchanged glances. Dan noticed that Micky Munt's remaining hand had an uncontrollable tremor.

'Crazy dreams,' Tommy said.

'Legs and arms growing everywhere — '

'Mad stuff. Just popping out of your body like something out of outer space.'

'Relief to wake up, to be honest.'

They both laughed.

'Will there be more operations?' Dan said.

'Lots, sir.'

'We've got to keep the weight off — '

'That's a bloody battle.'

'Can't let the stumps get sweaty or you get sores, and the prosthetics are frigging painful — '

'Get so hot, sir. You do, if you haven't got half of you. I get hot just thinking about it.'

Then they changed the subject and would not

return to it. How was old so-and-so? And X troop, and Y troop? Which troop had the most medals? Why wasn't Dan on Facebook? Why didn't he go on the Army Rumour Service website — they lived on it! They missed everyone and would come and personally duff up anyone in the regiment who wasn't missing them back. They'd be sure to. Couldn't tell what the future'd be yet, but they sure as hell had one. Tommy said he was thinking of teaching and Micky said what a bleeding pansy suggestion and hit Tommy lightly on his good arm, and Tommy said you watch it, you wait till I swing round your place in a specially adapted Porsche and see how pansy you feel like calling me then. You wanker.

'Don't worry,' they both said to Dan. 'We're used to it. Shit happens, sir.'

'What do you need?' Dan said. 'What can I get you? Smart phones?'

They tapped their pockets. 'Got them, sir. We need, we ask. Don't worry.'

Dan had stood up, towering over both of them. Tommy Stanway had once stood more than six feet in his socks. They grinned up at him. 'Thanks for coming, sir.'

'Please — '

'You should see us play volleyball, sir. We sit on our arses and chuck ourselves everywhere. It's a riot.'

Micky Munt had put his one hand out to Dan and said solicitously, 'You take care, sir,'

Dan finished his coffee. It had been unsatisfactory, thin and bitter and carelessly made. He crushed the paper cup in his hand, picked up the sandwich and got out of the car to drop both in a crooked overflowing litter bin bolted to the peeling wall of the forecourt. Then he got back in the car, switched on the ignition and drove out of the garage as fast as if he were being pursued.

There was nowhere, right now, to offload the excess energy of his emotions. He remembered an old soldier saying once, in an explosion of frustration after a complicated episode in his private life, 'I just want to go overseas, under orders and — and *kill* someone.' Dan wasn't sure about random killing, but oh, would he, at this precise moment, have welcomed the orders! If he were to get back to Larkford and find an email instructing him to report for immediate deployment on any mission, however insane, he would obey it with a fervour he had no measure for. As it was, he was confronted with getting back to a house that would have done nothing for itself since he left it — bed roughly made, coffee pot in the sink, sitting room untouched since the television-and-takeaway session of the night before — and a dog longing for company and exercise. There might — or might *not* — be a message from Alexa. There'd been nothing that day from her to his mobile. He wasn't actually sure whether he wanted to hear from her or whether this peculiar limbo land in which they currently seemed to be existing was preferable to the next stage, where decisions would have to be made and action taken. He beat the steering wheel with the flat of his left hand. She should have been with him today, she should have! If she'd seen those boys, seen their irrepressible cheerfulness and determination in the face of their injuries and disabilities, she'd get all her and Dan's stuff into perspective, she'd see the difference between the mountains and the molehills, he knew she would, he knew it. He'd tell her about going out of the place in a daze and finding himself sitting under a tree, hardly knowing how he'd got there, and she'd understand. Of course she would. He'd tell her what faith the boys had in the Army, how they knew the regiment would always look after them, and she'd look at him as she used to do when they first met, when she spoke of what he did, what his colleagues did, almost with reverence. Of course she'd get it!

Except equally, of course, she wouldn't. Not now. She knew all the downs as well as the ups, the minuses almost better than the pluses. She knew that the camaraderie and the determination could be as divisive to those outside the charmed circle as they were uniting to those within it. He put his hand up briefly across his eyes. He didn't think he'd ever let anyone see him cry and he wasn't about to start. In any case, tears were in no way an appropriate response for what he'd seen and heard. The response Dan would at that moment have liked to be able to indulge in was to be ordered straight back to Afghanistan to find whoever laid the booby-trap bomb that had blown Tommy Stanway's legs off, and skewer him to a mud wall with a bayonet.

He turned off the main road and swung the car up the lane that led to Larkford. It was getting dark. Beetle had been shut up in the house for the best part of six hours and would have his legs crossed, poor old fellow. The lane was empty, except for a solitary smallish figure in a hooded fleece some way ahead, carrying a bag over one shoulder and walking with purpose. As Dan came up behind the person, it dawned on him that there was something familiar about their shape and gait, and the bag with its jingling charms. As he drew level, he slowed the car and pressed the button to lower the window on the passenger side. It couldn't be — could it?

Dan leaned across. 'Isabel?' he said incredulously.

She turned her face a little, sliding it into her blue fleece hood. 'Hello,' she said.

'What are you doing here?'

'Walking,' Isabel said patiently.

Dan opened the door to let her in. 'Hop in. I'm on my way home.'

Isabel didn't move. 'No, thank you.'

'But — '

'I'm not going home,' Isabel said. She sounded unemotional, as if she was explaining something very ordinary to someone she hardly knew.

'Not — '

'No,' Isabel said. She began to walk again, not hurrying, but decidedly. Over her shoulder, she called, 'I'm going to Franny's! Rupert said I could!'

And then she began to run.

Mel Cooper's office was at the far end of a long institutional corridor, and barely bigger than a cupboard. It was late afternoon when Alexa arrived, and Mel was spearing cubes of mango out of a plastic box with a small disposable fork, and talking on the telephone. She waved her fork at Alexa and smiled, and indicated a chair just behind her, upholstered in grey vinyl.

'No chance, babes,' she was saying into the phone. 'Flat out all week, work presentation dinner Friday, can't miss. You're the one on leave. You come to me.'

Then she listened for a moment or two, put another cube of mango in her mouth and said amiably round it, 'Work it out, babes. Text me when you've decided.' Then she laughed and said, 'No. Never. I never miss you,' and clicked her phone off and dropped it into the slew of papers on her desk. Then she spun her chair round, her knees almost knocking into Alexa, and said, 'You came!'

Alexa nodded. 'I did.'

'Where are the kids?'

Alexa hesitated for a second, and then she said, 'With my parents. I can't be long.'

Mel swung back to her desk. 'Then come and look at this,' she said, touching her keyboard. 'Pull up your chair.'

'What?'

'Look,' Mel said. 'Look.' She was staring at her screen. 'I'm all fired up. We're starting a new survey. Look at that. Well, I knew dopamine was a neurotransmitter — '

'I didn't.'

' — but I didn't know it so imitated the effect of cocaine on the brain. Did you? And it's stronger in men. It's released when you solve a problem or win a game, so that might account for men getting obsessive about gambling or computer games.'

'Or war,' Alexa said.

Mel turned to glance at her. 'Or war,' she repeated. 'It's hard to live with someone always seeking a dopamine high, the big kick of endorphins. That's our study. That's my new project. Finding or even training the right people. We're embarking on a study of service kids having to live with traumatized fathers.'

Alexa said, as lightly as she could, 'Not before time.'

'Certainly not.'

'And maybe,' Alexa said, 'it'll help the wives too.'

Mel made a small dismissive gesture with the hand not guiding her computer mouse. 'They have the language,' she said. 'It's tough for them, but they do have a degree of power. The kids have no power, not much language and have to put up with the consequences of everyone else's choices. So I'm starting with the dopamine.'

'Why did you ask me to come?'

Mel looked at her screen. 'Why d'you think?'

'I don't know. It wasn't a very successful evening, with Kate . . . '

'Some things that needed saying got said.'

'But — '

'And,' Mel said, 'Kate said you were a good couple, you and your husband. If Freddie and I are serious . . . '

'Are you?'

'He's as good as they get,' Mel said.

'But?'

'I want to work.'

'And *I*,' Alexa said with emphasis, 'want to work.'

'Well, why don't you?'

'I can't. The uncertainty, the rules, the moving . . . '

Mel said, her eyes still on the screen, 'If you can't beat them, join them. That's what I plan to do.'

'What?'

'I'm doing this study. I'm going to specialize. I'm going to involve myself in *my* science applied to *his* profession.'

Alexa leaned forward. 'Did Kate . . . ?'

'Kate,' Melanie said, 'is going down to Larkford to see Gus. So you did hit home. She heard you.'

Alexa looked truly startled. 'Wow.'

In her bag, her phone started its urgent vibrating. She said, scrabbling for it, 'It's probably my mother.'

'She won't go back to him,' Mel said, taking no notice, her eyes still on her screen. 'She's done with all that. But she knows she left a car crash. She knows she's got to sort it out a bit.'

Alexa had her phone in her hand. 'Missed call,' it said implacably, and then, in slightly larger script, 'Mrs Cairns.'

16

Jack thought he had probably never been to Wimbledon proper. He'd only ever been to watch the tennis at the All England Club, trying to persuade Eka that there was global glamour there, despite all the old buffers in blazers and dated moustaches insisting that good manners should always prevail over spectacular, if occasionally discourteous, playing.

'Why d'you think you never have a British star?' Eka said after her second restless visit. 'I tell you. Because those old men live in the olden days! Nobody allowed to show temper! I show you temper. I getting out of this place right *now*.'

And she had, running in her perilous sandals with extraordinary skill through the crowds, leaving him to pant behind her, conscious of his physical ineptitude and girth in the wake of her gazelle-like grace. At least George Riley wasn't going to startle him by sprinting off somewhere unannounced. In fact, he seemed to be the complete opposite, shyly thanking Jack for coming and then confessing that he'd done a stupid thing.

They were sitting in a coffee place, almost at the top of the High Street, Jack painfully aware that it had cost George no effort at all to turn down a chocolate muffin with his cappuccino.

'What?' Jack said. 'You think it was stupid to be so generous to Alexa and Dan?'

'No, not that.'

'It was certainly,' Jack said, leaning forward for emphasis, 'unbelievably stupid and crass and bad-tempered for Alexa to react as she did.'

'I don't blame her.'

'I bet you don't. You're too nice.'

'We sprung it on her,' George said. 'Once Dad's got an idea in his head, you can't shift it. He was set on telling her. He was set on her falling on his neck and thanking him. He didn't give her a chance. I should have stopped him. I should have made him wait until we could suggest it to both of them.'

Jack leaned back again. 'You don't need to forgive her, you know.'

'I want to.'

'Have you seen Dan?'

George sighed. 'Briefly. I went down there. He hasn't been to see Dad yet.'

'They're a right case, the pair of them,' Jack said, 'aren't they? Hopeless.' He took a gulp of coffee. 'Why do we bother, I wonder?'

George gave him a half-smile. 'You know why. Why else did you ring me?'

Jack shrugged. 'Well, they're a load of trouble.'

George said shyly, 'We used to wonder if you were.'

'Me?' Jack said in amazement. 'Who did?'

'Me and the old man. We couldn't work out you and Alexa. We thought maybe Dan needed to keep a bit of an eye on you.'

Jack was laughing. 'Never in that way, mate. She never saw me as more than a comfort blanket. I'm as much of a threat to Dan as an armchair. What were you thinking of?'

George looked down into his coffee cup. 'He's my boy. And she's a great girl.'

'George Riley,' Jack said. 'Sir. I can't believe you thought anything so stupid. Or ever did anything stupid, either. Unlike the rest of us.'

George sighed. He smiled privately down at his coffee cup. 'I did, you know. I got myself in such a state the other day, I went out and found a house for them. After you rang.'

'You *what?*'

'Oh,' George said, glancing up, 'I didn't make an offer or anything. I just saw it, made an appointment to look round. What we're offering them'd cover the deposit.'

'Gosh,' Jack said admiringly. He ran a teaspoon round his cup to scoop up the remaining foam. 'Did you tell the old man?'

'No fear.'

'And?'

'It'd do,' George said. 'I'm not much of a one for houses, never have been, but I know what they've got now and they'd be better, really. Quite a bit of garden, for London. I could grow them a few veg.'

'George!'

George picked up his coffee cup and drained it.

'You've moved them in, in your mind, haven't you?' Jack said. 'You've seen a house and moved them in. I bet you've found a school for Izzy, haven't you?'

George said mildly, 'There's computers in the public library. And they're really helpful in there to pillocks like me who don't know how to get started.'

Jack struck the table. 'Well, I'm damned.'

'Even if she couldn't get into the High School,' George said in the tone of one used to having knowledgeable discussions about modern education, 'there's good state schools around, some with almost 70 per cent exam passes and all.'

Jack eyed him. 'George?'

'Yes?'

'She didn't mean to turn you down, you know. She doesn't want to refuse your offer.'

George sighed. 'So you said, on the phone.'

'She feels awful about the other day. Ashamed. I told her to get off her bloody backside and stop whining, I was really rough with her. And she knows she's got to do something. She knows it. And I think she will, I really do. That's why I gave in and said I'd come and see you. For her, really.'

George hesitated. Then he said, 'I'm — ' and stopped.

'You're what?'

George cleared his throat. He leaned across the table and said in a whisper, 'I'm scared she'll leave him.'

'A house wouldn't fix that.'

'It'd help.'

'No,' Jack said. 'It would only look as if it was helping.'

'D'you think — ?'

Jack put out one hand and made a tipping movement. He said, 'Could go either way right now. We're doing everything we can, aren't we? You're being nice to her, I'm being vile to her, Izzy and Dan are pulling her in opposite directions. Thank God, at least, for those twins. At least they're on three-year-old Planet Normal.'

'We've got to keep trying.'

Jack shrugged again. 'I know.'

'Shall — shall I — we — offer them the money again?'

'Maybe. No. No, don't. Yes. Yes — together. Offer it again when they're together.'

George pushed his coffee cup away. 'It's a nice house.'

'Where is it?'

George jerked his thumb behind him. 'Just up there in a terrace. Stone's throw from everything.'

Jack smiled at him. 'Can I see it?'

★ ★ ★

Even walking the short distance around the Quadrant with Beetle at his heels made Dan feel conspicuous. True, a lot of people were away, and another lot would have enough similar difficulties in their own lives to sympathize, but all the same, he felt exposed in a way that was uncomfortable and mildly humiliating, walking round to Franny's house in civilian clothes when most people — anybody within earshot of the garrison tom toms, which meant most people — would know that he was not only alone just now, but that his stepdaughter had run away from school a second time, and elected not to run home while she was at it.

He had been on the telephone for hours, since he had encountered Isabel at the roadside. Half the night, at least. Talking to Alexa, talking to Mrs Cairns, trying to talk to Isabel. He had found that he desperately wanted not to lose control of the situation, so he had managed to persuade Mrs Cairns that Isabel was better off not being immediately returned to school so close to the end of term, and — much harder — had convinced Alexa not to insist that her father drive her and the twins back to Larkford without delay.

'I must come,' Alexa had said. 'I *must*.'

He had gripped the phone. 'Please don't.'

'But Izzy — '

'She's where she wants to be. I've seen her. She's fine, she's well. She doesn't want any kind of drama and you racing back will be a drama.'

'It breaks my heart she didn't want to come home.'

Dan had paused before he replied, and then his voice came out in quite the wrong tone, too hearty, too confident. 'Mine too,' he said.

'Sounds it,' Alexa said sardonically. 'I'm going to ring Franny.'

'Please don't,' he said again.

'I'm afraid you can't tell me what to do about my own daughter. You're not to be trusted anyway, are you? I bet you knew what Izzy was planning and you chose not to tell me, because you knew I'd act on it and you didn't want the consequences of that. Did you? Well, you've been

found out, whatever fast one you've tried to pull.
You can't stop me. You've pre-empted me at the
school, you can't pre-empt me with my own
friends, too.'

'Go ahead then.'

'I will!' she'd shouted. 'I will!'

But Franny, to Dan's amazement and initial
relief, had said no.

'I'm not having Alexa here,' Franny said to
Dan. 'I've told her so. She can come when
Isabel's had her say.'

'Quite right,' Dan said approvingly, holding
the telephone. 'Just what I — '

'Hold on,' Franny said, interrupting. 'Hold on.
Don't think you're off the hook, Dan, not for
one minute. I need to see you round here. I have
something to say.'

'OK,' Dan said, reluctantly.

'In the morning,' Franny said. 'I'm not
working till midday. I'll see you here in the
morning. Andy won't be here.'

⋆ ⋆ ⋆

Her house, Dan thought, standing on the
doorstep, looked very unlike his own, despite
being almost a carbon copy. The garden was
ferociously kept, the windows glittered, but there
was nothing warm about it, nothing welcomingly
disordered or charming. And when Franny
herself opened the door, trim in tailored cords
and polished loafers, her expression was equally
uninviting. She looked past Dan at Beetle. 'He'd
better stay outside. Mine's in season.'

Dan turned to command Beetle, who lowered himself mournfully to the gravel and laid his chin on his paws.

'Come in,' Franny said.

'Fran, we're so grateful. We really are. I'm so sorry for the trouble.'

'She's no trouble,' Franny said. 'None at all. She's a dear. She's lovely. I'm flattered, in fact. It's a relief to know Rupe has even noticed a girl, let alone shown such good taste. Isabel is not, to my mind, the problem.'

'Ah.'

Franny turned on her heel and marched towards the kitchen. It was as tidy and charmless as the exterior of the house. Her dog, a small and lightly built black Labrador bitch, was in a basket by the back door, the lead attached to her collar tied also to the back-door handle. She didn't move when Dan came in. He stood just inside the door, on the shining vinyl floor, and took in the somehow reproving regularity of the room. Franny, who worked part-time as a house finder for a local estate agent, maintained she got all the house fixes she needed from her work and wasn't prepared to expend one ounce of emotional energy on four walls which would never belong to her, and which she would never, thank you very much, have chosen in the first place.

'Coffee?' Franny said sharply.

Dan attempted a smile. 'I don't think you want to give me any. Where's Izzy?'

'Gone with Andy to pick up Rupert's Christmas bike. Umpteen gears. You can have coffee if you want it, but what I'm going to give you, whether you want it or not, is a piece of my mind.'

'I thought as much.'

'So, with or without a mug of coffee?'

Dan wished suddenly and urgently for Izzy's return. A stab of jealousy at Andy's taking her to the cycle shop took him by surprise. He swallowed. 'Without,' he said. 'Fire away.'

Franny indicated a chair, its seat hygienically and glossily upholstered in plastic. 'Sit down.'

'I'm OK.'

Franny leaned against the nearest kitchen counter and folded her arms. She looked as unlike the friendly, smiling, easy-going Franny that Dan was used to as she possibly could. He stood where he was, on the far side of the kitchen table from her, trying hard not to stand to attention.

'I like Alexa,' Franny said. 'Make no mistake, my life here has been pretty well *made* by knowing Alexa. And Andy thinks a lot of you. But you just aren't looking, either of you, are you? You aren't listening. When Andy won't listen, I just go ahead and *do* it, whatever it is. But Alexa doesn't behave like that. She asks you. Or she waits for you to be ready to ask. But you never bloody are, are you? You just never, ever are.'

Dan's hand moved slightly, involuntarily. If he'd had his side hat in his hands — he vaguely wished he did have — he'd have been turning it slowly. It would have been comforting to have something to hold on to. He said, in too jocular a tone, 'My fault again, then.'

'No,' Franny said. She unfolded her arms and then folded them the opposite way. 'No. It's both of you. Neither of you are listening to Isabel.'

'But we *are*.'

'No, you're not. She really meant this, Dan. She's really unhappy. She really hates boarding school. She refuses to blame her mother, she refuses to blame you directly, but she just wants the same family life as Flora and Tassy get, she just wants to be at home with you and Alexa and the twins and the dog. And because you both make all decisions for her, and she can't bear the consequences of those decisions, and she can't get either of you to *hear* her, not really hear her, she takes matters into her own hands to try and *make* you see that she, poor kid, is in *pain*. And nobody should be in pain like that for no good reason. Especially not a *child*.'

'There — there was a good reason.'

'Good reason or convenience?'

'Oh, Fran.'

Franny stood upright and pulled her sweater over her hips. 'Lecture over,' she said.

'But boarding school isn't an ogre's den any more. Your boys love it.'

'My boys are much simpler mechanisms than Isabel. And like their father, they are sustained by action. Daily sport and regular food and sleep, and my boys are sorted. Isabel's different.'

Dan looked past Franny out of the window, where three yellow dusters flapped in a tidy row on a circular washing line. 'Yes,' he said soberly.

'She can stay here till Alexa gets back. She's

299

welcome to. Andy's chuffed to bits to have a daughter on loan. Someone else to show off to, since I'm not exactly a good audience any more, bless his heart.'

Dan switched his gaze to her face. 'Franny?'

'What?'

'How — how did Isabel have the money to get home?'

Franny looked at him calmly. 'Rupert sent it to her.'

'Rupert!'

'Yes,' Franny said. 'I asked her the same question and she told me. Then I rang him, and he confirmed it. As he said to me, it seemed the best thing to do.' She paused for a second and then she said, 'Hadn't you better rescue that dog of yours?'

★ ★ ★

The twins were crying. They had been weeping, on and off, since they woke up and realized that they were going home. Alexa had expected that they would be as they had always been, as she had supposed small children always were, thrilled to be going home to see Daddy, and Beetle, and even Isabel, who could invariably be produced as a trump card when a reward or an inducement was in order. But instead they had wailed and whined and become like floppy rag dolls when Alexa tried to dress them, and sat looking glumly at their untouched breakfast — pronounced their favourite cereal on all preceding mornings — with their thumbs in.

When her father — even her father! — sat down between them and attempted to coax in a mouthful or two, they had merely leaned against him, one either side, and indicated, round their thumbs, that they could not possibly be persuaded and, furthermore, they didn't mind how long it took to make that very, very plain.

In the end, Elaine had relented and put bananas and cereal bars in a plastic bag for the journey. She looked tired, Alexa thought, as tired as someone might well look on the fourth day of having five people in a flat designed for a formal two, and the ceaseless involvement in nurture required by two three-year-olds. Alexa's friend Prue, who had four children under eight to look after, said that she often felt like a tree entirely covered in woodpeckers. Elaine, still attired for the Marylebone Road but with slightly ruffled hair and a distinct air of discomposure, looked as if she might have been such a tree.

'Sorry, Mum,' Alexa said, wedged against the dishwasher in the tiny kitchen.

'I've loved it.'

'You've been fantastic. Really. But we're a lot to cope with. I know we are.'

Elaine took out the two bowls Alexa had just loaded into the dishwasher and put them back again at a slightly different angle. 'Daddy and I have loved having you.'

'Please, Mum. Please. Don't pretend we're easier than we are. Especially at the moment. It's — it's been a real break for me.'

Elaine straightened up and regarded her. 'You don't look as if you've had much of a break.'

'I will do. Promise. I just need to sort a few things.'

Elaine made a distracted, despairing gesture. 'All this business with Isabel.'

'I know.'

'You really can't — '

'Mum. Please.'

'I knew that would happen,' Elaine said. 'I knew it. The moment you told us that you'd met Dan and that he was a soldier. I said to Daddy — '

'No, Mum.'

'D'you remember, in Jakarta — '

Alexa put her hands over her ears. 'Of course I do!'

'Well, then.'

'Well nothing. Mum, I don't want to fight. Really I don't. Especially when you and Dad have been so generous. Really it's been a — wonderful stay.'

Elaine said sadly, 'I thought seeing Jack would do you good.'

'It did.'

'I — we rather hoped you'd marry Jack, you know.'

Alexa sighed. From the sitting room she could hear a steady whimpering setting in again. Was it Flora, or Tassy? She said, 'Mum, I didn't love Jack. I don't. Not that way. He's lovely, loveable, but not . . . not . . . '

'Not what?'

'Not like you love someone you agree to marry.'

Elaine looked away. She appeared to be

considering, with discomfort, the nature of the love you might ideally feel for someone you agree to marry. Then she said, as a statement rather than a question, 'And Dan was.'

'Yes.'

'And is?'

There was a fractional pause and then Alexa said, not wholly with conviction, 'That too.'

★   ★   ★

In Morgan's car, the twins fell asleep, their heads lolling forwards on the fragile stalks of their necks. Morgan drove with deliberate casualness, his right arm on the ledge of the window, just resting his fingertips on the steering wheel as if they had all day to meander pleasurably and relaxedly down to Wiltshire. Beside him, Alexa sat and tried not to make a checklist of all the things that needed confronting and dealing with at Larkford, or to think how these few days in London had demonstrated to her that it was no good being politely and even enthusiastically reactive any more, and that if she wanted even one of the things she had realized she could no longer live without — Isabel's happiness being paramount — she was going to have to take action.

'Omelettes and eggs,' Jack had said to her several times, increasingly irritatingly. 'If you want the omelette — '

'I know — I *know*.'

'Knowing isn't enough. You have to — '

'I know that too.'

She felt unfairly exasperated with him. He'd been amazing, smoothing her path back to her father-in-law — she hadn't yet had the courage to ring Eric, too — but she was worn out with being grateful to him, worn out with her own inability to handle herself at all times in a way she could be proud of, worn out at the prospect of walking back into the familiar patterns of irresolvable unhappiness at Larkford. Gazing out of the passenger window of her father's car, she wondered, with a kind of despair, if the green shoots of an idea that had popped up suddenly and miraculously in her mind in Mel Cooper's office, only to be overtaken immediately in favour of yet more anxiety and telephoning about Isabel, would prove to be merely another brief, hopeless illusion.

'It won't,' Morgan said, raising his voice very slightly above Radio Three, 'be as bad as you are thinking when you get there.'

She didn't turn her head. 'Want to bet?'

Her father put his left hand out briefly to touch her arm. 'Trust me,' he said, and then transferred his hand to the radio to turn up the volume. 'Now,' he said, 'which Beethoven symphony is this?'

★　★　★

Gus had been impossible to rouse for three days. Dan had left messages on his mobile, sent texts, and even been round to his house on two occasions, to find the curtains drawn back, the dog missing from the outside kennel, no car in

304

the drive and the door locked. Perhaps, Dan thought, he'd gone away. Perhaps he'd done something characteristically, energetically Gus-like, such as taking himself off to some outward-bound place in North Wales or the Lake District and blanking out what was going on in his head with outrageous physical challenges. And anyway, what with the Isabel crisis and Alexa coming back, thoughts of what had happened to Gus had to be pushed aside, not least because they were, if Alexa was to be believed, symptoms of the problem, if not partly the cause of it as well.

He had made an effort for Alexa's return. He had tidied the house, and ironed the pile of clothes in the specified basket, and fixed the dripping shower. He had spoken, pleasantly and without drama or asking questions, to Isabel, who had indicated that she would probably, but not definitely, come home when Alexa and the twins arrived. Then it struck him that there was no food. Well, there was the odd discouraging scrap of this and that in the fridge, but there wasn't new food, and certainly not the kind of small, bright, appetizing food that the twins would consent to eat.

He made a list, with decisiveness. Then he rounded up a number of responsibly reusable bags and got in the car and drove to the garrison village supermarket, and went round it, list in hand, methodically checking items off with a pencil as he added them to his trolley. He was amazed at how much there was. He was astonished at the size of the bill. As he was loading it all into the boot of the car, Mo came by, pushing her own trolley, and said cheerfully that she was glad to see him doing his bit and would he like to have a word with Baz some time, who thought a three-for-two offer was something to do with the porn industry.

Dan knew what was expected of him. He said, 'I don't know how you girls do it, week after week.'

'And it never gets to be anybody's idea of fun.'

'I can believe that.'

Mo glanced over her shoulder, as if to check that no one else was listening. 'I'll tell you something else you'll hardly believe.'

'What?'

'Gus and Kate.'

'Sadly, Mo, I do know about that.'

'No. I've just seen them,' Mo said. 'Together. She's back.'

Dan slammed down the car's tailgate. 'I don't think so.'

'I saw them, Dan. With my own eyes. Couple of hours ago I was driving out past the guardroom after delivering something for Baz — why do I do it? Why do I keep saying yes when he asks me to do something he could perfectly well do himself? — and they were coming in, in the same car. They looked — well, they looked OK to me.'

'Good,' Dan said shortly.

Mo let a beat fall and then she said, 'Alexa back today?'

Dan indicated the full boot of the car. 'That's what all that's for.'

'It'll earn you a few brownie points.'

'I need them.'

'You all do,' Mo said. 'Just by existing you do. Tell Alexa I'll call her. Tell her about Kate.'

Dan sketched a mock salute. 'Will do.'

Mo bent over her trolley and began to wheel it rapidly up the line of cars. Dan got in behind the wheel and put the key in the ignition. He fired the engine. He was not going to think about Gus. He was not going to think about Gus and Kate and whatever her return meant or didn't mean. He was only going to think about making it as easy for Alexa to come back as it could be, which would start, he had decided, with a full fridge and a full apology. And then he would see what she had decided to do. About everything.

★   ★   ★

In the driveway of number seven, the Quadrant was a car, already parked. Curses, Dan thought, they're here before me, before I've got the food in, before I've laid the table and found something to stick these flowers in. And then he thought, that's not Morgan's car, Morgan drives a Mercedes and that's a Volvo, a Volvo estate, the same colour as Gus's Volvo estate — actually, it is Gus's Volvo estate and there is Gus, getting out of it, looking like he'd rather be anywhere but here, and Kate, oh God, Kate, wearing an expression like thunder. Both the Melvilles. Give me *strength*.

He pulled the car in behind Gus's and yanked on the brake. Gus looked at Dan as he got out of the car. He didn't smile.

'Hi, there,' Dan said.

'Hi!' Kate called, climbing out of the passenger seat.

Gus said nothing. Kate came across the drive, past Gus, to greet Dan. He thought for a moment that she was going to kiss his cheek, and he couldn't stop her, but she halted two feet from him. She looked different, somehow, not exactly younger, but not so old as before either, despite her expression.

'Hello,' Kate said.

Dan nodded. His glance flicked to Gus.

'I'm sorry to surprise you,' Kate said. 'I'm sorry we're unannounced. Is Alexa back?'

'Any minute,' Dan said tersely.

'Good,' Kate said. She turned and waved an arm at Gus, as if indicating that he should come and stand beside her.

'This won't take long,' Kate said, 'but it's best you know before Alexa gets back.'

'Know what?'

'Gus,' Kate said. 'Gus. Come here. Come and talk to Dan.' She turned back to Dan and said, raising her voice a little, 'Dan, Gus has something to tell you.'

17

'Of course I can see you,' Mack said. 'You rang just in time. Mary and I are off to Scotland with the boy on Wednesday, so tomorrow's ideal. Come for a dram.'

'No, I'd rather come in the morning, if you — '

'Coffee, then. Come for coffee. Mary'll be thrilled. Bring your girls. All of them.'

'No, I'd rather just see you alone, if that's OK.'

'Of course it is,' Mack said. He sounded incapable of being put out by anything. 'Of course. See you at ten thirty, at Ranpur.'

So here he was, in barrack-room dress, in the drive of Ranpur House, at ten twenty-nine. The house reared up above him, solidly, uncompromisingly Edwardian, red brick with cream stone trimmings, the drive darkly shaded by a funereal stand of larch trees. On the sill of the bay window of the sitting room, he could see a jade tree in an oriental pot and two soapstone elephants tramping towards it, one on either side. Mack liked things symmetrical. It was probably one reason for choosing Mary as his wife. She was very pretty in as tidy a way as their sitting room ornaments.

She opened the door to him with a wide smile. She was wearing pressed jeans and a tight pink cardigan over a pink striped vest. She had pearls in her ears and her long, glossy curls were held off her face with a navy-blue velvet band.

'Dan! Lovely! Come in.'

She leaned forward to kiss him, exuding a breath of lily of the valley.

He said, 'Sorry to do this, when you're packing to leave.'

'Nonsense,' Mary said. 'It takes no time, packing for Scotland. It just means every sweater and waterproof in the house and praise be, no midge repellent needed in December.' She smiled again, her teeth almost luminous in the dark hall. 'How's Alexa?'

Dan tried to smile back. 'Round at Franny's.'

'No change there, then!'

'Absolutely,' Dan said, grateful for the formula.

Mary Mackenzie led the way into her sitting room. A gas fire was glowing with artificial flames and a coffee tray, complete with a plate of biscuits, was on a low table beside one of the twin sofas, stoutly upholstered in patterned chintz.

'Mack won't be a moment.'

'He's here,' Mack said.

Dan stood, immediately and involuntarily, to attention. 'Morning, Colonel.'

Mack indicated a chair. 'Morning, Dan. Sit yourself down.'

He put a hand on his wife's shoulder. 'Thank you, darling.'

'No trouble.'

'We won't be long.'

Mary turned another smile on Dan. 'I'm off to count gumboots.'

Mack leaned to kiss her cheek. 'Half an hour, sweetheart.'

He turned and bent over the coffee tray. The cafetière, Dan noticed, irrelevantly and idiotically, had a flowered porcelain lid which almost matched the sofas.

'Right, Dan,' Mack said, pouring, his back to Dan. 'What can I do you for?'

★　★　★

Franny had put Isabel to sleep in Rupert's room. This was exhilarating and slightly daunting in equal measure and Isabel wasn't sure if she should tell him by text that she was sleeping under his Arsenal duvet, below, among other things, a Dire Straits poster — pretty old, it looked — for *Brothers in Arms*. The poster intrigued Isabel, not for itself, really, but because Rupert had written out something in his own handwriting and taped it to the bottom edge.

Isabel knelt up on the bed to see what he had written, and saw that he had copied out some of the lyrics from the song, about the supreme brotherhood of bearing arms together, and then he'd signed his initials, RGW, as if he'd thought of the words himself, and dated them.

It made Isabel feel a bit odd, looking at it, the way she felt when Dan was in uniform and thinking about soldiering rather than his family. It was so weird, really it was, to be under Rupert's duvet, and being looked after by his parents, but at the same time realizing that what went on in Rupert's head could take him far, far

311

away to a place where no one, except other boys who felt as he did, could ever reach him. It was weird, but it wasn't frightening. It was quite exciting, really, even if she couldn't work out quite why. It was as exciting as putting her bare feet on the carpet where he walked, in his bare feet, when he was at home.

And then she got a text.

'Now u can tell Mum I need a new bed!' he wrote. 'It's crap isn't it.'

He knew! He was cool with it. It was empowering to have Rupert casually acknowledge her sleeping in his bed, just as being in this house with Franny and Andy was empowering.

'Will do,' she texted back laconically, and waited.

'Stay there,' he wrote commandingly, 'till I get back. x'.

She could hear feet on the gravel now below Rupert's bedroom window, and a familiar, lovely cheeping, indicating that the twins had arrived, and so had Mum. Isabel swallowed.

'You can stay,' Franny had said, 'as long as you want to. All you must be sure of is that if you do stay, you're not doing it to get back at your mother.'

Isabel shut her eyes, briefly. She was longing to see her mother. And the twins. Longing. And Beetle. It was just that in the past, giving in to that longing had meant a repetition of nobody listening, nobody making any changes. But this time, there were a few changes already, and Dan, at least, was trying to listen. He had not, for example, urged her to come home before Alexa and the twins returned.

She heard the doorbell ring and Franny's steps in the hall, and then the sound of the door opening and all the greetings and the twins squeaking and then Alexa saying, 'Isabel? Where's Isabel?'

'Upstairs,' Franny said.

'No,' Alexa said, in a different, more commanding tone. 'No. Stay with me — '

She was trying to restrain the twins. Isabel could hear them protesting, hear Tassy working herself up to one of her big screams.

'*Wait*,' Alexa said.

Her voice didn't sound very good, very steady. Tassy was making that noise like a siren now. She'd set Flora off, if she went on.

'Stop it,' Alexa shouted. 'Stop it!'

Isabel stood up. She glanced at the text again and then pushed the phone into her jeans pocket. Then she walked out of Rupert's room and along the landing until she could look down over the banisters to the hall. It was chaos down there, familiar chaos.

'Here I am!' Isabel called. And waited.

★   ★   ★

Mack watched Dan reverse competently out of the drive of Ranpur House, waved once to him in a single, economical gesture, and closed the front door. Then he moved briskly down the dark hall to the small room at the back of the house which he was using as a study, calling as he went, 'Just got a few work calls to make,

313

sweetheart!' to deter Mary from immediately coming to ask him what Dan had wanted, and shut the door behind him with even more emphasis than he had closed the front one. Mary, who had been so delighted when he got command — 'Oh darling, can you believe it! A cleaner and a gardener!' — was elaborately respectful of his closed study door, and he did not discourage her. When his own senior officer, Julian Bailey, had once said drily to him that as the Army didn't deliberately infantilize women it was a pity to do it oneself, he had simply pretended he saw no personal relevance in the remark. Mary's girlishness was not only abidingly charming to him, it was also useful. She would not, now, come into his study without knocking and calling out to ask if she might. And in return, he would, in the course of the day, find a small way in which to indulge her. It wasn't the kind of marriage that would suit the Baileys, he was sure, but it suited the current occupants of Ranpur House very well indeed, thank you.

Mack's study was a small shrine to the regiment. The lower halves of the walls held bookcases full of military and sporting books, and the upper halves were neatly and thickly covered with photographs and insignia. Some of the photographs were of Mack's military career, some of them featured his father and paternal grandfather, both Highland gunners, both staring out at him with the same inflexible directness. Against one wall was his orderly desk, with its computer, and in the centre of another, the half-glazed door to the dark back

314

drive of Ranpur House, above which Mack had instructed Robbo, the PT instructor, to install a pull-up bar.

Mack sat down at his desk and pulled the landline telephone towards him. It was his intention to ring Julian Bailey immediately and report on the most disquieting half-hour he had just had with Dan Riley, as well as asking Julian's advice as to what, if anything, should be done next. But then, with his hand on the handset, he hesitated. It came to him, suddenly and uncomfortably, that he might — in the heat of the moment, as it were — have said too much himself. He withdrew his hand. He must think. He put his elbows on his desk and his chin in his hands. He must re-run the interview in his mind, and think.

Dan had not so much come straight to the point as rushed at it. He had said — almost blurting it out — that he didn't think he could go on.

'Go on?'

'Soldiering,' Dan said. 'I just don't think I can. I just don't think I can ask — '

Mack had motioned him to silence. He had leaned forward, coffee mug in both hands, and said, in a very calm, steady and deliberate way, that they were all feeling the effects of returning from a particularly gruelling tour, and that it was desperately hard to change gear and desperately hard for the families to do likewise in their own way, and it had only been a few weeks, and although it was more than understandable to feel as Dan did, it was crucially important not to give

315

way to impulse or the difficulties of the moment.

Dan listened in silence. Then he said, not very coherently, that he couldn't go on asking everyone to make all these sacrifices because of him, and he could not be responsible for Isabel and Alexa's unhappiness any longer. And then he stopped again, drank some coffee and said suddenly, 'Anyway, I've lost faith.'

Mack put his coffee down. He said, incredulously, 'In — soldiering?'

'No,' Dan said. 'I adore it. It's my life.'

'Then . . . ?'

'I can't tell you.'

'What?'

'I'm sorry,' Dan said. 'You'll have to take my word for it. I've lost faith.'

'In yourself?'

'No.'

'In — in comradeship?'

There was another silence. Then Dan shook his head, like a dog getting water out of its ears. He said, mumbling, 'I just can't go *on*, putting them all through it.'

Mack got up. He walked to the window and surveyed the jade tree and the soapstone elephants. 'Is Alexa home?'

'Yes.'

'Does she know you are here?'

'No.'

'Does she know why you might be here?'

'No.'

Mack turned round. 'What would she say if she knew you were here?'

Dan said unhappily, 'She'd probably tell me

316

not to be such a bloody idiot.'

'Then why wouldn't you listen to her?'

'Because,' Dan said, 'she's had enough. So has Izzy. And I've had enough of letting them down like this. I can't go on with it. It breaks my heart, but I can't.'

Mack came back to the sofa. He sat down and leaned forward again, his elbows on his knees. He said, 'Are you ambitious?'

'As a soldier?' Dan gave a little bark of laughter. 'I was. Boy, I was.'

Mack said, 'You had a good tour of duty.'

'Yup.'

'Your third tour of duty.'

Dan nodded.

Mack linked his hands and stared at the hearthrug. He said, 'You're coming into zone for promotion. As you know. We'd be looking at your past battle planning as well as your achievements. You know as well as I do that you did a fantastic job with your sub unit. You hit all the bases. You are not a guy, Dan, who walks between the raindrops. You've had your opportunities to shine and you've taken them. You even — dare I say — have your patrons. Afghanistan is the ultimate test — and you have not failed it.'

Dan muttered something.

'What?'

'I just said, I'm afraid it's too late.'

'Is it?' Mack said with sudden energy. 'Is it?' He looked up from the rug, and gazed hard at Dan. 'Are you telling me, really telling me, that you want to throw in the towel just as you come into the zone?'

Dan stared at him. 'I don't have a choice.'

Mack jabbed a forefinger at him. 'I may be speaking out of turn. I may well be. But I can't stand to see you giving up, I can't stand it.' He leaned closer until his face was six inches from Dan's and said in a hoarse, urgent whisper, 'You're on target, mate. On target. To be pinked. Don't bloody give up at the *moment*. You hit the bull's eye!'

He shifted his position slightly now and put his hands over his face. Should he have said that? Should he? It was early December. The pink list wouldn't be out for two months plus. On that fateful Thursday in February, Julian would ring him and say something like, 'I'm aware that Dan and Gus both wanted and hoped, but only Dan got it,' and then Mack would have to confront Gus and a whole tribe of other triple-alpha, confident people who believed they could do anything and tell them that only Dan — But maybe it wouldn't, in the end, *be* Dan. Maybe, however great he'd been and might be, he wouldn't finally get promotion. And then *what* would Mack have done that morning, setting that hare running, raising those hopes? He balled his hands into fists and beat them lightly against his forehead. Why hadn't he kept his mouth shut? Why hadn't he heard Dan out and then rung Julian before he said another word?

There was a tap at the door.

'Only me!' Mary called, from the far side.

Mack got up from his desk and took a deep breath. He rearranged his features and his voice. 'On my way, sweetheart,' he said.

318

Isabel said that she would come home to play with the twins and help put them to bed, but that for the moment she would like to sleep at Franny's house.

'Just till Rupert gets back,' she said, 'and needs his bedroom.'

She hoped she had said his name really ordinarily. Alexa had flinched slightly, but had not said anything except that that would be lovely.

Franny said to Isabel, 'Are you sure?'

Isabel nodded. 'If that's OK.'

'It's OK by me.'

'Thank you,' Alexa said to Franny. She put an arm around Isabel's shoulders and held her hard. Then they ushered the twins out of Franny's house and walked home round the Quadrant and the twins rushed across the grass to the beech clump in the middle so that they could kick the leaves up and shout. Isabel wondered whether to join them, and decided not to. It was a risk, staying with Mum, that she'd ask all kinds of questions, but luckily the risk was worth taking and she didn't. Alexa just walked, and told her silly things the twins had said and done and how spoiled they had been in London, and then they were home, and there was Beetle, in a rapture of welcome, and Dan, in sort of uniform, looking very pale but laying the table and trying to smile. She smiled back at him but didn't cross the room, and he seemed to get it and stayed where he was, a bunch of forks in his hand.

Alexa said to him, 'You look very tidy.'

He shrugged. 'Barrack office stuff. Very dull. Good to see you, Izzy.'

'You, too,' she said politely.

'No Gus?' Alexa said.

Dan placed two forks precisely on the table. 'No Gus.'

'Franny said that Kate — '

'I know.'

'Have you seen her?'

'If you want to know,' Dan said, turning to get water glasses out of the cupboard behind him, 'I don't want to see either of them.'

'Really?'

'Really.'

'Oh.'

'Where are the twins?'

Alexa pointed out of the window. 'Coming. There they are.'

'Isabel,' Dan said, setting tumblers on the table, 'could you field them and get their hands clean, for lunch?'

'OK.'

Alexa said, 'This all seems very brisk.'

'What does?'

She gestured. 'All this table laying and uniform and hand washing.'

Dan looked at her. 'I've got to go into Salisbury.'

'Have you?'

'Yes,' he said. 'Dad's coming.'

'George?'

'Sorry,' Dan said. 'Sorry, but I said yes. He just rang. Half an hour ago. He said he just had an impulse, and was acting on it.'

'He never has impulses.'

'He's no trouble.'

'No,' Alexa said, 'no trouble. Oh, well.'

'Sorry.'

She shrugged. 'I don't mind.'

Isabel looked out of the window. The twins were running across the grass to the house, their hands full of wet leaves.

'He can have my bed,' Isabel said. 'I won't be in it, will I? I'll be in Rupert's.'

★ ★ ★

George was carrying a laptop case. It was as surprising as if he'd arrived carrying a Masai spear or a blow-up doll.

'What's that?' Dan said, indicating it.

'A laptop,' George said reasonably.

'I thought it was all you could do to pick up a telephone.'

'Ah,' George said. 'You have to speak to folk on telephones.' He looked round. 'No kids?'

'No,' Dan said.

George peered at him. 'You all right, son?'

Dan looked down at the car keys in his hand. 'Thanks for coming, Dad.'

'Not at all,' George said. He switched the laptop to his left hand and put his right on Dan's arm. 'When you rang — '

'Sorry about that.'

'What's to be sorry for?'

'Interrupting — '

George gave a yelp of laughter. 'What's to

interrupt in my life, I wonder? Pension day, beers with your granddad, lottery tickets Friday. Full schedule, I have. Not a minute to call my own. But you — ' He tightened his grip on Dan's arm slightly. 'You worried me, lad, ringing like that. I thought there'd been a crisis. For two pins I'd have hired a car and driven straight here, except I've let my licence lapse, haven't I? Not the only thing that's lapsed, moron that I am.'

'I told Alexa you'd rung. Not that I'd rung you.'

George said soothingly, 'Same difference.'

'I'd like to talk to you before we go back,' Dan said, still looking at his car keys and not his father. 'If that's OK by you. Cup of tea, maybe?'

★   ★   ★

Dan drove George to the centre of Salisbury and left the car in a side street just off the market square. Then he stowed George's rucksack and laptop under a blanket of Beetle's, and took him to a coffee shop where the other customers were all women, women with children or shopping or both, making the atmosphere uncontrovertibly, reassuringly domestic. Dan settled George in a booth with banquette seats and a plasticized menu on the table, and went away to the self-service counter to fetch tea for both of them.

While Dan was away, George watched a young woman at one of the centre tables feeding chips and some battered balls of something to her two small children with her fingers, and he wondered if she was a squaddie's wife, and if these children

322

had been born nine months almost to the day after her man got back from a tour. He remembered talking to an Army midwife in Germany once, who said that when the boys came back, she'd block out a whole month in her diary for nine months later. 'Regular as clockwork. Baby after baby. You'd think they'd never heard of precautions.'

Dan put two tall glass mugs of tea on the table.

George said, 'You said on the phone that nobody's ill.'

Dan eased himself into the booth, opposite his father. 'All right as rain.'

'That's what I told your granddad.'

'Did he ask?'

'What?'

'Why you were coming?'

George thought of his laptop, and the information it contained. 'He knows,' George said carefully, 'that I'll tell him what he needs to know. And he'll ask. Never been shy of asking.'

Dan picked up his tea. 'Unlike you, then, Dad.'

George shrugged. 'Maybe some of us are better listeners.' He glanced at Dan. 'I'm all ready to listen to you — if you want to tell me.'

Dan leaned forward, his hands wrapped round his tea, his shoulders hunched. He said, 'I'll give you the short version, Dad. The very short version. We'll leave out most of the last year. We'll leave out the training in Kenya for Helmand, and we'll leave out getting back from Helmand, and just focus on the here and now. It

323

amounts to this. Isabel keeps running away from school because she hates it. Alexa got offered a job she can't take because we might not be here much longer. I get let down big time by my best mate, which blows my mind, so I go and see Mack and tell him I can't put my wife and family through any more of this, and he says, steady on, don't chuck it all in right now because you're bang on target for promotion.'

Dan stopped and looked up at his father across the table. 'Sorry, Dad,' he said. 'Sorry, I just had to tell someone. It is, as the boys would say, doing my head in.'

★ ★ ★

It was almost nine o'clock when Alexa heard the car wheels crunching on the drive. Dan had texted to say that they were having tea, and then again a bit later to say that they were in a pub, and then a third time to say that they were bringing fish and chips home with them. In the meantime, she and Isabel had bathed the twins and read to them, put appropriately unfeminine sheets on Isabel's bed for George, and had several stilted small conversations in which any real communication was rendered impossible by Alexa's strenuous efforts not to ask questions.

When the twins' voices had finally subsided into slumber, Isabel had put on her blue fleece, hugged her mother and set off round the Quadrant to Franny's house with a torch, promising to text when she reached it. Just as she was leaving, Alexa had said impulsively and unguardedly, 'Don't you think it's all a bit silly, you sleeping seven doors away?' and Isabel had stared straight back at her and said, 'No,' in a voice that did not encourage further discussion.

She had texted five minutes later. 'Safe at F's. I love you.'

Alexa gripped her phone. How tempting it was to text back with whole paragraphs of questions and reassurances. But she would exercise restraint. It was, if she thought about it, not only her great life skill, but at the moment also her only option.

'Xx,' she typed back and pressed Send.

Now Dan and George were getting out of the car, lit by the half-hearted gleam of the lamp over the front door, and Beetle was tense with welcome in the hall. Through the window she could see that George was carrying his rucksack and what looked like a laptop case, and Dan had an armful of tidily wrapped paper parcels from the chip shop. She had laid the table — ketchup, vinegar — and made a salad. There were plates warming in the oven.

The front door opened and Beetle took charge of the greeting. Then Dan came into the kitchen, came straight across to her and kissed her. He smelled of beer. He said at once, 'Sorry.'

'It's OK,' she said automatically. She wanted to say, 'Does it occur to you how often we have that precise exchange?' but there was George behind him, in his old anorak, smiling at her, coming forward, kissing her cheek, beery too, but lightly, as if whatever he'd drunk had been automatically diluted by the mildness of his nature.

He said, 'Shouldn't be dumping myself on you like this again.'

'I like it, George, I really do.'

He stayed standing in front of her, still smiling. 'Better than last time we met, eh?'

Alexa shot Dan a quick look. 'Please don't — '

'He didn't know,' George said easily, 'did he? He didn't know anything.'

'What?'

George dropped his rucksack on the floor and laid the laptop flat on the table. 'We shouldn't have been so long in the pub,' he said. He seemed to Alexa to be in an unusual mood, much less diffident than his normal self. 'We shouldn't have had those second halves. Not really. It's just that there was so much to say, as it turned out.' He patted the laptop. 'I'd got things to show Dan, you see. I've probably jumped a whole row of guns, getting pictures of a house I've seen, and all, but I'd been planning to show you both together, that's what I had in mind. And then . . . and then . . . '

He looked at Dan, who was standing a yard away, still holding the fish parcels, and then he turned back to Alexa and smiled at her again. 'And then,' he said, 'it turned out you'd never said a word to him. About any of it. Had you?'

18

It was an impulse, really it was. One minute she was standing in the playroom, distractedly holding a pink plastic miniature saucepan and a Barbie doll with half her hair torn off, wondering where to put either, and, without really taking it in, watching the Brigadier's wife crossing the Quadrant with her spaniels, and the next minute she was out of the front door and sprinting across the grass, still holding the saucepan and the doll and shouting Claire's name.

Claire stopped walking, turned round, saw this distraught figure without a coat racing towards her and broke into a run herself.

'Alexa! Alexa, what's the matter? What's happened?'

Alexa stopped in front of her, panting slightly.

'The children,' Claire said. She indicated the Barbie and the saucepan. 'Is it the children?'

Alexa swallowed. She blinked. 'No. They're fine.' She gave Claire a weak smile. 'They've all gone swimming. With Dan. And — and his father.'

Claire peered at her. 'Then what is it?'

'I saw you — '

'Yes?'

'I was just — standing by the window, and I saw you. And the next thing, I was out here — '

Claire took a step forward. She put a hand on Alexa's arm. 'I was on my way home.'

Alexa said vaguely, 'Were you?'

Claire glanced at the spaniels. They had both flopped down in the grass when she stopped walking and were lying there, as limp as rugs. 'I was just taking these chaps back. And then I was going to make some coffee. Why don't we go and lock your house, and then you come back with me to have coffee too?'

Alexa eyed her. 'Well . . .'

'Leave a note for Dan,' Claire said. 'Tell him where you'll be. Julian'll be glad to see you, too.'

'Julian?'

'He's at home,' Claire said. 'Under my feet isn't in it. You'll be doing me a favour.'

Alexa looked down at Claire's hand on her arm. It was sheathed in a brown sheepskin glove, sensible and of quality. She felt ridiculously, enormously comforted by that neat sheepskin glove resting on her forearm. She raised her eyes and looked at Claire. 'Thank you,' Alexa said.

★ ★ ★

When Julian Bailey had been promoted to Brigadier, he and Claire had decided not to move house. He would be entitled, he knew, to something bigger, grander, one of those substantial houses overlooking the polo ground, but he and Claire felt that such a house would be distancing from the brigade, less communal, and in any case, they were very well suited where they were. Their present house had a small downstairs room where Claire could take the children she saw for speech therapy. She worked two half-days a week in the local hospital, and then saw her other clients — 'Not *patients*, Julian, not these days. Has it ever struck anyone that political correctness has become a form of censorship in itself?' — at home in this tiny room which she had furnished to resemble the primary-coloured children's section of a book-shop.

Her kitchen, by contrast, was neutral. Tidy, efficient, old-fashioned and neutral. Everything in it, Alexa thought as she looked round, had its place; there was even a custom-built wooden dog bed under the table, and a chair for Julian, close to the telephone and the table, but well away from any drawer or cupboard Claire might need to open.

He was in the chair when Alexa came in, reading a copy of the *Economist*, half-moon glasses on, spruce in a jersey and cords. He leaped up. 'Alexa! My dear!'

'I collected her,' Claire said, pointing the spaniels to their lair under the table. 'I was on my way home and there she was, and as we haven't had a sight of her since that lovely supper party, I brought her back with me.'

Julian pulled out a chair. 'Have a pew. Delighted.'

'Thank you,' Alexa said. She sat down. The table was shiny with varnish and completely bare, except for a blue pottery bowl of clementines.

Julian went round the table and pulled out the chair opposite. He said, sitting down, 'I'm glad to see you.'

'Coffee all round,' Claire said, stating not asking. 'And possibly shortbread, if I can find it.'

'How is Isabel?' Julian said.

Alexa looked at him. 'You remembered.'

'I don't like to make the same mistake twice, if I can help it. How is she?'

'Not good. I — we — are going to have to move her. She's home again.'

'Home!' Claire said.

'Yes.'

'You sound doubtful.'

'Well,' Alexa said, 'it's complicated.'

Julian said, 'Would you like to tell us about it?'

Alexa looked at him. 'No.'

'No?'

She said, as if explaining something to someone hard of hearing, 'Emotion and unhappiness are so suppressed round here. I'm out of the habit of talking about anything much. I really am. It all has to be kept so quiet, no boat must be rocked, there's no admitting that anyone's at the end of their rope, no confessing to an inability to manage whatever's thrown at you.'

Julian leaned forward a little. He said gently, 'My dear — '

'Please don't tell me — '

'I wasn't going to tell you anything. I promise.' He glanced up at Claire. 'Is that coffee coming along? Alexa, I think the time has come, really, for you to tell *me*. Don't you?'

Claire came forward and put three striped mugs on the table. 'Tell him,' she said.

Alexa glanced up at her. 'Tell him?'

'Tell him how it is. Tell him what you feel.'

'But — '

'Tell him,' Claire said, 'about going to see Walter. In Welfare.'

Alexa laughed.

'That's better,' Julian said, relieved.

'It was useless,' Alexa said frankly.

'*Useless?*'

'He's so nice. So kind. But he had nothing to say, nothing to offer me. Of course he hadn't! And he hates the job. They all hate the job, when they have to do it.'

Julian said, a little stiffly, 'I'm sorry to hear that.'

'You know it,' Claire said to him crisply. 'You all know it. No soldier wants to do Welfare. It's seen as pansy. That's why they don't do it for very long. That's why there's no continuity.'

Julian looked down briefly at the table. 'Ah,' he said.

There was a small awkward silence, and then Claire put a coffee pot and a small jug of milk on the table, and Alexa said, with an abrupt rush of energy, 'Actually — '

They both looked at her.

'Actually, what?'

'Actually,' Alexa said, her voice gathering conviction, 'I do have something to tell you. I do.'

She lifted her chin and looked past Julian's well-brushed head to a poster on the wall of Van Gogh's sunflowers, framed in black. 'I went to London — and I — I was offered a house.'

'A house!'

'In London?'

'Yes.'

'Will you take it?' Julian said.

Alexa transferred her gaze to his face. 'I might,' she said. She smiled. 'I might do a lot of things.'

Claire eased herself very quietly into a chair at the end of the table.

'And Dan?' Julian said.

Claire nodded. She put her hands round her coffee mug. She didn't speak, but there was something about her demeanour that Alexa felt was far from antagonistic.

Alexa smiled slightly at Julian. 'You'd better ask him yourself,' she said. 'It's no good asking me.'

★   ★   ★

When Alexa had gone, Julian Bailey followed his wife into her teaching room. She settled herself in front of her computer and he perched behind her, in a small red inflatable armchair intended for the children she was helping. They sat in silence for a while, Claire tapping on her keyboard, and then Julian said to her back, 'Do you think she's going to leave him?'

'I have no idea. Why didn't you ask her?'

'God,' Julian said, with sudden force. 'I don't know. Two of my best rising stars and their private lives are round their ankles! Gus and Kate. Now Dan and Alexa. I don't want to sound like the judge who didn't know who the Beatles were, but what the hell is going on?'

Claire stopped typing. She turned round and regarded Julian gravely. 'What do you think? I mean, consider how the picture — the whole picture — has changed since your father and my father were army cadets. You *know* what's going on, Jules.'

He sighed. He shifted himself tentatively in the inflatable chair. He said miserably, 'I do. I do. For my old dad, in the Cold War, military duty was simple and honourable, but these discretionary fights aren't the same. We choose them, they're morally complicated, and we're responsible for them. I know I have a unique duty of care as a result. I know it. I want it. I'm on duty for the brigade at all times, and yet here's this girl telling me that my families welfare officer is useless — '

'For *her*,' Claire said.

'She — '

'She only said for *her*.'

'What are you trying to tell me?'

Claire swivelled her desk chair round until she was facing him. It crossed her mind, briefly, that it might cheer some of Julian's junior officers to see him so disadvantaged, crouching there in a red balloon chair meant for an eight-year-old. She put the thought firmly to one side and said, 'I'm trying to tell you what Mrs Major Riley was trying to tell you. You can't treat the men as if they didn't have families. You can't pour all this thought and all these resources into the soldiers if you don't deal with their human landscapes too. You've got to open it all up. You've got — '

'I'm running a *brigade*, Claire, not a therapy session.'

'Soldiers are people. Their partners and children are people. Dan's habit of diplomatically not telling his wife alarming things is infectious and she's holding back from him now, too. There's no encouragement to talk, everyone feels they're letting themselves down if they do.'

Julian leaned out of the chair, causing it to squeak in protest. 'You've never said this sort of thing before.'

Claire examined the nails of one hand. 'Maybe I've never seen things the way I've seen them recently, before.'

'Like what?'

'Like these marriages. Like these wives who want careers, too, not just part-time jobs. Like — like what it's like, frankly, living in a situation whose vocabulary simply does not include the word compromise.'

Julian put out a hand and grasped one of his wife's. She gave his hand a quick squeeze and dropped it. He said, 'Claire, where should I begin?'

She swung her chair back to her computer, and then she said to the screen, 'I should start by going to see Alexa Riley again and asking for her help. It won't do any harm to *ask* instead of telling, for a change.'

★ ★ ★

It was years since Jack Dearlove had been inside Elaine and Morgan's flat. The last time, not long after Richard died, had admittedly been a bit of a strain, because Jack knew how much the Longworths were hoping he'd marry Alexa, and he knew even more certainly that she would never agree to it. He supposed he might, given a free rein, have married her if he'd been given the chance, and he supposed — quite often, actually, since then — that if they'd married, they'd have made quite a companionable go of it. But he thought, on balance, it was probably best that she, at least, had known her own mind. It was odd, now, to enter that luxurious, old-fashioned lift, in that luxurious, old-fashioned building, and recall that earlier Jack who'd last been there, full of an eager — it now seemed to him naive — certainty that he could make a difference. To all of them.

Elaine Longworth looked exactly the same to him, careful and conventional, greeting him with just enough warmth to be more than polite, but without the enthusiasm that might take her into the badlands of being effusive. Morgan, wearing the kind of tweed jacket that made men of Jack's shape look like comic characters out of P. G. Wodehouse, shook Jack warmly by the hand and led him to a cream sofa beside a glowing electric fire full of artificial coals, in front of a glass coffee table bearing an orchid in a porcelain pot and a precise stack of expensive books. Nothing had changed in the nine years. Nothing.

He looked round. 'Nice to see some things can be relied on!'

Elaine sat down opposite him. 'We had Alexa and the twins here, mind you.'

'I know.'

'It was amazing how the flat coped with them.'

'And amazing,' Morgan said jovially, 'how *we* did.'

Elaine looked at him frostily. 'We loved it.'

'Of course we did!'

'It made the flat come alive, having them. They were so sweet. And funny. They looked adorable in bed.'

Morgan made a tipping gesture with one hand towards Jack. 'Drink?'

Jack shook his head. 'I've sworn off it for the moment.'

'Good God,' Morgan said. 'What's brought this on?'

Jack considered. He had promised himself that he would not mention Maia. He knew that if he mentioned her once, he was very likely to go *on* mentioning her, and in the course of all those mentions he would give away the fact that he was trying, desperately, to lose weight, in order — in order to be worthy of her.

He looked at Morgan, gave a rueful smile and patted his belly briefly.

'Nonsense,' Morgan said heartily.

'Leave him alone,' Elaine said.

Morgan tried again. 'A very weak — '

'No, thank you,' Jack said. 'Nothing.' He touched the pocket of his leather jacket that contained his calorie counter, as if for reassurance.

Morgan said teasingly, 'Glass of tonic?'

'Leave it,' Elaine said sharply. She turned to Jack and said, in quite a different tone of voice,

'Thank you for coming, Jack.'

He ducked his head in acknowledgement.

'It's — it's just that we've been so worried. Ever since Dan got back. Of course, we don't want to interfere, but we'd like to help, if we can, if they'd like it too. We'd like — ' She stopped and glanced at Morgan, and then she said, 'And we've had old Eric Riley on the phone.'

Jack sat up straighter. '*Have* you?'

'He was so upset,' Elaine said. 'I couldn't understand him at first, I couldn't think what he was trying to say, he was half shouting, as he does, and it all came out backwards, but it was something to do with Alexa going to see them, taking my umbrella and forgetting it because they offered her money for a house or something, and all she did was burst into tears and rush off and there was my umbrella, still in Eric's bathroom. Do — do you know anything about any of that?'

Jack sighed. He looked at the orchid. How much happier it would be if it were still in Thailand. 'Yes,' he said.

Elaine leaned forward. 'So, it's true.'

'More or less.'

'But the house,' Morgan said. 'This house . . . '

Jack said cautiously, 'The Rileys were just trying to inject a bit of stability — '

'Have they *bought* something?'

'Oh no. No. They've just got some money put by, and George has done a bit of research.'

He smiled at Elaine. He didn't want to tell her about meeting George, about their visit to the terraced house with its bay windows and

337

seventy-foot garden, which George walked round with all the exclamatory optimism of an estate agent, pointing out the light and the ceiling heights and the proximity to Wimbledon Common. Jack had looked at the sad little kitchen and the antediluvian bathroom and sucked his teeth, and George had exclaimed over and over, 'Nothing that can't be fixed! Nothing can't be fixed!'

He said now, 'Like you, they couldn't bear to do nothing.'

Elaine looked down at her hands. 'It's so hard . . .'

'Yes,' Jack said.

Morgan took his reading glasses out of his top pocket and jabbed them towards Jack. 'And what, I wonder, have *you* said to her?'

Jack shifted a little. He said as vaguely as he could, 'I just told her to get on with it.'

'With what?' Morgan said.

'With deciding.'

Elaine glanced at Morgan. Then she said, 'That's what we're afraid of.'

'What is?'

'That she will decide.'

'Decide?'

Elaine looked at Morgan. He said, almost through clenched teeth, 'She'll decide to leave him.'

'Leave him!' Jack said. 'Leave Dan?'

'Yes.'

'Never,' Jack said. He felt his face grow hot. 'That's the whole bloody problem, excuse my French. She'll never leave him. She adores him.

It's taken me a while to realize it, but that's what it is.' He looked at them both, turning his face from one to the other. 'That is why — that is why she's so stuck.'

★ ★ ★

When Julian Bailey had rung, Alexa had supposed that he was ringing to speak to Dan, so it had taken some minutes for him to get through to her that it was her he wished to see, her he wanted to speak to. When she at last understood him, she immediately felt apprehensive.

'Can you tell me what it's about?'

'I would much rather be in your presence before I say anything further.'

Alexa had taken the call in her bedroom. She had gone upstairs to make the bed after the twins had had a prolonged post-breakfast jumping session on it. It looked as if the bedding had been stirred up by a giant spoon. She put a hand to her forehead. 'I can't quite think.'

'I'd be so grateful if you could see me before Christmas. I'm sure you have plans for Christmas.'

'I haven't even thought about it,' Alexa said, subsiding on to the edge of the bed. 'I don't even know where we'll be.'

Julian let a small silence elapse and then he said, 'I'd so appreciate just an hour . . . '

Alexa reached out and pulled a small green sock out of the tangle of bedclothes. 'Perhaps tomorrow — tomorrow afternoon?'

'I'll be there,' Julian said.

And now here he was. In the sitting room, leaning against Dan's Union Jack cushion, refusing tea or coffee or even water, and waiting for Alexa to stop fidgeting about around him and focus on the reason for his coming. She had moved from the arm of the sofa to the seat, and then to a chair wedged against the television. The children were out, at Franny's, to be part of a welcome-home celebration for Rupert and his brother. Dan had taken George behind the wire to see the new regimental gym. He hadn't asked her why Julian was coming. He wouldn't. She could see it in his face. He wouldn't.

'Settle,' Julian said now. 'Please.'

'I feel,' Alexa said, 'that you've come to tick me off.'

Julian spread his hands. 'That's the *last* thing I've come to do. Please sit somewhere comfortable. That doesn't look at all comfortable.'

'It isn't.'

'Then move. Please.'

Alexa stood up. 'Could we go into the kitchen?'

Julian rose too. 'I'd be glad to.'

Alexa walked in front of him into the kitchen. Even as she moved, she felt better. Being in the kitchen gave her a kind of small authority and took the formality out of the meeting. She turned. 'Now, will you have coffee?'

He shook his head. He said, 'I want your attention.'

'Why? What are you going to say to me?'

He said soberly, 'Nothing.'

'Nothing?'

'No. I'm here to ask you. I'm here to ask you what you want.'

'You don't mean it.'

'I do,' he said. 'I do. What do you want?'

She turned away from him and looked out of the window. He was still standing behind her. She said, not entirely steadily, 'You know about the negatives.'

'I think I do.'

'Do you want me to recite them again?'

'Only,' he said, surprisingly gently, 'if you do.'

She turned back to look at him. 'No,' she said, 'I don't. I'm exhausted by them. I'm worn out with battling against things I can't change.'

He said nothing. He was plainly just waiting. It occurred to her suddenly that he might be a very senior officer, he might — it was his job, after all — demand unquestioning obedience from his men, but he was a man, too; in a way he was *just* a man, standing there in his navy-blue cord trousers and rust-coloured sweater with his hands in the pockets of his waxed jacket, which she had omitted to ask him to take off and which he seemed to have forgotten he was still wearing. Clever, weathered, healthy face. Thinning hair. A man. A husband and father. Just a middle-aged man, in her kitchen.

'I had a few days in London,' Alexa said.

'Ah.'

'It didn't change anything, not there and then. But since I got back . . . '

'Yes?'

She said, not looking at him, 'I've had an idea.'

He waited.

'For — well, to help myself, but to help other people too. Army people. Army wives. And families.'

He leaned forward and rested his hands on the back of the nearest kitchen chair. He was looking at her now with a disconcerting focus. 'Yes?' he said again.

'It isn't enough, any more, just to follow the drum . . . '

'I know that.'

'And we can't go on being marginalized by what our men do.'

'I know that, too.'

Alexa made herself look straight at him. 'I'd like to train to be what Walter Cummings and his ilk don't want to be.'

Julian snapped upright. 'Good heavens. You mean — '

'I'd like to be the first female non-serving welfare officer in the British Army. The first of many, I hope.'

He spread his hands. 'My dear girl — '

'I need your help. Civilian women helping Army women.'

He regarded her. He said, 'But Dan — '

'It's my kind of compromise,' she said quickly. 'And if you think I'm a radical kind of Army wife, women like Freddie Stanford's girlfriend will make us lot look like dinosaurs.' She paused and then she said, 'Those bright girls your bright boys want to marry just won't put up with things as they are.'

He said slowly, 'And nor will you?'

'No. Not if I want to stay married. And I do.'

'Good,' he said emphatically.

'But I can't live any longer with no settled home and Isabel so miserable and — '

'I know,' he said. 'I know, I know.'

'I'm accepting the offer of the deposit on a house. I'm sending Isabel to day school.'

He put his hands in his pockets. 'Decided?'

'Yes.'

'With Dan?'

'Not — quite,' Alexa said carefully.

'Please tell him.'

'It's not up to me. He has to hear me. He has to come out of his soldier's cave or wherever he is, and *hear* me.'

'I've heard you,' Julian said.

'Have you? Have you really?'

He gave her his steady frank soldierly look. 'Really.'

'Right,' she said. She felt entirely in command of the moment. She tilted her chin very slightly, to issue her small challenge. 'Will you help me, then?'

19

Isabel was home. She had brought the twins back from Franny's house, plus her backpack, and had announced that she was staying, and that she would sleep on the airbed in the twins' bedroom until George went back to London. Alexa looked at her, then looked at the twins, expecting shrieks of excitement at the prospect of having Isabel in their bedroom, especially from Tassy. But neither Isabel nor the twins appeared about to explode about anything. They stood in a funny little row in the doorway to the playroom, silently manifesting a distinct and disconcerting solidarity.

'Lovely,' Alexa said politely, as if addressing mere acquaintances. 'I'm so glad you're home.'

'Me too,' Isabel said, and then motioned to her little sisters to follow her. In silence, Alexa watched them stump upstairs, Flora trailing the tattered rag of pram blanket that she still needed as a refuge in stressful moments. It had once been pink and white check. It was now a blurred grey.

Alexa went into the sitting room and looked at the dented Union Jack cushion where Julian had briefly sat. Then she went back into the kitchen and switched the kettle on. But the thought of tea was somehow not just unappetizing but entirely irrelevant, so she switched it off again and the kettle gave a great sigh, as if exasperated by the change of plan, and subsided.

'I will make some investigations,' Julian had said. 'Some enquiries. Ring some people.'

'Yes,' Alexa said, forcing herself not to add 'Thank you.'

He had paused in the front doorway. 'I may look to you like someone entirely resistant to change, but appearances can be deceptive. All I would warn you is that in the Army things don't happen overnight.'

She smiled at him but didn't utter a word.

'Are you,' he said, half-smiling back, 'tempted to say 'Please don't state the obvious'?'

When he was in his car, he wound the window down and added, looking up at her, 'I will be in touch. As soon as I have anything to report to you. You may be sure of that.'

It was a step. A small one, but the first one. And Isabel was home and Dan knew about George and Eric's offer. It was all, she told herself resolutely, progress. She was advancing by tiny steps. Might advancement even bring an improvement, however small? In what, exactly? Not, really, in relations with Dan. He knew about the offer of a house, but he had apparently decided not to react. Not to his father, nor Alexa. But she must cling to what small shreds of hope there were and tell herself resolutely that if he wasn't being at all communicative about it, at least he hadn't refused it out of hand, either, or lost his temper and shouted. He'd simply looked as if he was trying to grasp something alien and unwieldy, and that if he were interrupted in this intractable process, all his personal progress

345

— if, indeed, that's what it was — would go to waste.

Alexa gave a little exclamation of impatience. What use was it, fidgeting about down here when three of the four most significant people in her life were together, upstairs? She took the stairs two at a time and almost ran down the landing, halting in the doorway to the twins' bedroom. Her three daughters were sitting in a rough circle on the floor, and on the carpet in the centre of the circle sat the miniature teaset that Isabel had had when she was the twins' age, and which they were forbidden, as a general rule, to touch. There was a tiny cup and saucer in front of each child, and Isabel was pouring water into each of them in turn from an equally tiny teapot, gravely regarded by the twins.

'Hello,' Alexa said from the doorway.

Nobody moved or looked up.

'I just wondered,' Alexa said, aware that her voice had none of the firmness she had used while speaking to Julian Bailey, 'if I could join in?'

*   *   *

Dan had found a cart track going up a steepish ridge on the edge of one of the firing ranges. It was a flinty track leading up a bleak hillside, but the austerity of it suited his mood, and, in any case, Beetle thought it was terrific, and despite his age was trundling resolutely up the slope ahead of Dan, his tail signifying his enthusiasm. George had asked to be left back at camp, back in the blocks, where he had found someone whose father he had served with in the South Atlantic. In any case, there was no more, really, that Dan wanted to say to his father right now. He would, in truth, have liked George to go back to London, but George seemed in no hurry to go, and was full of benign certainty that this house scheme of his and Eric's would come off if he just kept nudging it along, like a dog with a ball. And Alexa, Dan had noticed with mounting tension, was doing nothing to discourage him.

Dan stopped for a moment and took several deep, deliberate lungfuls of air. It was cold up here, but exhilarating, and the views across the immensity of Salisbury Plain — those vast uplands where the Celts had grown the wheat that the invading Romans referred to as 'Celtic Gold' — were soothing to what the padre would almost certainly term his 'troubled mind'. It *was* troubled. He wasn't sure it had ever been so purely troubled, and the bizarre interview that morning with Gus had done little to quiet it.

Gus had asked to see him. He had rung and said, without any familiar preliminaries, that he'd be grateful if Dan could spare him half an hour.

'Sure.'

'Where?'

'Want to come here?'

There'd been a fractional beat and Gus had said, 'Not the best idea. Not here, either, actually.'

So they'd ended up in the coffee shop of a service station on the A303, among people eating egg and chips on their way to a West Country

Christmas, drinking cappuccinos sold to them by a girl in an insistently cheerful uniform, who would plainly rather have been anywhere else on the planet than where she was.

And Gus had started off by saying a lot of the things he'd said when he and Kate came round, saying them very fast, not meeting Dan's eye, repeating how gutted he was, how he'd never meant it to happen, it was just an insane impulse, how he was in such a state and Alexa was being kind to him and of course he thought she was a great girl, but not in that way, and Dan must believe him, he really must, he just felt like shit about it all, he really did.

Dan had stirred his coffee in its thick white cup and waited. He'd wanted to say, 'All that aside, mate, what about me? How d'you think it feels to be me without you to rely on?' But now that the moment had come and Gus was sitting opposite him, he couldn't somehow be bothered. It was pointless. It was too late. It was pathetic. And anyway, Gus was rushing on now, saying that all this stuff, everything that had happened since they got back, had stopped him in his tracks a bit, made him reassess, look at the wider picture. And the bottom line was that he couldn't do without Kate, he just couldn't. God knows, he adored the Army. Adored it. It was his life, it really was. But if he didn't have Kate, nothing else would have any value, not even the Army, he knew that now, not *even* the Army. He couldn't do it. He couldn't let her go. So he'd talked to her. Really talked to her like he wasn't sure he ever had, and he'd said he didn't care if she'd been seeing someone else, he didn't care what she'd done, he'd put up with anything, as long as she'd give him another chance to prove to her that she came first in his life and always would. *First*. And to his relief, she'd said OK, but — there's always a but, isn't there? — she said, but what, Gus, are you going to *do* about that? I'm not interested in more talk and easy promises, I'm only interested in what you *do* to change things.

Gus took a gulp of coffee, leaving a faint smear of foam on his upper lip.

'So,' he said, 'I've done it. I've actually gone and done it. I'm going to leave. It's bloody awful, but not as awful as losing Kate. God knows what I'll do, but we're going to London, all of us, we're going somewhere to start a new life and I've never been so panicked about anything in my entire life. But I know it's right. I *know* it. That's what I told Mack when I went to see him. I saw him yesterday. He'd got one leg in the car going off to Scotland, but he was pretty decent when I told him it was urgent and said he could postpone going for an hour or so. And when we got into his office and I told him, I almost had to field him falling over. He was pretty shell-shocked, I can tell you. In fact we were quite a pair, reeling round the room. I can't believe I've done it, I can't believe I actually went and saw Mack and told him. But I did. I did it, and I'm in bloody pieces and I'm not. I'm *not*. Because Kate is thrilled. She's thrilled with me. I can't remember her reacting to anything I've ever done the way she did to this.'

He stopped and, for the first time, looked up at Dan.

Dan said flatly, 'You've got coffee froth on your face.'

Gus took no notice. His eyes were shining, whether with tears or a kind of evangelical fervour, Dan couldn't tell.

'You can't imagine that, can you?' Gus said, staring at Dan. 'You just can't imagine what it's like going into Mack's office and telling him you're giving it all up for the wife and family, can you? *You*'d never think of doing that, would you, Dan? Not in a million years. Not *you*.'

After that — well, what could he have done? Grinned and said sorry mate, but old Mack was shell-shocked because you were the second of us in three days? Or, good idea, mate, because we aren't all going to get pinked, and it looks like me rather than you? Or, no grins, no revelations, just an honest, heartfelt reaction to the prospect of no longer having Gus to — to *talk* to? Especially with his own situation so unresolved, so unarticulated, so — so bloody lonely.

He whistled for Beetle. He had meant it when he told Mack that he didn't think he could put Alexa and the girls through any more of what his soldiering compelled them to cope with and endure. He had not only meant it then, he meant it now, up here on this windy ridge with the great plain unfolding in front of him, darkened with gorse and bracken in the foreground and criss-crossed with the precise pale lines of the tank tracks. But his meaning it was now tussling with the prospect that Mack had held out to

350

him, a more-than-prospect that Mack should probably never even have hinted at, but did because — and this was what was making it all so fiendishly hard — he really believed that Dan was in with more of a chance of being promoted to lieutenant colonel than almost anyone else at his level and with his experience. Mack would not have said what he'd said if he didn't believe it. And then he'd compounded his conviction by ringing Dan from a motorway service station somewhere in Westmorland, on his way to Scotland, and begging him not to do anything final, not yet, not till everyone was back at Larkford in the New Year. Please, Dan, please do nothing. Sit on your hands. Please.

Beetle came to Dan's side, carrying a stick with the air of one who has been asked to lead a royal procession bearing a sceptre.

'What to do?' Dan said to him despairingly.

Beetle looked sternly ahead. Stick-carrying allowed no room for the diversion of conversation.

'I probably couldn't have told Gus anyway,' Dan said. 'Not if he hadn't been tipped the wink, too. So at least I'm no worse off in that way. At least Dad knows, but it isn't fair to tell Alexa — '

In his jacket pocket, his phone began to ring. It would be Alexa, calling not to ask if he was OK — she had stopped doing that — but to ask if he would be back before dark because the twins —

But it was not Alexa. It was Eric. He lifted the phone cautiously to his ear. 'Granddad?'

'I expect,' Eric shouted, 'you'd forgotten you'd

bloody *got* a granddad, hadn't you?'

'No, I — '

'Where are you?'

'On a hill. Walking Beetle. It's a bit windy.'

'Get down off it,' Eric commanded. 'Get yourself somewhere where you can bloody think, and ring me. Ring me right back. Do you hear me?'

'Yes,' Dan said, closing his eyes, holding the phone hard against the side of his head. 'Yes. Are you OK?'

There was a short pause, and then Eric said, not shouting this time but with emphasis, 'Yes, lad. Yes, I am. I'm A1. It's you that bloody isn't.'

★ ★ ★

'Are you crying?' Tassy asked.

She and Flora were sitting on one side of the kitchen table, with squares of Marmite toast on their plates, looking at Kate Melville.

Kate had a mug of tea in front of her. She was wearing jeans and a sweater of Gus's and had tied a red bandanna over her head to keep her hair off her face. 'A bit,' she said.

'Did you fall over?' Flora enquired.

'*Flora* fell over,' Tassy said.

Flora started to wrench up the sleeve of her cardigan to show Kate her wound. 'It was *blooding*.'

Kate tried not to smile. 'I haven't got blood.'

'*Look*,' Flora said reverently. She held out a small, flawless arm with a barely discernible pink smudge across it.

'Gosh,' Kate said, peering to see.

'She yelled,' Tassy said. 'She yelled till all snot came out of her nose.'

'Enough,' Alexa said sharply.

Alexa wasn't sitting at the table, but standing by the kitchen counter, near the kettle. Dan wasn't back — no surprise there, then — and George had returned from the camp, having been given a lift home by someone or other, and had taken himself off with Isabel to Franny's house. Alexa liked George, even loved him, but she could not work out why he was staying so long, nor why Dan tolerated it and why she felt powerless to ask him why herself. She just knew that when she saw Kate Melville making for her front door, her only thought had been that she did not have the energy for such a visit. Dealing with George, and Dan, and her own current thoughts, was more than enough.

Kate had looked quite subdued, standing on her doorstep in a waterproof jacket and no make-up. She explained that Gus had gone to collect the boys at the end of their school term, and that she just wanted to come and explain what was going on.

'Of course,' Alexa had said. She hoped she'd sounded as neutral as she'd felt. She led the way into the kitchen, where the twins were already settled at the table.

'Tea?' she said.

Kate nodded gratefully. She sat down opposite the twins and smiled at them. They, pleased to have a diversion from the tedious business of having to stay on their chairs at the table while

353

eating, smiled back at her. Tassy knelt up in her chair and leaned down across the Marmite toast so that several squares of it got stuck to her jersey.

'Do *you* have snot?' Tassy said conversationally.

Alexa came across the kitchen, pulled Tassy upright and detached the squares of toast. 'I said enough. Now finish your tea.'

'We have,' Tassy began, looking at her sister for support.

'One more word,' Alexa said, 'and you will — '

'I don't mind,' Kate said, interrupting. 'It's a relief, actually. There's been so much big stuff to sweat that I'm really rather grateful for a bit of snot.'

Tassy and Flora began to giggle.

Kate said wistfully, 'I always wished I'd had a daughter.'

Alexa pushed a piece of toast into Tassy's mouth while it was open to giggle. 'Well, perhaps you now can.'

'Hey!' Kate said, startled.

'Fresh start, new baby . . . '

'But,' Kate said, 'I shall be the only breadwinner. For the time being anyway. Until Gus disentangles himself and finds something else to do.'

'Snot!' Tassy said, spraying toast out of her mouth.

'Stop it!'

Flora stood on her chair and began a little dance. Tassy watched her, cackling.

'It must be so lovely for them,' Kate said,

'having Isabel home.'

'It's lovely for *all* of us.'

Kate regarded her. 'You look different.'

'Better or worse?'

'Better. Definitely. It's such a relief, deciding things, isn't it? Even when the decisions are fraught with their own difficulties. I mean, what am I going to do with a Gus without his mates and his regiment?'

Alexa picked each twin up in turn and plonked them down on to their chairs again. Then she produced a damp cloth, wiped it briskly across both their faces and realigned their plastic plates in front of them. '*Eat*,' she said. She did not sound friendly.

Docilely, they picked up a remaining piece of toast each and put it into their mouths.

'Gosh,' Kate said admiringly. 'You *do* feel better. Impressive.'

'I wish you luck,' Alexa said, 'I really do. It's very brave of both of you.'

'I don't know about that. I don't actually know what's courage and what's guilt. For either of us. But we'll cobble something together, I'm sure we will.' She gave a sad little attempt at laughter. 'What's really pathetic is how disappointed the boys will be not to have Daddy as a soldier any more. No more the hero, just a common or garden grumpy old dad like anyone else's. They'll be so envious of you and Dan.'

'Don't wind me up, Kate.'

'I didn't mean to, I just — '

'What?'

'I just was wondering what's happened to you

355

to make you look so different?'

Alexa was still watching the twins. She shrugged. 'I've taken some decisions, like you. That's all.'

Kate waited a second or two, and then she said lightly, 'What decisions might those be?'

Alexa retrieved her gaze from the children and rested it briefly on Kate's face. Then she said, without smiling, 'Why do you think I would tell you before I even mention them to Dan?'

★　★　★

Dan had thought his grandfather intended to give him a hard time. He had expected ten minutes of bellowed exhortations to be a man, be a soldier, show some mettle, get a bloody grip. But Eric didn't seem interested in hectoring him about anything, didn't even seem particularly bothered about his and George's offer of money and the profoundly unsatisfactory reception their generosity had had. In fact, after only a few mildly contemptuous remarks about George's uselessness as an envoy if you wanted any mission accomplished that was more challenging than putting the kettle on, Eric switched into quite another mode, one that Dan had never encountered before and which made him sit there, in his parked car, his phone clamped to his ear, with his eyes shut, the better to concentrate.

The thing was, Eric said, that soldiering was a damn fine bloody thing for a man to do. It gave a man a purpose and an aim, and skills and comrades, and, above all, a sense of belonging, and a sense of value. You could take the most good-for-nothing bloody boy and turn out a loyal, serviceable, brave soldier in not much more than a year — even a modern boy with too much blubber on him from sitting around in front of all this PlayStation nonsense. He should know. His soldiering years, looking back, were his golden years. He wouldn't trade in one bloody second of those years, especially the ones in Aden.

But — and this was what he was getting at, ringing Dan like this — these days you had to think ahead. Far ahead. When he was a nipper, men copped it in their seventies, but now Dan could be looking at ninety even, *ninety*, thirty-five whole bloody years after he'd have had to retire from the Army, and he, Eric, wanted Dan to think about that. Never mind thirty-five years, think twenty-five. Twenty-five whole years after soldiering. 'You've got to picture it, lad, you've got to,' Eric said. 'D'you want to be like your own dad, maundering on in that miserable little flat with nobody to talk to but your senile old father and the lady in the launderette? D'you want to be like me, living like an old fossil, stuck in the past and going off to have conversations with the headstone put up to commemorate a brother I never bloody knew? D'you want that? Do you?'

He'd paused then. Dan waited in silence. Then Eric said, 'Because, you see, I was an only child, to all intents and purposes. Your dad was. You were. Alexa was. It's all very well when you're a nipper, but it's draughty when time goes on. And if you leave the Army, or you retire from the Army, you bloody well feel the draught. You can't keep those friends the way you can when you're all in the firing line and the man either side of you is all the world to you. You're brothers in arms then, but lay down your arms and it's another story, another story altogether.' His voice grew louder.

'But you're a lucky sod, Daniel. You're a lucky bloody sod. You've got four women in your life, four girls, and three of those girls'll grow up and have children, and you'll have people round you all your old age who don't love you because you're in bloody mortal danger together, they love you because you're you. And when you've been dealt a hand like that, lad, you don't want to go and bloody *risk* it. You don't want to cut off your stupid nose to spite your whole stupid, bloody *face*.'

When he stopped, there was a sudden and complete silence. Dan couldn't even hear him breathing. He waited a full minute, and then he said, unsteadily, 'Granddad?'

'I've got nothing more to say,' Eric said with finality.

'No. Yes. Granddad — '

'What?'

'Are . . . are you telling me I . . . I should *quit*?'

Eric sighed gustily from Wimbledon. 'Don't be so bloody ridiculous.'

'But I thought you were saying — '

'I was saying, take care,' Eric said, his voice

rising again. 'I was saying, don't risk your future. Don't decide a single bloody thing without deciding it together. That girl, Daniel, will be here when the Army's over for you. Or she will if you treat her right. And in the end, where would you bloody be, soldiering or not, without her?'

He'd rung off then, quite abruptly. He'd simply said, all of a sudden, that he'd said his piece and he'd had enough jawing on and he was going to make a brew, and Dan found himself holding a silent phone against his ear. Dan took a deep breath. The car smelled of dog, and he was cold, with the engine off and the heater with it. He flipped down the sun visor in front of him and inspected his face in the mirror on the back of it. He looked like someone he had never seen before.

He leaned forward and switched on the ignition. At once the heater and the radio came on, pumping warmth and sound into the car. He wanted to ring Eric and say thank you, but Eric would only shout at him and in any case he wasn't sure what he'd be thanking him for. Just — just for being there, for starters. For being there, and staying there, and not reproaching Dan for not yet going to see him, not being able to accept a gift, not being able, for far too long, to see the man for staring at the soldier.

He drove home slowly and parked the car in the drive. Then he got out and went round to lift the tailgate and assist Beetle, stiffened by lying still after his walk, down on to the ground. Passing the kitchen window on the way to the front door, he saw that the twins were sitting

359

meekly at the table and opposite them was Kate Melville, drinking tea. He definitely did not want to see Kate Melville. In fact, he did not want to see anyone right then but his wife and his daughters.

He opened the front door and ushered Beetle inside. He shouted, 'Home!'

There was an instant clamour from the twins, and above their noise he could hear Alexa's voice saying, 'Don't move from your chairs, don't move — '

And then he went down the hall and into the kitchen, Beetle at his heels, and Kate Melville half rose, almost nervously, as he entered.

'Dan,' she said.

He gave her a brief nod as he went past her, and then he went round the table to drop a kiss on the twins' swivelling excited heads, and then he halted in front of Alexa.

'Hello,' he said to her, directly.

She regarded him. He was looking down at her with absolute focus.

'I'm back,' Dan said.

'Yes.'

He put his hands on her shoulders and held her hard. He said again, 'I'm *back*.'

The twins scrambled to their feet and began to jump on their chairs, squealing.

Kate got decisively to her feet and moved towards the door. 'I'll go, I think.'

Dan didn't take his eyes off Alexa's face. 'Please,' he said to her, ignoring Kate.

'Daddy's back! Daddy's back!' the twins shouted.

The door of the kitchen closed quietly behind Kate. Nobody looked at it.

'And I'm listening,' Dan said. 'I really am. I'm back. *Talk* to me.'

20

In her bedroom, Isabel was listening to her iPod. She was listening to the Eurythmics, 'Here Comes The Rain Again', bootleg mix, which Rupert had added to her iPod for her because he said that the string playing was just so cool. He'd also downloaded Tensnake's 'Coma Cat' — 'Awesome,' he said reverently — and told Isabel, with the air of one sharing a considerable confidence, that his cousin Brett, who was Franny's sister's eighteen-year-old son, had come back from his first trip to Ibiza the previous summer and said that these two songs were on every club playlist, man, almost every one.

Isabel was listening to the music mostly out of manners, because it had been nice of Rupert to take the trouble for her, but she wasn't sure how much she liked music meant primarily for dancing to. And if she decided that she really didn't like it, she wouldn't pretend that she did, just to please Rupert. There was no need, any more, for that kind of reaction, not since she'd repaid him the ten pounds he'd sent to her at school, and spent enough time in his bedroom to get a much clearer idea of him as more than a myth.

She did like him, she was quite sure of that, and sometimes she liked him a lot. But he seemed to have lost the sheen of glamour he'd had when she didn't know him so well and just saw his name pop up on her phone screen. Maybe, she thought, lying back on her bed so that the beat of the music in her head was more comfortable, that was just as well. Maybe, you could be better friends with people, whether it was boys or girls, without the fairy dust of exciting strangeness making everything sparkle only as long as you kept it at a distance. Anyway, the idea of Rupert turning into the kind of friend that Jack Dearlove seemed to be for Mum was rather attractive, especially as she didn't have a brother. It also looked like a distinct possibility. He had texted her two jokes that morning already. She liked that.

The house was quite quiet. Isabel knew that Mum and the twins were in the kitchen, because Mum had said to Isabel that she deserved some time off from Tassy and Flora, and that she, Mum, would keep them downstairs and let them do one of their favourite things, which was cutting up with grown-up scissors instead of the blunt-ended children's ones which never cut anything properly. When Isabel went downstairs, she knew the kitchen would look like a gerbil's nest, a sea of random shreds of paper and cloth, and the twins would be red in the face from excitement and effort.

But she wouldn't go down just yet. It was oddly luxurious to be lying on her bed with the thump of music in her ears. Granddad had left a bar of milk chocolate for her, hidden under the pillow with the ten-pound note which had been so useful for repaying Rupert. He'd gone back to

London that morning, with Dan driving him, and Dan was going to stay with him for a few nights and see Great-Granddad Eric, and Granny and Grandpa Morgan, which was something, he'd said, standing rather awkwardly in the doorway to Isabel's bedroom, that he should have done weeks ago. Weeks. He'd then asked her — quite shyly, she thought — if she'd like to go to London with him.

Isabel had been fidgeting with all the infinite number of tiny china and plastic objects on the top of her chest of drawers when he spoke. She had managed to say, not at all fluently, that although it was really kind of him, and usually she loved the thought of going to London, she didn't think she would, right now, this time. But thank you.

Dan grinned. He said, slightly teasingly, 'I see.'

'It . . . it isn't Rupert.'

'Oh?'

'No,' Isabel said. Her face was getting hot, which was really annoying. 'No. It's — something I can't explain.'

'It doesn't matter,' Dan said. He sounded kind, but still amused. 'It really doesn't.'

Isabel had just nodded. Let him think it was Rupert, if he wanted. Better he should think it was Rupert than that she should have to admit that, having scored such a victory over school and been allowed to stay at home, she didn't want to let the spoils of that victory — Mum and the twins — out of her sight just yet.

It was Franny who had pointed out to her that she had won. They were folding sheets together, ready for ironing, and Franny had said quite casually, without catching Isabel's eye, 'I think you've punished your mother enough now, don't you? I think she gets it. I think she respects what you feel. It's never a brilliant idea to keep forcing someone to see what they can completely see already.'

Isabel went on searching for the corners of a duvet cover, to shake it out into a neat rectangle. She felt such a sudden flood of relief at being given permission to go home again that she had been afraid that she might cry. So she had just nodded emphatically, and swallowed hard, and focussed on the duvet cover, and Franny had eventually said in quite a different voice, 'You're a complete barometer for your mamma, aren't you? Wish my boys were, for me!'

And Isabel could laugh, and even if she only partly got what Franny meant, it was plainly a compliment, as it was when Franny came up to see her in bed, her last night there, and sat on the edge of the bed, and said she'd miss her.

'Who am I going to do the girl stuff with? It's been so great, having you.'

'I love it here,' Isabel said truthfully.

Franny smiled at her, and put a hand out and squeezed her nearest leg, under the covers.

'You should be at home, now, though. It's where you belong.'

'I know.'

'It'll be good to be back. You'll see. And it'll be different. They've made a lot of plans and a lot of them are very good, and you'll like them. It won't be perfect, mind, because nothing ever is perfect, and Dan really wants to go on being a soldier, like Andy does, and I think you know a bit about that kind of wanting yourself now, don't you?'

Isabel had simply said 'Yes' in not much more than a whisper. She imagined Franny was talking about the sort of wanting that amounted, really, to a need. The sort that made you who you were, the sort you *had* to satisfy, even if it sometimes elbowed other people's wantings out of the way.

'You see,' Franny said, gazing up at the Dire Straits poster on the wall above Isabel's head, 'your mum has had to find a way round that wanting. She's decided that she'd rather go round Dan than walk away from him, and even if it's wonderful for everybody, especially Dan, that she's chosen that way, it isn't going to be easy for her.'

Then Franny had stopped speaking, quite abruptly, and transferred her gaze from the poster to Isabel's face, and, after a pause, said in the upbeat tone Isabel was used to her using, 'Bend, not break. That's what you have to do. Bend, not break, if you're sure you've got the cake you really want to eat.'

★ ★ ★

The twins had been ecstatic to have her home — so ecstatic, in fact, that they had been quite sobered by her return, as if overdoing their reaction might cause Isabel to evaporate in front of their eyes, like a witches' punishment in a fairy tale. Even Tassy had been quite quiet and biddable, instinctively responding to the new atmosphere in the house of changes slowly heaving themselves up into all their lives, like some great monster of the deep turning over by degrees and causing huge waves on the surface, and making them all soberly aware that nothing was ever going to be the same again. One very different thing was being invited last night, while Granddad was watching television and the twins were asleep, to sit at the kitchen table with Mum and Dan, and being told that they had had a long conversation with Mrs Cairns and with someone from the Ministry of Defence about the Continuation of Education allowance, neither of which meant much to Isabel, and then, wonderfully, that she would not be going back to boarding school.

She looked at them both intently, one after the other. 'Not — ever?'

'No. Not unless you want to — you *ask* to.'

'I won't,' Isabel said fervently.

'Then it won't happen,' Dan said.

Isabel suddenly felt extremely shy. She whispered, 'Thank you.'

'Don't, Izzy. No thanks, no recriminations. No looking back.'

She said, picking at a grain of wood in the table top, 'So where will I go?'

'Well,' Dan said, glancing at Alexa, 'we can't be sure. Not just yet. We can't be sure of quite a lot of things . . . '

Isabel inspected the nail she had run along the table top. 'Like what?'

'Like exactly where we'll live. Or how much

we can all be together, sometimes. But for now, there's schools in Andover and a good one in Gillingham. Just while we decide.'

Despite everything Franny had said, Isabel had a little clutch of fear. 'Are you — ' she said, and stopped.

'Are we what?'

She leaned back in her chair, looked at the ceiling and said, very fast, 'Are you getting divorced?'

'No,' Dan said.

Out of the lower rim of her eyes, Isabel saw him take her mother's hand.

'No,' Alexa said.

Isabel slowly lowered her chin.

'Then what d'you mean about not all being — '

'I'm going to train, in London,' Alexa said. 'I'm going to train for something a bit like teaching but not teaching. That's what I want to do. That's what I want to happen. So we might be going to London to live, you and me and the twins.'

Isabel thought about this. 'And Dan?'

He was still holding Alexa's hand. He said, 'I'll come when I can. Whenever I can. As much as I can. We . . . might buy a house.'

Isabel was startled. 'A *house*!'

They both laughed.

'You make it sound an outrageous idea,' said Dan.

Isabel looked at him. 'Will you still be a soldier?'

'Yes,' Alexa said, for him. 'For now, anyway. For the moment.'

'But where will you live? Will you live here, by yourself?'

'No,' he said. Isabel could see from the whitened skin across his knuckles that he was gripping Alexa tightly. 'No, I won't live here. This house'll be for another family. When I need to be here, I'll stay in the mess. But I might be on a course at Shrivenham, or on exercise, or, heaven forbid, behind a desk in London. And I'll be with you four whenever I possibly can.'

Isabel pulled a hank of hair over her shoulder and inspected it, as if for split ends. 'OK,' she said.

'Is it?' Alexa said. 'Do we really have your permission to go ahead?'

Isabel took no notice. It was a good sign that they wanted to tease her, but she had no wish to encourage them.

She said firmly, 'A house.'

'Yes,' Alexa said, casting a glance round the kitchen. 'Our own house.'

'In London?'

'Maybe. Probably.'

Isabel brushed the tuft of hair in her hand against her cheek. 'What about Franny? And Mo? And Prue and Claire and everyone?'

Alexa gave a little sigh. 'They'll be all moving on, Izzy. Some time soon. Nobody stays anywhere for long, in the Army. You know that.'

'I like Franny.'

'We know you do.'

Isabel dropped her hair and said crossly, 'Franny, I said. Not Rupert. *Franny*.' She was willing them not to laugh.

Alexa said, 'Then you'll be pleased that we're spending Christmas with them. Two families together. And carol singing at Claire's.'

Dan lifted Alexa's hand to his mouth, and kissed it. He said to Isabel, looking at Alexa, 'Julian is very keen indeed on your mother.'

Isabel looked away. She thought of saying 'Yuck' loudly, but decided to let her expression do the talking instead.

Dan said, laughing, 'Have you had enough?'

She nodded, pushed her chair back and stood up.

Alexa was looking up at her. 'Are you pleased?'

She nodded again.

'It might mean two changes of school.'

'That's OK.'

'And friends, too.'

Isabel thought of Rupert's invitation to go bowling, in Andover, with a group of them. She was good at bowling. He'd be surprised at how good she was.

She said, rather loftily, 'I'll get new ones.'

'D'you know,' Dan said to Alexa, his voice admiring, 'I rather think she will.'

Isabel drifted away from the kitchen and went slowly through to the sitting room. Granddad was on the sofa with a newspaper on his knees and the television on, and his eyes shut. She watched him for a second or two.

'I'm not asleep,' George said.

She came further into the room. George opened his eyes and looked at her. 'They've told you, have they?'

'Yes.'

'You OK with it all?'

Isabel perched on the arm of the sofa. She swung a foot. 'I am.'

'Even though it's all so vague?'

'I'd rather that it was vague than horrible.'

'No more boarding school.'

'No!'

'Home every night to your sisters.'

Isabel slid off the arm of the sofa so that she was sitting next to George. 'Granddad?'

'Yes, pet.'

'Are you staying for Christmas?'

George chuckled. 'It would have been grand, but not this time. Another year, we'll see.' He leaned sideways and rapped Isabel's arm lightly with his reading glasses. 'D'you know what me and Great-Granddad Eric are doing? Do you? We've been asked over to your other grandparents, us four old fogeys in paper hats together pulling crackers. Your granny wants to cook a goose. I've never eaten goose in my life. It'll be something, don't you think?'

Isabel considered him. Of all her family, he got the gold star for being no trouble to anyone. She thought of the flat in the Marylebone Road and the silk lampshades.

'D'you want to go?'

He winked at her. 'D'you know, I don't mind.'

'Really?'

'Really. It'll educate me. Granddad Eric'll be shining up his shoes already. Maybe we'll have a sing-song. I might even' — he winked at Isabel again — 'get round to teasing your granny. When we've had a couple.'

Isabel smiled at him. She leaned sideways and kissed his cheek. 'I'm going up to bed.'

'Sweet dreams, princess. And thanks for lending me your bedroom.' He put his reading glasses on and picked up the paper on his knee. 'Look under the pillow when I'm gone,' he said. 'You never know what you might find there.'

★ ★ ★

Isabel pulled her earplugs out of her ears. There were extra sounds from downstairs, not just the usual noise of the twins making a commotion, but someone arriving, the door opening, pleased voices. Isabel laid her earplugs on top of her iPod and swung herself upright so that she could push her feet into her black ballet pumps — they were scuffed enough, now, to satisfy her — and shuffled across the room to open the door.

'Isabel!' Alexa was calling. 'Isabel! Come down. There's someone I want you to meet.'

She dawdled across the landing and looked down into the narrow hall. Alexa was standing below her, unbalanced by having Tassy on one hip, and Flora was jigging beside her, clutching one trouser leg. A bit further on, by the door, just beyond a wagging Beetle, was a young man with a pinkish face and neat Army hair, in jeans and a waxed jacket, and in front of him was a girl with fantastic hair and truly amazing boots that went right up over her knees, almost to the hem of a white wool coat that wasn't, really, any longer than a jacket.

Alexa glanced up at Isabel. 'Darling, come on

down. Come and meet Mel. Mel and Freddie.'

Mel manoeuvred herself past Beetle and came to the bottom of the stairs. She lifted the hair off her forehead and let it fall back again, slippery and shiny. 'Hi,' she said.

Isabel slithered down two steps. 'Hi.'

'You're Isabel.'

'Yes.'

Mel put a booted foot on the bottom step and smiled up at her. 'I heard about school. Congratulations.'

'Oh. Thank you.'

Mel turned her head and looked back at Freddie. He came forward towards the stairs, Beetle grunting beside him. The two of them stood there, looking up at Isabel. They seemed to her like two people in an advertisement for scent or shampoo, beautiful and gleaming, like perfect pieces of fruit.

Mel said, 'We've come to tell you all something, me and Freddie.' She glanced at him and giggled. 'We've come to show you . . . '

She pulled her left hand out of her coat pocket and brandished it, and something flashed in the air, the rainbow flash of a sudden small brilliance.

'Oh, wow,' Isabel breathed.

Alexa and Freddie were laughing. So was Mel. Alexa leaned forward, letting Tassy slip unevenly to the floor, and seized Mel's wrist. 'You did it!'

'Yes.'

'You said yes!'

Mel glanced at Freddie. He said proudly, 'She did.'

'Please don't say she couldn't resist you.'

'Wouldn't dream of it!'

'Actually,' Mel said, 'I wanted to. I just — wanted to. It began to feel nothing but perverse, purely perverse, not to.'

The twins were crowding round Mel now, jabbering to see the ring. Isabel slipped a few more steps closer to the bottom. Mel bent so that the twins could seize her hand, and over her back Alexa said to Freddie, 'Look after her.'

'It's all I want.'

Alexa gave him a little smile. She said, simply, 'You're a soldier.'

Isabel descended the last few steps.

'It's a *diamond*,' Tassy announced importantly. 'It's a real *diamond*.'

Mel straightened up and looked at Isabel. She said, 'You'll have one of these one day.'

'Not yet!' Alexa said.

She put an arm out and took Isabel's hand. She glanced at Mel. 'New beginnings . . . '

Mel nodded. She held out her hand and regarded her ring.

Alexa looked at Isabel. She smiled at her and squeezed the hand she held. 'New beginnings?' she said, and she looked very much as if she needed a reassuring answer.

'Yes,' Isabel said. She could feel herself nodding and nodding, like some stupid toy. 'Yes.'

We do hope that you have enjoyed reading this large print book.

Did you know that all of our titles are available for purchase?

We publish a wide range of high quality large print books including:
Romances, Mysteries, Classics
General Fiction
Non Fiction and Westerns

Special interest titles available in large print are:
The Little Oxford Dictionary
Music Book
Song Book
Hymn Book
Service Book

Also available from us courtesy of Oxford University Press:
Young Readers' Dictionary
(large print edition)
Young Readers' Thesaurus
(large print edition)

For further information or a free brochure, please contact us at:
Ulverscroft Large Print Books Ltd.,
The Green, Bradgate Road, Anstey,
Leicester, LE7 7FU, England.
Tel: (00 44) 0116 236 4325
Fax: (00 44) 0116 234 0205

Other titles published by
The House of Ulverscroft:

MARRYING THE MISTRESS

Joanna Trollope

Genie Watkins, a Birmingham kid, dreams of having a proper happy family like her Italian friend, Teresa. But it's August 1939. Genie hasn't reckoned with the outbreak of war, her already rocky family being split up and the strangely liberating effect it all has on her mother. Narrated in the cheeky, courageous voice of Genie, the disasters that follow display her powerful capacity for survival. Under skies darkened by blackout she tries to hold her family together, keeps up her spirits with her nan and glamorous Auntie Lil, shares her fears and hopes with Teresa, and amid it all discovers love . . .